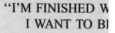

"My God, kitten, you are so lovely," he breathed hoarsely. "I must have been mad not to have married you long ago."

"Why didn't you?" she chided him lovingly.

He stroked her shoulders and breasts and gazed at her thoughtfully.

"I think you were too exotic for me to think of as a wife. A man would think of you only in terms of a mistress because of your beauty. When you look at me imperiously, you could be Russian; the black clouds of your hair and shape of your eyes remind me of an Oriental. You have the dainty hands and feet of a Balinese temple dancer."

She was in a dreamlike trance as his words revealed his enchantment with her. "At other times you are so sleek and pantherlike, you could even be Egyptian."

She smiled up at him. "It's Gypsy, my darling."

"My exciting, exotic *Irish Gypsy*."

TEMPTED

"Reaches new heights of passion, adventure, sensuality and storytelling . . . Remarkable . . . A romance of exceptional proportions. With each new novel, Virginia Henley tests her powers as a writer, and, as readers, we reap the splendid rewards. Let yourself be *Tempted* by this spectacular tale."
—*Romantic Times*

"A five-star book . . . a classic . . . Virginia Henley takes a first-class setting, peoples it with too-proud sensual characters, seasons it with some interesting plot twists and serves up a rip-roaring, old-fashioned good time . . . Scotland came alive as no other Highlander story has ever succeeded in doing for me . . . Superbly detailed and richly drawn."
—*Affaire de Coeur*

"Virginia Henley is at her best . . . She so vividly depicts the people and events of the time that the reader is transported back to that exciting period of history. Quickly, the reader becomes entwined in the emotions of the characters, feeling their love, hate, and passion."
—*Rendezvous*

"5 stars! . . . As rugged as the Highlands, as feisty as a Scottie dog, and as colorful as a field of heather."
—*Heartland Critique*

Other Books by Virginia Henley:

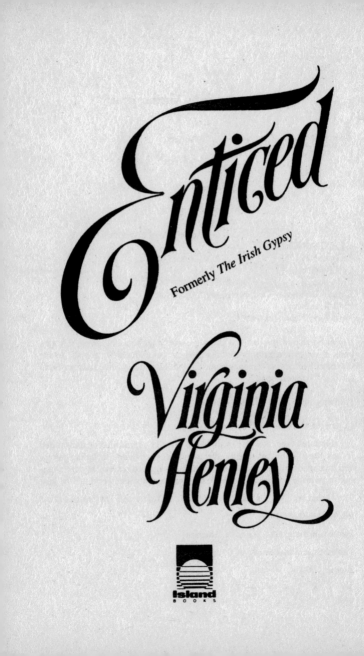

Enticed

Formerly The Irish Gypsy

Virginia Henley

Island
BOOKS

ISLAND BOOKS
Published by
Dell Publishing
a division of
Bantam Doubleday Dell Publishing Group, Inc.
1540 Broadway
New York, New York 10036

Formerly titled THE IRISH GYPSY

The trademark Dell® is registered in the U.S. Patent and Trademark Office.

ISBN: 0-440-21700-8

Printed in the United States of America

Published simultaneously in Canada

August 1994

10   9   8   7   6   5   4   3   2   1
OPM

For my mother,

L I L,

the Duchess

Chapter 1

Little Kitty Rooney sat contemplating two potatoes and half a turnip with disgust. Sighing, she cut the rot out of them and chopped them up into the black iron pot. She glanced apprehensively at the hearth where the meager fire threatened to go out any minute. Her grandfather, an old Gypsy called Swaddy by almost everyone, sat in the chimney corner, his gold earring reflecting the last dying flame. The door to the little cottage was flung open, letting in the wind and rain. "Terrance, God be praised!" she cried, "the fire's in its death throes."

She jumped down from her stool and helped her brother put some fresh peat, which he had been out to cut, on the fire.

"Faith, yer soaked again, Terrance."

"Aye, when will this bloody rain cease and desist?" wondered Terrance aloud.

"When pigs fly," laughed Kitty. "Hutch up, Grandada, and let Terrance get warm. He's drenched to the skin."

"Kitty, I can't wear these bloody boots much longer. They've such great holes in the bottom, they give me blisters."

"I'll mend 'em for ye, boyo; I'm right handy at mending boots," Swaddy bragged.

"With what, pray tell?" asked Kitty pointedly.

Terry shook his head, "Ah, well, I shouldn't complain about boots while you go barefoot, Kitty."

"Sure an' I'm used to it. Besides, 'tis summertime," she said and twinkled.

"Summer! When's the last time you saw the sun? Tell me

that, Kitty Rooney. The crops are ruined again, you know. The fields are so black and sodden, every vegetable is rotten,'' he said bitterly, sounding as if he were an old man rather than a child of eleven.

"Well, one good thing about the rain, I don't have to carry water from the River Liffey to cook with, although there's little enough left to cook,'' she said with resignation as she lifted the black pot onto a hook over the fire. "There will be a bit o' broth for dinner, but by the grace of God I don't know what we'll eat tomorrow.''

"Something will turn up, lass, don't worry your pretty head,'' said Swaddy from his corner. The brother and sister exchanged significant glances and Kitty rolled her eyes heavenward.

Terry wiped his nose on his sleeve. "They was getting the carriage ready at the big house.'' Kitty's head shot up. "They must be going into Dublin. I wonder what's up?''

"Himself must be comin', I suppose,'' he said and shrugged.

Kitty took down her shawl from behind the door and put it over her head. "Wait here, I won't be long,'' and she dashed out into the downpour, oblivious of her bare feet.

Kitty had lived her whole life on the one-hundred-acre estate of Squire O'Reilly, which was in County Kildare, about thirty miles from Dublin. The O'Reilly mansion was called Castle Hill, with its herd of Charolais cattle and sleek Thoroughbred horses. Jonathan O'Reilly was a wealthy Lancashire millowner over in England and only came to his Irish estate in the summertime. Castle Hill had live-in, year-round servants and its farm cottages were filled with his herdsmen and gardeners who planted crops and tried to make it a self-supporting estate. The Rooneys were not servants of the O'Reillys, but Gypsies who had settled on the land and had been allowed to stay. Kitty's mother hadn't survived Terrance's birth. Their Gypsy father in his grief hadn't been able to provide a stable existence for them and he wandered off one night, leaving their grandfather with the problem of their survival. They had been camping beside the River Liffey that night and ten years later they were still there.

Kitty crouched beside the stable wall in the downpour. She was still as a mouse, quite prepared to wait all day if necessary. The doors to the carriage house stood open and the coach had been wheeled outside. The men were harnessing the horses inside the stables because of the rain. Kitty waited. The stableman led out two horses and harnessed them to the coach, then went back for the other two horses. He said, "I'll get their feed." The driver said, "I'd better get four horse blankets, Tim. You know what the squire's like about his horses."

The men disappeared inside again, then Kitty saw two feed bags appear at the stable door and once again Tim went back for the other two bags. Kitty whipped one of the bags across her back and ran like the wind. She flung open the front door and said, "Here, milado, take this, it's pretty heavy."

With a grin Terry hoisted the feed bag onto the table. "All those oats! We'll have porridge for a week!"

Swaddy said, "Maybe you can make us some of them little oat cakes." Kitty shook out her wet shawl and hung it by the fire. "I'll put some of these oats to soak, but the best part is the leather feed bag. Now Grandada can mend your boots!"

Late in the afternoon the rain stopped for a short while.

Kitty said, "Come on, our Terrance, now's our chance for some milk."

"Will I keep him busy while you milk a cow?"

"No. I'll do the talking. You nip down to the bottom of the pasture; there's sure to be one or two cows down there now that the rain's stopped."

She climbed over the stone wall and shouted, "Hallo there, Jack Kenny!"

"Hallo, lass. I've to get the cows up before the rain comes on again."

"Hold there, Jack Kenny. I had a dream about you last night. Such a vivid dream, so lifelike. I believe you could call it prophetic!"

He stopped and listened, interested now. She was using the old Gypsy formula: Get your hook in to hold their interest immediately, then you could tell them any yarn. People never tired of hearing about themselves. "I saw you on a boat. You were going on a journey to another country. Then I saw a magnificent house, bigger even than Castle Hill. You made a great fortune and beautiful ladies admired you," she said with great enthusiasm.

He chuckled at the picture she had painted. "Sure now, lass, 'twas only a dream."

"Perhaps not, Jack Kenny. It all seemed as real as if I were seeing your future. Who knows what lies beyond the horizon?" she asked breathlessly. He laughed, pleased with the fantasy.

"Well, I must be off," said Kitty lightly. She skipped away and was halfway over the wall when he called, "Wait! Tell me more, Kitty."

Her laughter trilled out as she disappeared over the wall.

That night, after their grandfather had mended the boots, he reached for his fiddle. "No, no, Grandada, not tonight. I've things to discuss with Terrance."

"What's on your mind, Kitty?" Terry asked.

"Things are bad, Terrance; they've never been this bad before." He nodded and waited for her to continue. "We've been in the big house lots of times to look about and nobody's ever been the wiser. Why should some have so much and others have nothing?"

"By Jasus that's what I'd like to know," he agreed.

"We could slip in and pick out a couple of small objects they'd never even miss and you could take them and sell them," she suggested.

"Well, I could pinch a ride into Dublin from somebody surely now," he said and grinned.

"The only trouble is, I think the squire's coming tomorrow, so we have to act first thing in the morning."

"You're on, Kitty. I only hope the bloody weather is foine."

"Faith, but we'll have to be mighty careful, Terrance. If we're caught, it would mean a whipping at the cart's tail, or even transportation."

"Stop your blathering, Kitty. They've never caught us afore!"

The next morning they made their way around the east wing of Castle Hill and climbed a huge sycamore that reached past the second-story windows. Kitty was thirteen, but she was so small that she looked only ten. They were both extremely nimble and it took but a few minutes to reach a bedroom window, pry it open and swing over the ledge into the room.

As they stood quietly taking in the richness of the room thick carpet caressed Kitty's feet. They were alert for the sounds of servants as their eyes swept about the bedroom. The furniture was heavy black oak, polished to a mirror shine. A magnificent wardrobe stood in one corner with a full-length mirror upon its door. Kitty was drawn to it. She held out her skirts and curtsied prettily, then clapped her hand to her mouth before her laughter came trilling out. Terry climbed onto the big four-poster and gave it a tentative bounce. The walls held valuable paintings and the desk had a silver inkstand and a jeweled letter opener. A table beside the bed displayed all manner of small, attractive pieces that caught the eye and made Kitty's fingers itch to touch them. She selected a silver chased snuff box and a colorful paperweight. Terry opened the little drawer in the table and gasped as he seized a handful of gold sovereigns. The silence was shattered.

"What in Christ's name is going on here? Who the devil are you?"

Kitty looked up at the man who towered over them, looking at least seven feet tall.

"Patrick John Francis O'Reilly," breathed Kitty.

"Himself!" said the squire's son in a voice that sounded like thunder. She looked up into blazing blue eyes, arrogant nose and mouth and squared chin, and he gazed down at the most beautiful child he had ever seen. Her hair was a mass of over a thousand black silk ringlets as wild as a blackberry thicket, her mouth was naturally bright red and the wind and rain had given her patches of scarlet on her high cheekbones. Her eyes were a velvety brown with double rows of black lashes framing them. She gave Terry one warning glance, which conveyed he was to keep his mouth shut and go along with whatever story she concocted.

"Milord, I shall have to tell you the whole truth and throw myself on your mercy." She paused for dramatic effect, then launched into her tale.

"Me brother Terrance stole this here paperweight and this snuff box, but faith, ye can't blame the poor wee man, he hasn't eaten in two days."

She let that sink in, then continued, "When he brought them home and showed them to me I said, 'Terrance, 'tis a wicked thing you've done and we must put them back immediately,' and that's just what we were doing, milord," she said and curtsied. She noticed a slight twinkle in the bright blue eyes and thought, We are going to get away with it!

"I believe you, but thousands wouldn't," said Patrick O'Reilly.

"What the devil's going on up here, and what are these filthy little buggers doing in my house?" a loud voice demanded.

"The bloody squire!" muttered Kitty.

She might be able to fob off his son with a glib explanation—after all, he couldn't be more than twenty—but the bloody squire was a different kettle of fish. He was hard, cruel, selfish, with a terrible temper, completely used to having everyone obey him immediately and without question. He held his riding crop in the air, poised over Kitty, ready to bring it crashing down upon her head, when she blurted out, "Milord invited us in."

"You lying little bugger, what in hell would he want with the likes of you?" he demanded harshly.

Kitty gulped, then plunged on, "He said he'd give me a shilling if I'd pull me drawers down."

Immediate silence fell like a thunderbolt. Then Patrick threw back his head and roared with laughter. His father turned on him, "By God, I've put up with your drinking and gambling and whoring, but by Christ this is child molestation!" He slashed him with the riding crop. Patrick quickly took the whip from him but offered no rebuttal. The squire spluttered, "You'll go back to England tomorrow. You two get home before I send for the constable!"

Terry fled, but Kitty gathered her dignity about her and descended the wide staircase like a duchess. Only when she was outside did her feet take flight. She caught up with Terry and demanded furiously, "Why didn't you know they arrived days ago?"

He flashed her a cheeky grin and said, "Jasus, you're supposed to be the one with the second sight. I just about shit myself when Patrick O'Reilly caught us. He's a big bugger, isn't he?''

She tossed her head at the mention of the handsome young man. ''Arrogant bastard!''

Early the next morning Kitty was on her way to steal some more milk when a huge black stallion almost ran her down in the mist.

''You stupid child, I could have killed you.''

''Little you'd care! I thought you were being sent back to England,'' she taunted.

He laughed and said, ''I stopped taking orders when I was seven, and I think that probably applies to you too, from your cheek.''

She put her small nose in the air, tossed her curls and pointedly ignored him. ''Faith, you act like you own the place, instead of being . . .'' He hesitated.

''Gypsy ragamuffin?'' she finished for him. ''Well don't look down your arrogant nose at me, O'Reilly; someday I shall be a lady and have a carriage of my own!''

He threw back his head and laughed, ''Lady Jane Tut!''

''Lord Bloody Muck!'' she flung back.

''There's only one way to achieve your ambition, and that's to marry money,'' he advised her.

He laughed at the speculative look that came into her eyes. ''Nay, lass, you can't have me. I'm disinclined toward marriage to begin with, but when I do saddle myself with a wife, she'll bring me a bleachworks or a brewery at the least.'' He reached into his pocket and tossed her a coin. ''Here's that shilling I'm supposed to have promised you,'' he said with his eyes twinkling.

She was left standing alone and for once she hadn't had the last word; that was most rare for Kitty Rooney.

*   *   *

Jonathan O'Reilly sat with his son in the library. "Have you had a chance to assess the estate yet, lad?"

Patrick stretched his long legs to the fire. "Aye, father. Things aren't good, but remember, it's all the counties, not just this one."

"Quit beating about the bush. You know what I want to know. Is the place still able to support itself?"

"No. The crops are ruined. There'll be no food for the people and no feed for the herds. It'll all have to be imported. The tenants won't be able to pay their rents and they shouldn't be pressed into doing what's impossible!"

"That's all my arse of a tale!" O'Reilly shouted. "They have the use of the land, they should pay the rent."

"Futile," Patrick said shortly. "You can't get blood out of a turnip."

"Well, I'm determined to have this place support itself and not be a continual drain on my pocket. I'll sell some of the Thoroughbreds."

"If you could be farsighted, Father, you'd see that's exactly what you shouldn't do. You should increase the number of horses. It's the only thing you can make money on, and getting rid of them would put a lot of your people out of work. That's dangerous."

"Then where does the money come from?" he demanded.

Patrick shrugged and said, "You could use some of the profits from the mills, although if you were intelligent enough to look into the future you'd see that the mill profits should be turned back into improvements, new machinery and greater safety measures."

"Intelligent? That's what I sent you to that bloody London university for, and let's not get off on that tack about improving the bloody mills. I make a damned good living from them mills, so we'll just let it be. We're discussing Ireland at the moment."

"Yes, we'll discuss it and then you'll go ahead and do exactly as you please and not take any notice of the advice I try to give you."

"Oh, aye, we know there's only one with any brains in this family, but let me tell you I've got more common sense in my little finger than there is in that whole bloody university!"

"You could be right there. It's crammed with young men who are England's future and once they receive the finest education that's available in the world, they go off and race their horses and sleep with their mistresses and fritter away their fortunes gambling and never, ever, under any circumstances soil their hands with trade. But commerce is what makes England strong and if they applied themselves to making money instead of wasting it, we'd be the richest, most powerful country in the world."

"I always thought we were."

"How long will it last if everyone's as shortsighted as you?"

"All right, all right, try me. Give me a suggestion and I'll carry it out."

"If the people of Ireland have no food and conditions get worse, mobs will descend like locusts on estates like these and pick them clean. They will eat your prize cattle and strip your house bare."

"We'd call out the militia before things got to that state."

"They've almost reached that state. Those children were here to steal yesterday, so my suggestion is let them work for wages. Give the boy work in the stables with the horses and let the girl work in the kitchens."

"The thieving little buggers will steal me blind, and I'll have them off the place tomorrow!" he shouted.

"Goddamn it to hell, you old hypocrite, you said you'd carry out one of my suggestions! Talking to you is like bang-ing my head against the wall.'' He arose swiftly. ''Good night.''

''By Christ, my word is as good as my bond! Don't you ever insinuate otherwise!''

''Then it's settled,'' Patrick said quietly.

Kitty sat with a candle, poring over a dog-eared copy of *Etiquette for Ladies and Gentlemen,* the ladies' indispensable assistant. There were instructions on dress, behavior in the street, visiting, behavior at dinner, how to make introductions, how to make entertaining and amusing conversation. A whole section was devoted to the preliminaries for marriage, love letters, and ''popping'' the question. Kitty's attention was riveted, although she must have read them over a hundred times. Her eyes avidly scanned the words:

Cleanliness, absolute purity of person, is the first requisite in the appearance of a lady. Not only should the hands and face be kept clean, but the whole skin should be subjected to frequent ablutions. Better wear coarse clothes with a clean skin, than silk stockings drawn over dirty feet.

Kitty closed the book slowly. Two words at least had penetrated her brain and set her imagination on fire—silk stockings!

Chapter 2

The next two years were devastating for Ireland. There was famine in the land, babies died at their mother's breasts, women begged in the streets and men banded together to steal, murder and finally starve. It seemed the whole population became destitute and homeless.

Safe in Lancashire, Jonathan O'Reilly knew only that his Irish estate was a money eater. He had had it up for sale for over a year but there had been no takers. He had ordered the servants to pack everything inside Castle Hill and ship it to his London house in Cadogen Square. Long gone were the milky herds of Charolais. The few remaining horses had to be guarded night and day. Let it not be said that old O'Reilly didn't have a shrewd head on his shoulders, for while Patrick was busy at the mills, Jonathan made a quick trip to London and disposed of his Irish troubles swiftly. Upon his return he could not forgo the pleasure of bragging of his perspicacity to his son.

"You've done what?" demanded Patrick, thunder in his face.

"Signed a contract with the government to billet the militia at Castle Hill; and I've sold them the horses too," he added with satisfaction.

"Christ, don't you have a conscience, Father? How can you do this to your own people?" Patrick asked incredulously.

"My first loyalties are to England. I was born in Lancashire, not across the water, even though the name is O'Reilly."

"All the people who work for us in Lancashire are Irish. If word gets out, you'll be getting a late-night visit from the Molly Maguires. Do you want the mills razed?"

"That would be cutting off their noses to spite their face. Without the mills to employ 'em, they'll starve to death."

Patrick was appalled. "Your life won't be worth tuppence! You'd better move up to the London house and let me handle things here. The first dark night, they'll slip a knife between your ribs, or a mob could corner you and put the clogs to you."

The old man licked lips suddenly gone dry. Patrick proceeded, "There's only one way out. Instead of abandoning our people in Ireland, ship them over here to work in the mills. If you get them out fast enough, they won't know what you've done with Castle Hill."

Jonathan nodded his agreement. "I'll go tomorrow."

The door was flung open and a young woman of about eighteen swept in. She was very mature for her age, with a full bust and the same sensuous mouth as her older brother, Patrick.

"I'm not having the wedding in this godforsaken place, and that's absolutely my final word in the matter," she stormed.

"What bloody maggot have you got in your brain now?" the old man thundered.

"Patrick, do something with your sister before she gives me apoplexy!" Patrick smiled; he was very indulgent with his two sisters and in return both adored him. Julia was eighteen and her engagement was imminent, while Barbara, only twelve, still was in the schoolroom.

Patrick asked, "How would you like to be married from the London house? I've just been telling Father he should move up there for his health. It would be much more convenient for your fiancé's people, too."

"Oh, Patrick, you're such a darling," cried Julia.

"Why in hell should we do what's convenient for them toffee-nosed buggers?" her father stormed. "I'll never understand you, Julia, if I live to be a thousand. You could have had Walker's Tannery or Whitlam Brewery, but oh, no, nothing but aristocracy for you. Viscount bloody Linton. What good is he? Neither use nor ornament!"

"Listen to him!" she almost screamed. "All that matters to him is money!"

"You think money isn't important to that long streak of piss you're marrying? I've bought him for you and well you know it, so don't go turning your nose up at my money."

"Oh, Patrick, he's the most vulgar man in the whole world," she cried.

"Me? Vulgar? Wait till Viscount bloody Linton gets you in bed; then you'll know what vulgar is!" he shouted.

"You dirty old Irishman!" she shrilled.

"Don't you ever forget your name is O'Reilly, my lass. . . ."

Patrick was choking with laughter. "Father, your face is purple. Calm down. A minute ago you were near to a fit calling the Irish names, now you're near to a fit defending them. Julia, my love, you are magnificent when you're angry. I believe you provoke these quarrels on purpose just to flaunt your beauty before your menfolk." He steered her toward the door, and as he did so he whispered, "Start packing. It may take a couple of weeks, but I'll convince him to go to London." She threw her arms about him and kissed him.

"Father, you lose your temper too much. What's wrong with you these days? I think you're suffering from night starvation. What you need is a woman. Now, if you were in London I know this little place called The Divan. They bring you champagne while you make your choice from girls hanging from chandeliers."

"You think we don't have any whorehouses in Bolton? I don't have to go to London. I don't need to leave my own house. Any one of the maids would jump into my bed if I crooked my finger."

Patrick was helpless with laughter. "There isn't one of them that doesn't have a face like a boiled boot."

"Aye, there's method in my madness. You'd have 'um in your bed two at a time if they were pretty."

"And here was I thinking you always underestimated me," Patrick said with a chuckle.

Two days later Jonathan O'Reilly stood in the huge hall of Castle Hill amid all the people of the estate.

"Lock, stock and barrel; men, women and children—I own the mills where you will be given work, and the houses where you will live. I know some of you have relatives in Bolton and you will go to them. Get your belongings together today; no livestock whatsoever will be transported," he stated firmly. A great amount of conversation went up. People who had become hopeless now saw a way out. They were all willing to place their fate in his hands because the alternative was unthinkable. "Tim and Mick here will help you load your tackle on the wagons, just personal belongings now, no furniture. We'll start for Dublin first thing in the morning. You'll be on the boat to Liverpool overnight. Now then, Maggie"—he singled out Castle Hill's housekeeper—"about my dinner."

In the kitchen Maggie spotted Kitty slipping out the back door. "Not so fast, Miss Mischief. You can serve the squire his dinner. He'd have me running in and out like a dog at a fair, and your feet are younger than mine."

"I'll serve him if I can have something to eat," Kitty said impertinently.

"Faith, child, there's little enough, only a rabbit pie, but I'll share whatever is left of it with you."

Kitty washed her hands and face very carefully and put on a clean apron. In the dining room Jonathan O'Reilly looked askance at Kitty in her bedraggled skirt and bare feet, carrying in the big dish with her head bent over it.

"What's your name?" he asked. She lifted her head up and he thought, My God, she's got a face like a flower.

"Kitty, milord."

"I remember you. Don't think I don't. How old are you now?"

"Fifteen, Milord."

"The old Gypsy, your grandfather, has relatives in Lancashire, doesn't he?"

"I believe he does, milord."

O'Reilly's mind was trying to smooth a path for Kitty that led directly to his bed. "Mmm, the mill is a hard place for a little wench like you, so I think I'll make an exception in your case and find you a place in my household. You'll make a nice little maid—that is, of course, if you know how to do as you're told."

She seemed to hesitate.

"Well, what is it? Speak up!" he shouted.

"It's my brother, Terrance, milord. He's wonderful with horses, sor, You don't suppose you could find it in your heart to make room for him too, do you?" she asked imploringly.

He compressed his lips. "You drive a hard bargain, you little rogue."

She dimpled at him and he was surprised to hear himself say, "How would you like a piece of this rabbit pie?"

"Oh, yes, please, milord," Kitty said prettily.

She ate so heartily, yet with the daintiness of a kitten; he was fascinated just watching her.

"Have you no shoes?" he asked abruptly.

"No, milord."

"Mmm; well, all that will be changed when we get to Bolton. Here, have some more." He finished off the second bottle of claret he had had the foresight to bring with him. "With the proper food, we'll soon have you filled out."

She scraped her plate clean and arose from the table and bobbed him a curtsy. "Milord, I'm after packing up all our belongings. If you'll excuse me now, sor?"

"Run along, run along. You and your brother go with your grandfather to his relations, and I'll have the carriage sent round for you."

"Thank you, milord."

She took the empty pie plate back to Maggie, who said with dismay, "He's eaten the lot!"

"Yes, isn't he a glutton?" ventured Kitty before she slipped out the back door.

Patrick sat in the mill office with the foremen and over-seers. He was patiently trying to explain why he was in favor of abolishing the Half-time Factory System in the three mills that the O'Reillys owned. These mills were known as the Falcon, the Egyptian and the Gibraltar. Jonathan O'Reilly had named them thus so they would not sound Irish.

"It's sheer exploitation of child labor. After working in this damp, dirty, noisy atmosphere from six in the morning until twelve noon, these exhausted children are expected to go into the classroom. They probably fall asleep over their books, instead of learning anything."

One of the men spoke up, "If we didn't employ children, there would be more work available for men and women, but Mr. O'Reilly, your father, would never pay the extra wages that would entail."

Patrick raised his hand and said, "I'll handle my father. You tell the workers there will be no more children after the end of the month. Now, Saturday noon I want the machinery pulled down and cleaned properly. Workmen are coming in to install mechanical devices to the looms in the form of a warp-stop motion. It will up production considerably. I realize the workers always struggle to retain traditional methods of production against oncoming thrusts of technocracy and automation, but it will be your job to convince them of the wisdom of these changes. They will be immeasurably better off in the long run. Now, I'll be at the Falcon tomorrow and the Gibraltar the next day, if you need me."

He went into the millyard and unlocked the gates to let himself out. "Billy, why are these bloody gates always locked?" he asked the outside overseer.

"Orders, sir. I unlock the gates at five-thirty and lock 'em again at six sharp."

"But what if someone was late? They couldn't get in," Patrick pointed out.

"That's the idea. They don't work if they're late. That way they aren't late a second time. My orders are not to unlock them again until six o'clock at night."

"Well, here's some new orders for you, Billy. When you unlock these gates at five-thirty, don't lock them again until everyone has gone home. It's a mill, not a bloody prison!"

Later that evening Patrick let himself into the flat of Dolly Worthing; he had been paying for the flat the past six months. She was a pretty blond widow, well endowed with seductive curves.

"Why, Patrick, darling, I wasn't expecting you tonight."

He looked at her breasts, barely concealed beneath the filmy material of her negligee. He cocked an eyebrow and said, "Who were you expecting?"

"Why, no one, of course. Patrick, you are a vexing creature. You haven't been here for over a week, and then you come in and accuse me of being unfaithful." She pouted prettily.

"The thought never entered my mind until you put it there."

He had no illusions about Dolly. She would be faithful only as long as it suited her purpose. If she could find someone richer she would move along without a backward glance, he thought. But in truth he didn't give enough credit where it was due, because Dolly was mad for him. He was easily the most accomplished lover she had ever known, even though he always kept a part of himself aloof so that never, even in their most intimate moments, did he give himself completely. He poured himself a brandy, then pulled three or four envelopes from his breast pocket and threw them down on the sofa beside her. "What the devil are these, Dolly?"

"My letters. When you didn't come I wrote asking you what was wrong."

"Do you realize how irritating it is to be pursued and questioned about my whereabouts continually?"

She moved close to him and put back her head so that her lips invited him. Instead of kissing her he sipped his brandy reflectively. She was piqued; determined to arouse him, she slipped her hand down his thigh until it came to rest on the bulge at his crotch. He was easily aroused, but not nearly so easily as she herself. "Finish your brandy and come to bed," she whispered. He didn't appear to be in any hurry, so she slipped out of her negligee and stood before him naked. If only he would be subservient as other men had been. She wanted him at her feet, declaring undying love for the favors she would grant him, but he was too arrogant, too sure of himself for his own good. He put down his glass and followed her into the bedroom. He undressed slowly. She couldn't wait and helped him with avid fingers. His arms went around her and he kissed her slowly, expertly. She was

all over him, kissing, stroking, cupping him. He lay back
with his hands under his head.

"What's the matter, Patrick?" she asked, breathing heavily.

"Nothing. When you're in this mood, I might as well lie
back and let you do all the work; after all, that's what I'm
paying you for."

It was like a slap in the face. Hurt and angry, she withdrew
immediately.

"That's better," he said quietly, and set to work to win
her back into a loving mood. "I enjoy the pursuit, Dolly."

Afterward, as her breasts began to soften in the aftermath
of pleasure, he caressed her and murmured, "What kind of a
present would you like?"

She hesitated for only a second, "What I would really like,
Patrick, is to go to London with you next time you go."

He stiffened. "That's impossible! My sister is being married in a few weeks. It would be most improper."

"I see. Well, never mind; I have some dress bills that are
outrageous."

"You always do, to say nothing of the ones you run up at
the jewelers."

She knew he was tiring of her; there was nothing she could
do about it.

Chapter 3

When the immigrants disembarked at the Liverpool docks they were a sorry sight. The women clutched pathetic children and the men carried their meager belongings with an air of dogged resignation. Their faces were blank with tired hunger, but in every breast was the hope that things would at last get better. They were herded like sheep onto wagons, which O'Reilly had hired especially for their transportation to Bolton. Kitty stared about her, taking in every detail of the new country she had come to. It wasn't anything like she had imagined. She had pictured big houses, beautifully dressed ladies in carriages, magnificent shops, and wealthy men with dozens of servants. Instead she saw a dark, damp country where the predominating color seemed to be black. With each successive town they passed through, the atmosphere seemed to get bleaker. The houses were little and poor, row after row of them. The people were clad in black clogs and shawls, their faces grim, their bodies small and stunted. The buildings were black, the factories were black and there was black smoke everywhere. Gone were the beautiful green fields of Ireland.

In her scarlet skirt and shawl, Kitty stood out as the Gypsy she was. Her grandfather saw the look of dismay upon her face and asked kindly, "What's the matter, my little wench?"

"Everything is so dirty and so—so drab."

"Never mind, lass. Where there's muck there's money."

"Oh, Grandada, you have a saying for everything. But where are the big houses and the foine carriages?"

"Ah, now, you'll be meaning London. This is Lancashire, where all the manufacturing goes on. I expect this is where all the money is made and the people go to London to spend it."

Terry squeezed Kitty's hand. "Never mind, we won't be staying in dirty little streets like these. We'll be living at the squire's and he's bound to have a grand place."

Kitty said, "I feel so sorry for everybody. How will they get used to factory work?" Swaddy patted her hand and said, "Ye get used to hanging if ye hang long enough."

It was late that night before everyone was settled with the Irish families who lived on "Spake Hazy." Swaddy and his two grandchildren were left at his niece's house. Ada Blakely, a little woman aged beyond her years, made them welcome with hot tea and potato pie. Her husband, Jack, was not in evidence, and she explained that he always spent his evenings at the Dog & Kennel, a pub at the top of the street. She had five children, ranging from a girl of twelve to a new baby. All were in bed save the oldest girl, Doris, who couldn't take her eyes off the beautiful brother and sister who had been billeted on them.

"These little houses only have two up and two down. I don't know wherever you are going to sleep," Ada said, wringing her hands helplessly.

Kitty spoke up, "Terry and I can sleep down here, it will only be for tonight. Tomorrow, Squire O'Reilly is sending his carriage for us. We are to work at his house. Grandada is too old to go into the mill, but he will be a great help to you, I know. He's very good with children; he brought Terrance and me up from little babies."

"Maybe I could let you look after the little 'uns and I could get set on at the mill," Ada said hopefully to the old man.

After everyone had gone to bed, Terry lay down on the horsehair sofa, and Kitty sat curled before the fire reading her book, the only possession she had brought with her except for the family tarot cards. She read:

Never scratch your head, pick your teeth, clean your nails, or worse than all, pick your nose in company. Spit as little as possible, and never upon the floor.

Kitty put the book down and slipped into blessed sleep.

The carriage arrived early and Kitty was vastly relieved that the squire had kept his word. After a tearful good-bye the carriage took them away from the dark little streets and out toward the country. In the daylight Kitty could see that the town sat in a bowl and if you lifted your eyes to the horizon, it was surrounded by green moors.

"Oh, it's a town in a bowl, Terrance. That's why it's called 'Bolton'!"

The O'Reillys lived at Hey House. The carriage turned up a long drive bordered by huge rhododendron bushes, which were a mass of red bloom. Terry was let off at the stables and Kitty was led to the servants' entrance. The housekeeper looked her up and down and gave a loud sniff. "Irish Gypsy! I don't know whatever the master is thinking of."

Kitty thought, I'll have you eatin' out of my hand before this day is out, missus. Then she curtsied to the housekeeper and said prettily, "Pleased to meet you, ma'am. I can see I shall be happy here, you have created such a warm, welcoming atmosphere. No wonder the squire always speaks of you in such glowing terms when he comes to Ireland."

Mrs. Thomson showed a flicker of interest and Kitty pressed her advantage. "A treasure, that's what he's after calling you behind your back."

"Come and sit by the fire, child; have you no shoes?"

"No, ma'am, but himself told me to put myself entirely into your capable hands and you would do me proud."

"Did he indeed?" she simpered. "Here, let's have a cup of tea."

"Oh, thank you, ma'am. I can see by your face how kind you are. I can read your tea leaves for you when we are finished."

"Oh, how lovely, but don't tell me if it's anything bad!"

"Oh, nothing bad is in store for you, ma'am, I can feel it in me bones."

The housekeeper wore no wedding ring, so Kitty gazed at the tea leaves at the bottom of her cup and said, "I can see a letter 'T' here."

"Why, that's my name, Mrs. Thomson. How clever you are."

"I also see a man here who thinks of you constantly. He is waiting for an encouraging word from you."

Mrs. Thomson's mind went rapidly over the servants and the deliverymen.

"He is a man who is held in great esteem by everyone. He holds some position of authority such as doctor, or perhaps a man of the cloth." She swiftly glanced at Mrs. Thomson and caught her with a blush upon her cheeks. Ah, not far off the mark, thought Kitty shrewdly.

"We can't sit here all day gossiping. Here is a clean uniform for you, it's a little large, but what will hold more, will hold less. Now, you must keep all that hair covered up. Here's a mobcap for you. Now I must see what I can do about shoes and stockings, and then I'll find you something to keep you busy. I must admit I wasn't looking forward to training a new maid, but I think you'll do very nicely."

* * *

At lunchtime Jonathan sat down with his two daughters.

"Father, you look tired out," exclaimed Julia.

"No bloody wonder. I've crossed the Irish Sea twice this week. Do you realize how much it's cost me to transport that lot to Lancashire?" he asked.

"Father, it's simply not done to discuss money all the time, especially to ladies, and especially at table," she said repressively.

Barbara watched with horror as her father's face turned purple, and before he could say anything she begged, "Oh, please don't fight!"

"There now, you've upset your sister," thundered O'Reilly. "Why can't you be a gentle girl like Barbara?"

Julia rolled her eyes to the ceiling in exasperation.

"Where's Patrick?" he demanded.

"He's over at the Falcon today; he left a message not to go running down there this afternoon. You'd do better to have a rest instead."

"Why is it everybody knows what's best for me?" he thundered. "Barbara, sit up straight! Stop playing with your food! Julia, why is it you and Patrick are always giving orders and demanding your own way?"

"Because if we didn't, you'd bully us the way you bully Barbara. I hope you haven't forgotten the Leavers are coming for dinner tonight."

"That's good. Maybe you'll watch that sharp tongue of yours!" he shouted.

"You'll dominate the conversation and I won't be able to get a word in edgewise," she said and laughed.

He looked at Barbara. "It wouldn't hurt you to try to take part in the conversation at dinner tonight, instead of sitting there like you're posing for Lipton's pickle jars." He looked at Julia. "What do you mean, I bully her?" he demanded aggressively.

"Oh, why don't you go for a drive this afternoon? It's such a lovely day, it will soothe your nerves. But stay away from the mills."

Jonathan O'Reilly got dressed up and walked over to the stables. He ordered the carriage. He directed his driver to take him through town, and he sat back enjoying the fine afternoon. He felt good and his spirits rose as the carriage made its way through the center of town. He called to his driver to stop outside Ward's Florists, where he descended and bought an impressive bouquet of roses, carnations and snapdragons, then gave the driver an address he called up out of the past. He ascended the flight of stairs after confidently dismissing the carriage, with orders to return in two hours, and knocked on the door. "Hello, Dolly. Remember me?" he said and smiled.

"Why, Mr. O'Reilly," she said and smiled hesitantly. "I haven't seen you in ages."

"It must be nearly two years, eh, Dolly? These are for you, my dear."

"Won't you come in?" she asked a little apprehensively. She wondered if he had found out about her and Patrick and had come to make trouble. She smelled the flowers and opened the little card that came with them. Inside were fifteen pounds and it was suddenly very clear what he had come for. She had most of her bills paid for her and received many presents, but it wasn't too often that she received cold cash, and the temptation was too great to refuse. She smiled provocatively at him and said, "Come and make yourself comfortable, Johnny."

"It's rather warm today," he said as he divested himself of his coat and sat down.

"Would you care for a cold drink?"

"Some brandy would suit me better, lass," he said and winked.

"Help yourself then, Johnny. I'll just change into something a little cooler," she said suggestively.

Before he had finished his drink, she came back in a loose wrapper and as she sat down beside him on the sofa, the wrapper fell apart to reveal her long legs. He reached for her and gave her a deep kiss, then reached up and parted the top of her wrapper. "My, you have a fine pair of breasts, Dolly. They always did excite me."

She laughed throatily and removed his hands, which were squeezing her painfully.

He licked his lips and his breathing quickened considerably.

"I think we'd be more comfortable in the bedroom," she whispered. She took his hand and he trotted after her eagerly. He took off his waistcoat and she knelt in front of him and unbuttoned his shirt and slipped it off. She repressed a smile at the sight of his undervest on such a warm day, and lifted it over his head. She bent to remove his boots and her wrapper again parted to reveal her breasts. Jonathan quickly stripped the wrapper from her completely and put his mouth to her nipples. As she divested him of his pants, she noted that he was indeed ready for business; however, she knew that older men often lost their erections, so she didn't want to delay the action with too many preliminaries. She positioned herself under him and he began thrusting vigorously. As he did so, his face became an alarming shade of crimson with overtones of purple, and his breathing became labored.

"Johnny, are you all right? Here, why don't you lie back and let me on top?"

Patrick had finished his business at the mill. Remembering that the Leavers were coming for dinner, he decided to drop in on Dolly. He slipped his key into the lock and entered quietly. He could hear noises coming from the bedroom, so

he pushed the door open and stopped dead on the threshold.
Dolly's buttocks were rising and falling rhythmically and
Jonathan was groaning hoarsely. Patrick looked at them
coldly and said, "Father, I see you've taken my advice for
once." He paused and looked distastefully at Dolly's opulent
flesh. "Dolly, still doing all the work, I see. Don't let me
interrupt you, I'll let myself out." He placed his key on the
table and quietly left. When he got outside, he leaned against
the wall and laughed until the tears rolled down his face.

Patrick opened the front door to greet the Leavers.

"Hello, Patrick. Sorry my wife couldn't come tonight, but
her mother's ill, so she begged to be excused and she sends
her regrets."

"Well, I'm glad you and your son could make it, James.
You're looking very well." He shook hands with the two
men. "Ah, here's Father," he said, keeping a bland expression on his face as he looked the older man in the eye. The
table was beautiful and Julia was at her best, especially in
male company. Her wit sparkled and her conversation never
lagged.

Patrick was determined to use this visit to his advantage by
letting his father in on the changes he had been making at the
mill. If he could get James Leaver on his side, they would
overrule the old man. Barbara sat beside her brother, desperately trying to think of something to add to the conversation.
Finally she said, "This soup is delicious."

Her father glowered at her from across the table, and Patrick smiled down at her and slipped her hand into his. She
felt better immediately.

Patrick plunged in, "Father has abolished half-time for
children at the mill." Jonathan almost choked on his green
peas.

James Leaver looked pleasantly surprised. "That was a

courageous thing to do, John; commendable, highly commendable.''

Before his father could speak, Patrick went on, ''Mind you, it will cost him, but he's decided to be generous.''

''Will you have difficulty finding workers to replace them?'' Leaver asked. Patrick answered for his father, ''As a matter of fact that's another generous thing father has done. He's brought over all our people from Ireland at his own expense and he's giving them jobs at the mill.''

By the time Leaver and his son had finished complimenting Jonathan on his beneficence, O'Reilly realized Patrick had outmaneuvered him, so he decided to capitulate and bask in everyone's approval.

''Have you changed over your looms yet?'' asked young Leaver.

Patrick allowed his father to answer this time. ''Monday morning we start production with the improvements.''

''Do you think there'll be any trouble? Remember when James Barlow introduced power looms in his mill? The repercussions were terrible with the local hand-loom weavers.''

''If there is trouble, I'll handle it!'' said Jonathan darkly.

''Barlows—aren't they the ones who make the satin quilts?'' asked Julia.

''Oh, Patrick gave me a beautiful pink one,'' piped up Barbara, then subsided into blushes.

Everyone smiled at her except her father. He spoke up quickly, ''You two lasses can withdraw and leave us to our port.'' Julia bristled—she hated these customs that gave men the upper hand in all dealings with women, but Barbara was relieved to escape.

When the two girls were alone, Julia said, ''Are you packed for London yet?''

"No, I don't think Papa will allow us to go," answered Barbara.

"Nonsense! Patrick promised, and he always gets his way, doesn't he?"

"You mean *you* do, Julia," said Barbara, not afraid to be bold now.

Julia spied Kitty and said sharply, "Get my sister's trunks out and pack for London. Be very careful with her things. You're new, aren't you? Are you sure that you know how to pack?"

Kitty answered. "Yes, ma'am," and right away Julia sniffed, "Irish!"

"Please, ma'am, can you tell me where the trunks will be?" asked Kitty.

"My God, Irish, how am I to know? Somewhere in the attics, I imagine. You'll have to ask. You've got a tongue in your head, haven't you?"

Kitty thought, Begod, just as arrogant as that brother of yours, but then her heart skipped a beat at the thought of him.

"When are you leaving for London, ma'am?" asked Kitty politely.

"None of your business, Irish. I'm not here to answer your impertinent questions!" Julia pointed out.

"That's cause you don't know!" flashed Kitty, and Barbara laughed.

Julia slapped Kitty's face. She immediately retaliated and slapped Julia's face in the exact same spot. The two girls stood red-faced and glared. "How dare you?" Julia said incredulously.

Kitty said, "If you hurt me, I'll hurt you back."

Barbara held her breath, terrified of the outburst that would ensue, but Julia, being the unpredictable young woman she was, laughed and said, "At last! Someone with some spirit around here.'' She shook a finger at Kitty, ''But don't try my patience too far, Irish.''

By the sounds emanating from the dining room the men were deeply involved in their business conversation and would likely be hours. Barbara shrugged and said, ''I'll go and help Kitty.''

''Wait—don't leave. Let's play a game of cards,'' Julia suggested restlessly.

''Oh, Julia, you know I'm no good at cards; you always win,'' protested Barbara.

''I could read the cards for you,'' suggested Kitty.

''Do you mean tell our fortunes?'' asked Julia, her interest piqued.

''Oh, Kitty, are you a Gypsy?'' asked Barbara, wide-eyed.

''Yes and yes,'' confessed Kitty.

''Are you any good at it?'' asked Julia bluntly.

''I'm an expert,'' Kitty said, queening it over them. ''I can read palms, tea leaves, cards and the ancient tarot. I can even do it all in rhyme if you like.''

Julia handed her a deck of cards. ''Let's see.''

Kitty considered for a moment. Young girls usually were interested in young men and falling in love. ''We'll all three play this game. Each one of us shuffles the deck and picks out five cards. Then I'll give you the rhyme that goes with each card.''

''Me first,'' said Julia, taking the cards back from Kitty. She shuffled the cards quickly and with deliberation selected five cards, face down on the table. Kitty turned over the six of spades.

Your lucky color is turquoise blue,
Your lucky number is five times two.

The next card was the five of diamonds.

If you would be a rich man's bride,
Bake a cake with a silver coin inside.

The third card was the eight of clubs.

Love, wealth and power will be yours,
If every night you lock two doors.

"Ha!" said Julia with a laugh. "They won't even let me have a key."

Kitty turned over the fourth card: the king of spades.

If his name begins with J,
You will seldom get your way.

"Oh, however did you know Julia's future husband is called Jeffrey?" asked Barbara, amazed.

"It's in the cards," said Kitty.

"Well, I shall always get my way," asserted Julia. "That's the reason I chose him."

The last card was the queen of diamonds.

This week or next will likely bring,
Good luck and an engagement ring.

"Oh, we will be going to London after all," exclaimed Barbara.

"Barbara, it's just a silly card game," Julia said, but she was well pleased with Kitty's prophecies.

"Shuffle the remaining cards and pick your five," said Kitty.

Barbara hesitated. "You go first, Kitty."

Kitty shrugged and picked up the cards. The first one was the seven of hearts.

If a blue butterfly you see,
You are fated to sail over the sea.

"Heaven preserve us, I've just done that," muttered Kitty.

"Don't worry, you won't see any blue butterflies in Bolton," scoffed Julia.

"Now, that's a lie," said Kitty, "for you are wearing, at this very moment, an enameled brooch which happens to be a blue butterfly."

Julia looked down at her shoulder. "So I am. You made it up!" she said flatly.

The next card was the three of diamonds.

Three men, three men in love with you,
But only one will e'er be true.

She turned over the four of clubs.

His heart is black, he likes his fun,
So turn to one whose name is John.

"That's Father's name," said Barbara with a giggle.

"His name is Jonathan," said Julia sternly.

Kitty's fourth card was the knave of hearts.

Beware of Cupid and his darts!
Your fate is held by the knave of hearts.

Her last card was the queen of hearts.

The queen of hearts, the king of love,
A rose, a ring and a snow-white dove.

"Oh, that's beautiful," said Barbara. She took the cards, shuffled them rather ineptly and slowly picked out five cards. The nine of spades was the first.

At nine in the morning on Saturday,
You will be traveling far away.

The ace of hearts was next.

Your fate is sealed on a Thursday night,
Amid moonlight, flowers and pure delight.

The next card turned over was the ten of clubs.

When the sun goes down, for luck and love,
Hide a new penny in a velvet glove.

"You shouldn't tell her that. She'll go upstairs and do it," said Julia with a laugh.
The king of diamonds came up next.

First he kisses your fingertips,
Then love is sealed with scarlet lips.

Barbara blushed prettily. The last card was the two of clubs.

A Gypsy girl will tell you the truth—
You are fated to marry the love of your youth.

"Oh," gasped Barbara, going a deeper pink.
"What rubbish!" said Julia with a laugh. "You'd better get that packing done." When the other two girls had disappeared upstairs, Julia slipped out in the direction of the stables.

* * *

"Enough about the mills; how is the wholesale grocery business these days?" asked Jonathan.

"Oh, it's doing well, John, but it's my son here that's surprised me. You know he started that little soap works a year ago? Well, I can tell you he's come up with a soap that's better than anything you've ever seen."

James Leaver's son looked pleasantly embarrassed at his father's praise but conceded, "It is good. That's what I wanted to talk to Patrick about. You've got such good ideas on marketing products, I wanted your advice."

"To be a success you need only one thing—a good-quality product. But to be a phenomenal success you also need a good advertising campaign. Now, you start with a name that grabs the attention. What do you call your soap?"

"Why, it's Leaver's Soap, of course," interposed James Leaver.

"You need a more catchy name than that," asserted Patrick.

Young Leaver said, "Well, I have been kicking a few names around, but I'm afraid of looking foolish."

"It's your soap! Have the courage of your convictions," urged Patrick.

"Well, I think of it as 'Sun Light' soap."

"That's very good. A woman would like that. Your best bet at the moment is billboards. As many as you can get and the bigger the better. Keep it simple. In large letters that fill up the whole billboard you put SUN LIGHT SOAP and underneath in small letters put something like 'Best Soap in the World'; modesty doesn't count in business. Send salesmen to every major town and the orders will come in so fast you'll have to expand production. As soon as business warrants it, open an office in London. I can help you there with contacts."

"I don't want this advice for nothing, Patrick. I'll pay you a retainer."

"I'd rather have a one percent interest in your soap venture."

Jonathan winked at James. "He's got a head for business, that lad, probably richer than I am with his one percent of this and that."

"You can't beat quality, Father. In Lancashire we manufacture some of the best goods in the world. I'm thinking of exporting to America."

"Eh? What's this?" his father demanded.

"Oh, I've been talking to a shipowner in Liverpool, Isaac Bolt. If I bought half interest in a ship, we could take over our textiles from the mills and perhaps some of your soap. We have so many things that are manufactured right here in Bolton, I'd be spoiled for choice. Dobson makes the finest steam engines, and Webster makes water pumps and windmills. There's Springfield Paper Mills and Walmsley's wrought iron. In Bolton we make everything—chemical dyes, furniture, glass, leather goods, carpets, even coffins," offered Patrick. He continued, "I'm thinking of sailing myself. Then I could buy the best long staple cotton from the Carolinas." He allowed his father to digest all this.

James Leaver looked across at Jonathan O'Reilly and shook his head. "We thought we had big ideas when we started out, but if these two aren't careful, their names will go down in the history books," he said and winked.

"How am I supposed to run three mills while you go running off to America?"

Patrick said with a laugh, "Ah, well, it won't be tomorrow, Father."

Kitty lay in her small iron bed on the third floor and went over every pretty article she had packed. She pretended the clothes were hers. She was deep into a fantasy now. She swirled around the ballroom floor in the most exquisite creation, and all heads were turned in her direction. Ladies whispered about her behind their fans and she looked up into her partner's adoring eyes, and her partner was none other than . . .

Suddenly a stone fell onto her face. The drowsy sensations of near sleep she had been enjoying vanished immediately. She sat up quickly.

"Psst, Irish."

Kitty leaned out the little dormer window and saw Julia on the driveway below.

"I'm locked out, Irish. Come and open the front door without rousing the house." Kitty was shocked at Julia's behavior. "I have to be up at five o'clock. How dare you wake me up at this ungodly hour, you selfish girl!"

"Please, Irish?"

"Me name's Kitty!"

"Please, Kitty?"

Kitty crept down the two flights of stairs and quietly opened the front door for her. The look she bestowed upon Julia was one of tight-lipped disapproval. Kitty had no idea what she had been up to, but instinctively knew it was wrong.

Julia looked at Kitty and said, "You look like you've been eating pickled Bibles." They both giggled and then shushed each other. By the time they climbed the stairs and Julia reached her room in safety, they were firm allies.

Chapter 4

On Monday morning, Jonathan O'Reilly was up at dawn and on his way to the mills, determined to take the reins back in his own hands. First at the Falcon, then at the Egyptian, and finally at the Gibraltar he had called in the men before work began on the new machines and made it clear that in return for this technical innovation, management would claim a substantial reduction in wage rates. The men were surly and instead of producing more work they produced considerably less. Trouble was brewing ominously, but it wouldn't erupt until after working hours, when they could get together and decide on a plan of action.

Patrick, blissfully unaware of his father's intentions, decided to let him have the running of the mills to himself and went off with a friend to a horse race.

Kitty emptied the bucket of dirty water after she had scrubbed the kitchen floor and Mrs. Thomson took pity on her. "It's almost ten o'clock, child. Mr. Parker will be here to give Miss Barbara her lessons. They are from ten to twelve each morning in the library. You be the chaperone today. Take your duster in there and after you're finished, just sit quietly until the lessons are over."

Mr. Parker was a thin, ratty little man dressed in a shabby but genteel fashion. Kitty almost pitied him until she saw he enjoyed the way he could make Barbara cower. He insisted that she could not give him verbal answers, but that she must write everything down on the slate.

Kitty moved about slowly so as not to attract attention as she went about the room dusting. When she came to the grandfather clock, she moved the hands ahead an hour, then moved over to the bookshelves and continued to dust.

"Now, Miss O'Reilly, seeing you are hopeless in mathematics, we will put it aside and do spelling, and let me tell you, young woman, every time you make a mistake you will write it out one hundred times. That should keep you busy all evening, for from what I've seen, your spelling is as atrocious as your mathematics."

Kitty opened a dictionary and with her voice low and her back toward Barbara and Mr. Parker, she began spelling the first word for Barbara. Kitty said quickly, "Just put down what I tell you, he can't hear me, you know, he's as deaf as a doornail. That's why he makes you write everything on the slate."

They finished the list of words and she handed him her slate to be checked for mistakes.

Kitty kept her face to the wall. "You mustn't be afraid of him, Barbara. He probably threatens to tell your father about you, eh?"

"Now take a fresh slate and make proper sentences using the following words." Mr. Parker was clearly annoyed that Barbara had made no errors for which she could be punished.

"Employer," Mr. Parker dictated.

Kitty said, "Put down: Does your employer know you are deaf?"

"Employee," he continued.

"Put down: Employees should not bully little girls." Kitty moved silently over to the desk behind Mr. Parker, picked up his pocket watch and altered the time to match that of the grandfather clock.

"Employment," intoned Mr. Parker.

"You are about to lose your employment," whispered Kitty.

The tall clock chimed twelve and Barbara arose to hand him her slate.

"Where are you going, miss?"

She pointed to the grandfather clock and he looked thunderstruck. He took his pocket watch from the desk, checked it and looked up, thoroughly bewildered.

Barbara curtsied, handed him the slate and disappeared as fast as her legs would carry her, but Kitty lingered behind to see the look on his face when he read the slate.

He looked down at the sentences and his pallor went from dirty white to dirty gray. He spluttered, "Little bitch!"

Kitty held the feather duster to her ear like an ear trumpet and shouted, "Eh?" before following Barbara from the room.

After the evening meal Jonathan went off to his club and Patrick decided to visit the theater. He very seldom told Bradshaw to bring the carriage to the front door, but usually went to the stables and coach house himself because he liked the atmosphere there. He had won a little on the horses and was in a good mood, blissfully unaware of how incongruous he looked in frilled shirt and tall silk hat, fondling the muzzle of one of the carriage horses. Patrick caught sight of Terry and somewhere in the recesses of his mind he was vaguely aware that he was familiar. "Who's this?" he asked Bradshaw.

"That's the new lad I was telling you about this afternoon. The squire wants me to teach him how to drive the carriage, but to my way of thinking, he's not old enough." Bradshaw couldn't hide the fact that he didn't want any competition, and Patrick hid a grin. "He can come along tonight," he said, winking at Terry, who was delighted with the plans. Patrick knew it would annoy Bradshaw, but Patrick also remembered what it felt like to be denied things because you were too young. Patrick sat in his box at the theater considering the chorus girls very carefully. When he had made his selection he was just about to send a note backstage when the bookkeeper from the Gibraltar mill lifted the curtain and entered the box.

"Mr. O'Reilly, thank God I've found you. There's trouble at the mill. I went up to the house, but your father was out and they told me where I would likely find you."

Patrick stiffened. "What kind of trouble?"

"Well, your father cut the wage rates today and there's an ugly crowd gathered outside the mill. I can't control them."

"Let's go," said Patrick, gathering up his hat and gloves. He stepped inside the Man & Scythe Pub and caught Bradshaw's eye. Terry followed them to the pub's coachyard, where the carriage was parked. "Gibraltar Mill, and hurry."

The well-lit streets of the town center were soon left behind as they drove into the poorer district. The carriage rumbled over the greasy cobbles of the dark street. Despite the poor light, they could see that a large crowd was gathered. The bookkeeper was very nervous. "You can't tackle them on your own, sir; they're a bunch of mad buggers. You know what the Irish are when roused, nothing but brutes and savages. Oh! Beggin' yer pardon, sir."

Patrick's teeth showed like a wolf's. "I suppose we are," he said reflectively. A crowd of men, women and children hurled curses and abuse when they spotted the carriage. They brandished bottles, bricks and assorted clubs as Patrick looked out from the carriage and saw their hard-set features.

"Put the clogs to 'im! Blood-suckin' bastard!" and a woman's shrill, "The old pisspot, let me get me hands on 'im!"

Patrick's tall figure emerged from the carriage and someone shouted, "It's not the O'Reilly, it's Patrick!"

He looked into the anger-filled faces where usually he saw only despair.

"I won't let my father cut wage rates and that's a promise. Now disperse and go home. You know you are breaking the law, or do I have to read you the Riot Act?" They stood back silently from the tall man. His evening dress told them clearly that they were slum rats and he was of the ruling class. He continued, "The saying is that the Irish would rather fight than eat, but I don't believe that. I think putting food on the table is more important to you than rioting. Now take my word about the wages and go."

Slowly the crowd started to melt away. Patrick let out a relieved breath and cursed his pigheaded father. "By Christ, you can always tell a Lancashire man, but you can't tell him much!" He glanced around. "Where's Bradshaw?" he asked Terry.

"The minute the carriage stopped, he made himself scarce. I'm after thinking he was scared shitless, sor."

"It looks like we've seen the back of them all, but before we go I'd better make sure there's nobody lurking about in the millyard. You'd better stay with the horses, lad."

Patrick went around the back of the mill, heard and saw nothing and turned to retrace his steps when a dark figure from the shadows darted out and attacked him. It all happened so quickly; Patrick grappled with the burly figure and saw the blade's glint just in time. He recoiled sharply and the knife that was intended for his heart slid against his breastbone and was diverted upward through the breast muscle. The impact felled him, and his attacker took off over the mill wall into the blackness. Terry thought he heard a scuffle, but he was loath to leave the horses alone. When Patrick didn't return he knew he had no choice. When he saw him, Patrick was struggling to his feet.

"Yer bleedin', sor!"

"Rather badly, I'm afraid. Here, take my scarf and wad it up against my shoulder."

Terry helped him to the carriage, terrified that he would expire before he could get help for him.

"Do you think you can drive?" asked Patrick.

"Of course I can drive. Just tell me where to find the doctor, sor."

"No. I don't want this news spread all over Bolton. Just get me home." Inside he fell back against the squabs. As the carriage jolted over the cobbles, the pain became almost unbearable and a couple of times he had to force his eyes to focus on a point in front of him to keep from passing out. Terry drove like a demon and soon he swept up the driveway to Hey House and helped Patrick up the front steps. Terry put his fingers to his mouth and gave an ear-piercing whistle. Three girls came running.

"Kitty, get some boiling water and bandages!" Terry shouted.

Julia cried, "My God, what's happened?"

"He's been stabbed," said Terry shortly. Barbara screamed.

Julia said, "Bring him upstairs."

Patrick leaned heavily on Terry's shoulder as he climbed to his bedroom and sank into a wing-backed chair gratefully. Barbara was before him on her knees clutching him, her face blanched so white Patrick feared for her. "Don't faint, sweetheart. Go and sit quietly over there. Everything will be fine."

"My God, look at the blood! Stay still, Patrick, you're getting it on everything!" cried Julia. "I've got to get the doctor."

"That's what I say, miss," Terry said firmly.

"No, Julia love, please. I want to keep it quiet," gasped Patrick.

Kitty came in with the bowl of hot water and towels; her

heart was in her throat with fear for him. She knelt before him and said to Terry, "Take off his coat and let's see how bad it is."

Patrick looked down into her face and thought he was hallucinating. Tears made her eyelashes spiky. He said, "Well, I'll be damned—Lady Jane Tut!" Terry eased him out of his coat, and Julia took scissors and cut away the shirt, which now was crimson. Kitty's heart contracted as her fingers gently washed the ugly wound. Patrick never took his eyes from her. Her lips were slightly parted and her breath quickened. He was so close to her he could see the tiny blue veins in her eyelids and smell the wild heather fragrance of her hair. It was as if he were alone with her; the babble of Julia and Barbara faded away from his consciousness. Her closeness was like an aphrodisiac. His nostrils quivered and his hand went without volition to her curls.

She sprang up and said, "It's not going to stop bleeding on its own; we'll have to bind it tightly. I'll fetch a clean sheet to tear it into strips," and she was gone.

Patrick looked at Terry with recognition. "That's where I've seen you before."

Julia said, "I'll fetch Mrs. Thomson and send a message to father's club."

"You'll do no such thing, Julia. I don't want that bloody woman fussing over me—I've got three now! As for Father, he won't be long. Now, Terry, be a good lad and pour me some brandy."

Kitty darted in, tearing the sheet into strips. She began to bandage him by wrapping them around his chest and over his left shoulder. When her fingers came into contact with his bare flesh she lowered her eyes and tried to keep from blushing. His closeness disturbed her; she couldn't think straight with his eyes on her. She finished tying the bandage and rose to her feet. Patrick sipped his second brandy and the fiery

liquid spread its fingers across his chest. His head felt impossibly light. He grinned down at Kitty. "I thought you were
going to be a great lady with a carriage. How come you're
only a maid?"

She looked into his mocking eyes and couldn't bear the
arrogance she saw there. She leaned slightly forward, placed
her hand upon his bandaged wound and squeezed cruelly. He
went white from the pain and only just managed to hang onto
consciousness.

"If you hurt me, I'll hurt you," she told him softly. Desire
flamed up in him. He could have taken her right there on the
floor in spite of his sisters' presence and the awful pain.

Jonathan O'Reilly came into his son's bedroom like a
pasty ghost. His usual high color had drained away with
dread of what he might discover. He began shouting to cover
that fear. Patrick glanced over at Barbara and knew she
shouldn't be subject to the harsh words that shortly would be
hurled about.

"Julia, take Barbara to her room; she's had enough excitement for one night."

Jonathan shouted, "Why in hell isn't the doctor here?"

Patrick kept his voice level. "I don't want a doctor; I don't
need a doctor. It's only a scratch."

Kitty immediately covered the crimson bowl of blood with
a towel. She curtsied to Mr. O'Reilly and left the room.

"We'll get the police. Not only are we going to put this
assassin behind bars, but whoever it was who started this
business, whoever it was who incited them to this behavior. . . ."

Patrick's head ached vilely and his vision blurred slightly,
but he pointed an accusing finger at his father and shouted,
"Goddamn it, that was you!"

The old man's jaw sagged open at the vehemence behind the words.

"I won't have the police involved in this, or the doctors. I don't want it spread from one end of Bolton to the other. Tomorrow I have to put right what you set wrong. I have to tell them that there will be no wage cuts and I have to gain back their confidence. Now hear me well, Father, for I'm fatigued. They tried to kill me because they thought I was you! It's not safe for you here, and tomorrow you'll take the girls and go down to London."

Jonathan O'Reilly sagged visibly. He looked at Terry and said quietly, "Let's get this lad into bed."

Kitty returned with a brass scuttle of coal to replenish the fire.

"I'll sit up with you tonight," Jonathan said firmly.

"I want everyone out of this room immediately. I can't stand another minute of this bloody hand-wringing. You'll have me buried before morning. Kitty! Fetch me some fresh water before you leave. Good night, Father." He pulled up the covers to his chin and closed his eyes.

Kitty returned with a supply of drinking water and a lovely crystal goblet on a silver tray. Patrick's hand gripped her wrist firmly and he pulled her toward him. They stared fiercely into each other's eyes for long minutes. His mouth was dry and he couldn't keep his thoughts clear. As he gazed at her she saw the arrogance leave his face for the first time since she met him. Her eyes softened, then also her heart. He mumbled thickly, "I don't think I should be alone." She placed her hand on his fevered brow and whispered comfortingly, "Neither do I."

Patrick fell into a doze and Kitty curled up in the armchair by the fire. In about an hour he was thrashing about the bed so wildly that she feared he would open the wound again. She tried to hold him still but it was impossible. He was

extremely fevered, so she held water to his lips and he drank
avidly. She bathed his brow, but still he would not settle, so
she brought a chair over to the bed and sat holding his hand
and murmuring soothing words. Gradually he grew calmer
and fell into another fitful doze. Another hour passed this
way and then he began to babble and became completely
delirious. She stayed with him all night, giving him water,
washing his face and hands and comforting him as best she
could. She daydreamed that he would fall in love with her
and ask her to marry him. She had seen the loving, generous
way he had with his sisters and longed to be included. She
was determined to learn all she could and improve herself.
She already copied the girls' table manners and speech and
decided that the first thing she must do was get rid of her
Irish brogue.

The hours wore on and Patrick finally fell into a more
peaceful sleep. In the early hours of the morning she felt his
brow and he seemed to be much less fevered. She put more
coal on the fire, curled up in the chair and fell asleep. She
awoke because she heard someone calling her name. Light
filtered into the room and she blinked quickly and went over
to the bed.

"Kitty. Thank you for staying with me. It couldn't have
been very pleasant."

"Are you feeling better, sir?"

"Yes, thanks to you. Listen, Kitty, when my family comes
in I want you to tell them I had a very peaceful night."

"But you didn't, sir," said Kitty.

"I want you to lie for me. Otherwise they won't go to
London."

Jonathan O'Reilly came in wearing a dressing gown, followed by Mrs. Thomson with a breakfast tray. Patrick tried to

conceal the distaste he felt for the food before him as his father hovered anxiously about the bed.

"How are you feeling, lad?"

"Quite well, everything considered."

"What sort of a night did you have?"

Patrick turned to Kitty with a conspiratorial look. She curtsied to Jonathan O'Reilly and said quickly, "He had a very peaceful night, sir. I stayed just in case he became ill."

"Good lass," Jonathan said. "A couple of days in bed and you'll be right as a trivet."

"It won't work, Father. I'm on my way to the mill and you're on your way to London." As Jonathan started to fume, Patrick said, "I'll make a bargain with you, Father. If you leave for London, I promise to get this looked at by a doctor friend, and after a couple of days seeing that the mills are running smoothly without any hitches, I'll follow you. No later than the weekend; that's a promise. When you get to London I want you to complete plans for Julia's wedding. Plans must be made."

"If you keep your word about seeing the doctor, I'll take the girls," their father said grudgingly. He turned to Mrs. Thomson. "Tell the girls to get packed; this will be a real surprise for them."

Kitty spoke up, "They've been packed for days. We're all ready to go."

He smiled at the "we," secretly delighting in the thought that she would be going with them. "In that case, young lady, you can come and help me pack." Left alone, Patrick arose from the bed and stood still for a few minutes with his eyes closed until the room steadied around him. He was in pain, but for the most part, he could ignore this. It was the condition of his rubbery legs that worried him. He rang for Terry, who helped him to bathe and shave and then helped him to dress.

"How do I look to you?" he asked Terry.

"Pale," he said bluntly, "but you look like you're in control."

"I want you with me today. Kitty's going up to London with the girls."

Terry hesitated a moment, then said, "The old man's got his eye on her, and she don't know about men and things. She thinks he's just being kind to her."

Patrick smiled and said, "Don't worry about Kitty. I intend to take very good care of her."

This statement only added to Terry's worries about his sister, but he had sense enough to keep his own counsel.

In spite of the girls' pleadings, Jonathan refused to leave until Patrick returned from the mills. He showed up in the middle of the afternoon much annoyed to see the huge traveling coach still on the driveway. He wanted only to seek his bed, but he now realized he'd have to undergo a torrent of questions he didn't feel like answering.

"Father, if you'll come upstairs where we can be private, I'll answer all your questions," he said curtly and ascended the steps.

Terry sought out Kitty, glad that he could have a few words with her before she left.

"Did he find out who stabbed him?" she asked breathlessly.

"Oh, aye. A few coins in the right hands soon put him in touch with the bastard, but, Kitty, it was the most curious thing. They came to an understanding and Patrick told him he wanted him on his payroll."

Kitty laughed and said, "He must be planning to get rid of somebody."

"By God, I wouldn't put it past him."

"Terrance, I want you to go and see Grandada and tell him I won't be able to see him for a while."

"I'll tell him. Kitty, you're changing! You don't even talk the same, and I don't like the way O'Reilly looks at you."

"Oh, don't be afther worryin' yerself about Patrick O'Reilly. I've got plans for him, I have an all, an all," she said in a thick brogue.

"Saints preserve us," muttered Terry.

Patrick was thankful the day was over. His wound had been attended to and the new bandage was much more comfortable. He lay in bed going over the events of the day, but Kitty's image kept intruding in his thoughts. With a sigh, he gave up the effort and let his mind dwell on her more fully. She was extremely beautiful. She excited his senses as no female had ever done. She was small and dainty as a kitten. All her movements were graceful, almost exotic. Her face was exquisite and her eyes flashed fire and held his attention with a seductiveness he knew was unconscious. He fantasized how he would like to make love to her. He realized she was very young, but he hoped that once he had aroused her sensuality, he would have the pleasure of satisfying all her hungers. His imagination slowly stripped her naked and his hands could feel her body's smooth contours. He thought of kissing her slowly—her mouth, her breasts, her navel, her mons veneris. He felt his loins tauten, his manhood rise and his testes ache. He knew he would never be able to sleep in the state into which he had worked himself. He savagely threw back the covers and poured himself a stiff drink. "Damn her eyes," he cursed.

Chapter 5

By rights Kitty should have been almost immobilized with the shock of coming from the bog to the City of London, but she absorbed everything like a sponge and seemed to thrive. The London house was very grand. There were a butler and two footmen who were the required six feet tall, as well as numerous other servants. There was a *chef de maison* rather than a housekeeper. Kitty learned to keep out of the way but she also managed to observe the visitors who came calling. The plain-faced Jeffrey Linton seemed to be wrapped around Julia's little finger, but Kitty thought privately that there was more to him than met the eye. She expected that once they were married he would assume a quiet authority that would keep Julia in her place. His mother and father were obviously titled upperclass, and the necessity of making a connection with "trade" was distasteful to them, but they swallowed their pride and accepted Jonathan O'Reilly because of his vast wealth.

The date for the engagement party was settled and it was decided to have the wedding in October. Julia insisted that Kitty have a new brown dress and cloak so she could accompany her about London in her many shopping expeditions. Kitty loved to go with Julia to the Burlington Arcade, running north off Piccadilly. There were thirty-one specialty shops in the arcade, which was known as London's most exclusive shopping thoroughfare. While Julia dreamed over the rings in S. J. Rood's Jewellers, Kitty coveted the beautiful tablecloths in the Irish Linen Company, the cashmere shawls, the folio cases in the Unicorn Leather Shop and the

56 *Virginia Henley*

gleaming lead crystal in the windows, all the while rubbing
elbows with the British upper crust. It had great Regency
charm and a "Beadle" in full dress of frock coat and trousers, which was like a policeman's uniform; in effect he was
a policeman. The prices were pretentious and often outrageous and Kitty longed to be able to go inside and spend
lavishly.

The servants did not take to Kitty and gave her the most
menial tasks, but she carried them out and didn't complain.
She knew they were jealous because she went about with
Julia and Barbara, and the old man always had a smile and a
kind word for her, saving his bad temper for the other servants. One of the housemaids said, "She's a real bleedin'
apple polisher." "Ha, tool polisher, more like! Have you
seen the way the squire looks at her?"

Jonathan had promised that if Julia met him at the Silver
Vaults, he would buy her a full service of sterling for twenty-
four. It was understood that any party larger than this would
be catered. Tradesmen from the various guilds were falling
over themselves to bring samples of their wares to Cadogen
Square, but O'Reilly could not resist a bargain, and he knew
the Silver Vaults contained magnificent heirlooms from the
aristocracy, who had had to sell when their coffers became
depleted. "We wish to go to 11 Charterhouse Street, which is
just off Chancery Lane," she explained to the cabby.

"Yes, ducks—I know where the Silver Vaults are, believe
it or not," the old Cockney replied cheekily.

Once inside the Vaults, Kitty was transported to seventh
heaven. Every conceivable article that could be made from
silver was to be found there. Some of the precious articles
were only being stored, but most of it was for sale. Jonathan
O'Reilly was already being shown around by a salesman
when the girls arrived and Julia had a hard time picking what

she fancied. The more ornate, ostentatious articles appealed to her father, while Julia realized the plainer pieces with a simple monogram were in much better taste and would meet the approval of her in-laws. After Julia had selected a tea service and some soup tureens, she wandered over to the antique jewelry and inspected several pieces. One was a silver bracelet with silver coins alternating with tiny silver bells, and it tinkled deliciously when it moved. Kitty felt an overwhelming desire to possess the bracelet. Never before had anything quite taken her fancy as this little trinket did. She was quite content to wait for the large silver pieces that would someday grace her own table, but the idea of waiting for some future mythical bracelet to grace her wrist sat all awry with her. She wanted this bracelet, and she wanted it now! She tried to push away the longing, but the more she denied herself, the stronger grew her compulsion to own it. That covetous feeling quite overpowered the petty one of self-denial and without ever seeming to have even glanced in its direction, she was filled with elation as her fingers caressed it inside her pocket.

Jonathan O'Reilly insisted on paying cash for everything and loved to pull out large rolls of banknotes before clerks, especially those with clipped, upper-class accents who pretended they were doing a favor by condescending to wait on you.

"Where shall we deliver the silver?" inquired the salesman.

"We'll take it with us." The clerk was taken aback, and O'Reilly added, "My carriage is outside with two great lanking footmen idling about doing nothing. Just step outside and fetch them," he directed. "Kitty, show him where." She bobbed prettily and started to climb the stairs to the street level. The clerk spoke from behind her. He had dropped the Mayfair accent and spoke to her in Cockney. "The old bleeder's takin' it wiv him coz he's scared of bein' diddled. Fancy him tryin' to be a nob! Well, you can't make a silk purse out of a sow's ear, can you? His bleedin' daughter pinched one of them bangles when I 'ad me back turned, but never mind, I just added the price onto his bill, and that way everybody's happy, eh?" He chuckled.

Kitty smiled happily. "Yes, everybody," she agreed.

The day of the engagement party approached and Patrick had not arrived, to everyone's consternation. There were a lot of preparations required and Kitty was nearly run off her feet. The household was in chaos without Patrick. In one way or another every detail seemed to depend on him. Their father's temper lacerated everyone's nerves to ribbons and it was feared that in Patrick's absence, nothing could be accomplished. He arrived the day before the party. Julia flung open the door for him, kissed him soundly and blurted out, "Thank God you're here! You must do something about Father and, oh, yes, I want you to mount me; the horse Father has supplied is a positive hack—I'm ashamed to death to be seen on it."

Barbara came flying down the stairs and rushed into his arms. He picked her up and swung her around, completely ignoring his recent wound. She blushed profusely when she saw Terry struggling in with the luggage. She lowered her voice and whispered urgently, "Patrick, you will allow me to attend this party, won't you? And please make Father get us a dancing instructor. I absolutely must know how to dance before the wedding."

All he needed to do was be there, and miraculously everything fell into place. His eyes went up the staircase until they found the one he was looking for. He put Barbara down and gazed up at Kitty, only just visible over the banister. She looked down longingly as if she would like to be lifted into the air too. He thought, "She's been deprived all her life. God, how I'm going to enjoy lavishing her with luxuries. I'll smother her with affection and pamper every whim once we get this damn engagement out of the way."

Kitty, ashamed to be caught peeping through the railings for a glimpse of him, put up her chin and slowly descended the stairs. She kept her eyes carefully lowered and started to help Terry with the luggage. Patrick was horrified and beckoned the two footmen with an imperious finger. He said coldly, "See that this child doesn't carry anything heavy again."

Halfway up the stairs one footman said to the other, "Damnation, I was going to slip up to her room one night, but it looks like she's a private crumpet!"

The other shrugged and said, "When the maids are nicer lookin' than the daughters, you know they have to be warmin' the master's bed."

They were dining *en famille* that evening and Julia, animated even more than usual, was doing her utmost to cause another dinnertime brawl.

"Patrick, I shall just die, just simply die, if Father starts in tomorrow night on his old theme of 'I'm a self-made man; I pulled myself up with my own bootstraps.' "

Barbara eyed her father fearfully as his jowls turned purple and he began breathing heavier, but Patrick put in coolly, "Julia, I know we're beyond the pale because our dirty fingers dabble in trade, but sometimes I think you should look to your own manners instead of concentrating on Father's. While you're cataloging his faults, you've overlooked his generosity toward you. I'm afraid you've been sadly spoiled, and I'm guilty in that department. I think I'll have a quiet word with Jeffrey."

She wanted to pull the tablecloth off and smash dishes, she

wanted to throw the contents of the soup tureen over him, she wanted to fly at him and scratch his eyes out, but she knew better than to tangle with Patrick when he was in this quiet, cutting mood. Barbara's dinner was totally ruined now that her brother as well as her father was hostile; she tried to conceal her sniffling behind her napkin. Without glancing in her direction, Patrick said, ''That noise is unacceptable at table. You may go to your room.'' Barbara fled; Julia followed.

Jonathan O'Reilly looked down the table at his son and felt uneasy.

''What's the matter, lad? Is your wound plaguing you?''

He shook his head and said, ''A bit tired, I suppose. It's just these women—they're all the same, they always want something.''

''We've both spoiled them because they've no mother, but who spoils us, eh, lad? Anyroad, tell me about the mills. Who did you leave in charge?''

''I know you trust Tom Connors, so I put him over all three mills. If things work out well, I think you should leave him as manager to take some of the load from your shoulders. I'm putting my money into that shipping venture I told you about with Isaac Bolt, and I'm seriously considering going to America on one of the trips.''

''Maybe I should sell the mills and retire altogether,'' Jonathan mused.

Patrick was shocked; though he agreed completely with that suggestion, he had never thought to see the day his father would propose it. ''Well, there's no hurry. Once Julia's married, perhaps you can think about it more seriously. I certainly intend to invest any future monies in London rather than the North; perhaps you should do the same.''

* * *

On the day of the engagement party Kitty was up at five o'clock. She was told to light the kitchen fires and when she discovered all the coal scuttles empty, she could have cried with vexation. She hated going to the cellars for coal, as there were always rats, but worse than the rats was the degrading nature of picking up the filthy cobs with her hands to fill the scuttle and then heaving it up the stairs, a job much too heavy for her. The chef had a hired helper for the day, so naturally he had to establish total authority by throwing a temperamental fit of pique. The chef demanded the flagstone floor of the huge kitchen be scrubbed before he set foot on it, and this job fell to Kitty. While she longed for the fancy jobs such as making exquisitely patterned butter pats and putting silver balls on the pretty *gâteaux,* in reality she got the job of gutting and cleaning the fowl. She only thanked God that someone had had the foresight to pluck them the day before. So while the other maids helped make canapés and hors d'oeuvres, she sat with a bucket of guts between her legs and pinched her nostrils together as best she could to prevent her gorge from rising. She silently prayed that Julia would need her for something and call her away from all this, but of course the girls were busy with their own preparations. Their gowns were to have final fittings and each spent over two hours with the hairdresser. After lunch she was put to work cleaning vegetables. Her hands were in water so long they became crinkled and red. When at last she was finished, she wiped them on her apron and surveyed them with dismay. She shrugged; there was no alternative but to steal some of the hand lotion from Julia's room next time she passed that way. Kitty longed to find a concealed hide-away where she could observe the guests, but due to a mild conspiracy of the other servants she was placed at the sink once again. At first she took pleasure in handling the fine crystal glasses and china plates, but after she had stood at this task four hours without respite, her legs began to ache painfully. Her hands stopped being red and wrinkled and turned white and bloated. Kitty felt sorry for herself. She hated them all. She could imagine the music and the laughter in the big salon that stretched across the whole front of the house, and vowed that when she was rich and gave parties she would always remember the poor drudges belowstairs who had to do all the dirty work. She wasn't allowed to go up to bed until after one o'clock in the morning, and her weary legs could hardly carry her up the back stairs to the attic. The thought of arising again at five appalled her, and she thought enviously of Julia and Barbara, who could stay in bed until noon if they fancied.

Patrick was up early about his own affairs the next morning. He took a lease on a small but smart establishment in Half-Moon Street and sent a note around to the employment agency setting out his requirements for a lady's maid, informing them he would be around the next day to make his selection. He kept the appointment promptly and made his choice from the three women they had lined up for him.

"Mrs. Harris, the lady you will be looking after is rather young and your duties will be quite light. Naturally, I have a daily to do the heavy work and I think I'll get you a cook too. Here's the address. Can you start tomorrow?"

"Yes, sir. Is there just you and your wife, sir? Are there any children?"

He smiled and said, "The lady is not my wife, Mrs. Harris. I won't be residing there, I'll only be a visitor."

She grasped the situation immediately. "I see. So it's simply a matter of looking after the lady's wardrobe and attending to her toilet and hair and accompanying her shopping, and of course keeping an eye on her as regards other gentlemen callers?"

"Precisely, Mrs. Harris. I think we understand each other perfectly."

Patrick had asked Jeffrey to call at two o'clock and was pleased to see the butler usher him into the library at precisely that hour. Julia was in a fit of pique because when she had hinted to her father about a house in London for a wedding present, he had told her flatly they could live at Cadogen Square; he had been adamant about not wanting the expense of another household in London. Patrick poured them both a glass of Scotch and water, sat behind the library desk and indicated a seat for his future brother-in-law.

"Jeff, I hope you won't take me wrong, but I feel I have to speak. I would hate to see you set off on the wrong foot with Julia."

Jeffrey held himself stiffly, not knowing what to expect.

Patrick drank half his glassful in one swallow and continued, "You should start out as you mean to carry on, and that's to take the upper hand."

Jeffrey was surprised at the words.

"Julia is used to dealing with two very strong-willed men, and yet she is able to get her own way most of the time. If she were to come up against anything softer than an iron will, she would walk all over you; worse, she would devour you," Patrick emphasized.

Jeffrey said carefully, "It would be nice to be master in my house, but it will not be my own house, will it? Julia will control the purse strings."

"Wrong! Father will control the purse strings and you can only avoid that in the way I myself did; make yourself financially independent of him."

Jeff opened his mouth to speak.

"Ah, don't object before you hear me out. I realize England's ruling classes haven't soiled their hands with trade in the past. The Regency saw to that, but we are coming into a new era now that Victoria is on the throne. England owes its strength to manufacturing.''

Jeffrey said quietly, ''I wasn't going to object. I would jump at the opportunity to prove myself, in spite of my family's objections.''

''Excellent! Now, I've been giving some thought to you and I believe that the one occupation that wouldn't put you beyond the pale is that of wine merchant. You have the entrée to society and you could introduce and promote new brands of wine, especially champagne. I am about to acquire part interest in such a company, Stowils of Chelsea. Your help will be invaluable. What do you say?''

''I should be honored to join you in any endeavor you have in mind. I'd be a fool to refuse; you are always such a resounding success.''

''Thanks for your confidence. I abhor snobbery. It's like cutting off your nose to spite your face. I remember at Oxford I was the best damned oarsman they'd ever had, but I was barred from entering the Royal Henley Regatta because I'd worked with my hands. I had the satisfaction of seeing my school defeated because they dispensed with my services.''

Jeffrey thought, I wouldn't want Patrick O'Reilly for my enemy. ''So let's shake on it, and I'll be in touch with you. Don't forget my advice concerning Julia,'' he said with a wink.

Chapter 6

Jonathan O'Reilly was expecting a shipment of wine and liquor from the distillery to replenish his stock. When it arrived he looked over the invoices, signed the receipt and told the two delivery men to put the cases in the cellar.

An angry Kitty had been sent down for coal. She vowed that she would never do this degrading chore again, promising herself she would appeal to Patrick if there were any repercussions. The men stacked the cases of wine at the top of the cellar steps and as Kitty hauled the heavy coal scuttle through the door she collided with the wine and sent eight cases crashing to the floor. The girl was rooted to the spot with horror. "How many's broken?" she finally whispered.

"All of 'um! Eight dozen, that's ninety-six bottles, you clumsy bitch!"

She stood in a wine-red pool with shards of glass stretching clear across the kitchen floor.

"Oh, my God, whatever shall I do?" she asked piteously, and the tears ran down her cheeks and dripped into the pool.

Patrick, followed by most of the servants, came to investigate the crash. "What in Christ's name is going on here?"

The men spoke up together, "It was her fault, gov'nor. She crashed into the wine with that bleedin' coal scuttle. Who's going' to pay for this breakage that's what I'd like to know."

Kitty dared not look up at Patrick. She trembled with the overwhelming knowledge of the havoc she had wrought.

Patrick's voice had a cutting edge that brooked no disobedience.

"Clean it up instantly. Replace the order and bill me. Kitty, come!" He ushered her from the kitchen and up the broad staircase to his bedroom. The tears were still coming as she climbed each stair with trepidation in her heart. Her mind was going over the alternatives rapidly. Would it be best to deny that she had done it, or disclaim responsibility because the cases were stacked improperly, or would it simply be best to throw herself on Patrick's mercy and hope he wouldn't deduct the cost of the wine from her year's wages? He closed the door quietly and stood looking down at her. He took a large white handkerchief from his pocket, put a finger under her chin to lift her face and then very gently wiped away her tears.

She eyed him warily.

"Kitty, I can't bear to see you a servant. Let me take you away from all this." For one glorious moment she thought he was going to ask her to marry him, until a little voice of reason told her it wouldn't be that easy.

"What do you mean?" she whispered.

"First of all, Kitty, tell me what you want to do," he urged.

She knew he was not referring to the wine, but to life. She took a deep breath. "Everything! I want to see, smell, taste, touch everything. I want to do everything, go everywhere, experience it all," she said with passion.

"Then we are alike," he smiled. "I have a little house in Half-Moon Street. Would you like to go and live there? Learn how to be a lady, wear pretty clothes and have servants of your own?"

"Are you sure it would be all right for me to do that?"

"Oh, yes, it's done all the time, I assure you."

"When can we leave?" she asked quickly.

He laughed and said, "Now, if you like."

She thought happily, He does want to marry me, but first I have to learn to be a lady.

She dashed upstairs to the attic for her cloak. She slipped her tarot cards into her reticule, retrieved her bracelet from under the mattress and didn't even pause to look around the room. Her heart was singing. She wanted to slide down the banister, but when she saw Patrick waiting at the bottom for her, she quickly decided that it would be unladylike.

She leaned back against the velvet squabs of Patrick's well-sprung carriage and closed her eyes for a second to control her excitement.

He kept glancing at her and smiling, while keeping an eye on his driver.

"Where are we going?" she ventured.

"I'm going to take you to Madame Martine's in Bond Street. A very chic Paris dressmaker. Probably the only time she saw France was from Dover on a clear day, but her clothes are unsurpassed."

Kitty laughed and asked, "Is she very expensive?"

"You will be delighted to know her prices are shameful. It will very likely cost me an arm and a leg before I get out of there, but don't let that stop you from picking anything you desire."

She threw him a mischievous glance from under those long black lashes and said with a laugh, "I won't disappoint you!"

He held her eyes for a moment and said, "I'll hold you to that promise," but she quickly lowered her eyes and fingered the tiny bells on her bracelet. His eyes clouded momentarily. "Kitty, where did you get that?" he asked.

"I can't tell you," she said prettily.

"Damn it, Kitty, I won't have you accepting presents from other men. I wasn't even aware you knew any men except

Father and me. Father! That's who bought your little trinket, isn't it?'' he demanded.

''Well, I suppose you could say that,'' she answered carefully.

He looked at her sharply, the rake of his jaw thrust out angrily. She felt frightened of him when he ◄was angry. ''What did you do in return for the bracelet?'' He almost sneered.

She cast down her eyes and whispered, ''I stole it when we visited the Silver Vaults.''

The crack of his laughter startled her. Relieved that his dark mood had passed, she laughed with him. His lips brushed her forehead and he said, ''You're incorrigible!''

She was disturbed by his closeness. It was pleasant but instinctively she knew his behavior was a little too familiar. She looked down at her lap and fingered the plain material of her dress. Suddenly she burst out, ''I hate brown!''

''So do I,'' he agreed.

''Then I'll never wear it again,'' she vowed.

Madame Martine welcomed Patrick effusively. She remembered him very well, as only a few days ago he had brought his sister in and spent a good deal, promising he would soon return with his younger sister. She whisked Kitty away to a tiny fitting room, leaving Patrick to sip sherry as he relaxed on a blue satin, Louis XIV love seat. She dressed Kitty in a child's pink organdy dress with frilled white pantaloons showing beneath and swept her before Patrick. *''Ta soeur!''*

Patrick's eyes met Kitty's and they both went off into peals of laughter. ''You look delicious, my sweet, like icing on a cake. *Madame,* I assure you this is not my sister.'' He smiled charmingly. ''May I suggest something a little more sophisticated? She will need everything—underwear, dresses, negligees.'' Madame Martine realized her *faux pas* instantly. She had taken them for brother and sister because they had the same vivid, dark beauty.

Kitty spoke up, "I look much younger than I really am, *madame,* and I should like some grown-up gowns with plunging necklines. I'm almost sixteen." Patrick had the decency to flush as Madame Martine's eyebrows rose. In her business one couldn't afford scruples, but she felt morally justified in her decision to charge him double for everything. She started with day dresses in exquisitely sprigged muslin, then gowns for evening wear that had been made up for other customers. *"Mademoiselle* is so petite I will have to get the girl to pin it tighter."

As soon as she left, Kitty, who was standing on a raised platform in front of Patrick, lifted her skirts to show off her legs. "Look, Patrick—silk stockings, just like I've always longed for!"

His loins went taut and he began to stiffen. She had only intended to show him her ankles, but elevated as she was he saw the shapely calves and caught a glimpse of her bare thigh, that very exciting area above the garters where the stockings left off and the most intimate part of the female began. He was acutely aware of the savage pulsing of blood into his shaft.

"They come in all kinds of shades. May I have some pink ones and some flesh-colored ones?"

"And black," he said huskily, as he shifted position to ease the tightness of the cloth of his trousers. Kitty only had eyes for the pretty shoes with bows across the toes and tiny high heels. They made her feel different as she strutted about in them. Most of the dresses would have to be delivered when they were finished, but many of the articles of lace underwear, shoes, stockings, etc., were boxed up and ready to be taken with them. Madame Martine came out of the dressing room to have a private word with Patrick. She carried three or four transparent nightgowns in delicate shades over her arm, which she indicated. "She absolutely refuses to try any of these on, *monsieur*."

"Why?" asked Patrick, puzzled.

"She simply refuses to believe a lady would wear such a thing to bed. She says nightgowns have to be made of flannel to keep you warm."

Patrick laughed. "Wrap them up; we'll take them."

When they left the shop Kitty was wearing a yellow silk organza, which fell in ruffles down the back over a crinoline. Her hair was gathered up at one side with a bunch of silk primroses and she carried a parasol to match her dress. She insisted on wearing two pairs of frilled gloves at the same time. "See how pretty the double rows of frills are?" she asked Patrick.

"Like your eyelashes," he murmured.

She loved the compliments he had suddenly begun to pay her, but his voice was so intimate that it made her blush. She couldn't escape the feeling that he knew something she didn't. She was anticipating what would come next and could sense his anticipation, but vaguely she felt they were not anticipating the same things. Suddenly her attention was drawn to a man beating his horse in the street. Without a moment's hesitation she wrested the whip from him and laid it about his back with a sweeping stroke.

"Now you know what it feels like!" she said passionately, her eyes blazing.

Patrick was momentarily stunned at her actions, but gallantly backed her up in condemning the carter's treatment of the poor beast. Out of his past came a picture of his pretty Irish mother taking a whip to some fellow for his insolence.

"What a difference your new clothes make. Suddenly you have the confidence of a duchess. Lady Jane Tut to the very life!'' he teased. He helped her into the carriage and gave instructions to his driver. He sat opposite her so that he could view her to advantage. ''You saw yourself in a mirror at Madame Martine's so you must realize how very beautiful you are.''

''Yes, I do look beautiful, don't I?'' she asked ingenuously.

''As a matter of fact, you are a very showy female. In Lancashire we have an expression, 'You pay well for dressing.' Now wherever I take you, all the men will be staring at you, and I'll hate every moment of it.'' The glint in his eyes belied his words.

''You're teasing me!'' said Kitty with a laugh.

''On the contrary, my dear, it is you who are teasing me,'' he said softly.

His eyes lingered on her lips until she said breathlessly, ''Why do you keep looking at me like that?''

''Like what, Kitty?''

''Well . . . like I look at food when I'm very hungry— sort of longingly.''

He took her hand and put the tips of her fingers to his lips. ''I would love to eat you,'' he said suggestively. ''Just one taste would satisfy me.''

She looked at him very seriously and said, ''Patrick, you know that's a lie; nothing would satisfy you but the whole.''

He was startled for a moment and wondered if she realized she had just made a very racy pun. It was hard to tell with Kitty. One moment she was all little girl; the next she could do or say something so sexually provocative, he became hard instantly.

The carriage went downriver past the Tower of London. ''Oh, let's go to the Tower, please, Patrick.''

''How can I refuse you anything when you ask so prettily? However, first I think we are in need of sustenance.''

The carriage stopped at Wapping Wall outside the Prospect of Whitby. "Oh, isn't this a public house?" she asked doubtfully as he helped her down.

"Yes, it's a pub, the best on the Thames. It has been here since 1509."

"Well, do you think it quite proper for me to go into a place like this?"

"Well, some ladies would refuse, but this morning you were the girl who wanted to go everywhere and experience everything, weren't you?"

She tucked her arm in his and smiled up invitingly. "What are we waiting for?"

He led her upstairs on the riverside. It was high tide and the Prospect stood on tall timbers, out in the river's waters. Kitty received many admiring glances and she noticed that she was the only woman in the room. Patrick ordered for them both. They had pâté, whitebait and trout broiled in heavy butter. "In the last century, thieves and smugglers frequented this place. The hangman too—the public execution area is just across the street."

She shuddered. "The atmosphere is strange here."

"Wait until you go up in the Tower," he promised.

Instead of white wine to go with the fish, he ordered her mead and mulled wine for himself. "Do you like it?"

"It's delicious," she said dreamily. "I feel like Queen Guinevere, sipping mead."

"Much more beautiful," he assured her.

He took her to the Tower as he had promised and guided her toward the Jewel House.

"There are three floors of armor, but you must be prepared to climb to each floor, and then coming down there's over a hundred winding tower stairs to the exit, so please, sweetheart, can we skip the armor today?"

"Oh look, there's one of the ravens. You must bow to him, Patrick."

He laughed, "I'm Irish too, or have you forgotten?"

"I can feel the sadness here, can you?" she asked wistfully.

"Of course; and evil and pain, but don't let it spoil our day. Come, look at the jewels, they will really thrill you."

Kitty was in thrall as she viewed the crowns and scepters encrusted with precious gems.

He whispered in her ear, "Do you like diamonds, Kitty?"

"I like pearls," she said softly.

"Pearls are for tears," he protested.

"To be Irish is to know the world will break your heart before you're forty."

"My God, it must be this place. Let's get out of here," he said, laughing.

They were driving past Green Park when he said, "Half-Moon Street is just across the park."

"Oh, could we get out and walk the rest of the way?"

"Of course, sweetheart." He told his driver to deliver the packages to Mrs. Harris in Half-Moon Street. "Tell her we'll be arriving shortly. You can return the carriage to Cadogen Square, I won't be needing you again today."

He took her hand as they strolled through the beautiful park. Kitty put up her parasol and almost skipped along at his side. "Oh, Patrick, this has been the happiest day of my life."

The sun was sinking behind the trees and people were making their way home after an outing in the park. They received many cold stares and there was much tut-tutting as they strolled hand in hand in a public place, seemingly lost in a world of their own.

Before they reached the top step, the door was flung wide and Mrs. Harris was curtsying to her new master.

"Good evening, Mrs. Harris. This is your new mistress, Kit . . . er, Kathleen Rooney."

"Good evening, ma'am." She sketched another curtsy. "All your packages arrived and I've taken the liberty of unpacking them in your bedroom, ma'am."

Mrs. Harris was very pleased when she saw how young Kitty was. She felt certain she would be able to take the upper hand. It was plain to see his nibs was badly smitten with her, as he couldn't take his eyes from her for more than a few seconds at a time. She knew he would have a formidable temper if aroused, so she hesitated over her next words for fear of spoiling his obvious good mood.

"Milord, I'm sorry to have to tell you, but the cook never showed up today."

"Well, never mind, Mrs. Harris. Fortunately Shepherd's Market is just two steps away round the corner. Ye Grapes can provide us with a light supper, if you would be good enough to step round there for me?"

"My pleasure, sir," she answered, relieved that his easygoing mood had not altered.

"The wine you sent arrived this afternoon. I put some of it to chill."

"Did it arrive intact, no bottle broken?" he asked, winking at Kitty.

"Oh, Patrick," Kitty said with a laugh, "that seems a lifetime ago; I can't believe it was only this morning."

"Come, let me show you your new home while Mrs. Harris sees about our supper." It was clearly a man's establishment, with a richly patterned oriental carpet, a wine velvet couch and two leather wing-backed chairs in front of a small fireplace. There was a beautifully inlaid writing desk, but the whole effect was softened by masses of flowers Patrick had ordered. This sitting room was one floor up from the reception hall where they had entered. It was a tall, narrow house, and above the sitting room on the third level was a spacious bedroom. The bed was enormous, with brocade hangings that matched the heavy curtains at the tall windows. The wardrobe and tallboy were in a polished red mahogany, and the pile on the rug was like plush velvet. Patrick opened a door off the bedroom to show Kitty the bathroom.

She was utterly delighted. "Oh, a bath just for me! This is the nicest room of all; I'll spend all my time here."

He was delighted at her pleasure in everything.

"Oh, who picked out all this beautiful soap and dusting powder?"

"I did, of course," he said with a smile.

She stripped off her gloves and washed her hands with the rose-scented soap. "Mmm, smell me," she invited, holding her hands up to his face. He buried a kiss inside her palm and quickly closed her fingers over it. She was delighted at such a pretty trick. When they went downstairs to the sitting room, Mrs. Harris had laid out a cold supper for them. She was glad to see they were in a playful mood; that meant bed right after they'd eaten and she would be free to go belowstairs to her own room for the rest of the evening.

Patrick carved the bird and poured the wine. Later he peeled a peach for her. It was the first time she had ever seen a peach in her whole life. She decided she liked them excessively. He led her to the couch to finish their wine. He looked deeply into her eyes and offered a toast. "To this moment, and the moment yet to come," he said meaningfully.

She was acutely aware of his nearness and thought, "This is what it would be like to be married, just the two of us alone."

He said huskily, "What would you like to do?"

She looked at him from beneath her lashes and said, "Will you let me play with your . . . watch?"

There, she had done it again! Her words were erotically

suggestive, as if she were a practiced coquette, while at the same time she looked at him with innocent, trusting eyes. A desire such as he had seldom felt before swept through him. He murmured Robert Burns' lines:

> Honeyed seal of soft affections,
> Tenderest pledge of future bliss,
> Dearest tie of young connections,
> Love's first snowdrop, virgin kiss.

He crushed her to him. The scent of her breath excited him further and his mouth came down upon hers longingly.

She sprang up quickly, confused. "Do . . . do you have a key of your own?" she stammered.

"Of course."

"Good. Then you can let yourself out when you're ready to leave. I know you'll excuse me, but I'm just dying to take a bath in that beautiful tub. Oh, Patrick, I can never thank you enough for what you've done. Good night!" she said quickly and ran from the room.

Patrick chuckled to himself and rang for Mrs. Harris. "Milady has decided to take a bath. She's used to doing everything for herself, so you will have to insist on helping her if she tries to dismiss you. Oh, and, Mrs. Harris, try and hurry her along to bed, won't you?" he said with a wink. He removed his jacket and waistcoat, stretched out his legs and lit a long, thin cheroot.

"I'll draw your bath, ma'am," said Mrs. Harris.

"Oh, please call me Kitty, won't you? Fill the tub right up and pour in some of those lovely lavender bath salts. I feel very extravagant tonight." Kitty tied up her curls with a satin ribbon and sank into the perfumed water up to her chin. The hot water gave her a sensuous feeling. Although Kitty did not

know what it was exactly, she knew it was an extremely
pleasant sensation.

After ten minutes Mrs. Harris came in and picked up
Kitty's clothes and laid a white gossamer nightgown out for
her.

"Where did you find that?" asked Kitty, surprised.

"It was in one of the boxes that were delivered. Mr.
O'Reilly picked it for you."

"I can't wear that. It's indecent! Bring my petticoat back,
please."

"Nonsense. Put the nightgown on before he comes up. I
think he's been patient long enough."

"Hasn't Patrick left yet?" asked Kitty, surprised.

"Of course he hasn't left—he's spending the night."

"But where will he sleep?" puzzled Kitty.

"With you, of course," Mrs. Harris answered firmly.

"But men and women don't sleep in the same bed," said
Kitty, shocked.

"I don't know what game you're playing, miss, but you'd
better slip into that nightgown and pop into bed or we're
going to have one angry young man on our hands."

Kitty was furious. "I will not put that thing on. Bring my
clothes."

"Then you'll have to get into bed naked. He'll soon have
you in that state anyway."

"Mrs. Harris, you are an evil woman and I don't want you
here."

"Listen to me, dearie. You an' me have a good thing going
here if you'll just be sensible. All you have to do is open your
legs for him and he'll give you anything you ask for. On the
other hand, if you cross him, he looks like he could be a very
nasty customer."

"Oh, I won't listen to such wicked talk," Kitty said, close

to tears. She stepped from the water and dried herself on the big white towel.

"Where are my clothes?" she demanded.

"You'll never find them," asserted Mrs. Harris.

Wildly, Kitty opened drawers and pulled out their contents, but she could only find nightgowns and undergarments. Tears of frustration filled her eyes. Realizing how undignified she must look, scrambling about for clothes, she ran back to the bathroom and swept up the white nightgown. It was slit down the sides and fastened with delicate ribbons. She put it on furiously and Mrs. Harris approved. "That's better. It was designed to give a man pleasure."

Kitty caught a sob in her throat and ran downstairs to the sitting room.

Patrick's cheroot glowed in the darkened room and Kitty ran to him. "Patrick, thank God you are still here!"

"My darling, what's wrong?" he gathered her close and she hid her face against his chest.

"It's Mrs. Harris. She's an evil woman. She's been saying such wicked things to me. Oh, you wouldn't believe the things she said."

Mrs. Harris appeared in the doorway and said, "I'm sorry, sir, but she wouldn't go to bed. I can't understand what's upset her so much."

"You may leave us, Mrs. Harris. She'll be all right with me," he told her coldly. She bobbed a curtsy and disappeared.

"My darling, what's the damned woman been saying to you" he asked soothingly.

"I . . . I can't tell you," she whispered.

He reached over and turned up the lamp. Kitty gasped as the light flooded over her dishabille.

He raised her face and demanded, "Tell me instantly what she said to you."

"She said . . . she said that men and women sleep in the same bed. I've never heard of such a thing," and she began to cry again.

He kissed her forehead and smoothed her hair. "Kitty, when people love each other, they do sleep in the same bed." He stroked her back gently until her tears subsided. He had her gentled now and he didn't want her to see the naked desire in his eyes.

"I love you, Kitty. Do you care for me a little?"

"Patrick, you know I love you." She looked up at him and the tears spiked her eyelashes. He bent forward and took her mouth possessively. When she pulled her lips away from him she saw the tip of his tongue. Would he dare to put his wicked tongue in her mouth?

"You go to my head, kitten." His voice was husky and his hands slipped inside the folds of her gown and caressed her body. My God, wasn't it just like a man to want to touch a woman on her most shameful parts!

With an air of ownership, he leaned forward to kiss her again, but she brought up her hand and slapped his face. His teeth glittered in a wicked grin and he laughed deep in his throat. "I denied you nothing all day. Now you seek to deny me everything, selfish little wench."

His hands moved upon her body possessively, knowingly, as he tried to remove her nightgown.

Her deep modesty was so outraged she escaped his embrace and fled toward the stairs. He was after her in a flash and she could hear his laughter and knew he was enjoying himself more every moment.

"A female runs away just so that the male will chase her." He grasped her ankle with strong fingers and she could go no farther up the stairs. "You were quick enough to display your ankles at the dress shop. I think you enjoy teasing me, Kitten." He sat down on a step and pulled her down into his lap.

Slowly, tentatively, his hands slid up her legs, inching the nightgown higher and higher, until her limbs were exposed to his avid gaze. "You have beautiful legs, sweetheart. And what are these pretty curls between them?"

"You are going to ravish me!" she gasped as the full realization of her plight dawned on her. "My God, Grandada warned me about ravishers!"

He was startled for a moment and lifted his hands from her body. She fled up the steps into the bedroom and quickly put the width of the bed between them.

"Is that all they've told you about what happens between a man and a woman?" he asked incredulously.

She saw a softening in his eyes and begged, "I had such a beautiful day. How can you spoil it for me like this? Oh, Patrick, please tell me it's just a game you are playing with me." She looked at him imploringly.

"Sweetheart, of course it's a game. It's a love game. It's a grown-up game. Let me teach you how to play. You can't be a little girl forever. It's time for you to become a woman."

"I'm afraid," Kitty protested.

"My little love, there's nothing to be afraid of. I promise I won't hurt you. I just want to kiss you and hold you," he coaxed.

She shook her head. "It's wicked."

"Kitty, there's nothing wicked about love. Kisses are beautiful things. Every one different, just like snowflakes. Let me show you." He noted her slight hesitation. "You are shy because you've never been alone with a man before, and that thrills me more than words could ever tell you. I thank God that you come to me pure and innocent. That's the way it should be. Trust me to cherish you, Kitty."

She wanted to believe him. Wanted it with all her heart. She loved Patrick and had wanted him to love her since she'd seen him in Ireland, years ago. She cursed her own ignorance. He was so educated, so worldly, how could she ever hope to become his wife unless she let him teach her every thing she should know? She let him come around the bed to her and take her in his arms. Slowly her arms lifted about his neck and Patrick dipped his head to take her lips. She did like to be kissed, she admitted. Other things about him were powerfully attractive and exceedingly pleasant. She liked his smell. She liked his strength. It would keep her safe against the whole world. Her hand touched his face. He was so masculine, her fingertips felt the roughness of his beard in spite of the fact that he shaved every day.

She heard him groan and suddenly his hands pulled off her nightdress, leaving her completely nude. Immediately she ran around to the opposite side of the bed. She stared in disbelief as he unbuttoned his shirt and tossed it aside.

"If you come to my arms willingly, I promise to make love to you in a way that will not hurt you."

When she saw that no appeal would turn him from having his way, a searing anger spread along her veins. "No one has ever said 'no' to you in your whole life! You are so accustomed to having your own way, you think it's the natural order of the universe. I will fight you to the death, you arrogant bastard!" she spat.

His teeth gleamed against his dark face as he stripped off his "inexpressibles," and her eyes widened as she saw the column of his hard phallus stand up rigidly from his groin to his navel. In her fury, she had forgotten her nakedness and Patrick knew she was the most exquisite, exotic creature outside of paradise.

"You are flaunting your beauty for me like an angry pagan goddess. Your body was made for love!"

They posed for a moment, facing each other. With a swift movement he reached across the bed and grabbed her, then she was clawing, biting and scratching him savagely. He held her down on the bed with both wrists clamped securely above her head and brought his lips down to touch hers. He breathed, "My wild Irish Gypsy." He knew this seduction was going to be the most exciting thing he'd ever done. He'd gentle her with sweet kisses until she clung to him. Then he'd awaken a flicker of desire, which would burst into flames and consume them both. He took her mouth exultantly because he could smell victory.

The taste of her lips had the tang of wild honey. He slid his mouth across hers, molding the curve of her lips with his. The desire he felt for her was white-hot. Naked, beneath him, her effect stunned him. The passion she aroused in him was blinding, dizzying. He meant to be gentle, meant to awaken her sensuality slowly, meant to seduce her with tender kisses and caresses, but his hunger for her blazed out of control like wildfire.

Kitty lay still while Patrick kissed her. The shock of being naked on a bed with a man above her was almost staggering. The things he was doing to her, coupled with the breath-stopping nearness of the man felt delicious. In fact, the pleasure he was bringing to her body felt so wonderful she knew it must be sinful and wicked beyond belief. In her distress at her own carnality, she began to pant.

Patrick felt a thrill when he saw her breathless with desire. She was no longer fighting him, she was yielding to him sweetly.

His hot breath teased her silken skin as his mouth slid down her throat and across one very round breast. It was as firm as an apple and he knew he must taste it.

Kitty's thoughts ran about like quicksilver, writhing with the conflict of opposing desires. At all costs she knew she must not take the very thing she desired. She wanted Patrick. She wanted his love and protection, but the raw lust she saw in his dark face frightened her. It frightened her because she knew with the age-old knowledge of Eve that he created a matching lust in her, and once that devil inside her was released, there would be no controlling it.

Kitty felt her very senses being drugged by the dark whisper of skin against naked skin. He was all hard muscle, scalding heat and surging male hunger. He aroused sensations in every inch of her silken skin as her young body responded to his virile sexuality. He was bad and wicked and sinful and he was on the verge of making her bad and wicked and sinful.

Suddenly, even his mouth became hard and he crushed hers savagely. Kitty took his bottom lip between white pointed teeth and bit down hard. He cried out in pain, then kissed her so brutally, her whole mouth was bruised. Her eyes flashed fire as she sought a vulnerable place to wound him. She saw the scar on his shoulder, pink and tender, barely healed over where the knife had been plunged in. She arched her body up to him and sank her teeth in his wound deeply.

He screamed with the raw agony of it, then as if pushed beyond endurance, he wedged her thighs apart and impaled her with one plunge. He increased the depth and speed of his thrusts. She was so hot and tight inside, he had never experienced such ecstasy. Each time she moved, her muscles gripped the shaft and sent quivers to the tip.

The mating was elemental, like a great force of nature. Patrick was beyond thought. When she writhed and cried out it excited him to madness. He would have sold his soul to sustain and prolong this cataclysmic intercourse but some instinct told him she had endured enough, so he did not delay his climax. It came like an explosion that rent his body with great shudders and left him totally satisfied and sated. He rolled his weight from her and quickly gathered her to him with gentle, protective arms.

Kitty was in a state of shock. All the fight had gone out of her. It was too late now. They had both committed a terrible sin. She was as much to blame as he. She lay numb, knowing she should have somehow stopped him. How ironic that now when she needed to be comforted and enfolded in warm, loving arms, they were *his* arms that were offering her succor.

Patrick murmured endearments against her hair. "Kitten, I'm sorry. You received no pleasure from it at all, did you? If only you hadn't fought me, it would have been so much easier for you. Next time I promise to be gentle and tender and bring you exquisite pleasure."

His words threaded through her brain. She knew he was entirely capable of bringing her exquisite pleasure. He would have done so tonight if she had not fought like a tigress against it. She flinched at his talk of next time. She knew that if there ever was a next time, she would be lost. She would offer herself for his taking. Her virtue was gone and she felt covered with shame because of her own secret longings.

Patrick gently kissed her ear and murmured, "I think perhaps you were too young after all."

His words tore down her last defenses and she curled into a ball and sobbed uncontrollably into the pillow. She made an effort to leave the bed, but he drew her back into his embrace. With one muscular thigh across her legs, his arms possessively held her captive. "Sleep now," he said firmly.

Chapter 7

Terrance ran up the steps in Half-Moon Street and pounded on the door. After the second pounding, Mrs. Harris opened the front door apprehensively. "I must speak with Mr. O'Reilly," Terry said breathlessly.

"I don't dare disturb him. I would lose my job." She had heard the screaming and carryings-on upstairs and she wanted no part of it.

Impatiently, Terry pushed past her and ran upstairs to the sitting room, Mrs. Harris following him, wringing her hands. Finding the room empty, he took the next flight of stairs and pounded on the bedroom door. He called out, "Patrick, I must speak with you."

Patrick quickly got out of bed and went to the door naked. Kitty sat up in bed and cried out, "Terry!"

"How the devil did you know where to find me?" Patrick demanded.

"You know I try to keep my eye on Kitty. I knew you were bringing her here."

"Terry, you came for me," she cried thankfully.

He lowered his eyes from his sister's nakedness. "No, I didn't come for you. I came for Patrick. Your father's had a bad turn. The doctor thinks it's a stroke."

Kitty said accusingly, "You knew what would happen to me, but you let him bring me here."

"It's better than being a servant, isn't it?" Terry flared.

"No, it's just the same! I'm like a chambermaid who must be obedient to my master's demands, except I'm to be paid with pretty dresses instead of wages." She saw her clothes where Mrs. Harris had hidden them under the bed. Patrick was almost dressed, so she begged, "Wait for me. I'm going back with you. Mr. O'Reilly will have need of me."

"Kitty, I need you too. Stay here, please. I'll go to Father."

"I hate you! I'll always hate you for what you did to me. I can't bear to stay here another minute."

Terry looked at Patrick angrily and said, "Did you have to be so brutal?"

"Yes, damn it, she's like a wildcat. Would you like to see the bites she inflicted to my wound? If there had been a knife within her reach she would have plunged it in and spilled my guts rather than submit to me!"

Kitty said to Terry, "You ought to kill him for me!"

Terry regarded her with the smoldering arrogance of the Gypsy male and said, "You challenged his manhood—he had to master you."

Patrick asked him, "Did you bring the carriage? Good! I'll drive; you go inside with Kitty."

In the dark interior of the carriage she realized for the first time in her life that men and women were natural enemies. She knew without a doubt that Patrick would always conquer her in any physical encounter; therefore her weapons would have to be more devious and subtle.

Upon arrival at Cadogen Square, Patrick turned the carriage over to Terry for stabling. Patrick tried to help Kitty alight from the carriage but she brushed past his proffered hand and swept up the steps and into the brilliantly lit salon.

"Where have you been?" demanded Julia, looking them over speculatively.

Kitty's yellow organza was badly creased from the hurried carriage ride, but she held up her chin and said, "Is there anything I can do to help Mr. O'Reilly?"

"The doctor still is with him, so we won't know what to

do until he gives us our instructions. Go and make us all some tea, Kitty; that should make us feel better,'' said Julia. Barbara sat unhappily in a corner with red-rimmed eyes. Patrick spoke up quickly, ''No, Kitty may go and tell one of the servants to make tea, but she no longer is here in the capacity of a maid. She may share in father's nursing duties, but that's all.''

Kitty went to find a footman to order the tea, feeling grateful toward Patrick and at the same time hating herself for feeling that gratitude.

As soon as she was out of earshot Julia said, ''Well! Don't you know it's bad form to keep your mistress under the same roof as your family?''

Patrick glared at her with ice-cold eyes for a moment and Julia paled and realized she shouldn't have spoken to him so boldly.

He said quietly, ''Kitty has refused to be my mistress. You'd better keep a civil tongue between your teeth when you are speaking to me, miss. Now be good enough to tell me what occurred with Father.''

''Well, it really all started this morning. Father got into the most violent argument with two draymen who came to make a wine delivery. Somehow ninety-six bottles were smashed and Father demanded they replace them at their own expense. The shouting match went on for hours. The whole household was in a state of upheaval. At lunchtime he still hadn't calmed down. The men were long gone, but he kept at it with Barbara and me for his audience. I swear he covered every conceivable subject, from the inefficiency of the British working classes to the folly of putting a woman on the throne. He drank deeply at lunch and I suspect carried on throughout the afternoon. Just when everything seemed to have quieted down and settled back to normal he clutched his head and fell to the floor. It took us forever to get him upstairs and into bed. We sent for the doctor immediately but he didn't come for ages and ages, and you know the rest. I was going mad, not knowing where you were, but Terry said he would find you.''

Patrick ignored this latter part of her speech and said, ''I think I'll go up and speak with the doctor. Terry said something about a stroke. I imagine that's what he has had. He does tend to live at the top of his voice, doesn't he?''

Kitty came back into the room and Julia said to her, ''Well, Irish, you've more sense than I gave you credit for, rejecting our Patrick. He thinks he's God's gift to women, you know. Now then, what I have to figure out is how to keep this business from affecting my wedding plans. If he dies now, I'll kill him!'' She laughed at herself. ''Well, that's Irish if I've ever heard it.''

Barbara cried, ''Julia, how can you think of yourself at a time like this?''

Julia looked at Kitty and said, ''You know, don't you? A woman has to take care of Number One first. Men will always sacrifice our wishes for their convenience. A woman is expected to give all for love, but what man is willing to do that? If a woman doesn't take care of herself, no one else will. I'm a survivor and so is Kitty. You, my little gutless wonder, will fall by the wayside because you've got a wishbone where your backbone should be! For God's sake, stop sniveling. Ah, here's the tea. I think I'm going to have some brandy in mine. How about you, Kitty?'' Kitty nodded her appreciation and Barbara piped up, ''I'll join you, by God.''

Patrick went quietly into his father's bedroom to find the doctor just closing his bag. ''Ah, Mr. O'Reilly, glad to meet you, sir. I'm very pleased to be able to tell you that your father's stroke was a slight one. He's settled quite comfortably now. He'll be in a very heavy sleep for the rest of the night, but that's quite natural. His eyes have a great deal of blood in them. It will take a few days before his system drains it away. I can't be sure if there will be any paralysis until I check him tomorrow.'' He glanced over to the bed and beckoned Patrick outside the room. ''Now, I don't want to worry you unduly, but these slight strokes sometimes are just warnings, and quite often days or weeks later they are followed by a massive stroke that either totally paralyzes or kills. All you can do is keep him warm and quiet.''

Patrick saw the doctor to the front door and came back to answer the questions his sisters would put to him.

''The doctor says he's been very fortunate and it's just a mild stroke. I'll sleep in Father's room tonight and I suggest you girls go to bed and get some rest. You can take over tomorrow. You know what he's like when he's ill—you'll be run off your feet fetching and carrying.'' He looked at Kitty. She was deathly pale and swaying on her feet. A great wave of protectiveness swept over him. He wanted to pick her up and carry her to bed. He wanted to cradle her against his heart and beg her forgiveness for being such a swine to her. He swore he'd make it up to her, but now wasn't the time. He decided the kindest thing he could do was leave her alone, so he said good night and went to his father.

Jonathan O'Reilly was a tough old man and within a few days he was recovering satisfactorily. The only noticeable effect the stroke had had upon him was that his speech was slightly slurred and one corner of his mouth was lifted a little. This gave him an appearance of perpetual amusement, which was, if anything, an improvement of his rather harsh features. As the three young women moved about his room administering to his needs, they cracked jokes and gave him the acerbic side of their tongues if his demands grew too outrageous. Even Barbara learned to answer him back. This treatment did a great deal to aid his recovery. If they had spoken in subdued whispers with an air of polite deference, he would have feared his death was imminent. They never saw Patrick during this time. He slept within calling distance of his father every night, but arrived home so late and quit the house so early each morning that no one saw him. As soon as he knew his father was going to recover fully, he plunged back into his business endeavors with unflagging vigor.

Jeffrey Linton sought him out anxiously to see if the wedding plans would have to be altered. Relieved when Patrick told him the wedding could go ahead as planned, he invited Patrick to his club in St. James's Street for the evening.

"I thought you needed a title to walk into the hallowed halls of White's."

"To become a member, perhaps, but you would be coming as my guest," said Jeffrey.

"Wasn't it Beau Brummell, upon being invited to Manchester, who said, 'Gentlemen don't go to Manchester'? By the same token, factory owners don't go to White's."

"Come now, Patrick; only last week you told me the ideas of the Regency were dead. You're not afraid of being snubbed, are you?" asked Jeffrey politely.

"Afraid? Me? You must be joking! I'll pick you up at nine."

They entered the card room and to Jeffrey Linton's great surprise, Patrick was hailed heartily by Sir Charles Drago. "Patrick! Christ, it's good to see you. I didn't realize how much you could miss London until I started seeing some familiar faces."

Patrick clapped Charles on the back. "Martinique, wasn't it? Is your term of governorship finished, then?"

"Martinique went back to France after the Napoleonic Wars, my boy. It's St. Kitts. I've another three years yet, but my health hasn't been what it should be lately, so I returned for a few weeks. Damned tropics eat a man's vitals."

"Sorry, Jeffrey, this is Sir Charles Drago. I went to school with his younger brother Kevin. Charles, this is Viscount Linton, soon to be my brother-in-law."

"So you're popping Julia off this season, are you? I could use a wife to look after me in my declining years. You've got another sister, haven't you?" He winked.

"She's only thirteen, I'm afraid. Ask me again in three years' time when you return from the islands," Patrick said and laughed. He turned to Jeffrey. "Don't look so astounded that the likes of me knows the likes of him. We're both Irish and we're both from the North. His father is the Duke of Manchester."

Charles Drago was about thirty-nine. He was a square, thick-set man with wavy dark hair showing the first trace of silver. He was handsome in a full-blooded, florid way. The tropical sun never had bronzed him, but only burned him until his skin peeled, and then repeated the process over and over again until had the color of a boiled lobster. He contrasted greatly with the rest of the English nobility currently in the room, who looked more the color of oysters, thought Patrick privately.

Charles told Jeffrey, "This young man has a knack for making money. I can spare about thirty thousand pounds right now; how would you like to invest it for me? I'll wager you've something cooking at the moment."

Patrick said, "Well, I've acquired part interest in Stowils Wines, and Jeffrey here is introducing a new line into society for me. Now, the vineyards that produce this wine are in St. Emilion at Château Monlabert, and they're currently on the market for about a hundred thousand pounds. If the three of us throw in an equal amount, we could get them as an investment. Charles and myself will be silent partners and Jeffrey here can describe himself as the *directeur*. Why, Jeffrey, you'll be entitled to fly a flag with the company's coat of arms, a *fleur-de-lis* and a lion or some such device, and you can honeymoon at the eighteenth-century château. All your snobby friends will try to wangle invitations, and Julia will adore you for investing her marriage portion so wisely.''

"Do you think it's quite the thing for me to use Julia's money?" Jeffrey said stiffly.

"Don't be so squeamish, man," urged Patrick. "You'll have to put up with all the disadvantages of marriage, so you might as well enjoy its advantages."

"How many acres?" asked Sir Charles.

"Fifty acres planted in Sauvignon and fifty in Merlot. They produce a full-bodied red *premier grand cru*. I also think champagne is the coming thing here in London. Soon it will be as popular as it is in Paris. Especially if we keep the prices outrageous," added Patrick.

The acquisition of the château was accomplished without Patrick having to set foot outside London.

Kitty's youthful vitality soon reasserted itself; however, she was troubled in her mind. She wished she could have gone to her grandfather for advice and understanding. She dreaded a confrontation with Patrick and knew that so long as they were both under the same roof, meeting would be inevitable. She was glad that the drudging tasks of housework had been replaced by the lighter tasks of nursing and realized that it was a step up on the social scale. The doctor was pleased with O'Reilly's improvement but was very strict with regard to his diet and absolutely forbade him intoxicants. He was allowed out of bed a few hours a day now, and he spent these complaining bitterly to anyone who would listen. When Kitty brought him a bowl of clear soup, he pulled his face and began another tirade.

"I'd rather be dead than live on gruel for the rest of my life! Bloody doctors! No smoking, no drinking, but did you ever see one who practiced what he preached? Fornicators!"

Kitty said thoughtfully, "I wonder what your own doctor would say? The one in Bolton, I mean. He might suggest that we feed you up to get your old strength back."

"Do you think so? Kitty, try to smuggle me something more substantial from the kitchen, there's a good lass."

"Well, it's very difficult with that chef down there and then there's always that butler poking his nose into everything. Now, if it were your housekeeper in Bolton, Mrs. Thomson, I wouldn't have any trouble at all," she said sweetly. She saw the wheels begin to turn. She had planted the seeds of suggestion, all she had to do was wait until they took root.

Another week passed in which O'Reilly seemed to have returned to normal, except for tiring easily. He called his children together for a conference. "I've been thinking, and I've decided I'd be much happier in me own home, in me own bed," he said, coming straight to the point.

Julia looked alarmed. "But, Father, we can't return to Bolton now. It's less than a month to the wedding."

"Now, who said anything about *us* going back? I'm talking about *me*. You can manage without me at the wedding. Patrick can give you away and then fetch Barbara home to Bolton after the wedding."

Secretly, Julia was relieved. She was ashamed of her father, and if his presence were removed, her social life would be vastly improved.

Patrick questioned, "Are you sure you will be well enough for the journey?"

"I'm fit as a fiddle, or will be once I get back on my own midden. I'll take young Kitty with me. She's a good lass and pleasant to look at."

Patrick's mouth tightened. "I'll get you a nurse, Father."

"Keep your nurses—I'll take Kitty, thank you. We deal very well together," Jonathan said firmly.

"I'll send her brother along with you then, but I have my doubts about such a long coach ride. It will take at least twenty-eight hours from London to Bolton and even allowing an overnight stop in Leicester, that's at least two fourteen-hour days on the road. I think you should go by rail. These new locomotives cut the traveling time in half. If I get you settled in a railway carriage first thing in the morning, you'd be home by nightfall. What do you say?"

Jonathan stroked his chin reflectively. "Well, I wouldn't say 'no.'" He tried to veil the look of excitement that sprang to his eyes at the thought of trying out this new method of transportation.

"Good; I'll arrange your tickets. When would you like to go?" asked Patrick.

"Tomorrow," Jonathan answered without any hesitation whatsoever.

Late that night all Patrick's thoughts centered on Kitty. He had kept away from the house during the daylight hours because being under the same roof as the tempting beauty played hell with his peace of mind, to say nothing of the physical effect she had on him. His inventive mind built one fantasy on top of another relentlessly and he knew he was besotted with the beautiful little baggage.

A dozen times he'd almost gone to her room in the dead of night. Her exotic beauty lured him like the moon lured a lunar tide. The one taste he'd had merely whetted his appetite so that each night he felt more ravenous than the last. He was in one hell of a state. He'd tried easing his hunger with other women, but soon knew the only cure for what ailed him was Kitty . . . Kitty!

Perhaps it was for the best that she was going back north. At least he'd be able to concentrate on business again. But he felt so reluctant about letting her go. He wanted her back at Half-Moon Street as his exclusive property, but she pretended she'd have none of him and he'd be damned if he'd go down on his knees and beg her!

On the other side of the house Kitty lay awake thinking of Patrick O'Reilly. In spite of his wickedness he was the only man she would ever want. If he'd ask her to marry him, she'd say yes in a flash, but fat bloody chance there was of that. He just wanted her for his fancy piece and she was relieved she was leaving for Bolton before she gave in to temptation.

She dashed a tear away before it dared to form and wrapped her arms about her aching breasts. Then she sighed and gave herself up to her dreams, which with any luck would fly her to Patrick's waiting arms.

On the station platform Kitty was rather nervous of the huge iron monster, chugging out clouds of dirty smoke, ashes and cinders. The noise was a clattering assault on the eardrums and everything was confusion and disorder as baggage was loaded before the passengers. Kitty carried a lap robe for over O'Reilly's knees and a wicker lunch basket of food. Suddenly a cinder blew into her eye and she let out a little scream and tried to rub it away.

"Don't do that," Patrick commanded. He took out a white linen handkerchief and lifted her face without so much as a by-your-leave and extracted the foreign body. The moment he touched her, Kitty began to tremble. As he looked into her

eyes, she blushed a deep pink and lowered her eyelashes.
"Look at me," he ordered. Her eyelashes fluttered upward
momentarily and he said, low, "Do you forgive me?"

She caught her lip between her teeth but could not speak,
so she shook her head vehemently. "To hell with you then!"
he said savagely.

Soon the dirty buildings fell away and they were traveling
through green hills and then fields of golden ripe wheat,
dotted with red poppies. Farmers were haymaking and the
scenes were so peaceful that Kitty fell into a sort of daydream. In a way she had hated to leave the excitement of
London, and she hadn't enjoyed saying her farewells to the
girls last night. Barbara, bless her, almost had been in tears.
Julia was so full of the wedding, of course, she could think of
nothing else. Kitty, realizing the next time she saw Julia, she
would be a married woman, felt it her duty to forewarn her of
what to expect from Jeffrey. She broached the subject by
asking, "Julia, aren't you just a little bit afraid of marriage?"

"Afraid? Of course not," she said and laughed. "I can't
wait. Married women have much more freedom, you know."

"I suppose so, but you will be expected to share your
husband's bed," persisted Kitty.

"Oh, no, I shall insist on my own bedroom. Oh! I know
what you're hinting at—the intimacy business," laughed
Julia.

"Oh, Julia, don't laugh. It will shock you so deeply. You
have no idea what it's like to be with a man that way."

"Don't I?" Julia arched her brows. "What quaint notions
you carry around in that head of yours, Kitty!"

She was brought abruptly back to the present as Jonathan
O'Reilly shook her arm for the second time.

"Yer off somewhere wool-gathering, lass. Be a good girl

and open that lunch basket and let's see if we've got 'owt worth eating, eh?''

There was some cold chicken and some small jars of calves' jelly for invalids. A dozen small red tomatoes had been carefully packed to keep them separate from the russet apples.

"What muck!" Jonathan complained. He brought out his wallet and handed some money to Terry. "Here's a quid, lad. At the next station go and get us some pork pies and a bottle of hock."

Kitty almost protested, then realized that he would have his way no matter who put forth objections. However, an hour after he had partaken of the heavy pork pie, he was rolling about with indigestion.

Kitty was very anxious for him. "Mr. O'Reilly, you don't think you are having another stroke, do you?"

"Nay, lass, it's the wind. Next stop get me some peppermints. Ask for Mint Imperials; they should do the trick. I'm often plagued with wind. You know, life's funny—when I was a little lad I went hungry many a time, and now that I can afford anything I like, it doesn't like me. By gum, I'm feeling poorly."

By the time the little party wound its way to Hey House, all three were suffering from exhaustion. Terrance soon made himself scarce and after Mrs. Thomson helped Kitty get O'Reilly to bed, Mrs. Thomson took her into the kitchen, where a bright coal fire blazed.

"Take a load off yer feet, child, and I'll get you a cup of tea. If himself rings in the next half hour, you just ignore him. He can be a mithering old devil."

"Oh, Mrs. Thomson, I'm glad I'm back," said Kitty helplessly.

"They say that there London just seethes with vice. It's

nothing but a den of iniquity. Did anything happen to you out of the ordinary?''

Kitty looked at the bright eyes, avid for a juicy tidbit. She said slowly, ''Just one thing: I stopped being a little girl.''

Chapter 8

October 1 was a cool, clear day. The wedding went off without any hitches until the reception was well under way. Julia followed Patrick from the crowded salon into the library, where they would be alone.

"My God, Patrick, how could you keep it from me that Sir Charles Drago is a widower, and here in London again? Do you realize when his father kicks the bucket, he'll be the Duke of Manchester? Just think, I could have been a duchess! You made me settle for a viscount," she accused.

"I ought to take my riding crop to you, you mercenary little bitch! How can you say such things when you've just exchanged vows? By God, I wouldn't wish you on a fine man like Charles; he deserves better. Have you taken the trouble to thank him for that magnificent set of Wedgwood china? Thank God I don't have the managing of you anymore. Damned women are all alike—want your cake and eat it too!"

"Well, there's no need to be offensive to me, Patrick. I swear, I think you must be foxed," she hissed as she swept from the room.

Patrick sought out his friend in the crowd. "Society weddings are all alike, dead boring."

Charles finished off his drink and set the glass aside. "I'm just back from Drago Castle. Things are bad in Ireland, Patrick."

"I know. Father shipped all our people to Lancashire to

work in the mills. Not a very rosy future, but better than dying in the streets.''

''County Armagh is very bad. Of course, we've a lot more people than you, but they're leaving in droves. They clustered about me thick as flies for news of the West Indies. I've advised any who can beg, borrow or steal passage to go. Some of them are willing to indenture themselves for years in lieu of passage. It fair breaks my heart to see them leave their native sod. It's hard work on a plantation, but there's plenty to eat and they'll never be cold again.''

''Charles, you *are* depressed. After we get rid of the happy couple, let's go along to Madam Cora's and sample some of her soiled doves.''

Charles would rather have died than admit to Patrick that he hadn't been able to perform with a woman for over a year now. He knew it was from the dissipation of life in the tropics. Too much liquor; too many native women. Overindulgence had rendered him impotent, but he said quickly, ''Delightful idea! What could be better than good music, good food, good wine and a bad girl?''

In the early hours of the morning, Jeffrey lay awake with his hands behind his head. Despite the maidenly modesty Julia had displayed, he knew that he hadn't been the first. She had enjoyed it just a little too much for that. It was an age of complicated standards, where one type of behavior was accepted from men, but the female population was sharply divided into two groups. Bad girls were expected to be lustful, but good girls weren't supposed to know anything about sex whatsoever. In polite society, trousers were called inexpressibles, underwear was referred to as unmentionables and legs were whispered of as limbs. It was an age of hypocrisy where even piano legs were covered. Thus it was a shock to Jeffrey to doubt his wife's chastity. A quiet and prudent man, he decided some things were better left unsaid. But he also decided he would never give her the opportunity to be unfaithful to him. He would get her with child immediately, which would give him the upper hand by putting her at a physical disadvantage. He began to feel better. After all, there were advantages besides her money. Having a responsive, passionate woman in bed with you, especially when that woman was your wife, was a thing to be desired. He reached over and ran his hand possessively down her back and over her buttocks. She roused from sleep, turned toward him and opened up to him eagerly.

Jonathan O'Reilly did not consult his doctor in Bolton. After spending the first day home in bed, he arose as usual the second day and went to the mill.

Kitty seized the chance to go visit her grandfather. She took her tarot cards so he could give her a reading. She was too superstitious to read for herself.

"What burden is weighing your shoulders down, lass? Unload it."

Kitty, relieved to have a sympathetic ear, blurted, "I was seduced . . . against my will!"

Her grandfather looked at her keenly. "By the father, or the son?" he asked shrewdly.

"Patrick John Francis O'Reilly," she whispered.

He nodded, "Good. Better you should have your first experience with a young stallion like that."

"My God, men are all alike. You all stick together!" she shouted wildly.

"Gently now, little one. Young men are virile; it's a fire in the blood. They lose control once they're teased and aroused."

"I didn't tease and arouse him!" she said indignantly.

"You were born with the instinct. You fan your great

lashes and they sweep across your cheeks, then you flutter them upward and smile, so a man's heart turns over in his breast. Your sharp, little white teeth show between your parted lips, then the tip of that pink tongue darts out so a man would die just to put his mouth on yours. You sigh so deeply your titties swell over the neckline of your gown and your black silk curls bounce about your shoulders so a man's fingers can't resist the impulse to play with them. You are too tempting for any man with red blood in his veins.''

Kitty was speechless. Was this the picture she presented to the world? He was exaggerating, like every Irishman who ever drew breath, but only a little, she finally had to admit.

''So there's no use crying over spilled milk. Is he going to set you up?''

''I don't want to be his mistress. I hate making love! But oh, I wish he would marry me.'' Her own words shocked her, for she had not realized until this very moment that she still loved him in spite of everything. When a man entered a woman's body, he penetrated her soul and left behind a trace of himself that could never be completely erased.

''Be sensible, Kitty!'' He spoke sternly for the first time. ''Patrick couldn't marry you if it were his dearest heart's desire. A man in his position has a responsibility to his family to marry well. He's related to the nobility through Julia's marriage now. Surely you wouldn't expect him to sacrifice himself for a Gypsy wench who serves in his house as a scullery maid?''

''Don't be so brutal,'' cried Kitty, her face white with pain.

''Life is brutal, Kitty. We have happy moments and happy hours, but not happy lives. Come to terms with it, learn to bend with the wind or be broken by it,'' he said quietly. ''If you dislike being intimate with a man, choose someone older. Older men aren't filled with the burning lust that plagues young men. Choose a man who will not be demanding in bed and before long you will be so unsatisfied you will crave a man with vigor.''

"Will you read the cards for me?" she asked.

"I'll do the Celtic cross." He began to turn over the cards, speaking as he laid them out.

"Queen of swords—very dark coloring—many clouds and storm warnings, nothing will come to her easily.

"King of pentacles—self-made man, king of all he surveys, an authority figure, one who won't be managed by a woman.''

He turned the third card. "The Lovers—but alas, it's reversed. Means unrequited love, lovers' quarrel, breakup, separation.''

He turned the fourth. "The Star—idealism of the young, wishing on a star.''

He turned the fifth card. "The fool—you have a choice in life—no matter which path you choose, there lies your destiny; learn by your mistakes.

"The magician—symbolizes the four elements: earth, air, fire and water. Your destiny will include all four.

"Death . . .''

"Stop! I don't want to hear any more," cried Kitty.

He gestured to her to be quiet as he peered intently at the cards. "It could mean a physical death, but also that things get worse before they get better. Always remember, Kitty, death is followed by resurrection.''

Kitty looked dismayed. "I shouldn't have bothered. I only wanted to know about marriage.''

He chuckled and took her palm. "You'll have at least three husbands; it says so right here.''

She shook her head, still distressed but trying to smile. "I've got to get back now. Take care of yourself, Grandada.''

* * *

Jonathan O'Reilly fell into the habit of dining with Kitty every evening. Then they would play dominoes.

"How about half a crown on this next hand, lass?" said Jonathan, laughing. "But what will you put up?"

"Oh, I don't need to put up anything; I'm going to win!" She was as good as her word and deftly pocketed the half crown.

"By gum, you're sharp. You've been in the knife drawer again. I'd like to see the man born who could outsmart you, Kitty. You're just like a tonic, lass." He beamed at her.

"You really have made a remarkable recovery. I can't get over it. It's as if there never was anything the matter with you," marveled Kitty.

"Very likely wasn't a stroke in the first place," scoffed Jonathan. "Doctors like to make you think you're sicker than you are, then they can stick you with a big bill. I wasn't born yesterday. There's not many as can put one over on me." He winked. "Like you, eh, Kitty?"

"Oh, you really were ill, Mr. O'Reilly. Your aura went the most ghastly shade of brown."

"My aura? What's that, lass?"

"Well, you know, it's the light that surrounds you. The color can tell all sorts of things about your health and your character."

"That's just Gypsy hocus-pocus. Surely you don't really believe in all that."

Kitty said with a laugh, "Don't tell me you aren't superstitious—you're always throwing salt over your shoulder when you spill it and you go around knocking on wood."

"You've caught me out," he said and smiled. "Tell me about this aura."

"Well, while you were ill it turned muddy brown, but now it's gone to a sort of pale orange shade, so you are a lot better. When you are in full health and running the mills and ordering everyone about, it glows a bright yellow. That shows you have a lot of energy. When you lose your temper, the edge becomes tinged with red."

"Me? Get angry? Never!" he protested. "Tell me: Does everyone have one of these auras?"

"Yes. Julia's is red and Barbara's is a lovely shade of blue."

"What's yours?" he asked.

"I've been told it's a pale violet," she said, and thought silently, and Patrick's is a deep, vibrant purple. She suggested, "Would you like me to read your palm for you?"

He offered his hand, palm up, fingers curled upward.

"Right away I know you are careful with money. Your hand is cupped to keep what you already have. If you fling your hand open with the fingers spread, it means that money just runs through your fingers. Do you see the difference? You have a very square hand. That means you are practical with a good deal of common sense. Your palm is longer than your fingers, which shows you are a doer rather than a dreamer. You would have made a success out of any line of work you went into. Your thumb is very strong and thick at the bottom. That means you like to be the boss. Your mound of Venus is very fleshy."

"Where's that?" he questioned.

"Here, this fat pad at the base of your thumb. That means you love luxury. You overindulge in food and other things. The tips of your fingers are a little blunt, which indicates that you are stubborn and would have your own way if it killed you." She laughed.

"Enough of my character. What about my fortune?" he prompted.

"You've already made your fortune, Mr. O'Reilly. As to your future, all I can tell you is the usual Gypsy hocus-pocus. You will meet a dark, mysterious stranger. You are going on a very long journey. You will be granted three wishes," she joked.

There was only one wish he was interested in. Kitty had been on his mind a lot lately. He wanted to obey his longings and give in to the physical impulse of fornicating with her, but he was fearful of getting a taste, then having the sweets withdrawn, to leave him starving. She'd be off with the first rich young blade who propositioned her. What did he have to bind her to him? "Bugger it, I'll ask her to wed me," he decided. "My children will play hell when they find out," he thought, and his face lit up with anticipation at the thought of the scenes they would create. He didn't want a life of furtive sex, hurried gropings in the dark and creaking floorboards to alert the servants. No, by God, he wanted to be able to pull her onto his knees and fondle her in front of everyone if he so fancied. After all, how many years did he have left? He was going to throw his cap over the windmill. They'd say he was in his dotage, but let them! Meanwhile he'd be enjoying that silken little wench.

The next day he put up the mills for sale. Bugger it all, he would retire! At dinnertime he could contain himself no longer. "You have it within your power to make an old man very happy, Kitty. Will you wed me, lass?"

She was taken completely off guard. The idea never had entered her head. She knew he had come to depend on her company and he was able to be himself and relax and be comfortable in her presence.

"I . . . I don't know what to say," she said honestly.

"Say 'yes,' lass. You won't be sorry," he urged.

"Well, I'd like to see my grandfather before I give you my answer. I'm not yet sixteen you know, Mr. O'Reilly," she temporized.

"Mmm, that is a bit young, but I think your grandfather

can be persuaded to give his consent. Why don't you nip around and see him tonight? Do you want me to come with you, love?"

"No, thank you, Mr. O'Reilly, I think I'd better go alone."

"Call me Johnny," he urged.

Kitty faltered. "I . . . I couldn't."

"Well, Jonathan then. Go on, try."

"All right, Jonathan."

"That's it, love. Now you go and get your cloak and I'll order the carriage for you." He patted her knee in a fatherly fashion.

Kitty's head was in a whirl. All she could think of was that she would be Patrick's stepmother. If she agreed to this marriage it would put her out of Patrick's reach, and at the same time be a subtle revenge. She would have a lovely home and an easy life. Jonathan O'Reilly had always treated her kindly. He was quite old, but hadn't her grandfather pointed out what an advantage that could be? He obviously just wanted companionship because he was lonely. She probably could have her own bedroom, as Julia intended to do. When Kitty arrived at the little shabby house, she asked the driver to wait for her. Inside she found her grandfather bathing the children before a meager fire as Ada sat nearby, huddled pathetically. Kitty noted her swollen body. "Is your time near, Ada?"

"I've another month to go yet, bless you, but it moves about so much, I swear it's got four arms and four legs."

One of the children started crying from hunger and Kitty felt guilty that she had life so easy these days. She quickly felt in her dress pocket and came up with the two half crowns she had won from Jonathan at dominoes. She pressed the money into Ada's palm, but she shook her head. "Give them to your grandad. My husband would have them off me for drink before you could say Jack Robinson,'' Ada said pathetically.

"I have some news. Jonathan O'Reilly has asked me to marry him and I'm so confused I don't know what to do.'' She appealed to her Grandad.

He looked at her for a few minutes, then shook his head. "Nay, lass, you must decide your own future. I won't advise you either way.''

Ada got to her feet very deliberately and took Kitty's hand. Ada spoke earnestly. "He might not advise you, but I will. You'd have to be daft to refuse to wed a millowner. That's riches beyond your wildest dreams! No worries about where your next stick of firewood is coming from, or mouthful of bread. You're bound to outlive him and be left a rich widow. Remember this: All men are selfish and have violent tempers and know how to make a woman miserable, so you might as well marry one with money. All cats are gray in the dark, if you know what I mean.''

Kitty looked at her poverty-stricken surroundings and made up her mind.

It was getting late as the carriage made its homeward journey. A thought crept into Kitty's brain which she couldn't dispel. When Patrick brought Barbara home and learned that Kitty had agreed to marry his father, there was always the chance that he could not bear such a thing to happen and would demand that she marry him instead. At Hey House silence greeted her and she realized everyone had gone to bed. She lit a candle in the front hall to guide her up the stairs and as she moved quietly past Jonathan's bedroom, the door opened and a voice asked, "Is that you, Kitty?''

"Yes, Mr. . . . yes, Jonathan. I'm late because I stayed to help put the children to bed,'' she apologized.

"Come in, lass, I'm that impatient for your answer. I've been waiting hours."

He had a robe over his nightshirt, but Kitty had seen him in this state of undress many times while she had been nursing him. She set down her candle on a table by the window and said shyly, "I've decided to become your wife."

"Sweetheart!" he cried and enveloped her in a smothering bear hug.

"Please, please, I can't breathe," she cried, horrified, but his mouth came down on hers, suffocating her even further. His mouth was soft and flaccid and she shuddered with distaste. His hands took hold of her buttocks and squeezed and pressed her against his hardening member. She gasped and tried to pull away, but he was a robust old man with much more strength than she had dreamed possible. "No, no, I beg you, Mr. O'Reilly, you must stop!"

He was very excited and tried begging her. "Don't deny me, sweetheart. Just let me put it in."

"No, no, let me go!" she implored, repelled by his crudeness.

"Don't fight me, Kitty," he begged. "Can't you understand how I need you?"

He had her on the bed now, his great bulk on top of her. It was like a nightmare. Kitty couldn't believe that this was happening to her. She had thought that nothing could be worse than Patrick's ravishing, but he was so physically attractive and his touch had made her quiver, while this assault only made her shudder. His face hung above hers. The mouth with the unnatural lift at the corner leered down at her, as his hands grappled with her long skirts to raise them above her waist.

"Hurry! I can't wait much longer! Open your legs!"

Her fear turned to fury. She spat full in his face. Now he came on like an angry bull. His hamlike fist tore her drawers off and he hoisted his nightshirt to facilitate his entrance. His pubic hair was sparse and bristled against her soft skin. He lunged against her, but she was so small, only the tip of his weapon entered. He raised himself up to make another plunge and Kitty was off the bed like a shot. With amazing swiftness he was at the door before her, barring her way. She ran to the window and panted, "I'll scream the house down!"

"No one would dare come into my bedroom, screams or no screams."

"I'll shout 'fire!' " she threatened.

"But there is no fire."

She grabbed up the candlestick. "There is now!" She set the curtains ablaze and as he rushed forward with his water jug, she ran from the room and straight out into the night. She ran about four miles altogether until she stood outside Ada's door, taking in great gulps of air before she finally found the courage to knock. Her grandfather answered the door. He had been talking to Terry.

"What's the matter, Kitty?" Terry asked as he jumped up and ran to her.

"What happened, child?" asked her grandfather.

She shook wildly. She was so agitated, he didn't press her for an answer, but led her to the sofa and wrapped his old overcoat about her.

"I'd better get back to the house and see what's up," said Terry.

Her grandad rocked her gently and smoothed back the tumbled hair from her face. Her body trembled uncontrollably, but as the realization of her close escape dawned on her, she calmed a little and laid down her head to rest. After about an hour Terry returned wild-eyed. Kitty sat up wearily as he came to the couch.

"Did you lose your job because of me, Terry?"

He shook his head. "He's dead, Kitty!" Terry blurted.

She crossed herself. "Mother of God, how?"

"His bedroom caught on fire."

"My God, he wasn't burned to death, was he?" she asked, horrified.

He shook his head. "Oh, no, he soon had the fire out. It was after that in all the confusion, he must have had another stroke and dropped dead."

"They'll say I killed him!" she cried.

"Well, we never can go back, that's for certain sure," said Terry.

Chapter 9

For the first week Kitty was afraid to go outside for fear she would be picked up by the police. Gradually, as time elapsed and nothing happened, she began to relax a little and returned to her usual good cheer. Her immediate needs were pressing. She had one dress, one shift, one pair of shoes and stockings, but no drawers. How was she to get the things she needed with no money and no job? The poverty in the Blakely household was unbelievable. She sat and thought for over an hour, then resolutely put on Ada's shawl and went out the back door. She walked up the back streets until she came to a line of washing. Swiftly she unpegged two pairs of navy blue bloomers and a pair of black cotton stockings, and was back home in under ten minutes.

She tried everywhere to get a job, but there were signs posted at most places that read: NO IRISH NEED APPLY. She heard that Constantine's, a modern drapers, was opening a new shop in the town center and needed girls. She had the sprigged muslin dress, which when washed and ironed would do very nicely, but she needed something warm to go over it. She went to a secondhand shop and looked through all the cloaks but they seemed too shabby; then she spotted a gray velvet pelisse that was just her size. She hunted among stacks of hats and feathers until she found a small gray bonnet. The pelisse and the bonnet took her last penny, but she left the shop feeling elated.

She needed ribbon to trim the bonnet and make it look half decent and she knew exactly where to find some. She walked home past Deane Churchyard. There, on a fresh grave, stood the ugliest wreath Kitty had ever seen, but it had a marvelous mauve satin ribbon on it that lit up Kitty's face with delight.

She got up very early the next morning, heated some water in the kettle and washed her hair. When it was dry, she put on her outfit, knew she looked pretty and hurried down to Constantine's. A well-dressed young man, two very plain-faced young women and an older woman with a hooked nose that looked like it was trying to detect a bad odor stood behind the counter. Kitty approached the gentleman, but the older woman pushed forward and said, "Could I be of service?"

"I'm applying for the position of shop assistant, ma'am," Kitty said politely.

"May I see your references?" the woman said coldly.

"I've never worked in a shop before, ma'am. I was in service," Kitty said and hesitated.

"Irish?" the woman inquired, her nose seeming to discover where the odor was coming from at last.

For a fleeting moment Kitty thought she would deny it, but she lifted her chin a little and said, "Yes, ma'am, I'm Irish."

A hush fell. The others were listening intently. The woman gave her a pitying look and said, "I'm sorry, you wouldn't be at all suitable, and besides everyone knows that all Irish girls are bags!"

Kitty felt a lump rise as her throat constricted and tears threatened to come to her eyes, but "No, by God, they won't see me cry," she swore. She looked them all up and down in turn and said, "Well, in that case, you can all kiss my arse; the north side of it!" She flipped up her skirts at the back cheekily and sailed from the shop with her head in the air.

"It'll have to be one of O'Reilly's mills, I'm afraid. They're the only ones who will hire the Irish," said Ada.

"Can I call myself Kitty Blakely when I go for a job? I don't want the O'Reillys to know where I am."

" 'Course you can, lass," Ada said.

Kitty went around to the Falcon and was hired in the knotting room. The first thing she had to do was trek to Uncle Joe's once again and pawn her sprigged muslin, shoes and gray velvet pelisse. She picked navy and white striped pinafores and a pair of button-up boots.

She entered the knotting room with great trepidation. Counterpanes hung from long tables. She was shown how to pick up alternate fringes and twist them into knots, making sure the edges were uniform and even. This was an easy task; however, a lot of the goods were shoddy and manufactured from poor yarns. To give them a more substantial finish so they would sell, the cloth was soaked in a vat of sizing and then dried quickly between hot rollers. This process filled in the weak spots and holes, but it made the fringes stiff and sharp. Before the end of the day, Kitty's finger ends were rubbed raw and spots of blood smeared on the counterpanes. These were immediately classed as "damaged" by the examiner and she received no payment for them. Thus Kitty embarked on that period of her life when she saw daylight only on the weekends. The knocker-up would tap on the bedroom windows with his long pole at five in the morning and she would clatter off to the mill with the wave of humanity that swept down the street and through the mill gates by five-thirty each day. Inside the mill, the hot-oil stench of the machines always made her nauseated at this hour and the incessant clatter of the big machines gave her a headache until she learned to block out the noise. The rooms were kept very hot and damp, as humidity was needed in the processing of cotton so that the threads wouldn't break so easily and to keep the fibers floating in the air to a minimum. Kitty soon was promoted to the weaving sheds to help a more experienced woman who ran four looms. Her job was "tenting." The large room held hundreds of towel looms, which belted to and fro at top speed. Kitty was intimidated by the noise and frightened by the flying picking sticks and unguarded straps that whirled the machinery. Between the rows of machines the alleys were so narrow they were warned always to pass a machine with their backs to it; never their faces. It was an incredibly dirty atmosphere and after working her twelve-hour shift she went home to wash her overall and her hair every night. She was careful always to wash the machine oil from her black cotton stockings because she had seen some of the other girls' legs and they were covered with masses of pimples. Her job as a tenter was to rethread the empty shuttles. She noticed that many girls did it with their mouth and sucked the thread through the shuttles. Although this was faster than using your fingers, Kitty could not bring herself to do it. For one thing, if there were different colors in the cloth, your mouth became daubed with different hues of dye, and for another thing, Kitty noticed that the girls who did this had rotten front teeth as a result. The first hour of the working day was spent in a dull, silent stupor, but then everyone would thaw and the fun began. The girls were a laughing, joking, happy group. They played jokes on each other and had a bit of fun. While the machines were going it was too noisy for a lot of talk, but they had worked out a system of winks, nods and gestures that conveyed a welter of meanings. The mill workers were vulgar and convulsed each other with rude stories. Kitty soon learned that birth, death and sex were spoken of openly and treated as normal, everyday occurrences, which, after all, they were. She learned to laugh at the coarse jokes and sometimes told them herself. They were protective of one another, and the first day she was warned never to go behind the tent frames with the overseer, no matter how he tried to maneuver her back there. As Kitty stood by the loom watching for the first empty shuttle, the overseer came up to her with a note in his hand. "Kitty Blakely, you're needed at home," he announced with distaste and dropped the paper as if it were contaminated. Kitty realized he knew she had to go home because another baby was being born, and everybody knew the Irish produced too many babies. She found Ada huddled over on a chair, clutching her black shawl about her with one hand and the other doubled into a fist pressed into her side.

"Why isn't there any fire?" asked Kitty.

"There's no wood."

Kitty went into the back kitchen and brought back the ax. She picked up a chair but put it down again because they had only two. Then she remembered the back panel of the dresser was hanging loose, so she used it to light the fire. Then she ran for the midwife. She didn't have to go far, as midwives were almost as plentiful as pubs in that neighborhood.

Mother Byrum was a little, round woman. She always had her bag ready by the door and came along with Kitty without delay.

"Why isn't there a bed set up down here?" Mother Byrum demanded.

Kitty said, "They were all born on the kitchen door, Ada says."

"Oh, yes, I remember now. Well, give me a hand, girl. Don't stand there like a dressmaker's dummy."

They unhinged the door and set it up with a fairly clean sheet over it.

"Now I want hot water, girl. Put the kettle on the hob. The first thing I want is a cup of tea!" She hung up her shawl and pulled a chair up to the fire. "Who's got your other kids?"

"Big Florrie across the street is keeping them until tomorrow," Ada answered weakly from the makeshift bed.

"Not Mrs. Piece-out-of-her-nose?" asked Mother Byrum, scandalized.

"Why does she have a piece out of her nose?" asked Kitty.

The midwife shot a significant look at the woman in labor. "The bad disorder! Mind you, it's not her fault. Her husband's the doorman at the Music Hall and he knocks about with the chorus girls."

Ada could hold back no longer, but Mother Byrum finished her tea before she proceeded.

"I won't need any help with the delivery, so stay clear, but you'll have to clean up afterward. That's not my job."

Kitty nodded her understanding and sat gazing into the fire. She blocked out the screams of hard labor by concentrating on the crickets chirping behind the fireplace. She could imagine it was a pet bird and the fireguard was its cage. A voice cut into her reflections, "I think there's more than one —yes, it's twins!" "Oh, my God, no!" protested a weak voice. In a remarkably short time the midwife was saying, "There now, it's all over. There's one of each. Which do you want to keep?"

"The boy every time," answered Ada.

"What about *her?*" whispered Mrs. Byrum, gesturing toward Kitty.

"She won't say nothing," came the low answer.

Kitty wondered wildly if they meant what she thought they meant. There was a sharp slap and a frail cry and the midwife placed the boy child with its mother. "Here, wash this." She handed Kitty the dead baby, and she took the pitiful bundle into the kitchen. She saw it and felt it, but her mind was numbed, and she automatically carried out the task of cleansing it. She dressed it in a nightie she had made the week before, and not really knowing what to do with the lifeless creature, laid it on the kitchen shelf. She went back

into the other room and the midwife pushed an enamel bowl
into her hands. "Empty this and wash these blood-soaked
things. I'm off now. By the way, remind himself I haven't
been paid for the last one yet!"

To Kitty's relief the older children came in from school
and she kept busy feeding them, and then to make sure they
wouldn't wander into the kitchen, she shooed them out to
play in the front street. She made Ada a cup of tea and then
timidly crept into the kitchen to see if there really was a baby
on the shelf. Its face looked waxen and she decided it looked
like a doll.

"It's only a wax doll," she whispered.

After she washed the blood-stained linen and cleaned up,
the kids were home from school for the day.

"You're staying at Big Florrie's tonight," Kitty told them,
so they trooped across the street.

"Kitty, will you go over and give Big Florrie some help?
Jack will move me upstairs when he comes in from work."

Kitty not only put Ada's kids to bed, but also looked after
Big Florrie's brood. When it began to go dark Kitty said,
"I'd better go back now. It's getting late and Jack will be
home."

She walked slowly back across the street. Jack Blakely met
her at the door and handed her a parcel done up with newspaper and string.

"Take this to old Tommy Ferguson, the night watchman at
the mill down the street. For two shillings he'll pop this in
the furnace. Tell him it's a dead dog." Kitty took the pack-
age and started off down the street. She saw the string and
felt the newspaper, but her thoughts would not penetrate the
wrapping. She turned her mind instead to Christmas, which
was only a week away. Old Tommy was just inside the millyard. She looked up at him, held out the bundle in one hand

and the money in the other, but no words would come. Old Tommy relieved her of her burdens. "Another dead dog, eh?" he said with a broad wink and ambled off inside.

The week passed quickly and great excitement filled the children's hearts on December 25. Kitty and Doris washed eight grubby hands and four little faces. Kitty ran a dinner fork through the girls' hair and they were off to the Queen's Street Mission for the charity Christmas dinner. Each child was given a meat pie, a toasted raisin cake and a mug of tea. Then Mr. Poppawell, the revered benefactor, came in to hand out the presents.

"Did everyone get a meat pie?" he asked, beaming.

"Yes, Mr. Poppawell," they answered in unison.

"Did everyone pull a Christmas cracker?"

"Yes, Mr. Poppawell."

"Did everyone fill a brown paper bag under the table to take home?"

"Yes, Mr. Poppawell," they chorused innocently.

"Well, you can all empty them out, that's not what you're here for!"

All the children lined up and Mr. Poppawell and his helpers started to hand out the presents.

"Do you see that pretty girl over there?" he asked his assistant and indicated Kitty. "She's spent all morning looking after five of them. Save that big box for her. She looks like a good girl, and I bet she never gets much." Kitty was handed the large box. With shining eyes she lifted the lid and looked into the face of a wax doll. Her throat constricted, and a bluish tinge appeared around her mouth. She shook her head woodenly and tried to hand it back, but they pressed it upon her with fond insistence.

After she had taken the kids home, she walked three miles until she came to a field. She scratched out a shallow grave with a stone and buried the baby in its cardboard coffin.

There were no flowers to gather, so she broke off two low branches and placed them in the form of a cross on top of the little mound.

By spring Kitty drooped and yearned incessantly for a bit of green Ireland. The long, hard winter had made her frail. The roses were gone from her cheeks, leaving a ghostly pale shadow of herself behind. Her grandad was worried. "Terry, on Sunday I want you to take your sister up on the moors. Get you both out in the fresh air and sunshine to blow the cobwebs off you."

So they took some bread and cheese and a bottle of water and went up on Belmont Moors.

"What do you want to do?" asked Terry, eyeing a pretty stretch of water known as the Blue Lagoon.

"I want to run along the top of the stone walls," said Kitty eagerly.

"Well, that's pretty daft. Dangerous, too!" said Terry, laughing.

"I know, but these stone walls remind me of Ireland. If it gives me pleasure, why should I not do it?"

He lifted her atop a stone wall and she ran like the wind, never missing a step where the stones had tumbled and left treacherous gaps. She came to a hawthorn tree in blossom and stood inhaling the heady fragrance as if she never would have enough. She looked down from the tree and was surprised to see a young couple lying in the tall grass. When she realized they were making love with passionate abandon, she ran back to Terry as fast as she could.

"We'd better go back that way. There's a couple in the grass up there."

"Oh, what were they doing?" Terry asked.

"What do you think they were doing?" she asked flatly.

"Oh, that?"

"It's disgusting! She actually looked like she was enjoying it, too."

"Well, you know. Kitty, there's not much privacy in these little houses. What is a young couple to do when they're in love and have nowhere to go?"

Her eyes slid sideways to him. "Have you ever forced a girl to do that?"

"Most of 'em don't need forcing. There's a lot of girls like it, you know. In fact, they say there's something wrong with the ones who don't."

This was a novel idea to Kitty, and she turned it over and over in her mind. Perhaps the girl had been doing it for money, but she quickly rejected that idea. When a man offered a woman money he wanted it then and there; only lovers would have taken the time to find a beautiful setting for their mating.

As summer wore on, Kitty was given some more machines to mind in the spinning room. At first she thought she would never be able to keep up with the voracious machines, but she was bright and quick, and soon it seemed she'd been doing it for a lifetime.

Kitty's life was not pleasant, but she was determinedly cheerful, looking forward to her Sundays as a chance to rest and play, doggedly getting through the rest of the week, doing her job as best she could.

By the time her seventeenth birthday had passed she realized that the notion of the mating of men and women had become less traumatic for her. For nearly two years she had lived in an atmosphere where sexual relations were open and natural and accepted by all. It was hard even to think of such a thing as romance.

Another winter passed, but not without taking its toll. Kitty was far too thin, with eyes almost too large for her face.

Her figure, which at one time had been very nicely rounded, almost disappeared. Her breasts became so small she considered padding her bodice, and her bottom became narrow and flat. The long hours and poor diet not only had taken the glow from her skin and the sheen from her hair, but also had robbed her of that sparkling vitality she always had in abundance. Her wit was honed and her tongue sharpened, but she became so physically weakened that often she was dizzy.

Chapter 10

Patrick had a strong desire to find Kitty after his father's death. He questioned Mrs. Thomson and the other servants, but they could not or would not furnish him with any details that might lead to her whereabouts. As Patrick had no idea that Kitty and Terrance had relatives in Bolton, the pair seemed to have vanished into thin air. Perhaps they had gone to another town, or back to London, or even returned to Ireland. At last he began to realize that if she cared for him at all she would not have left him without a trace. He didn't blame her; he blamed himself. What he had done to her was unpardonable. Eventually he stopped searching every crowd for a glimpse of her beautiful face. He felt that if she wanted to be free of him, the least he could do was leave her in peace. Her image still lingered in his memory, and if he did not keep himself busy every hour of the day, she came back again and again to haunt him. Sometimes in bed, the dark room would be filled with that unique fragrance that always lingered about her hair—a mixture of wild roses and peat smoke; then he would curse himself for a fool. If only he hadn't ravished her, but taken her gently, awakening her desire and giving her pleasure and rapture with his touch.

He put the mills up for sale, as he definitely had decided to sail for America on his merchant vessel's next voyage. He sold the Egyptian for a very large sum, but offers on the other two mills didn't meet his expectations, so he decided to keep them until he got his price. Patrick had noted that the best cotton they received from the Carolinas had been marked "Bagatelle Plantation," and he intended to journey there and buy up the whole crop if possible. He threw himself into arranging the cargo and was impatient at the amount of time this consumed. At length he was free to depart for Liverpool to see the various goods loaded and make final arrangements before departure.

Patrick found that he loved the sea. He welcomed the needed change. The air was invigorating and the male-oriented environment of the ship was rough and ready and made possible an easy camaraderie that he fell in with comfortably. When they made harbor in Charleston, Patrick discovered that vessels from England were eagerly awaited, and the goods he had brought were snapped up quickly for fantastic prices.

He had written to Monsieur LeCoq at Bagatelle Plantation, telling him of his proposed visit, and he carried an invitation in his pocket that the LeCoqs had extended to him. He bought a carriage and horses to convey him. When he arrived at Bagatelle he was amazed at its size and opulence. This was not the ''trifle'' that its name indicated. The plantation must have covered ten thousand acres. There were endless rows of slave cabins and hundreds of slaves. The magnificent Georgian mansion set in vast formal gardens took his breath away. He drove his carriage up the long, circular driveway; half a dozen slaves waited to take care of his horses when he stopped. The house was white with an upstairs gallery that swept across the whole front of the building. The lawns were like jade velvet, with each shrub trimmed to perfection. Patrick counted over a dozen gardeners plying their trade. A liveried majordomo complete with powdered wig opened the door to Patrick. Patrick handed his calling card to the servant, who placed it on a silver salver and disappeared up a magnificent wide staircase. The female house servants were dressed in striped cotton dresses with bright cotton tignons covering their hair. Quite a number appeared in the short space of time Patrick was kept waiting, and he realized it was out of curiosity to get a good look at him. Suddenly a female appeared at the top of the staircase. She was the most striking woman Patrick had ever beheld. She was a Juno, statuesque, almost as tall as himself. A Titian-haired beauty with a slightly hooked nose, Patrick thought she bore a striking resemblance to Elizabeth I. Their eyes met in mutual amusement as each acknowledged the other's critical inspection. He stared at her magnificent breasts, well displayed in the low-necked black gown, and her sensual mouth. She stared at the thick saddle muscles of his thighs, unconcealed by the tight trousers, and her glance lingered on the bulge of his crotch, which was satisfyingly large even in his unaroused state. She spoke up then; her voice was low, with an attractive French accent.

"Jacquine LeCoq, Monsieur O'Reilly."

"I've been looking forward to meeting you, *madame,* and your husband, Monsieur LeCoq, who extended me such a gracious invitation."

"My husband, Monsieur O'Reilly, was laid to rest two months ago." She paused dramatically.

The knowledge somehow didn't surprise him, perhaps because she had given the immediate impression of being in command. He murmured his condolences, but he had known as soon as she imparted the news of the death that she was not sorry. He wondered why. Freedom? Money? Power? Yes, definitely power! he thought.

"You must call me Jacquine, *monsieur.* Let us move to a sitting room on the shady side of the house and let me offer you a cool drink."

The tall glass of Bourbon filled with crushed ice was delicious to Patrick's parched throat.

"Your home is very beautiful, Jacquine, but I must admit I am having difficulty adjusting to the climate."

"It is a trifle humid, Patrick. At this hour of the afternoon any sensible man or woman would be between cool sheets for a rest, no?"

Somehow he was not surprised that she had brought up the subject of sex before they had even finished their first drink.

"I find it more than a trifle humid, my dear; it's more like a steam bath."

"That's why our gentlemen wear white suits in the tropics. Have you nothing lighter you could change into?" she suggested.

"Alas, *madame,* where I come from, men's fashion is black, and I'm afraid I would feel foolish in a white suit."

"The English are said to be very set in their ways; however, I must confess I enjoy doing things in the French way," she said as she directed her eyes to his lap. She licked her lips to add emphasis to her words. He stirred and began to enlarge and the corners of her lips lifted in triumph with the knowledge of her power.

He said pointedly, "I'm not averse to experimenting. Are you, Jacquine?"

She smiled and said, "I'll wager you ride well, Patrick."

"I have stamina. I don't tire easily," he promised.

"In that case, I shall enjoy mounting you." She paused again for effect. "Tomorrow we will inspect the plantation. We should ride in the morning while some coolness lingers, then we can rest in the afternoon . . . perhaps?"

He bowed. "I am at your service, my dear lady."

She summoned an elderly black man. "Titus, show Monsieur O'Reilly to the front guest room and tend to his needs."

Titus ran a bath for Patrick and laid out fresh underwear and a white frilled shirt on the bed. While Patrick bathed, his suit was taken away to be brushed and pressed. Patrick had always been used to having money, but he had never seen it so lavishly spent. He estimated that house, kitchens and garden must employ over fifty servants. The rooms were filled with the most exquisite and expensive furniture Europe had to offer. The chandeliers were breathtaking, the drinking glasses were the finest lead crystal. He had no doubt now what would bring top prices when he shipped his next cargo.

Dinner that evening was probably the most delicious Patrick had ever eaten. It was French cuisine at its finest. A delicate bisque, crab quiche, shrimp coquilles, coq au vin surrounded by delicately flavored mounds of plantation-grown rice. Everything was served on the most ornate Georgian silver dishes and Sèvres china. The two of them were served by six slaves, albeit unobtrusively.

Patrick came straight to the point, buying and paying for Bagatelle's whole cotton crop. Only half was picked and baled, but he made arrangements for the rest to be shipped as soon as it was ready. She chided him for his impatience. "A southern gentleman wouldn't have brought up the subject of business until he'd enjoyed our hospitality for a few days. Tell me, Patrick, are you always in a hurry?"

"When I know what I want, I walk a direct path toward it, and I'm not always a gentleman," he warned her.

"That's good, for I'm not always a lady," she parried.

"The plantation intrigues me. Would you mind if I took a walk this evening?"

Outside in the darkness the air was hot and damp, but it had a softness to it that he had never felt before. Insects, frogs and crickets made up a midnight band, and singing could be heard in the direction of the slave quarters. The air was heavy with the fragrance of night-blooming flowers and the moss-hung trees made romantic, ethereal shadows. The atmosphere made him think of love, and Patrick was haunted by fleeting glimpses of Kitty. An overwhelming longing came over him that made a tightness in his chest and elsewhere. He mentally shook himself for a damned fool. Jacquine was within arm's reach. No child this, but a mature woman whose passion would match his own. He went back to the house and climbed the stairs to his room. He decided he wouldn't go to her, but make her come to him. If she wanted it as much as he thought she did, she would come!

He removed his coat, unbuttoned his shirt and slipped off his shoes and stockings when there was a soft tap on the door.

"Come in, *chérie*," he called.

To his amazement a small black girl took a few steps into the room and reluctantly closed the door.

"What would you like?" he asked, puzzled.

"I have to do my duties, sir," she said shyly.

"What are your duties, child?" he inquired.

"Whatever you desire, sir."

He looked at her and suddenly he knew why she was there. Another southern tradition for him to sample.

"What is your name?"

"Topaz, sir."

"Come, Topaz." He beckoned her to the light. She was not a pretty girl, but she was very young and quite obviously inexperienced from the frightened looks she cast upon him.

"Did your mistress send you to me?" he asked curiously.

She hung her head. "Yes, sir. She picked me for your bed wench. Please, sir, don't whip me?" she pleaded.

He put his finger under her chin and raised her face until their eyes met.

Fear, like he had seen in Kitty's eyes, mingled with mute pleading. He smiled kindly at her. "I won't whip you, Topaz. I won't hurt you in any way. You are very sweet and very lovely, but there is nothing I desire from you, sweetheart. You may leave now. Go to bed. Don't worry about your mistress. I will explain to her."

Relief flooded her features. In that moment of kindness she felt real love for him and she fell to her knees and kissed his hands. He gently disengaged himself and raised her hand to his lips before he held the door open for her to leave.

Patrick wondered if this was some kind of test Jacquine had devised for him. He did not know if he had passed or failed, and he didn't really give a damn. He went out onto the gallery to smoke a cigar. He had not been there long when he sensed rather than saw Jacquine. He stood perfectly still and let her approach. She was wearing a filmy black negligee that showed her white skin through even in the dark. He waited until she spoke first. "You did not care for the companion I chose for you, Patrick?" He crushed out his cigar and pulled her to him roughly.

"I choose my own bedmates, Jacquine! Stop fencing with me. There's no need to play cat-and-mouse games."

"I enjoy crossing swords with you, Patrick. You have such a formidable weapon." He picked her up and carried her to his room. He lifted her as easily as if she had been the lightest weight imaginable and laid her full length on the bed. He removed his shirt and pants and stood before her for inspection.

"Tell me what you like; name your poison." He grinned down at her.

"You mean like a menu, Patrick? Whatever I fancy, served any way I like?"

"Exactly! I will satisfy your hunger for you."

"Well, first of all I like it on the floor, *chéri*. Then I want to be assaulted and battered as hard and as long as you can stand it."

His love play consisted of biting her nipples and almost bruising her body with his hard hands. She groaned and writhed in pleasure and demanded he penetrate her immediately. He gripped her body with hurting hands and bruised her mouth with his, bringing blood. He mounted her with a brutal lunge and thrust himself to the hilt. He was just as rough, savage and brutal as she wanted him to be and she reached peaks of ecstasy with the pleasure-pain. He kept at her until she couldn't take any more for the moment and begged him to stop. He ignored her and thrust harder until she crossed her strong, well-muscled legs around his body and squeezed until she almost cracked his ribs. He withdrew, but strangely he had found no release with this insatiable animal. They rested for a few minutes, panting against each other. Their sweat plastered their bodies together, and when she reached for him, thinking she would have to cajole him to arousal for a second bout, his burning, hard erection jumped and quivered to her touch.

And so it was all night as he gave her whatever she desired.

As he bathed and dressed the next morning, Patrick wondered what made her so insatiable. Was it because she had been starved for so long without being satisfied, or was she always like that? He suspected the latter was true and idly wondered how she would manage until her year of mourning was up and she was free to marry again.

As Patrick and Jacquine rode together, he realized the vast scale of this plantation and became quite covetous. Five thousand acres were planted in cotton, and even though the yield was only one bale per acre, it was almost 100 percent profit because each crop provided seed for the next and the labor was virtually free. The plantation was totally self-sustaining. Vegetable crops covered many acres and these fed the slaves as well as the big house. All the swampland was cultivated in rice. The land had an intricate drainage system which took off water, stored it and returned it to the rows of green shoots as required. He immediately thought of Ireland and knew that with such a system successful crops could be produced from the black, sodden soil.

He thought, in fact, if only I could transplant this whole place to Ireland—without the black slaves of course—it would be paradise on earth.

At the farthest point from the house they kept livestock, hogs, chickens and turkeys, which provided the meat for the plantation.

He watched Jacquine from the corner of his eye. She guided her horse with an iron hand and clearly enjoyed the feeling of power the large animal gave her. He knew in that moment that all this could be his. If he asked her to marry him, he would be master of all he surveyed.

Whenever he saw Topaz, she gave him a shy smile and hurried away before the mistress could catch her. Patrick stayed a week and at the end of this time he was thoroughly sated with Jacquine and his nightly jousts. Her animal magnetism had ensnared him in the beginning, but the excesses began to jade his palate and the fascination was beginning to wear thin. At breakfast one morning he told her flatly that although he had enjoyed her hospitality, he had business awaiting him in New York that he dared delay no longer.

"Well, Patrick, you know when my period of mourning is up. Will you return by then?" she asked boldly.

"I promise you, Jacquine, that I shall return by then. I shall want your next year's crop, and perhaps other things, by then."

They understood each other completely. He knew what she was offering, and she was being generous enough to give him ample time to consider whether he would accept or reject it. In truth, at that moment, Patrick did not know what his decision would be.

He drove back to Charleston, and the ship sailed up the coast and into New York Harbor. He had come to see if it was feasible to start up branches of successful English companies. James Leaver wanted to start manufacturing his soap in America, and Patrick was on the board of directors of two other companies that had their eyes on America. New York was a thriving city. A new word had just been coined—"millionaire"—and Patrick thought it would be no bad thing to be. Fortunes were to be made in banking and railroads and gold mines. It was indeed a land of opportunities and he was determined to seize them all.

Chapter 11

Patrick was away eight months before he returned to England, and before he left Liverpool he sunk more money into another merchant vessel that he would fill with exports and sell at handsome profits. By the time he arrived in London, Julia had produced her first child and was determined not to have any more for a while. Barbara was beside herself with joy at the sight of her brother and longed to go home to Bolton with him. The cotton from Bagatelle would have arrived by now anyway, and he was anxious to see the quality of the goods it would produce.

His lawyer told him of two new low offers on the Falcon and advised Patrick not to sell. Determined to find out what was wrong at the Falcon he decided to have a talk with his manager and go over the books. When Patrick got there he called a meeting of the manager, the foreman and the overseers and asked for their reports. Production was down, there was discord between the workers and the bosses and Patrick wanted answers. At first they seemed to walk on eggs with him; finally someone with guts spoke up.

"Well, I'll call a spade a spade, if none of the rest of you will! We've had some accidents recently and the place has a bad reputation. It's been nicknamed 'Cripples Factory,' if you want to know the truth."

Patrick listened intently. "You mean the machines are old and unsafe?" They all nodded grimly. Patrick knew he was guilty of the things he had accused his father of. He had put back no money into improvements since he had taken over almost two years ago. Commerce without morality was a deadly sin and it would have to be corrected without delay.

Kitty had had no breakfast that morning. She set her machines in motion automatically. She was lightheaded, but it was a feeling that always seemed to be with her. Her face had taken on a resigned look and she feared that the mill would prove to be a lifetime sentence with no escape. It all happened in an instant. She squeezed past a machine facing it, rather than putting her back toward it. The great leather belt caught hold of her overall and flung her up into the air, with the material catching on the great cog wheel. She screamed wildly. The fact that the cotton dress had been washed so many times saved her life. The thin, almost rotten overall ripped clean down the front and her limp, unconscious body fell to the oily floor. The accident siren sounded and the hair on the nape of Patrick's neck stood on end. He ran from the office toward the spinning room where the commotion was coming from. He elbowed his way through the crowd of girls and looked down at the crumpled figure that seemed too small to be a human being. It was a minute before recognition hit him.

"Kitty, my God!"

The impact was like a blow to his solar plexus. The room was so hot and humid he could hardly breathe and sweat broke out on his face. He looked down at the striped cotton dress and suddenly to his horror he was back on the plantation and Kitty was just as much a cotton slave as those black people had been. He picked her up tenderly and carried her to the office.

"I'll run for the doctor, Mr. O'Reilly. Lay her down here," the foreman said.

"No, no. I'd rather you drove me home. I don't want a doctor from around here." He was alarmed at her waxen pallor. He quickly lifted her into the carriage and gently laid her against the squabs, keeping hold of her hands and chafing them clumsily. Kitty regained consciousness twice in the carriage, but her eyes only flickered open momentarily without focusing, then closed again as she lapsed back into unconsciousness. He flung open the front door and called, "Barbara, Mrs. Thomson, come quickly."

"What is it? Oh, Patrick, you've found her!" cried Barbara.

"She's hurt badly, I fear. Mrs. Thomson, is Julia's room made up?"

"Of course, sir. Where did you find the poor little lamb?"

He was white, his mouth a grim line, and his eyes terrible to behold.

"I found her working at the mill. There was an accident. I've no idea how badly she's hurt. Stay with her while I get the doctor. I hate to leave her, but that's the fastest way to get help. Pull back the covers, Barbara. Keep her warm and don't leave her for a second."

He was back within fifteen minutes. The doctor said, "Help me disrobe her so I can see how much damage she's sustained."

"No! Barbara, help Mrs. Thomson undress her, and for God's sake, be gentle." He looked apologetically at the doctor and said, "She's frightened of men."

"Indeed?" he said dryly. "Then I will ask you to leave the room until I complete my examination."

Reluctantly, Patrick left and closed the door behind him, but stood on the landing outside the door in a state of miserable anxiety. Twenty minutes later the doctor came out.

"She's been in an industrial accident at your mill, hasn't she?"

"How did you know?"

"Good God, man, I haven't always been a society doctor. I

started out in the slums. Her color gives her away, like a prison pallor.''

"What's the extent of her injuries?" he asked apprehensively.

"Well, she's in shock. She has a concussion, a dislocated shoulder, a large gash on her leg that I've just stitched and multiple bruises, cuts and abrasions. Apart from all this she is in a weakened, run-down condition and her blood is very low. She's seen more dinnertimes than dinners, and the work she's been doing has been far too heavy for her. It sounds grave, but all she really needs is food and rest. I think the concussion will go away on its own if she's left quiet, but I'd like you to come and hold her while I try to put her shoulder back into its socket. Would you ladies step outside now for a few minutes?" the doctor asked.

Patrick lifted Kitty gently and put his arms about her firmly. The doctor took hold of Kitty's arm. "This will hurt her a great deal." He gave her arm a terrific wrench, and her eyes flew open and she screamed.

"Patrick," she said weakly, "where am I?"

"You had an accident at the mill, love, but the doctor says you'll be all right. Try to sleep now. We'll look after you."

"I'll ease the shoulder with a sling and be back to check her again tomorrow." The doctor hadn't been gone ten minutes when Terrance appeared and demanded to see his sister.

"The doctor tells me she is going to be all right, Terry, but she needs nursing and decent food and I intend to see that she gets it. Where have you been living? Why on earth was she working in the mill?"

"Haven't you seen the bloody signs posted, 'No Irish or Dogs Allowed'?" he asked bitterly.

"Go home and get your things together. I know Kitty wouldn't have a minute's peace of mind if you were still at the mill after this accident."

* * *

With the good food and bed rest she received, Kitty's condition improved rapidly. Barbara was delighted because she had few friends her own age; she insisted upon doing everything for Kitty. A great relief filled Patrick as he watched Kitty blossom under their ministrations, and his guilt fell away. He was determined that this time he would not make such a mess of things. He would go about his wooing slowly and patiently. He forced himself to attend to business each day and only allowed himself half an hour each evening with Kitty. It was beginning to work. Already she looked forward eagerly to his arrival, and he took much pleasure watching her face light up at the sight of him. He kept a great deal of distance between them, at least half the room, and let his eyes convey his tender feelings toward her. He sent her flowers every other day and set about the courtship with a master plan, paying attention to the minutest details, and slowly but surely Kitty began to respond. Never once did the idea of marrying her enter his head.

One day he took Terry into the library. "Would you like to become a mill foreman, Terry?" he asked tentatively.

"I hated every minute I had to spend in that place. Besides, nobody is going to take orders from someone who hasn't turned sixteen yet."

"You need more education, you know. How would you like to go to school?"

"School? Me? Don't be daft! That's out for certain sure."

"Talk about gratitude and biting the hand that feeds you! Stubborn bloody Irish! I knew a lad who came here from Ireland and joined the British army just so he could become a deserter!" Patrick shouted.

They both burst out laughing, and Patrick shook his head in resignation.

"I fancy horses!" stated Terry without hesitation.

Patrick leaned back in his chair and thought for a few minutes.

"I'm going to give it out that you and Kitty are distant cousins of ours from Ireland so I can't have you working as a stableboy. I'll tell you what: I have a friend with a large racing stable over at Doncaster in Yorkshire. Would you like to learn to be a trainer? I have more than a passing interest in horses myself. Learn everything you can! When you return we'll see what we can do about acquiring some decent horse-flesh and enter a few races ourselves."

Terry's face lit up brilliantly. "Your smile is exactly like your sister's when she's getting all her own way," he said and laughed.

Patrick came home one day to find that Kitty had been downstairs for the first time. Her figure was rounding out again and her hair was a mass of shiny curls, prettier than it had ever been because of her improved diet.

"You're looking very well, but you still tire easily, don't you?"

"A little," she admitted shyly.

"I think you should be carried up to bed, don't you?" he asked softly.

She hesitated a moment, blushed prettily and nodded her agreement.

"Terry, come carry your sister up to bed. I think she's done enough for today." Patrick hid a smile as a look of disappointment came into her face.

Soon the girls were riding every day and the large house was filled with their happy laughter and madcap antics. One afternoon he returned early from business and discovered both girls filthy, wet, their dresses torn, their shoes and stockings forgotten on the riverbank where they'd been wading.

"You've been running around like two Gypsy girls all summer. Not that it probably hasn't done you a world of good, but I really think school is in order."

"Oh, Patrick, no, I hate lessons!" protested Barbara.

"What you need are different kinds of lessons, like dancing and singing and all those female accomplishments that turn hoydens into civilized young ladies. Six months is all I'm asking—I won't separate you, you can be together."

The girls eyed each other and then nodded agreement. "If you insist," Barbara said, "we'll go to the same academy for young ladies that Julia went to, and then you must promise to take us to London so we can meet some young men and begin to enjoy life!" Kitty hid a smile at the anger that distorted Patrick's features at the mention of young men.

"I want both of you to be on your best behavior tonight. We're having some very important guests for dinner. Mr. Haynsworth, who owns the oldest bleaching firm in England, is trying to interest me in some new scheme: It's strictly business, but you've driven past their place at Rose Bank and you know how posh they live, so for God's sake don't disgrace me."

They raced upstairs and pulled every article of clothing from Julia's wardrobe and clothespress that she had left behind. They spread them over the bed and Kitty made her choice easily. It was a gown of red velvet, low in the neck, very full in the skirt. She would have to nip in the waist and take up the hem, but it would be worth the effort. They went through Barbara's clothes, but she rejected everything. "This pink is so childish, and pale blue is insipid, don't you think? You've no idea how wealthy the Haynsworths are. I think there's a son and a daughter, and I don't want to look like a schoolgirl in front of them," she lamented.

"Well, let's look at Julia's things again," suggested Kitty.

Barbara decided upon an antique-gold taffeta that rustled

deliciously and agreed that they would keep out of Patrick's sight until the last minute in case he decided they were dressed too boldly for their age and ordered them to change. When the girls finally came downstairs, Kitty knew she looked well because Patrick couldn't keep his eyes from her. Her lips and breasts invited a man's mouth, her curls were too much of a temptation to leave untouched and she had such a saucy, knowing look in her eyes tonight. When the guests arrived, Kitty was surprised at how much Samuel Haynsworth reminded her of Jonathan O'Reilly. He had thick gray side whiskers and the same thick-set body. He was another self-made man, of which Lancashire boasted so many, and his speech and mannerisms were almost identical to Jonathan O'Reilly's.

The son was another type completely. He was a slim blond with lazy-lidded eyes which gleamed with unconcealed lust when he beheld Kitty. Patrick regretted the table arrangements that seated Keith Haynsworth next to Kitty, but it was too late to change them. He introduced his sister Barbara, then quickly passed Kitty off as "our cousin Kathleen."

Patrick hardly paid attention when he was introduced to Grace Haynsworth, a colorless young creature who could only be described as plain. Patrick was hard pressed to pay attention to what Samuel Haynsworth was talking about, for every time he looked down the table toward Kitty, Keith Haynsworth was whispering to her. First she would look shocked, the next time he looked she would be blushing and then damn, blast and set fire to it all, she would be laughing up at him. Once again he turned his attention to the older man, only to be distracted by Barbara's giggling. He looked up to see Keith Haynsworth bring his hand from under the tablecloth. The moment he did so, Kitty gave his hand such a vicious jab with her table fork it drew blood, and Keith had to cover it quickly with his napkin. It looked like Kitty was able to look after herself, but her table manners were appalling. Patrick turned to Grace Haynsworth on his left, and the contrast between the young women struck him forcibly. She wore a simple white gown and her halo of golden hair made her look innocent and virginal. She was quiet and poised and showed breeding in every line. Patrick thought she was the kind of young girl a man should choose for his wife. She'd make the perfect mother for a man's children. Even though her face was plain, it was sweet and serene, and Patrick thought she'd probably be complacent also, as he couldn't imagine her making a scene.

"Would you ladies like to leave us to our port now, so we can get down to business?" Samuel Haynsworth asked bluntly.

Patrick noted the rebellious looks but was pleased to see how graciously their guest arose and excused herself. Grace had been named well.

Keith stood up from the table and said, "I'll entertain the ladies while you discuss your business."

Patrick was damned if he was going to allow him free rein with Kitty. He put a viselike grip on the young man's shoulder and said, "Sit down. You won't want to miss this excellent new port. It's from my own vineyards in France," he lied smoothly, then turned to face the older man.

"Well, Patrick, I've been toying with the idea of a model mill. Modern, streamlined, the very latest machinery. A really large place capable of employing about a thousand people."

"I think that's a marvelous idea, but it would take a lot of planning and a lot of money," said Patrick, showing immediate interest.

"Well, of course I wouldn't attempt something of this scale on my own. I'd have to get a few partners."

"Our mills employ only about a hundred or so. What about housing the employees?"

"We could build a model village close to the mill with an institute for the workpeople and suchlike."

"I see you've been giving it a lot of thought. You'd need a large tract of land to begin with."

"That's the one thing I've got plenty of. I own all the land at Rose Bank and half of Barrow Bridge."

"Who besides myself were you thinking of approaching?"

"Well, I had thought of Gardiner."

"Good choice. How about Bazley?" suggested Patrick.

"Of course! I knew you'd have some good ideas."

"Would you object to London backing?" asked Patrick.

"Of course not. What do you have in mind?"

"Well, I'd suggest we get plans drawn up and publish some drawings in the *Illustrated London News*. Might even get someone in the House interested; they're forever on about improving the workingman's condition in industry. Now's their chance to do something constructive about it."

"You'd have to handle the London end of things."

"No problem there; just tell me when you're ready."

"Well, hold on a bit. All I really wanted was your ideas on the feasibility of the plan. I'll kick it about for a while and get back to you."

After the guests had left, Patrick said, "I was subjected to an appalling display of bad table manners tonight. I think you will both benefit from six months at school. If you'd taken the time and trouble, and if you had an ounce of common sense between the two of you, you could have behaved like Grace Haynsworth tonight."

"Colorless!" pronounced Barbara, defiantly.

"Whey-faced!" said Kitty jealously.

"As a matter of fact, you both looked rather vulgar beside her," Patrick said, and left them both with their mouths open.

Chapter 12

Patrick wasn't sure why he had suggested Kitty go away to school; he only knew he could not live under the same roof with her and not have her. His concentration had been shattered and he had developed a physical ache that would not go away, yet he held back because he knew Kitty was not quite ready. Hoping that absence would make her heart grow fonder, he had decided upon the school as a means of polishing her rough edges a bit. Once she was removed from his immediate proximity, perhaps he would be able to concentrate on his business again. Because of the large profit they were making with their wine venture, Patrick had been approached by a food company which wanted to improve its profits. Hind Food Company had its main head-quarters in London but had many plants all over the country. It was bigger than Lipton's, Lyons and Tate & Lyles all rolled into one. They even had a network of food processing plants in New York, Pittsburgh and Chicago. This company did pickling, bottling and the new process of canning food and had new plants springing up everywhere. Patrick knew that anything connected with feeding a nation would be prof-itable. He took the job on in London and the boardroom often was startled with his unusual suggestions. He discov-ered that the organization was being run under the mandate of providing as many jobs as possible. Small plants stretched across the country. He closed some down entirely, merged others and expanded the operations in the larger centers. He had been hired to raise profits, and he could only do this by making the organization tough, lean and efficient. He stopped the manufacture of some brands that didn't sell well. He planned to cut the prices to the farmer for his crops and standardize the measure of food going into each jar. It was a long-range plan, but after the first quarter the figures showed improvement. Patrick succeeded in fixing Disraeli's interest in the model mill and village Samuel Haynsworth had proposed and when the Christmas holidays arrived Patrick returned to Bolton quite pleased with the progress he had made in London.

He went outside when he heard the carriage approach, bringing Barbara and Kitty home for the holidays. Barbara flung herself upon him in the usual manner whenever they had been separated. She was full of chatter, telling him everything with her first breath. He heaved a sigh of relief as she ran into the house to greet Mrs. Thomson. Then there was only Kitty. Their eyes met and held, he reached for her hands and she alighted from the carriage in a dreamlike trance. Neither spoke, but drank in each other with their eyes as if they would never have enough. Slowly he drew her to him and bent to take her lips. She opened her mouth to say something, but he stopped the words with his lips, and her breath became a sigh.

"I missed you so," he whispered.

Then they were sitting around the roaring fire, laughing, telling stories, drinking warm mulled wine. Barbara rattled on, oblivious of the lingering glances Kitty and Patrick were exchanging.

"At first the girls were such snobs, you wouldn't believe it, but Kitty made up such outrageous stories, she was treated like the Princess Royal and we were the most popular girls at school."

"It's good to have you home. The house will be lonely when you return," he said meaningfully, his eyes on Kitty.

Kitty looked at Barbara. "You might as well tell him, Barbara. He'll find out sooner or later anyway."

Barbara handed him a letter from the headmistress, which he took and read carefully. It was couched in polite euphemisms, but it boiled down to the fact that they could not return to school because of their disruptive influence on the other girls. Barbara was relieved to see the corner of Patrick's mouth quiver. He looked up. "Well, imps, what was it got you expelled?"

Barbara spoke up quickly, proving the old adage that when under stress, women confess. "I don't know exactly if it was Kitty's Gypsy dances—they're really quite shocking, you know—or if it was her stories about her devastatingly handsome lover who ravished her."

Kitty gasped and said, "Barbara, how could you?" and ran from the room.

Barbara looked at Patrick in bewilderment. "Well, really, he was only imaginary. I thought those stories wouldn't make you nearly so angry as the time we dressed up as boys and then got locked out all night."

"Where the devil did you sleep?" Patrick was angry despite his resolve not to be.

"In the stables, of course," said Barbara matter-of-factly.

"And to think you used to be a little milk-and-water miss who was afraid of her own shadow."

"Yes, and got bullied for it too! Since I decided to be more like you and Julia, I've enjoyed myself immensely!"

"Tell Kitty to come downstairs immediately. No, take this note up to her." He scribbled on a piece of paper.

Kitty dabbed her eyes and read the note: "Lady Jane Tut: I can see there is no necessity to return to school. You are more polished and refined than I ever dared hope. Signed: Lord Muck."

Kitty laughed in spite of herself but wouldn't show the

note to Barbara. The girls came back downstairs and Patrick informed them of his plans. "Seeing you don't have to go back to school, we might as well go down to Julia's. I have to see Samuel Haynsworth tomorrow, but after that I have business in London. We can pick up Terry on the way and take him with us for Christmas." Barbara blushed furiously and Patrick said lightly, "These Rooneys are the very devil, aren't they?"

Patrick went out to Rose Bank to see Samuel Haynsworth. Patrick received the grand tour, not only of the house, but also of the bleachworks. Haynsworth looked sideways at Patrick and said, "Whoever marries my daughter will have half interest in all this!"

"A full partnership? What about your son, Sam?"

"No interest in the business whatsoever. Besides, he got all his mother's money when she passed away. I'll need someone to leave all this to, so I've decided it will be my daughter and my son-in-law—when I get one, that is." He coughed discreetly.

Patrick was left in no doubt as to whom Samuel Haynsworth had in mind and he decided it was worth careful consideration.

When they arrived at Julia's in Cadogen Square, Yuletide preparations were in full swing. Patrick had no doubt about what he wanted for Christmas. He made plans immediately for a private rendezvous and was more excited than he ever remembered, even as a boy.

Kitty too was more excited than she had been in years. She was filled with anticipation for what Christmas and the New Year would bring. She had a feeling in her very bones that one phase of her life was about to end and a new one begin. Patrick had rescued her from a life of drudgery and had nursed her back to her full vitality. He had even paid to send her to a young ladies' finishing school so that she would be an acceptable wife. Though at first he had behaved very circumspectly with her, now he made no secret of the fact he was irresistibly attracted to her. Whenever their hands touched accidentally, heat leaped between them. When he looked at her he became smoky-eyed, then his pupils would turn black with desire.

Though it made her blush furiously, she knew he became physically aroused whenever he came close to her. Now that she was older it didn't frighten her, it made her breathless with excitement. She often caught him gazing at her mouth or her breasts and longed for the moment he would crush her lips in a demanding kiss. When he spoke to her his voice became husky with need.

Kitty imagined she was in a worse state than Patrick. She hungered for him. When he came close her pulse speeded up erratically, her breath became faint and jerky and her throat went dry. His faintest touch turned her skin to ice, then fire, and filled her with delicious tremors. When she spoke to him her voice became low and whispery and she loved to watch the devastating effect this had on him. She knew he couldn't possibly wait much longer.

Patrick invited Kitty to dine with him on Christmas Eve at Clifford's Inn, Fleet Street. The moment she stepped into the closed carriage with him she knew the time had finally arrived. It was small and private and heart-stoppingly intimate inside as Patrick took the lid off a large box and shook out a silver fox cape.

"Here's one of your Christmas presents, darling," he murmured, holding it out for her.

"Oooh," she cried with delight, removing her dark wool cloak. Then she slipped into the fur he held out and allowed him to wrap it about her. Womanlike she blew upon the fur to admire its thickness and rubbed her cheek against it sensually.

Patrick hardened instantly. For several moments he throbbed savagely as his hot blood surged into his shaft until he thought he would explode. He felt a driving desire to strip her naked, lay her back upon the fur and take her right here in the carriage. With an iron will he tamped down his scalding desire. If she even guessed the things he wanted to do with her, she would bolt from the carriage.

Patrick removed his arms from her and moved back across the seat. He did not dare to leave his hands on her or he would lose control.

Kitty could not hide her joy from him. "Thank you, Patrick," she whispered and gave him a radiant smile.

Clifford's Inn was a small, elegant hotel and Kitty was enchanted with the Christmas tree decorated with feathered quail, sleigh bells, tartan bows and glass balls hand-painted with bird scenes. Her eyes shone with expectancy in the flickering candlelight.

"Have I told you how beautiful you are tonight?" She smiled and shook her head. The other diners could feel the current of their mutual attraction. His loins were melting with longing, and his deep desire for her showed to everyone. After the meal he took her hand and led her upstairs. He unlocked the door to a beautiful set of rooms. The walls were paneled, the floor covered in a Turkey red carpet and there was a magnificent hand-carved fireplace filled with blazing logs.

"I reserved the bridal suite for us," he said, closing the door and slipping his arms about her.

She looked up at him joyously. "For tonight?" Praise God, they were going to be married tonight! Her arms lifted about his neck and as he swung her about, the silver fur slithered to the floor. He bent his dark head to capture her lips. Beneath his, her mouth softened and parted and she recalled with amusement how shocked she had been when he had first touched her with this wicked tongue.

Patrick swept her up in his arms, then moved toward a comfortable chair before the fire. He cuddled her on his lap as his lips brushed the tempting black tendrils at her temple.

Kitty sighed deeply; she had everything she had ever needed for happiness: a full belly, a warm fire and Patrick John Francis O'Reilly. She traced her finger along a heavy black eyebrow, then brought it down to follow the slant of his arrogant jaw. She didn't know if she loved him in spite of his faults or because of them, she only knew that she loved him with every fiber of her being. She was dizzy with love. When her finger lovingly traced his top lip, Patrick bit it playfully. She immediately lifted his hand to her mouth and bit one of his fingers in return. "If you hurt me, I'll hurt you back," she said wickedly and Patrick groaned at the fierce arousal she always produced in him.

He knew he must go about his seduction with a little more finesse than last time. Though he was ravenous for her, he knew he must starve a little longer while he kindled her desire and fanned the flame until she was white-hot. One hand caressed her shoulder as the other stole to her breast. He heard her swift intake of breath that told him his touch gave her pleasure.

Kitty could feel Patrick's manhood, hot and hard, beneath her buttocks. She knew now that sex was primal, elemental and above all natural between lovers who were insatiably attracted to each other. With a knowledge as old as Eve's, she knew she was ready for this man to make love to her. The sensations he aroused were delicious as she clung to him, heady with the smell of his man-scented skin.

Patrick's fingers began to undo the fastenings of her dress.

Kitty kissed him and stayed his avid hands. "Darling, you mustn't undress me until after the chaplain's been."

"Chaplain?" he murmured huskily.

"Aren't we being married tonight?" she asked faintly.

"Married? I should hope not! Where would the fun be in that?" He saw a pulse beating in her throat and put his lips to the spot. "When I marry, it will be for convenience, to some respectable daughter of society who will be tied to the household and children. I don't want to spoil your body with babies, Kitty. I want you all to myself, free to come to France with me and to America next time I sail."

She felt like she had been doused with a bucket of cold water. "I won't! I can't! Take me home!" Kitty's Irish was up. Her eyes glittered dangerously. "If you touch me, I swear I'll kill you!"

"Stop playing games with me, Kitty. I'm not blind. You want me every bit as much as I want you." He moved cautiously to the right to block the door. "Darling, you'll have all my respect and honor and anything else you want." He touched her cheek longingly. "Let me spoil you."

Her eyes narrowed with fury. "You've already spoiled me! Or to use correct English, I should say despoiled!"

Goddamn and blast everything, it was happening again. Patrick hung onto his temper. He tried a new tack. He'd never begged a woman before in his life. Now he did. "Kitty, darling, yield to me. I swear I'll give you anything . . . *anything!*"

"Give me a wedding," she said stubbornly.

"I'll give you *anything* but that, I promise."

"Patrick O'Reilly, you've got a blind spot when it comes to marrying me. I'll swear you lace-curtain Irish are the most bigoted sods on earth, but you're worse than most. Even your father had the decency to ask me to marry him."

"My father?" questioned Patrick, angry now.

Kitty ignored the subject. "Ever since you brought me out of Ireland I've been branded with poverty, charity and humiliation and they are burns that never come out!" she shouted.

"What the hell do you want, wench?" His temper was completely gone now.

"I won't be your paid whore! I want a respectable marriage!" she cried.

His eyes smoldered and he sneered, "In that case we'd better look about us for a suitable husband for you."

The silence remained unbroken on the carriage ride back to Cadogen Square. The face that she loved above all others had a closed look that she could not penetrate.

After that, they avoided each other as much as possible, but when they were forced together because of the Christmas celebrations, they were dangerously polite to each other.

Julia had been planning a New Year's Eve ball for some time and she was delighted that Patrick would be there for it.

"I hope you have invited some eligible young men for Kitty and me," said Barbara hopefully.

"There will be plenty of young men, but I don't know anyone who would be willing to marry a penniless girl like Kitty," scoffed Julia.

"Why, Julia, Kitty is very beautiful and I was reading of the Gunning sisters only the other day. When their mother brought them out of Ireland they were so desperately poor they had only one fancy dress between the two of them and only one at a time could go out. Elizabeth was so beautiful the Duke of Hamilton eloped with her after knowing her for only a month."

Patrick looked up from his morning paper and said dryly, "He was a notorious drunkard who gave her two children in quick succession and made her life hell." Barbara lifted her chin and said, "But that's the best part. He drank himself to death at thirty-three and Elizabeth immediately married the fifth Duke of Argyll. Maria did even better; she married an earl.''

Julia retorted, ''Romantic nonsense! Kitty will get plenty of offers, but they won't be for marriage.''

Patrick was nettled enough to reply, ''You're very catty, Julia. I happen to know Kitty could have been your step-mother! If she'd married Father he would likely have left her everything and you would have been disinherited.''

Both girls were left with their mouths open.

Julia had invited a crush of her friends, and all Jeffrey's relatives were there. Kitty was deluged with invitations to dance and the moment the music stopped she was sur-rounded by men. Her eyes often sought out Patrick, who was never at a loss for female admirers. The young ones hung about him, giving him shy glances and blushing furiously when he spoke, but the older, married women vied with each other for his attention. They sent him bold invitations with their eyes and bodies and didn't even bother to conceal their blatant desire.

Kitty sought out Terrance, who had just danced with Bar-bara.

''What's wrong, Kitty?'' he asked.

''Oh, it's just awful. I'm going to stay close by you two. You have no idea what the men here are like.''

''Who? That fellow you were dancing with? What the devil did he do?''

''He kept trying to kiss me,'' she said indignantly.

''I'll just go and have a little word with him,'' said Terry angrily.

''Oh, no, don't. It wasn't just him. The last one danced me behind those potted ferns and put his hand down my bod-ice.''

"Right here in front of everyone?" asked Barbara, scandalized.

Just then a small woman approached Barbara with a young man in tow. "There you are, Barbara, dear. Do you remember me from the wedding? I'm Amelia Brownlow, Jeffrey's cousin, and this is my son, Simon. I've been simply dying to introduce you two. Simon, this is Julia's sister, whom I've been telling you about."

The fair young man with lazy eyes smiled and bowed before Barbara. "My pleasure, ma'am."

Amelia looked pleased with herself and said, "Well, I'll leave you young people to enjoy yourselves. Have fun!"

Simon looked amused. "Mothers! Thank heavens she's gone. Please forgive her. She's bent on matchmaking, I'm afraid." He looked at Kitty and Terrance standing together. "You must be brother and sister. The resemblance is most striking."

Barbara said, "Kitty and Terrance Rooney, our cousins from Ireland." He bowed before Kitty. "May I have this dance, ma'am?"

Kitty did not hesitate. He was only about eighteen and she thought she would be able to handle someone her own age.

"To tell you the truth, we were just going to find a quieter room somewhere. We really aren't enjoying ourselves in this crush."

"My sentiments exactly! Why don't we get some refreshments from the supper room and retire to a quiet spot, the library perhaps, and have a party of our own?" His smile was so disarming, they fell in with his suggestions immediately. They piled their plates high with an assortment of delicacies and each took a cup of punch and went down the east wing to the library.

Simon spotted a decanter of brandy and brought it to the fire. "This will taste better than that awful concoction they call punch!'' Simon saluted Kitty with his glass. ''You are a very refreshing change from the young women my mother usually introduces me to. They all say something very witty such as 'Shouldn't you be in school somewhere?' ''

''Well, shouldn't you?'' said Kitty, laughing.

''Sent down from Oxford, I'm afraid.''

''We've just been expelled from school ourselves,'' said Barbara with a laugh.

''Good! I can see we have a lot in common.''

''What do you do now that your school days are over?'' asked Kitty.

''Amuse myself, and others too, I might add. I think I shall make a career of it.''

''Are you independently wealthy, then?'' asked Kitty.

''Not exactly rolling in it, but I'm just marking my time until my uncle, Lord Crowther, sticks his spoon in the wall. Then I'll inherit the fortune and the title,'' he said and smiled.

''How convenient for you,'' said Kitty, amused. ''So your mother isn't in the market for an heiress for you.''

''No, but she is trying to get me married off. Says a wife is exactly what I need to settle me down a bit.''

''Surely you don't want a wife at your age?'' asked Terry.

''What I want is freedom, but I'll never have it until I get rid of Mother.''

''But if you married you'd have two women running your life instead of just your mother,'' pointed out Terry.

''Oh, no; once she fobs me off with a wife, she's bound for Europe. Can't wait to fold her tent and silently steal away,'' said Simon, laughing. Simon looked at Terrance and then at Kitty. ''I don't suppose you'd like to take me on? You are in the marriage market, aren't you?''

''Of course she is,'' said Barbara.

"I've no dowry. I'm just a poor relation," said Kitty with a laugh.

"Your face is your fortune. You attract men like a flame attracts moths. It comes naturally to you," smiled Simon.

Kitty blushed and drank her brandy to cover her embarrassment.

"Will you come out with me tomorrow, Kit?" Simon asked abruptly.

Terry spoke up. "She doesn't go out alone."

"Well, let's all four of us go somewhere, then."

"Oh, let's go, Terry. It would be great fun. What will we do?" asked Barbara.

Simon eyed Terry for a minute, then suggested, "We could go to Tattersall's and look at the horses."

Kitty said, "That was a shrewd hit, purposely designed to get Terry on your side."

Simon grinned and said, "Now something to amuse the ladies. Let's see. There's a spot up the river that is frozen where people are skating. There's all sorts of booths set up, chestnut sellers and fortune tellers."

"Oh, yes, please," begged Barbara.

The brandy was going to their heads and Kitty said, laughing, "You do exactly what I do, Simon."

"What's that, Kit?" he drawled.

"Plant seeds in people's minds and watch them flower."

He gave her a knowing wink.

"Kitty, tell our fortunes now," Barbara begged.

"I thought we were going to get our fortunes told tomorrow, down by the river," protested Kitty, but she felt in her pocket and pulled out her tarot cards, which she had been consulting earlier in the day. "I'll do Barbara and Simon. Terry doesn't like them," offered Kitty.

"What do I do?" asked Barbara.

"Shuffle the cards and while you are doing it, make a wish

and also ask a silent question which can be answered 'yes' or 'no.' Now divide them into three piles with your left hand and choose one of the piles.''

Barbara picked the one in the center.

''I'll do the wheel of fortune, so place seven cards in a circle. Let me explain a little,'' Kitty said, knowing that Barbara loved this ritual. ''These cards tell about life and death, good and evil, love and hate, strength and folly, success and failure, truth and falsehood; the whole of human experience. The cups represent love, the pentacles represent money, the wands refer to your work, and swords are the unlucky suit.''

Barbara solemnly laid out the cards.

Kitty turned all seven face up before she began the reading. ''Oh, Barbara, your cards are good. I can tell you right away that the answer to your question is 'yes' and you definitely will get your wish. The first card, strength, represents you, yourself. It shows a woman closing the jaws of a lion. The symbolism means that true strength lies in gentleness. You have a spiritual power that is stronger than material power. The second card, the king of swords, stands very close to you. It represents an overly stern father who inflicts verbal abuse on his children. The next card, the six of wands, means the triumphant resolution of all your difficulties. Eventually you will realize your hopes and desires by utilizing your quiet strength. The seven of pentacles is the fate or luck card. With the two of cups following, it means you will be lucky in love rather than in games of chance. The two of cups, which shows a young man and a young woman holding a loving cup, is the beginning of a romance or flirtation. It is also a time card; your wish will come true within a two. It could mean two weeks, two months or even two years. The knight of wands always has dark hair and dark eyes. He is the romantic knight in shining armor who will come into your life. Your last card, the sun, is a wonderful card filled with joy. It shows you have a sunny disposition and when combined with cups and pentacles means the beginning of a long-lasting relationship."

"Oh, Kitty, you're wonderful," said Barbara, laughing.

Simon picked up the cards and reshuffled them. "God, I hope mine aren't all sweetness and light," he teased.

Kitty frowned as she turned Simon's cards face up. She didn't like them. "The answer to your silent question is 'no'; however, you will get your wish. The card that represents you is the knight of swords. An aggressive young man, headstrong, reckless, self-destructive, quick to take offense. This is followed by the chariot, which usually is a good card, but when it is reversed like this, it means self-indulgence, dissipation of energies. It also hints that perhaps soon there will be a scandal."

"Ah, the plot thickens," said Simon, laughing.

"Your third card is the hanged man. It shows a young man hanging upside down from a cross. Notice that he is neither nailed nor tied to the cross, so he can free himself at any time and straighten out if he really wants to. This is followed by the seven of wands. All sevens imply change. Social matters are disrupting your homelife. The four of cups means you have lots of friends, many parties, drinking and good times."

"Ah, better and better," said Simon with a grin.

"The ten of swords has many meanings," said Kitty.

"What an awful card—the poor man has ten swords stuck into his back," said Barbara.

"It's not always a death card," assured Kitty. "It can mean the dark arts, the underworld. When coupled with the hanged man it means you have gotten so deeply involved in wrong activities you cannot find your way out. The devil means more self-indulgence and being chained by materialistic values. Your possessions can come to possess you if you put money before people."

"My character is laid bare!" grimaced Simon.

The library door opened and Patrick came in with a married woman. "Sorry, we thought this room would be empty," Patrick apologized.

"That's obvious," said Kitty stiffly. "Simon, I should be delighted to go with you tomorrow. Shall we go back to the party now and leave these older people to themselves?" Kitty asked tartly.

Barbara and Kitty were sharing a room and when they were in bed, Kitty asked, "Who was that with Patrick tonight?"

"Just one of his flirts, I imagine. Probably sowing the last of his wild oats before he settles down," she said, giggling.

Kitty caught her breath. "What do you mean?"

"Well, nothing's been said, of course, but I think he has his eye on Samuel Haynsworth's daughter, Grace."

"What makes you think that, Barbara?"

"Fabulous dowry, bleachworks and all that, she's wallowing in it," Barbara said and yawned.

"I should have thought he'd prefer someone prettier than Grace Haynsworth," said Kitty in a small voice.

"And I thought I was naïve! Patrick will always have a pretty face tucked away somewhere. Marriage won't put a cramp in his style."

Try as she might, Kitty was unable to fall asleep as she thought about what Barbara had told her. Kitty prayed silently, Help me to get over this terrible hurt . . . help me to stop loving him.

Chapter 13

When Patrick arrived at Cadogen Square for the third consecutive evening at the same time as Simon, Kitty, Terry and Barbara, he shouted at Julia, "For God's sake, they're like two pairs of Siamese twins! Don't you think Barbara's becoming too serious about this Simon Brownlow?"

"Men are so obtuse," said Julia, laughing. "Barbara has eyes only for Terrance Rooney, my dear."

"Good God, don't you think you'd better put a stop to it then?" he demanded.

"You needn't get your shirt in a knot. Barbara fully realizes an unequal marriage is beyond the pale, and I assure you it's all very innocent."

"So I suppose that means young Brownlow is dangling after Kitty!" he exploded.

"They're just four children having a little fun. All they ever do is laugh and play silly jokes and go racking about the town sightseeing and wearing off all that vulgar energy people have before they reach twenty."

He sighed and said, "I suppose you are right, Julia. I must be getting old. It's just that I have to go to Bolton again in a couple of days. The Rose Banks project has to be completed before they break ground next month. Perhaps I'd better have a word with Barbara before I go, just to be on the safe side."

After breakfast the next morning, Patrick managed to get her alone for a few minutes before she went jaunting off for the day. "Barbara, I want you to behave yourself while I'm away. Don't go off alone with young Terry. There's safety in numbers, remember, so just stick close to Kitty and you'll be fine." He hesitated, then said, "By the way, this Simon chap behaves himself, doesn't he?"

"Oh, yes, that's why Kitty likes him so much. He isn't forever sending her mooning looks and touching her and stealing kisses. We're all such good friends," Barbara said earnestly. Patrick looked relieved.

"Are you planning to get engaged, Patrick?" asked Barbara, avidly curious.

"To whom, pray, Miss Inquisitive?"

"Grace 'Rose Banks' Haynsworth, of course," said Barbara, laughing.

"I could do worse," he said noncommittally.

"Aren't you going to say good-bye to Kitty?" she asked tentatively, watching his face closely.

"I've run after Kitty for the last time! She knows I'm leaving. She'll have to come to me, not the other way round," he said finally.

While the girls awaited Simon, who was taking them to Madame Tussaud's, Barbara said to Kitty, "I managed to worm out of Patrick that he's planning to get engaged on this trip North."

Kitty's heart constricted painfully, but she strived to sound disinterested as she murmured, "Really?"

"I asked him to say good-bye to you, but he said you'd have to chase after him this time."

Kitty seethed with indignation but was determined not to let it show. "Barbara, men are like carriages—one doesn't have to go chasing after them because there will be another one along any moment."

Samuel Haynsworth was closeted with his daughter in his office.

"Now listen to me, Grace. This is our last chance. Patrick

O'Reilly is coming down this weekend and I want to make absolutely sure of him. He's a genius for ramrodding new ideas through, but if I lose him, I'll lose Gardiner and Bazley too. You know the bleachworks are so debt-ridden that I've come close to bankruptcy.''

"That's been entirely due to bad management, Father. It's not your fault."

"It's my fault because I put the wrong people in charge. But your brother is out now and that's why I'm so desperate to get O'Reilly. He's aggressive and hard-nosed with nerves of steel when it comes to taking chances in business. If he's behind it, Rose Banks will be a roaring success and put an end to our financial woes. The least you can do is help me snare him!''

"Father, Patrick O'Reilly can have any woman he wants."

"Exactly! And that's why it's going to take more than looks and blushes to interest a young stallion like him. A little slap and tickle won't satisfy a lusty man, Grace. Get him into bed, girl! There's no man breathing who's a match for a woman with her mind set.''

That same afternoon Patrick had been having an interesting discussion with Messrs. Gardiner and Bazley. He was surprised that they were toying with the idea of withdrawing their support from Rose Banks because of the state of Haynsworth's affairs. Patrick managed to assure the two millowners that their venture would be an unqualified success. He was annoyed with Samuel Haynsworth. The state of the business didn't bother him very much, because he knew with proper management it could provide a lavish living, as it had in the past. That Haynsworth had tried to put one over on him by keeping him in the dark about his financial troubles didn't sit well with Patrick. At dinner he avoided a frontal attack but decided to observe Haynsworth more closely. Sam's manner was so bluff and hearty that Patrick had a hard time hiding his amusement. It was glaringly obvious that the older man was pathetically trying to cover up something, and Patrick relented toward him because he was reminded of his father. His attention fell on Grace. She had the angelic look of a girl just emerged from the convent. He wondered how he could get her into a receptive mood without wounding her delicacy. He pondered whether he was doing the right thing to contemplate marriage to her. Would she shrink in horror at his touch, her maidenly modesty outraged? He thought, Well, I must get over the first hurdle. "Would you like to show me the plants in the conservatory, Grace? Your father tells me you know all their Latin names."

Her innocent blue eyes fixed on his as she smiled her acceptance and arose from the table.

"Like a lamb to slaughter," thought Patrick irreverently.

For the first time in years Patrick was a little unsure of himself. Should he declare himself first, or let his actions speak for him? As they stood in the green twilight admiring an exotic orchid, he gently drew her to him and softly touched her lips. Her tongue darted into his mouth expertly and he was so amazed that he wondered if it had really happened or if his imagination was playing tricks on him. He decided to put things to the test once more. Very tenderly he drew her toward him and gave her a chaste kiss, but she slid her body against his so invitingly it was obvious this wasn't her first encounter with a man. Patrick was at once shocked and intrigued. It was like making love to a nun; arousing because of its sinful quality! He was fascinated to see how far she would be willing to go.

Samuel Haynsworth came to the door of the conservatory in his hat and coat and announced, "I have to go out. I promised to visit an old friend of mine who's confined to bed. Grace will entertain you. Why don't you take Patrick upstairs to your sitting room? I'm sure you'll be much more cozy up there.''

''All right, Daddy. Don't hurry back on our account. I'll keep Patrick amused,'' she promised and rubbed against him again. It was so patently obvious that they were being left alone together, Patrick thought that perhaps Haynsworth was trying to palm off not only a damaged business but also a soiled daughter.

Grace took his hand and led him upstairs to her rooms. She didn't stop in the sitting room, but went straight through to her bedroom. Patrick noted with cynicism the lack of servants, but he was too consumed with curiosity to hesitate. She startled him with the swiftness of her disrobing. No shy flower, this. Patrick thanked Providence that he hadn't proposed to her before taking the liberty of kissing her. Her body was very pale and fragile-looking, her pubic hair blond and baby-fine. He was still reluctant to defile a "good" girl. Grace deftly took him in her right hand and manipulated his shaft until he was erect and throbbing. He took over then, forcing her back against the pillows. As her passion built, she began to whisper the most obscene words that Patrick had ever heard from a woman's lips. The effect was so erotic both to her partner and herself that she came before him with a great convulsive spasm that forced him to withdraw.

''Don't worry, my love, I'll do it this way.'' She went on her knees to him and took his shaft into her mouth. Patrick was too far gone to protest. He found it impossible to take the passive role even in oral sex, so he held her head and thrust and plunged violently to reach his climax. Confronted with such a paradox, he was at a complete loss and took refuge in anger.

''My God, you know more tricks than a prostitute from a Soho brothel. A girl with your upbringing should be ashamed. I took a riding crop to my sister when I found her fooling with the stableboys. What the hell has your brother been thinking of to allow you to learn such things?''

She laughed and said, "My brother?" with such contempt and irony that Patrick immediately was aware of their sordid relationship and he was sickened. "My brother started giving me lessons when I was ten," she told him bluntly.

He shook his head in disbelief. "I would have put money on it. You really had me fooled. I thought you a virgin. Grace, I was actually going to ask you to marry me, even though I'm well aware your father has been in financial difficulties. Oh, yes, I knew he was trying to put one over on me." He laughed at himself. "I'd no idea you were trying to put one over on me, too. Marriage now is out of the question. You do realize that, don't you, Grace?"

"I understand, but oh, God, Father will kill me for losing your backing," she said wretchedly.

"No such thing. I still shall work with your father on this new mill project. It's a very sound investment. Your family's finances soon will turn around for the better. But our personal relationship can't continue. You can tell your father that I'm engaged to another, if you prefer."

"Thank you, Patrick," she said quietly.

"Thank you," he said with a grin, his good humor returning, "thank you for everything!"

After he left the house, he just walked and walked. His ideas about women had just received such a jolt that all his previous thinking had been turned upside down. Grace had looked like a madonna and had turned out to have no morals at all, while Kitty with her bold looks and saucy manners was innocent as a kitten. How blind he had been! He was so conditioned to believe that an unequal marriage was worse than a loveless marriage. That was ridiculous! He loved Kitty; nay, he adored her. When he got back to London he would go on his knees to her and beg her to marry him. What an insufferable bastard he had been to her, thinking her beneath him for wedding but not for bedding. He'd put an announcement in the *Morning Post* and have the biggest wedding of the season. He'd flaunt her before all London. The women might not accept her into society for a while, but there wasn't a man breathing who wouldn't envy him.

At Madame Tussaud's Kitty felt miserable. Simon was egging Terry on to steal one of the waxwork figures and set it in Queen Boadicea's Chariot near Big Ben. Kitty found it childish and couldn't conceal her irritation.

"I know," Simon said. "Why don't I take Kit home and you two stay and enjoy yourselves." Kitty allowed herself to be persuaded. She didn't exactly have a headache, more like a heartache, and she felt miserable. When they reached Cadogen Square, Julia had gone on her afternoon round of visiting and the house seemed quiet and lonely.

"Simon, to be brutally frank, I'm not up to entertaining you in the drawing room. I want to go to my bedroom and be comfortable," she pleaded, longing to be alone with her thoughts of Patrick.

"Then that's exactly what we will do. I know the very thing to get rid of your headache and lift you out of the doldrums." He winked at her and went over to the wine table and removed two decanters and two glasses. He started up the stairs for all the world like he owned the place and she was the guest. "Come on. Last one up is a coward!"

Simon poured the wine and she sat gazing into the fire, desperately wondering how she would face it when Patrick brought his wife home. "Kit," he said softly, "have you thought any more about my proposal?"

"Oh, Simon, how could you possibly get Cromwell past the Tussaud guards?" she said impatiently.

"No, Kit, I mean my proposal of marriage."

She looked at him for a long time. How easy it would be to say "yes" and run away from this house and live happily ever after. She found she couldn't lie to him.

"I don't love you, Simon. I like you, but I don't love you," she said honestly. He threw back his head and laughed. His beautiful teeth shone in the firelight.

"Kit, I don't want you to love me. I just want to be friends. The moment I produce a wife to look after me, Mother will depart for Europe and leave us both in peace."

Kitty pondered this for a moment. "But, Simon, you're forgetting Terry."

"I'm not forgetting Terry for one moment. He'll come to Surrey with us. I wouldn't have it any other way! There's plenty of room—beautiful countryside to hunt. I always have bachelor friends staying with me; he'd fit right in. We'll be very informal, Kit. We can do exactly as we damn well please." He said persuasively, "Doesn't the idea of being Lady Crowther appeal?"

"I'd be lying if I said it didn't, but Simon, listen to me. I'll have a friend for a husband, a lovely country house, a home for my brother, freedom to do as I please, money and a title after your uncle dies. But what is in it for you?" she asked pointedly.

"Kit, you are very beautiful. All my friends will be mad about you. You'll make a delightful hostess for me in Surrey and get rid of my mother for me." He plied her with more wine and she looked at him owlishly. "There's a piece of the puzzle missing, Simon. There has to be something else in it for you. All men are selfish," she told him solemnly.

He topped up her wine and said with a laugh, "Kit, you are too shrewd by far. I'm afraid I shall have to confess all and throw myself on your mercy."

"Aha! I knew it," she said triumphantly.

"My uncle makes me an allowance. However, I can't manage on it.'' He looked her straight in the eye and said, ''When I marry, it will double.'' He lifted his glass to salute her.

Kitty began to laugh, distracted from her ever-present thoughts of her love for Patrick and her sure knowledge that she was about to lose him.

He grinned and said, ''I told you I was an amusing devil.''

Suddenly the door was thrown open and an outraged Julia stood on the threshold.

''Entertaining young men in your bedroom is simply not done in my home, Kitty. What a shameful example you set for Barbara, to compromise yourself in this shocking way.''

Simon said smoothly, ''I've just asked Miss Rooney to be my wife.''

''And I've accepted him,'' Kitty said imperiously, her face unnaturally flushed from the wine and the things Julia had said.

''Oh, my dear, how lovely. Simon, let me be the first to congratulate you.''

Julia was all smiles now. Everything was wonderful. Simon was smiling happily and Kitty thought she was going to faint.

When Simon told his mother that Kitty had agreed to marry him, she nodded her head rapidly, showing her approval. ''I know you can't bear to take my advice, but I'm giving it nonetheless. Do it right away before she changes her mind. Go to one of those wedding chapels, The Great Chapel, I think it's called, in Curzon Street. She's only a poor cousin, you know, and I don't suppose they'd give her a lavish wedding anyway, and you can't possibly afford anything showy. You're in debt up to your eyebrows and the house in Surrey is so heavily mortgaged it's a wonder it doesn't sink through to China.''

"For once I think you have the right of it," he agreed thoughtfully.

"The moment you get that certificate in your hand, present it to Lord Crowther's man of business and your new allowance will start. I only hope to God your wife will have sense enough to curb your excesses, Simon."

"If you think that, I'm afraid you don't know me very well," he said in a mocking tone.

"Simon, I don't wish to know you very well," Amelia shuddered delicately.

He bowed to her. "In that case, Mother dear, you may start for the Continent immediately."

"Not until you are legally married and a decent woman is ensconced in your home. If Lord Crowther got wind of your wild behavior, he would cut you out of everything, and then we'd both suffer."

"I'll see to the necessary arrangements today, so stop worrying."

Chapter 14

Two days later Simon picked up Kitty, her brother and Barbara. When the carriage pulled up in Curzon Street, Simon said, "Kit and I are getting married this afternoon and you can be our witnesses."

"Simon, whatever gave you an idea like this? It doesn't seem quite right to just run off and get married," Kitty protested.

"Kit, you know the O'Reillys will be relieved if they don't have to put on a fancy wedding for us. Besides we made a bargain; don't cry off now."

"Kitty, you daren't do this; Patrick will kick up a hell of a stink!" protested Terry, who was appalled at the thought of Kitty marrying Simon.

"Daren't? Are you implying I must have Patrick's permission before I decide my future?" she demanded.

"Why, you know how Patrick feels about you, Kitty," said her brother.

"How does he feel about you?" demanded Simon.

"He thinks he owns me, but I'm about to prove him wrong."

Barbara cut in, "Nonsense! He's busy with his own marriage plans to Grace Haynsworth. What possible difference can it make to Patrick?"

"True!" said Kitty with a toss of her head. "Well, why are we sitting here? We have a wedding to attend."

It was only when the minister was intoning the words to the marriage service that Kitty came to her senses. He looked more like an undertaker than a man of God. The flowers didn't even look real. The sing-song voice was asking her to pledge away the rest of her life to this young man she hardly knew. She thought wildly, What am I doing here? The day had blank spaces in it for her. Now they were back in Cadogen Square and she didn't remember one moment of the carriage ride. Simon was speaking. She must make an effort to hear what he was telling her.

"Pack your bags. I'll pick you up in an hour."

The next thing she knew, she was being scolded and congratulated by Julia, "Oh, dear, you don't have anything that vaguely resembles a trousseau. But never mind; when you're Lady Crowther you'll even take precedence over me."

Kitty ignored this patronizing remark and folded her old flannelette nightgown.

"Oh, you must have something a little more alluring than that thing," said Julia. "I'll get one of my silk embroidered ones for you. Now, don't protest, for I insist."

Kitty packed her toilet articles and Julia came back with the nightgown.

"You have no riding habit," said Barbara.

"Oh, dear, I'm a positive ragbag; I never should have consented to this marriage in the first place. I don't know whatever I was thinking of."

"Nonsense, every single girl in the world who marries believes she's just made a dreadful mistake, but by tomorrow you'll feel differently, believe me."

As the tears threatened, Kitty said quickly, "Thank you very much for everything; you've both been very kind to me."

Terrance was waiting below with a small bag that contained his few belongings. He hesitated. "I've written a note for Patrick."

"Oh!" Kitty said, startled.

"I just thanked him for everything and said I didn't want to leave him but I was going with you to take care of you."

"Don't you think Simon will take care of me?" she asked uncertainly.

"I don't know," he answered truthfully.

Simon arrived and good-byes were said. Kitty was relieved to get away, but when she got into the hired carriage she was surprised to find two young men occupying it.

Simon laughed and said, "Isn't it the most marvelous thing? I ran into my two very best friends in the world, Brockington and Madge, and they insist on coming with us so we won't be moped, stuck in the country."

Kitty murmured, "Hello," then added, "Did you say Madge?"

"His name's Talmadge, but you can call him Madge; we all do," said Simon.

"Indeed I won't! Madge is a girl's name! What's your first name?" Kitty smiled.

"Vivian," drawled the tall, thin youth, and the other two became engulfed with laughter, as if this was a most particular piece of wit. Kitty smiled too. "I see. I suppose I'd better stick to Madge then, like everyone else does."

"Oh, by the way, Mother wishes you luck and sends you her keys," said Simon.

"So she's finally cut the leading strings, eh, old boy?" grinned Brockington.

"Completely washed her hands of me. You'll have to play dragon now, Kit." Once again the young men went off into gales of laughter.

"I have a splendidly romantic idea," Madge suggested. "Why don't we go to The Elms by water?"

"Could we?" demanded Kitty excitedly. "Is The Elms on the river?"

"Of course it is," said Simon. "Tell the driver to take us to the river."

Brockington opened the little connecting door and told the driver, "Westminster Bridge."

"What the hell did you tell him that for?" asked Madge disgustedly. "We're much closer to Lambeth Bridge."

"Vauxhall!" put in Simon.

Terry hesitated. "Excuse me, gentlemen, but I believe we're closest to Chelsea Bridge."

" 'Course we are," said Brockington. "Are you foxed, Simon?"

"I'll tell you what it is, Brocky," said Simon. "You both got into the sauce before you even met me."

When they arrived at the waterstairs, Kitty couldn't believe all the baggage they had among them.

"Wedding presents," Madge winked at her, touching his nose to indicate it was a secret.

They hailed a barge and the waterman held it steady while they all climbed aboard. Kitty was excited by the smell and sounds of the Thames. Simon told the waterman he would show him the dock he wanted when they arrived. "It's between Weybridge and Chertsey."

"Not a bit of it," said Brockington. "It's after Hampton Court but before Chertsey."

"You're both wrong," insisted Madge. "everyone knows the waterstairs are at Richmond, Kingston, Hampton Court, Wheybridge and Chertsey."

The waterman shook his head as he pulled on the heavy oar, "Yer awl right, mates, so why argue? Westward ho!" he called out.

Kitty was shocked at the shabby condition of The Elms. There was a beautiful center staircase with three bedrooms upon each side, upstairs. Downstairs there was the kitchen, tiny breakfast room, dining room, lounge and a library-*cum*-gaming room. It was a little gem of a house with mullioned windows, but its furnishings were almost dilapidated. The draperies were faded and rotted from the sunlight. The chairs were all worn and frayed—some covers even hung in tatters —and the carpets in every room were threadbare. Moreover, the whole place needed a thorough cleaning.

Kitty remarked to Terrance, "I'm ashamed to have guests here when it's in this condition, but they don't seem to mind. It makes you wonder what sort of homes they are used to."

Terrance chuckled and said, "Didn't you know they're both lords?"

"Saints preserve us," exclaimed Kitty, astounded.

All the men took themselves off to the stables, so she opened her gifts alone. She was disappointed to discover the wedding presents were a case of wine and a case of brandy.

Simon hadn't even assembled the servants for her to meet, so she went toward the kitchens in search of someone. She found an old woman nodding over a small kitchen fire. "Hello, I'm the new Mrs. Brownlow. Could you ring for the other servants? I'd like to meet my staff."

The old woman looked at her shrewdly before blurting out, "There's only me and Hobson, me old man. He does the outside work."

"But, Mrs. Hobson, who does the cooking?" asked Kitty.

"I do," said the old woman.

"Then who does the cleaning?" asked Kitty.

The old woman's eyes kindled and she let out a crack of laughter. "Nobody, as ye can plainly see for yourself!"

"But that's terrible. We must hire some girls from the village," suggested Kitty.

"Girls from around here wouldn't come," she stated flatly.

Kitty was puzzled. "But why not?"

Mrs. Hobson shook her head. "Goings on," she said enigmatically.

"What sort of goings on?" asked Kitty blankly.

"That's for me to know and you to find out, missy," cackled the old girl.

Kitty decided to take a higher hand with this disrespectful servant.

"There will be five of us for dinner. I'll leave the menu in your hands, Mrs. Hobson—after all, I don't want to start interfering on my first day—but let me assure you that if I don't find things to my satisfaction, I shan't hesitate to make some changes round here."

"Well, let me assure you, Mrs. Brownlow, that unless me and my husband get some of the back wages that is owed us, we shan't hesitate to make some changes round here."

Kitty was immediately contrite. "Oh, I'm so sorry, Mrs. Hobson. How much does Simon owe you?" she asked bluntly.

"Three months to the day."

"I'll speak to him about it right away," she promised, then silently changed it to tomorrow. She emerged from the kitchen to see Brockington streak up the stairs after Madge, both discarding their clothes in a shockingly abandoned fashion.

"Drunk as lords," Simon joked as he caught the shocked look on her face. "Actually they can't wait to get into their riding breeches and do a bit of hunting. We'll be back for dinner. Amuse yourself."

"Simon, hang on a moment, please. I know we have an understanding that we won't live in each other's pockets, but you haven't even shown me to my room."

"Sorry, Kit," he grumbled, "don't turn into a tiresome female. Just pick any room you fancy. Oh, one word of advice. This lot always uses the rooms to the left of the stairs, so if I were you, I'd take the right.''

Terrance came in from the stables shaking his head.

"Mr. Hobson must do his job as ably as Mrs. Hobson," remarked Kitty.

Kitty lit fires in every room. She went over the house from rafters to the cellar and poked her nose into every cupboard. She found a meager supply of coal and put some in a skuttle and carried it into the lounge. A mental picture of herself came into her mind and she sank into the nearest chair. "Hauling coal again," she gasped with laughter. Oh, if I don't laugh, I know I'll cry, she thought wildly. What on earth have I gotten myself into?

The atmosphere was pandemonium. The dining room was echoing with laughter when she went in. Mrs. Hobson served them an almost inedible meal. There was a watery broth followed by a tough boiled fowl. The vegetables were sparse and the bread stale. But the young men ate heartily and proposed toasts liberally, so the little dinner party seemed a resounding success. They moved on to the library and immediately set up a card table.

"Come on, Terry; you too, Kit. Nothing beats a good game.''

"I'm sorry, Simon, I don't enjoy cards, probably because I don't know how, and Terry doesn't have any money."

"Nonsense. I'll stake him," Brockington said grandly. They insisted that Terry sit down with them. Kitty soon became alarmed at the amounts they were gambling, but she knew it was pointless to argue with men who had imbibed too much, so in desperation she told Simon that she was going up to bed. She looked at him apprehensively. His mouth curved into the nicest smile and he looked impossibly young. She put on the silk embroidered nightgown Julia had given her and waited. The only face that Kitty could see was

Patrick's. The mouth that could be cruel and passionate, the arrogant nose and smoldering eyes haunted her. "Oh, God, I love him so," she cried out loud.

The din from below grew louder until it became an uproar, but still Simon did not come. The racket continued and Kitty began to relax. Eventually she drifted off to sleep, but Simon never came.

Patrick hadn't removed his coat before he asked for Kitty.

"Oh, Patrick, the most exciting thing, Kitty eloped yesterday!" said Julia.

"With whom?" he thundered.

"Why, Simon, of course."

"Goddamn it, woman, how did you allow such a thing to happen? Is Amelia still in town?" he demanded.

"Why, yes, I think so," she faltered.

He grabbed his hat and departed. It was a man incensed who confronted Amelia. "If we act immediately we can get this thing annulled," he said firmly.

"You must be mad! They had my full consent. Why should I wish the marriage to be annulled?"

"I wish it and that should be sufficient," he thundered.

"You can't bully me, Patrick O'Reilly, so save your breath. Kitty is all I could wish for in a wife for Simon. The marriage is perfectly legal and there isn't a damn thing you can do about it. I wish you good day, sir."

He turned on his heel and left. Julia received the full brunt of his temper.

"For God's sake, calm down, Patrick, and consider this rationally," she pleaded. "Kitty received an offer of marriage and she jumped at the chance."

"You pushed her into it, to get rid of her," he accused at the top of his voice.

"I did nothing of the sort. They are well suited in age and make a lovely couple."

"Has he taken her to The Elms?" he asked ominously.

"Yes, they are on their honeymoon and you mustn't go bursting in on them."

Patrick then did something he'd never done before. He slapped her. She ran from the room in tears.

Then he had Barbara to contend with. She flew to her sister's defense and attacked Patrick head on. "Don't you dare to breeze in here and blame Julia for what is a direct result of your own high-handed behavior! You're the one who went merrily off to engage yourself to Grace what's-her-face and left Kitty with a broken heart. Now you return and find she has contracted a marriage with an eligible man of her own age instead of finding her prostrate with grief and pining for you. So you fly into a jealous rage and slap Julia."

He looked as if he were about to slap Barbara too, but she went on heedlessly, "I think Simon must love Kitty very much. He took her without dowry, without hardly a stitch to her back, if it comes to that. He's not very flush in the pockets until he comes into his uncle's money. He could easily have had Lord Brockington's sister, who has about thirty thousand a year, I believe."

"Good God, it would take twice that amount to get rid of her in the marriage market," he hooted.

"Anyway, it seems to me you're playing dog-in-the-manger. You wouldn't marry Kitty, but you don't want anyone else to have her. Well, you're making a damned cake of yourself, because it's a *fait accompli* and that's that!"

Patrick did what every other man would do under the circumstances. He got drunk. It didn't help. His temper was savage with everyone and everything. He called Kitty every vile name he could lay his tongue to. Patrick was cut to the heart that she preferred Simon Bloody Brownlow to himself.

He felt totally betrayed. Bitterness ate at him relentlessly. Finally he vowed to put the little jade out of his mind by throwing himself into his work and he again made plans for a voyage to America.

Kitty saw very little of Simon the first week of their marriage. He spent all of his time with his friends, mostly outdoors. Since there were not enough horses for everyone to ride, Kitty didn't attempt it. She helped Mrs. Hobson with the cooking, knowing the fare was more appetizing when she took a hand in it. At the end of the week, when Madge and Brockington returned to London, Kitty was glad to see their backs. They got drunk every night and spent their evenings gambling; she did not think they were very good influences on Simon. He begged them not to leave, and he was lifeless and despondent for the first few days after they were gone. Then Kitty got a great surprise: A horse was delivered from Tattersall's. She was practically on the verge of tears when she learned it was a wedding present from Patrick. "Oh, how can I ever thank him?" she exclaimed.

"Don't thank him, thank me," grinned Simon. "I dropped him a note, giving the hint about how poorly mounted you were," he boasted.

Kitty was shocked. "Simon, you shouldn't have done such a thing. How humiliating! I don't want anything from Patrick."

"Nonsense! Just think of all the money he has. I couldn't possibly make ends meet if it weren't for the benevolence of my friends. Madge always supplies the wine and Brockington the brandy. Put all those useless ideas to the back of your head, Kit, and decide what you're going to call her," Simon urged.

Kitty shook her head. "I'll call her Brandywine for the obvious reason that's the only other wedding present I re-

ceived.'' She put out her hand to fondle the soft muzzle and
tears stung her eyelids as she thought of Patrick. ''I . . . I
have no riding habit, Simon,'' she faltered.

''Oh, stuff! There's trunks full of riding breeches and
jodhpurs I had when I was a boy. Come on, we'll find something that fits you,'' he urged.

''Oh, Simon, I couldn't wear breeches. What would people say?''

''What people? There's none to see but me.'' He took her
by the hand and led her up to the attics, where the trunks of
old clothes were stored. He piled her arms high with buck-
skins and velvet breeches and lace-edged shirts. She tried
them on and was both delighted and dismayed that they fit
her. His eyes showed his pleasure at her appearance. ''If your
hair were shorter, you and Terry could pass for twins,'' he
said and laughed. ''Stay right where you are, Kit, and I'll get
the scissors.''

''No, no, you mustn't!'' she protested.

''Come on, Kit, be a sport. What a famous joke. Let me
cut off just a little?'' he coaxed.

''Simon, no! I don't want my hair cut off. Come back
immediately!''

Simon came back, but not before he had found a pair of
scissors. To Kitty's horror, she realized that Simon was perfectly capable of doing something to her against her wishes.
She protested and begged, but he held her down. Laughing
like someone having the greatest fun in the world, he brandished the scissors above her curls. She grew alarmed at
Simon's odd behavior and finally agreed to let him cut just a
couple of inches off the bottom.

Kitty could see that Simon became easily bored and restless. She realized that he was shockingly immature. One afternoon when she was riding with Simon, he said he'd catch
a rabbit for their dinner and produced a ferret from his sad-

dlebag. Kitty hated ferrets. She dismounted and began to run through the trees.

"Kit, come back. Don't be such a baby," he said with a laugh.

"No, I hate them. They're so long and slinky and their little red eyes frighten me."

"Coward!" he taunted. "Come and see how well trained it is."

"No! It's cruel to the rabbit to put those horrible things down their warren. It almost frightens them to death and I don't want to watch!"

He began to chase her. She screamed and ran as fast as she could to get away from him. She knew he had a sadistic side and was capable of anything once he caught her. She fell to her hands and knees to try to escape in the underbrush, but with a pounce he was on top of her and she was struggling blindly against him. She gave a huge sigh of relief when she realized Simon was empty-handed, and they lay with him sprawled on top of her. By accident his hand came in contact with her breast. He drew it away quickly.

"Kit, you're all breasts in these damned shirts of mine. Why don't you bind yourself so you don't wobble about so much?"

Kitty was really surprised and said indignantly, "I'm a woman, not a boy," and as soon as the words were out she realized that was exactly what Simon wanted. He called her Kit, a masculine version of her name. He wanted her in pants and he even had cut her hair. She brooded on this with a vague uneasiness. By Thursday night Simon could stand the solitude of the country no longer. He informed Kitty and Terrance that they were going up to London. "Brockington's mother is giving a ball. You must be the most ravishing woman at the party. I want you to come too, Terry. My clothes should fit you. Let's go up now and find you something really elegant," Simon insisted.

Simon took Kitty to Harridge's, the most expensive shop in London, where she spent a very pleasant hour trying on magnificent ball gowns. Kitty's choice hovered between the mauve chiffon and the misty rose silk, but Simon insisted upon a very low-cut white ruffled gown with a silver tissue overdress. It was extravagantly priced, but Simon waved away her protests. They went to Brockington's bachelor establishment in Jermyn Street.

"Couldn't miss your ball tonight, old man. I would like a hairdresser for Kit, though. Can't have her looking like a country bumpkin, can we?" said Simon with a laugh.

"Remember that er . . . friend you used to have? Frenchman, wasn't he?"

"Pierre!" they said in unison, smiling like two conspirators.

"Let's go and round him up. You come with us, Terry," said Simon.

Pierre was one of the strangest creatures Kitty had ever seen. He was extremely effeminate and she thought perhaps he was even wearing lip salve. He had eyelashes that vied with Kitty's, and when he spoke with his quaint accent, he gesticulated wildly. He had no difficulty, however, in making a creation of Kitty's curls. It was piled high on top, and a false piece cascaded down one shoulder. The style suited her gown to perfection. Kitty couldn't understand why Simon had picked a gown that displayed her breasts so obviously when at other times he found them distasteful.

When they arrived with the son of the house, they were given a very warm welcome and Kitty found herself looking for *that* face in the crowd. She was both disappointed and relieved that he was not there. She was soon surrounded by handsome, rich young men on the make. As Terrance stood on the edge of the ballroom and observed the scene, he was sickened as he realized Simon was using her as bait to attract these young men. What Terrance didn't realize was that he himself was part of the bait. With such a pair of attractive drawing cards, Simon had no difficulty rounding up half a dozen young men for a country house party for the following week. Brockington was engaged for every night of the coming week, but promised to come down to The Elms when the rest of the young men were expected, and promised to bring Madge with him.

"I've told everyone to ride down because I can't mount them, Brock."

"Never mind, Simon. Someday you'll have the best stable in Surrey."

"Well, like King Charles, he's an unconscionable time a-dying," said Simon, laughing. Simon made one stop on the journey home. Kitty thought it had something to do with providing entertainment for the invited guests. They stopped at a game farm that sold every kind of wild fowl chicks, such as snipe and partridge, and when Simon loaded a wooden box onto the gig she assumed it contained birds he was going to stock the woods with at The Elms.

Kitty didn't have a chance to speak with Terry until after dinner, when the effects of the brandy had overpowered Simon.

"What was it?" asked Kitty, drawing Terry to the far side of the room.

"A fox!" he answered, "a little vixen. A female fox gives off a scent that can be picked up from up to a hundred miles away."

"Of course. He wants to attract foxes for a hunt. It's too cruel! You must let the little fox go free," she asserted.

"Kitty, I don't approve of such practices either, but I don't think we should interfere." He hesitated. "I'm not worried for myself, love, but Simon is your husband and he can be very unpredictable. I wouldn't like him for an enemy and I shouldn't like to see him vent his temper upon you. I'll take him up to his bed," Terry murmured. He lifted Simon from where he lay sprawled by the fire and carried him upstairs.

Kitty wasted no time, but went directly to the stables. The small red creature blinked her eyes once, then like a cat's eyes the pupils slitted and the amber iris remained large and round. The vixen drew back into the corner and wrinkled her nose and bared her teeth in a snarl. Kitty chuckled softly. "I won't hurt you, my beauty." She took one of her hairpins, and using the two prongs pressed tightly together, inserted the points under the latch and forced it apart. The vixen knew instinctively what was expected of her. Without a sound she slunk into the night.

The next morning Kitty was still abed when she heard Simon's angry voice. He came up the stairs and flung open her bedroom door without ceremony. It was the first time he had ever seen her in bed.

"Which one of you did it? You or your damned brother?" he demanded.

Kitty didn't bother to dissemble. "It wasn't Terrance; I did it."

His face was white with anger as he moved toward the bed. "Do you know how much that vixen cost me? She was in heat. She would have attracted every fox in Surrey."

"When I saw her, I took compassion on the little trapped creature. Please forgive me, Simon."

"I am going to punish you," he threatened firmly.

She pulled the covers up around her neck, feeling alarm for the first time. "You wouldn't dare!" she asserted.

He didn't waste his breath arguing with her, but grabbed her wrist and pulled her struggling from the bed. He had a wiry strength which when fueled by anger she could not withstand. He dragged her facedown across his knee and lifted her nightgown to expose her bare buttocks. She was outraged and humiliated to be handled in this manner, but she found herself defenseless. Simon raised his hand and slapped her bottom with full force. The first smack carried such a sting it brought tears to her eyes and a cry to her lips. Slowly and deliberately he went about his business, and her cries and pleas fell on deaf ears.

Suddenly she felt his organ grow hard against her belly and she twisted her face up to look at him in surprise. His eyes were rolled back, and he was in a frenzy of sexual arousal. The intimate touch of their bodies repelled her. She tried to contain her cries because they were obviously giving him pleasure. Her bottom was red-raw where the blood had been drawn to the surface. She feared she would faint from the pain, when all at once he threw his head back and all his muscles twitched and heaved in a spasm that left him limp. Simon's blue eyes smiled under lids heavy with sensuality. His mouth was soft and relaxed, his whole face was smooth from satiety.

Escaping his grip was no longer a problem. She locked herself in the small bathroom. She bathed her bottom with warm water until gradually the pain became bearable. This had confirmed her every fear that Simon was abnormal. She understood all too well why his mother had been so anxious to marry him off and leave for parts unknown.

Mrs. Hobson appeared as soon as Simon had departed, so she could investigate Kitty's cries. When she saw Kitty's eyes, red from crying, she pressed her lips together and asked, "Has he been practicing his abominations on you?"

"No. . . . Yes, but please don't let my brother know, Mrs. Hobson. Let's just keep it between the two of us."

Mrs. Hobson looked at her conspiratorially and whispered, "I know some spells I could let you have."

Kitty immediately was diverted. "You mean witchcraft?" In spite of herself she smiled. "We have something in common. I'm a Gypsy, you know. I have a few curses of my own."

Warming to the subject, Mrs. Hobson confided, "As a matter of fact, I've already worked a spell on him. It only remains to see if it works."

"What did you do?" asked Kitty, amused.

"I buried five blue marbles," she replied in hushed tones.

"Did you call down the dark powers of Nebo?"

"No. Is that a witch?"

"Never mind. You're probably better off not knowing," answered Kitty. "Perhaps the most sensible thing we could do would be to ask Mr. Hobson to put a bolt upon my door," suggested Kitty.

"Practical common sense." She patted Kitty on the shoulder. "You'll survive this, my lass."

"I don't know, Mrs. Hobson. It's a hard world where the gentle can be eaten alive before they have time to grow an iron carapace."

Chapter 15

Kitty kept to herself as much as possible while the young men were there; however, Simon made it plain to her that he did expect a hostess at the dinner table each evening. She became adept at keeping them in their place with a word or a look. She had a native wit and she developed a cutting edge to her tongue. Before the meal drew to a close, they usually had imbibed enough for their hijinks to begin, and Kitty excused herself as soon as was politely possible. She could hardly believe the juvenile nonsense that amused them.

For Kitty the week passed without incident until the last day of their stay. She breakfasted early to avoid everyone, but as luck would have it, two of the young men were up before her. Her interest was caught when she overheard Ninian say, "That was the most ingenious peephole I've ever looked through."

"I agree," replied Basil. "When they are in the ceiling like that, you get a view of the whole bedroom; nothing is hidden."

"The most glorious black curls!"

"Tantalizing buttocks."

Kitty was outraged to think she had been spied upon while undressing, and by the sounds of it at Simon's instigation. Her dander was up now and she was damned if she would tolerate such behavior beneath her roof. She stepped into view and said, "Well, the more fools, the more fun, so they say. You can both pack up and leave now, and that goes for the rest of your stupid friends," she ordered.

"I'll tell you what it is, Basil: She's jealous," jeered Ninian.

"No, just low-bred," drawled Basil, whereupon Kitty sent him a ringing blow across his ear and stormed from the room.

What she needed was a brisk ride and some fresh air, she decided. She put on riding breeches and a jacket and took up her riding crop. Simon burst into her room and she could see immediately that he was as angry as she was herself. He wore only a silk dressing gown negligently belted and as he advanced upon her she knew he had nothing on beneath it.

"You've insulted my friends and I intend to punish you for it," he threatened. Kitty was damned if he was going to thrash her bare bottom again, so she struck out at him with the riding crop. His eyes got that certain gleam in them and he became instantly aroused. Kitty hit out at him again and his robe fell away from his body, exposing his erect member to the horrified Kitty. She lashed out with the quirt, forcing herself to stand her ground.

"The elastic of my patience just snapped! Get out! Don't ever enter my room again under any circumstances. If your precious friends are so important to you, you'd best get the hell to London after them, because I can't bear the sight of you."

"Maybe I will," he said menacingly, but all the fight had gone out of him. After she had bathed and changed, she discovered that Simon had departed for London and taken Terrance with him. A swell of relief swept over her and she fervently hoped he would stay away for a month. As she sat arranging her hair, Mrs. Hobson came to her, upset and agitated.

"Mr. Hobson has been looking worse and worse since I buried them blue marbles, ma'am. I do fear that the spell has come back on me. What can I do?" she pleaded. Kitty fully realized that Mrs. Hobson had fallen prey to the only danger that spells and superstition represented. If one believed in them, only then could they do any harm.

"Mrs. Hobson, you must dig up the marbles immediately," she urged.

Mrs. Hobson shook her head. "It did no good. I dug them up yesterday, and this morning Hobson took to his bed. I don't like the looks of him. You must take the spell off! You're a Gypsy—you can help me," she said fervently.

"All right, Mrs. Hobson. It's really very simple."

Kitty's mind raced as she sought out a little ritual that would convince the woman. "You must take the front-door key and place it in your Bible. Mr. Hobson will be better almost immediately."

"Will it work?" she asked hopefully.

"Oh, yes," Kitty assured her firmly. "Keys are ancient magic symbols and placing one in a Bible can lift any spell."

A week hadn't elapsed before Simon returned with more dissolute friends in tow. They were gambling in the library, and his pockets were empty, so he put up Kitty for grabs. Only the thought that he had lost again angered him; he gave not a fig for what he had lost.

"Christ, you're a lucky dog, Savage!" the winner was told by his companions.

"Fortune favors the bold, so I'm told," the cruel-looking youth retorted. He added with a sneer, "I hope your wife measures up better than this stuff we're drinking. It tastes like stallion piss!"

Simon eyed Duke Savage sullenly. Duke wasn't as far gone in his cups as the others, and although the thought of Kitty whetted his appetite thoroughly, he was shrewd enough to realize Simon would be jealous. Simon would reason that whatever the Duke and Kitty could enjoy, the Duke and Simon could enjoy more!

Duke Savage also realized Kitty's brother Terry would present a problem. They all expected Duke to collect his bet tonight so the rest could get their kicks as voyeurs, but Savage had a better plan. After everyone had left for London tomorrow, he would double back and take her at his leisure.

Terrance knew better than to act anything except indifferent. When the revelers got to the point in their drinking where he wouldn't be missed, Terrance slipped away to warn Kitty.

"Terry, I thought nothing Simon did could shock me anymore, but I was wrong."

"Well, the Duke of Savage is the one who has won you."

"Terry, he isn't a duke. That's just his nickname," she answered unhappily.

"Do you know, Kitty, I lie awake at night, planning to kill Simon."

"Oh, God, Terrance, not you too? Promise me you won't do anything foolish? I'll figure a way to get us out of all this. Anyway, Duke Savage is a more pressing problem than Simon. I'll be sure my door is bolted tonight. Come with me now and we'll make sure no one's hiding in that hideous wardrobe. It frightens me to death. I swear I'll get it moved tomorrow." She kissed him good night, then firmly threw the bolt and didn't undo it again until after the hour of noon the next day. By this time all had departed for London and she was left alone with the Hobsons. Mr. Hobson had fully recovered as a result of Kitty's "magic," and the couple would gratefully do anything Kitty wished.

"Mr. Hobson, I would like you to go over to the farm and get a couple of those really hefty, strong farmboys for me. I want that big wardrobe moved out of my bedroom. I don't have many clothes anyway, and that thing gives me the shivers.''

''I'll go over now, then, and get a couple of the lads. You might have to wait until they're finished their chores.''

''I might as well walk over to the farm with you. We need some eggs,'' said Mrs. Hobson. ''I'll just go and get my basket.''

It was a warm day and as Kitty was getting a drink from the kitchen she heard an unfamiliar step behind her. She whirled about to face Duke Savage. In one illuminating second that seemed suspended in time, his purpose became crystal clear. Pretense would have been ridiculous as she looked at the sensual curve of his mouth and knew he was already aroused.

''I'm not alone here,'' lied Kitty.

He cocked an amused eyebrow. ''On the contrary, my dear, I've just seen them leave for the farm. We are completely alone.''

The air of lust in the room was almost tangible. His face was brazen and knowing with an unmistakable leer.

''To pay a gambling debt is a point of honor,'' he whispered, and a lynx at bay could not have given her a crueler glance.

''Honor?'' she mocked. ''I'll swear you know little of honor.''

''I know much of other things, sweetheart.'' He reached out easily to encircle her waist and draw her body up against his. As his hand covered her breast, she let out a piercing scream, so he quickly bent his head and cut off the sound by covering her mouth with his. He did not release her mouth until he thought she might be in danger of suffocation. He then proceeded to tell her what he intended to do with her in graphic words, hoping she would relish the hinted indecencies. She was trembling now, but feared to fight him in case she enflamed him to madness. She hoped that by keeping calm she could postpone the violence that seemed inevitable. He caressed her breasts and whispered, "I bet you enjoy a good roll in the hay, don't you, sweet? I know Simon's no bloody use to you. You must be mad for it by now."

Kitty made a desperate effort to break away from him.

"You're not struggling, are you?" He pulled up a straight-backed chair and forced her down upon it none too gently. He took off his neckcloth and bound her wrists to the chair behind her.

"Like a spot of bondage, do you?" he teased.

He was standing behind her and Kitty shuddered with re-vulsion as she felt him pressing his erection against her back. He came around to face her, his eyes upon her mouth. "With a little cooperation on your part, we can get the first thing I want done without untying you or even mussing up your clothes." His fingers started to unbutton his trousers.

Although Kitty had had no experience of this sort of thing before, she was left in no doubt of his meaning. She raised her eyes to his and said very clearly, "Duke Savage, if you put that thing anywhere near my mouth, I promise you I shall bite it off! I'll maul it so badly it will never work again. It will give me the greatest pleasure to ruin you for life!"

He knew she meant it, and a grudging admiration came into his eyes. "Come then, I'll take you up to bed. That way we'll both enjoy it."

He lifted her in his arms and started for the stairs when Mr. Hobson came in with two young giants. Duke Savage set her on her feet at once as one of them asked, "Was there something you wanted us to shift, ma'am?"

"Yes, this gentleman. Kindly take him off our property and give him a bloody good beating."

Savage turned pale green. "They wouldn't dare. I'd press charges!"

"Shut your cake hole!" one of the farmhands said bluntly.

"Are you sure that's what you want us to do, ma'am?"

Kitty looked Savage straight in the eye and said sweetly, "Put the boots to him!"

Terrance was determined upon his course. He wasn't going to let one more day pass without informing Patrick of Kitty's plight. As soon as they arrived in London Terrance gave Simon the slip and wondered whether it was better to try to catch Patrick at home or at his office. Terrance finally decided to try the latter, as he probably spent as little time as possible under his sister's roof, even though the house in Cadogen Square was his.

Patrick greeted him with raised eyebrows. "Terrance! Your very presence tells me something must be wrong."

Terry nodded miserably. "It's about Simon." He hesitated.

"Go on," Patrick said shortly.

"He's not normal—he's queer! He sleeps with other men."

Patrick stiffened. "Wherever did you hear such filthy rumors?" he demanded.

"They aren't rumors," Terry said quietly.

Patrick looked at him with disbelief. "How do you know?" he demanded.

"How the hell do you think I know?" shouted Terry.

Patrick went pale. "My God, why didn't you tell me sooner? He hasn't harmed her, has he? She doesn't share his bed, does she?"

"No, she has her own bedroom, but he uses her as bait to attract young men and she is in constant danger from them."

"I'm sailing for America before the week's out. Why the hell didn't you come sooner?" shouted Patrick. "I'll just have to put the sailing date ahead for another week. You must have known it was a mistake from the very beginning. Why didn't you inform me earlier?''

''Kitty doesn't know men have sexual relationships with other men, but she knows Simon isn't normal. He calls her Kit, a boy's name, and he has her wandering about the place in boy's riding breeches. He even cut her hair like a boy, but it's growing again.''

''Terry, go at once to Cadogen Square and have them pack me a bag. I have some things here I must attend to, but I can leave for Surrey in about two hours.''

''I'll go back to Simon and make sure he stays in London. How long will you need?''

''Give us a week alone, if you can. After that I'll have to leave. Take Kitty and stay with Julia until I return from America, but be assured the problem of Simon will be eliminated. Permanently.''

Kitty rode out a little way from the house, dismounted and sat down with her back against a tree in a little glade on the edge of the forest. The bridle jingled as her horse cropped the grass beneath the leafy arches. The trees sighed and murmured to each other in the slumberous, gentle wind. She sat with unseeing eyes, trying to come to a decision about her future. She knew she could not remain with Simon any longer, but she was unsure of where she should go. Kitty longed to go home to Ireland, but the prospect was bleak and she realized she probably would fare better if she went to London and tried to find some kind of employment. What she really wanted was Patrick. The flowers lifted their faces to the sun and filled the air with their languorous perfume. Her eyes lifted heavenward, brimful of tears when Patrick caught his first glimpse of her. Screened by the thick-budded foliage, he gazed breathlessly upon her, entranced by her beauty, dewy-eyed and languid. He saw how the thin ruffled shirt clung to her shapely body, and he was filled with desire. Her horse whinnied softly to him; she was startled into awareness. The sight of him took her breath away. She thought for one fleeting moment that he was only a vision, but her heart lifted with such a wild surge that she knew he was real.

"Kitty, how are you?" he asked softly.

Her heart thudded in her chest, and a solid lump came into her throat when she tried to speak. She hesitated, then said with stiff pride, "Things are marvelous, couldn't be better . . ." but could go no further.

They looked into each other's eyes and in that moment their souls touched. Patrick held out his arms to her. With an incoherent cry she stumbled into them and sobbed out all her troubles against his chest. His arms were comfort and safety to her. Nothing could hurt her now, so secure did she feel against the firmness of his shoulder. When she had cried herself out, he lifted her chin until her eyes met his.

"I want you to go and change into a gown for me. Your breeches are so tantalizing I won't be able to keep my hands from you, and we have a great many things to talk about before I make love to you."

Her eyes widened in apprehension, but before she could voice a protest he set his mouth to hers and kissed her with all the pent-up longing he had known since they had been apart. She clung to him with a desperate need of her own. He was the first to withdraw from the kiss, but only long enough to whisper, "I love you, darling."

"Oh, Patrick, I've always loved you," and their mouths fused again.

He caught her in his arms and lifted her against his heart. Desire overpowered him, his hands were hard and fierce and her sweet, moist mouth trembled as she whispered, "Your embrace will crush me."

He set her down gently. "Forgive me, darling. It won't be like last time. I promise I won't hurt you. I want you to be my wife. You belong to me and no other. Repeat with me a simple marriage vow, 'I receive you as mine.' "

She clasped him close, beset by sudden fear. "What if Simon returns?"

He said simply, "I'll kill him!"

Kitty changed into her one pretty gown. It was pale lavender silk which flowed and billowed sensuously as she walked.

Mrs. Hobson wrung her hands, exclaiming over and over that she'd never be able to feed such a fine gentleman, until finally Patrick took her by the shoulders and said kindly but firmly, "We don't care what we eat, ma'am, all we want is to be together. Nothing else matters."

She bobbed a curtsy and disappeared.

The day had been warm, but as the evening lengthened into shadow, the air emitted a slight chill, so Patrick lit a fire. There was nothing stronger than tea to drink, so after dinner they sat before the fire and Kitty poured Patrick a cup and handed it across to him, thinking all the while, if only we could do this for the rest of our lives.

"Darling, I have to tell you right away that when Terry found me I was about to leave for Liverpool. My ship was to sail tomorrow for America."

"Oh, no," she whispered in despair.

"Love, don't be upset. I'll put off the sailing for a week. I've thought of taking you with me, it would be paradise, but too selfish of me. You could come only as my mistress while you still are married. That would distress you and leave you open to gossip and insult. When I come back, we'll be married properly," he said confidently.

"But how can that be?" she asked uncertainly. "You don't really mean to kill Simon, do you?"

He avoided answering her directly, as he knew that was exactly what he would do if Simon stood in their way. He waved his hand airily, "There are many ways: divorce, annulment. . . ."

"But . . . to get an annulment you have to be able to prove . . . that your marriage never was consummated. . . ."

He stiffened. "My God, Kitty, he didn't touch you, did he?" he demanded fiercely.

"No, he didn't, but you did!"

He relaxed and laughed at her fears. "My darling, you don't suppose I'd let you face the indignity of an examination, do you? You are so innocent! Money is simply exchanged for the certificate you would need to obtain the annulment."

"You mean a bribe?" she asked.

"Of course!" He sat back in his chair like a young, bronzed god setting the world straight.

He was triumphant and high-spirited, and he exuded confidence. Under this man's protection she would never be afraid again.

"I'll be going to Bagatelle Plantation in the Carolinas for their cotton crop, and then on to New York to the Hind Food Company offices. Someday I hope to be president of our American branch. How would you like to live on Millionaires' Row in New York?"

"I could be happy anywhere with you," she said shyly.

"You are my darling little girl, but you mustn't look at me like that or we won't get any farther with our plans."

"How long will you be away, Patrick?"

"That's the devil of it. You can never be sure with an ocean voyage, but if I'm lucky I could be back in four months. You can't stay here, of course; you must go to Julia in London. I'll explain to her that you will be coming and you must have no contact whatsoever with Simon. I'll be right back.'' Her eyes widened in surprise when he returned and held out a gun to her. "It's a Colt .45, recently designed in London. I shall teach you how to use it.''

"I'm not sure I want it, Patrick. Guns are for killing,'' she protested.

"It's simply for your protection. My God, how can I bear to leave you, knowing how vulnerable you will be?'' he demanded.

"If it will make you feel easier, I will keep it by me, of course.''

"Darling,'' he whispered. He set down the gun on the tea table and pulled out a long leather wallet. "I've some money for you here. Five hundred pounds is all I have with me, but that might meet your needs. If not, Julia has a line of credit at one of my banks and I'll instruct her to let you have whatever you need.''

"Five hundred pounds is more than I've ever seen in my whole life,'' Kitty exclaimed.

"It may sound like a lot, but I'll be gone for months, sweetheart, so you will have to be very careful with it.''

She took the bank notes and put them in her reticule. As she moved he thought how slender and delicate her wrists and ankles were. She was so exquisitely fragile, he knew he would need a will of iron to keep from ravishing her the moment he touched her. Desire almost overpowered him. His need for her was so intense it was more pain than pleasure.

She stood hesitant in the gathering shadows. Her small foot peeped from the perfumed mystery of her silken skirts and he was transfixed by the spell of her haunting beauty. The next instant she was in his arms. He lifted his hands and interlaced her hair; his thumbs brushed the velvet of her cheeks. He lifted her faintly parted mouth to him.

"Darling Kitty,'' he murmured and she looked into his

deep blue eyes with apprehension. "I receive you as mine," he whispered. An ancient unsolved mystery, a fragile, haunting, whispered vow.

"I won't unless you wish it, beloved," he swore, but it took every ounce of willpower he possessed.

"I'm finished with childhood. I want to be a woman," she whispered back.

He lifted her tenderly and carried her up the stairs. One eyebrow, like a raven's wing, went up to question which was her chamber, and she indicated with her eyes which door to open. Instinct told him she was far too shy to make the first move, so without hesitation he undid the small lavender buttons of her gown. He drew aside the fabric and kissed her on the curves of her breasts. She loved the look of adoration on his face as he slipped off her gown and undergarments and lifted her onto the wide bed. The room was filled with moonlight so he didn't light the candles out of consideration for her, but he promised himself they would make love with every light blazing before their week was up. He took off his tiepin and cuff links and placed them on the table by the bed next to a little pot of violet-scented face cream. He undressed quickly and slipped in beside her, gathering her into a very tender embrace. He knew that tonight he held the key to Kitty's future enjoyment of her own sexuality. Gently, he drew back the cover and gazed at her. Her nipples and aureoles were such a deep bronze color, they excited him until the blood pounded in his head and made him dizzy.

"My God, kitten, you are so lovely," he breathed hoarsely. "I must have been mad not to have married you long ago."

"Why didn't you?" she chided him lovingly.

He stroked her shoulders and breasts and gazed at her thoughtfully.

"I think you were too exotic for me to think of as a wife.

A man would only think of you in terms of a mistress, because of your beauty. When you look at me imperiously, you could be Russian; the black clouds of your hair and slant of your eyes remind me of an Oriental. You have the dainty hands and feet of a Balinese temple dancer.''

She was in a dreamlike trance as his words revealed his enchantment with her. ''At other times you are so sleek and pantherlike, you could even have a drop of black blood in you; Egyptian, perhaps.''

She smiled up at him. ''It's Gypsy, my darling.''

''My exciting, exotic Irish Gypsy.'' He lowered his mouth to hers worshipfully. He kissed her eyelids, her temples, her throat and lingered over each delicate breast. He wooed her with honeyed words as his hands moved across her waist, tracing small circles around her navel. He stroked her thighs and finally the soft black curls on her mound of Venus. She drew in her breath quickly at his touch, but before she could protest he said, ''Shh, my lovely, try to relax.'' She was fever-dry to his touch, so he used a tiny drop of the violet-scented cream and with sensitive fingertips traced the folds between her legs. ''Tell me what you like, darling,'' he urged, and his fingers gently probed again. ''Does that give you pleasure?''

''Mmmm.''

He increased the tempo of his movements and could tell she was becoming aroused. ''Does that excite you, sweet? It excites me!''

She moaned with pleasure, and with deft fingertips he brought her to climax. She arched against his hand as the strange sensation reached all the way to her toes. It was the first time she had ever experienced sensual pleasure and she was filled with the wonder of it. Patrick held her very closely and whispered such words of love, she felt her very bones would melt from the delicious sensations that swept through her. He was in no hurry; he forced himself to savor her enjoyment without marring her pleasure with his haste. He held her to his heart and stroked her back. Her arms swept up behind his head and when she moved her body closer to fit it to his, she gasped at his enormous phallus, swollen with passion. He soothed her fears away with caresses and words of love. He began to kiss her, gently at first, then more demandingly. His skillful lovemaking worked its magic until she became aroused again, and the intensity of her mouth matched his own. Gently he placed her on her back and crouched above her in towering excitement. A searing white heat shot through him at the first contact of their bodies.

"I can't, Patrick! You're too big!" she cried.

"Yes, you can, darling. Open your legs. That's right. Now kiss me." He would not be denied now, and firmly penetrated her trembling body and achieved his heart's desire. She was surprised to feel the delicious sensations arise again so swiftly, but this time magnified a hundred-fold. When she felt certain she could not bear such intensity one moment longer, he brought them to climax with a few swift thrusts and they lay in each other's arms, savoring their mutual ecstasy. He cradled her possessively until they both slept.

Once, in the dark before dawn, Patrick awakened and looked down at the beloved face next to his on the pillows. Desire flared instantly through his loins. He bent his head to seek her lips, then stopped himself. He did not wish to give her a disgust of his male appetite, so sighing, he closed his eyes and willed the fire in his blood to cool.

When the morning sunlight patterned the bed with its delicious, warm rays, Kitty panicked. My God, the words he'd whispered and the things they had done seemed shocking in the light of day. He was the master and she the servant, and now that he had had his way with her, he might discard her, toss her aside with all respect gone. She wanted to bury her blushes in the pillow but could not resist one swift glance through her lashes. Patrick was gazing at her. He adored her with his eyes. Relief swept over her. She sprang up joyously and kissed him repeatedly, saying, "Oh, Patrick, I love you."

"Say it again, Kitty. Again and again! Foolish little darling to think you could get away from me. You are mine. Mine! I'll keep you. You'll never get away. Never! Never! Repeat the vow you made me. Only love me, and I'll manage all the rest!"

Kitty was filled with such power she feared her heart would explode.

Later that morning Patrick made them fishing rods and they set off for the trout stream. They wrapped the fish in leaves and baked them to a tender golden brown. When they were finished, Kitty lay with her head in his lap. The heat made her drowsy and each time Patrick bent to kiss her, delicious sensations ran through her body, and they repeated a hundred times the whispered promise, "Tonight!" They strolled upstream to where it was dammed off a little. He urged her to swim with him, but she was too shy to strip and play in the water naked. He refused to go in without her, and pressed her so insistently she promised that she would swim with him before he went away. When their fingers touched, or their eyes met, everything was forgotten except the magic of belonging to each other. Time ceased to exist for them. Day blended slowly into night and they exulted that at last they would be sharing a bed.

In the aftermath of passion, she asked, "When it can be so beautiful, why did you ravish me that first time?"

"I was a selfish fool, my darling. I suppose I wanted to put my mark upon you so indelibly that you would always remember me even if you were with another. I wanted to master you, but I was the one who became enslaved."

Each night it was different for them. Sometimes their love was wild and hot, almost an assault of the senses. At such times Kitty surprised him with a passionate ardor that equaled his own. Then the next evening she came to the bed shyly, in a pristine white nightgown, making her look like a young novitiate, and a tenderness swept over him, along with a deep desire to protect her always.

Sometimes they fantasized about what their married life would be like. "If we go to America, I'll buy you a mansion on Millionaires' Row. I'll cover you in jewels and silks and thoroughly enjoy showing you off."

She spoke with her lips against his, "Can I have my own carriage?"

"Lady Jane Tut," he teased between a dozen tiny kisses.

"We'll entertain every night. I'll be the most famous hostess in New York," and she traced the outline of his lip with the tip of her tongue.

"Not every night; I'll want you to myself," he said possessively.

"Oh, Patrick, perhaps Julia won't want me, under the circumstances. After all, I'm still married to Simon. Julia probably will feel awkward and object to my living there."

"My dear Kitty, I am the paymaster in that house, and I will have things exactly as I wish them."

"Patrick," she chided, "you are so arrogant!"

"Lord Muck, eh?" he laughed.

"Exactly!" she agreed.

"That's not being arrogant, that's being masterful. Let me show you," and he pinned her beneath his body so there could be only one outcome.

One evening they discovered some Gypsies camped by the woods.

"I can dance like that. Would you like to see?" she whispered to Patrick.

"Very much," he said, caught up in her excitement.

She picked up a tambourine and began to undulate slowly. The beat of the music began slowly and deeply. A young Gypsy male came over to Kitty and began to partner her in the dance. He was very slim and swarthy and his teeth flashed white whenever their eyes met. They moved closer and closer in the hypnotic rhythm, never quite touching, and as Patrick observed the possessive look the Gypsy bestowed upon Kitty, he thought, "And she called me arrogant!"

The music speeded up and they whirled faster and faster. Her skirts swirled higher and higher about her bare legs until Patrick felt his anger build with the music. He felt a jealous rage grip him as he watched the pair fit their body movements to each other. He strode up to Kitty, took her arm in a grip of iron and commanded, "Come!"

"You are angry. Didn't my dancing please you?"

She knew very well what emotions plagued Patrick at this moment, but she wanted him to tell her of his jealousy.

"Your dancing aroused me, but it aroused him too, as you very well know," he ground out.

"He was just a boy," she said and laughed.

"He felt a man's desire for you."

"Darling, you're jealous," she whispered.

His mouth came down upon her savagely and she clung to him, savoring his brutality. "Come!" he commanded.

"Where are you taking me?" But she knew.

"You promised me," he asserted as he urged her onward toward the swimming place. She didn't protest when he began undressing her with impatient hands. Soon all her loveliness was revealed in the moonlight and he drew in his breath sharply at the picture she made. He stripped quickly and towered above her, not to be denied. The water was momentarily forgotten in his urgency, and she reached out to touch the quivering organ. Her fingertips ran along the entire length, which grew hard and rigid at her touch.

"Darling Patrick, never be jealous. You're the most beautiful man in the world."

"Kitten, desire and anger are a deadly combination. I'm warning you, there'll be no holds barred this night."

She licked her lips in anticipation as he pulled her down into the grass. She felt her own pulse merge with the earth's beneath her body. He intended to make violent love to her, then bathe together. After their swim, he would love her yet again.

It was three o'clock in the morning. Kitty stood by the window, looking down into the garden. Tears made silver streaks down her cheeks. Patrick roused from sleep to find the bed empty. Quickly he slipped out of bed and came up behind her. "Sweetheart, you'll catch cold. What's wrong?"

"How can I bear it? Tomorrow you'll be gone and I may never see you again," she said, sobbing. "There could be a storm at sea, or you could catch a fever in America, or what about Indians?"

"Indians?" He laughed incredulously. "Oh, sweetheart, your Irish is showing. Don't expect the worst; expect the best! I'll be back before you know it and by that time Simon will be out of the way and we'll be married immediately." He made a mental note to seek out the young hothead who had stabbed him in Bolton and give him a certain job to do.

"Come and be warm, love." He picked her up without protest and carried her to the bed. Instead of tucking her beneath the covers he stood her upon the bed before him and removed her nightgown. She shivered slightly as the cool air touched her naked skin, then shuddered convulsively as his warm breath teased her breasts and his hot mouth took possession of the impudent crests that thrust boldly forward like tiny spears.

His rough tongue began to lick her aureoles, then he took the entire crown into his mouth and sucked fiercely. A low moan broke from her throat that sent prickles along the back of his neck. He wanted to hear the love cries she would make when his mouth plundered her woman's center.

His powerful hands gripped her waist firmly as his mouth moved down her rib cage, then across her belly.

Kitty no longer felt cold. Her blood had heated to molten gold, flowing through every vein like liquid fire. She gasped as she realized his goal. Surely even Patrick could not be so boldly wicked as to put his mouth *there.*

She tried to pull back from his mouth, but his iron hands gripped her like a vise, holding her for his ravishment. The kisses he bestowed upon her were so thrilling she threaded her fingers through his crisp, black hair and arched herself against his lips.

He murmured against her hot center, "Beautiful, beautiful." His love words aroused her to a passion she had never experienced. His thumbs moved down to open her center and his tongue plunged inside to curl about her tiny jewel.

She was sobbing now at the exquisite torture of his scalding mouth as he licked and thrust, licked and thrust, exploring every secret crevice of her womanhood. Every nerve in her body responded to the hot center where he plunged so deeply with pure sensual enjoyment. Suddenly she became hot and wild and insatiable. She was all Gypsy, all woman, as she threw back her head and screamed her joy in a splendidly uninhibited frenzy of sexuality.

Patrick pulled her down beneath him. He knew she had experienced one delicious climax and he intended to arouse her immediately to another and satisfy her with the fulfillment of being hard and deep inside her so that his body could feel every last tremor.

After their explosion, neither of them could bear his withdrawal. Her hands clung to him desperately. "Don't leave me, I may never have you again," she sobbed.

"I'll take you with me in the morning. I'll not leave you here to brood unnecessarily," he said firmly.

When morning arrived, however, fate had conspired against them, and Mrs. Hobson had come down with an ague.

"I can't leave her alone, Patrick. It's best this way. All my fears have fled with the sunlight. You go and make things right with Julia, and as soon as Terry returns, we'll leave for London, I promise."

They both felt pain at parting. However, both knew it would be worse to drag it out endlessly. With one passionate embrace that implied a promise never to be broken, he was gone.

Chapter 16

Kitty was left in a blissful state of hazy euphoria. Everywhere she went recalled scenes of Patrick's presence. She smiled tenderly when she remembered the whole afternoon they had lain in the tall grasses of the meadow. Each time she had kissed Patrick, the corners of his mouth had quivered deliciously. She kissed him twice as often after this discovery, just for the pleasure of watching her lover's mouth. She hummed a pretty song as she made lunch for her and Mrs. Hobson and carried it in to the ailing woman on a tray. "I want you to figure out how much you are owed and also what we owe the farm for our food." The accounting came close to a hundred pounds and Kitty paid willingly, eager to be rid of the long-standing debts. After lunch, she decided to have a washday. There was a lot of bed linen as well as her own personal things that must be washed before she could pack everything. She would be ready when Terrance arrived, so there would be no delay in following Patrick to London. She tidied the kitchen and then packed all her belongings. She went to bed thoroughly exhausted and fell into a deep sleep. Suddenly something awakened her. It had sounded like someone in distress. Kitty could have sworn the cries came from her brother, Terrance. Carefully she got out of bed and removed from the dresser drawer the pistol Patrick had given her. Her hand tightened upon the gun as she silently moved forward and opened the door. The sight that met her eyes made her stagger back in horror. Three nude men were before her. Brockington held down Terrance while Simon bent over the boy. A motionless tableau etched itself indelibly upon her mind as she realized what was happening.

"Christ, Brocky, she's got a gun! Take it from her!" Simon ordered. She saw Terry's face, the tears of pain and rage, and at the same time Brockington launched himself against her and grabbed for the gun. She either had to let go, or squeeze the trigger. She did the latter. Silence filled the chamber after the loud report. A surprised look on Simon's face was captured for all time as the bullet entered his head and gaped like a third eye in the middle of his forehead. She thought irrelevantly, *Patrick told me I was going to be a widow soon. I wonder how he knew?*

The metallic scent of blood filled her nostrils, but she was nowhere near fainting. Terrance slid out from under Simon's dead weight and reached for a dressing gown to cover his nakedness. He was shaking from head to foot.

"You've murdered him!" screamed Brockington as the realization of the situation finally penetrated.

"You caused the gun to go off, you are the murderer, Brockington," she said as calmly as she could. She knew she had pulled the trigger and she was glad, but she had sense enough to realize that this influential young lord who stood before her must be implicated. Kitty still held the gun pointing toward Brockington. He proceeded to be very sick on the carpet.

"Are you all right, *acushla?*" she asked Terry softly, compassion almost choking her. He nodded, then blurted, "Only he touched me." He began to cry again.

"God! Please try to be calm and tie him up for me. I'll send Mr. Hobson for the doctor."

"Let me get dressed, at least," begged Brockington, pathetically.

"I caught you naked, and naked you'll remain until I'm done with you."

She knew this would keep him at a disadvantage, for once he got the upper hand she would just be the servant girl, and he would be the ruthless lord.

"Terry, go along to my room and I'll just see if I can find you some brandy." She reentered the dead man's bedroom. Without looking at the corpse she crossed to a side table and took one of the decanters from it. As she passed in front of Brockington, now tied securely to the chair, she threw him a look of contempt.

"I didn't hurt Terry," he pleaded.

"You were waiting your turn," she said with deadly calm. "I never understood why he married me until this moment. It was so he could have Terry, wasn't it?"

"Before anyone sees me, please clean this awful mess," he begged, indicating where he had been sick.

She gave him an incredulous look. "Me? Mop up your vomit? Not bloody likely!" and she stalked out with the brandy.

When the elderly country doctor arrived, Kitty took him upstairs and led him into her own bedchamber, where Terrance was awaiting them. Without any preliminary explanation or beating about the bush she said, "My young brother has been assaulted, Doctor. Will you kindly examine him and see if there is anything you can do for him?"

The doctor was shocked. "My dear young lady, is it necessary that you should have been informed of such unsavory goings on? Kindly leave us and I will attend the patient."

She bit back a cutting retort. After all, she wanted this man on her side. It wasn't too long before the doctor emerged. Once again he hesitated. "I must know, Doctor, I am responsible for him. Please be plain with me."

"There will be no permanent physical damage, I am glad to say. He is in shock. A couple of days' rest and if you don't treat him as if he were a leper, he should do very nicely. Who did this thing to him?''

''My husband,'' she said quietly.

''He should be shot!'' he stormed.

''We are in agreement. I'm afraid there's more, Doctor. Would you come this way?''

They entered the room and Dr. Fielding staggered back at the sight before him. ''God in Heaven, what's going on here?'' he demanded.

Brockington began to babble something incomprehensible and the doctor looked to Kitty for an explanation.

''I will tell you exactly what happened, Doctor, and it will be the *truth,*'' she stressed. ''I was awakened in the middle of the night by a cry of distress. It sounded like my brother, but he and my husband were away in London. I took my gun with me for protection while I investigated. I found this man and my husband raping my brother. I know there is a word for men like them, but I do not know what it is.''

''They are pederasts,'' the doctor said sharply.

''Brockington here tried to wrestle the gun from me and it went off accidentally, killing my husband. He insists it was my fault, and I could insist it was his fault, but the truth of the matter is that we are both equally to blame.''

There was a hushed silence. Then the doctor went over to Simon's body and carefully examined it.

''I'm Lord Brockington. Tell this woman to untie me immediately,'' he demanded.

Kitty went over to him and undid the ropes that held him. He immediately began an undignified scramble into his clothes. The doctor shook his head. ''This is highly irregular, highly irregular!'' he stressed. ''You must realize I can't just sign a death certificate. I wouldn't know whether to call it 'accidental' or 'death by misadventure,' but that's beside the point. The police should be called.''

Brockington protested, "Good God, man, we can't afford a scandal like that. My father could ruin you," he threatened.

Kitty said, "I will abide with your decision, Doctor, whatever it is."

He looked at them for a few minutes, considering different possibilities and then said, "The best I can do is consult my colleague, who is the coroner for this district. Whether or not he will call an inquest, I don't know. I'll be around tomorrow and bring Dr. Grant-Stewart."

"Otis Grant-Stewart?" asked Brockington. "Why, he's a friend of my father's!" Kitty could see his confidence returning and tried not to panic. These upper-crust types would close ranks and she would be destroyed.

"Thank you, Dr. Fielding. I appreciate your coming so promptly," she said as she showed him out.

Kitty felt drained of emotion. Mrs. Hobson helped her to lift Simon. Strangely, the bullet hole looked small, there was very little blood, but when they lifted his body, they saw that the back of his head had been blown to pieces. She washed him, then dressed him in the clothes he had worn in London. She felt physically numb, but her mind raced wildly, filled with thoughts of Patrick, Terrance, Simon, Brockington, the doctor and the coroner who would arrive tomorrow. Her mind went blank for a moment and she admonished herself, "Think! What will you say when the doctor arrives? When Brockington and Grant-Stewart put their heads together, I'll be the poor Irish scapegoat." She realized the odds against her were overwhelming. She was cynical enough to realize they would have much in common and she would be the outsider. Even if they weren't acquaintances, it was two men against one woman, and she didn't stand much chance.

She took a tea tray upstairs and went into the bedroom that Lord Brockington used on his frequent visits. He was lying on the bed, staring up at the ceiling. "I thought you probably could use a cup of tea. I know I could.'' She tried to keep the weariness out of her voice. She sipped the tea and began softly, ''Does your father know that you are a . . . a pederast?''

He looked at her defiantly, but when she steadily held his gaze, his eyes slid away and he shook his head ''no.''

''This will hurt him very much, won't it?'' she said gently. ''If I were you, I think I'd get across the Channel until all this blows over. I've got some money I could let you have,'' she offered.

Her generosity awoke his first sense of shame. ''I can't leave you to face the music alone.''

''I'll be truthful with you, Brocky. We're in one hell of a mess, but I think I'd be better off alone. If they think you've sloped off and left me to it, they'll only see that I'm female and helpless.'' Then she added as a clincher, ''I've got a hundred pounds you can have if you go tonight.''

''Get it!'' he shouted. ''You don't mind if I borrow a mount, do you?'' Relief washed over her in great waves as the fingers of the dawn crept up the darkened sky. She looked down and was amazed to see that her clothes were blood-stained and crumpled. She had to force her legs to move. She must bathe and change before the worthy doctors arrived.

They drove up in a carriage at midmorning and Kitty greeted Dr. Fielding with an air of innocent trust. She felt Otis Grant-Stewart scrutinize her from head to foot. She looked pleadingly at him and her mouth began to tremble. ''Doctor, Lord Brockington has fled and taken all my money with him.''

He looked startled. ''If that is true, you should have called the police. I told you last night the police ought to be called in.'' She gave a pleading little look to Dr. Grant-Stewart. ''But the police would cause such a nasty scandal. I don't wish to protect Lord Brockington, but I was thinking of his father.''

''Quite right, my dear, quite right,'' said Dr. Grant-Stewart. He cleared his throat and murmured, ''Ah, Dr. Fielding has quite graphically explained what was going on here last night, I just want you to tell me about the shooting,'' he prompted.

''Thank you, Doctor. I was holding the gun and I was so shocked by what I saw that Lord Brockington easily took the gun away from me. As he did so, it went off and killed my husband.''

Dr. Fielding gave her a quick glance at this alteration in her testimony.

''Could I see the body?'' asked Dr. Grant-Stewart.

''Of course, Doctor.'' She turned to Dr. Fielding with a smile. ''Would you have another look at my brother, Doctor? You did such a wonderful job of calming him down last night, I don't know what I would have done without you.'' He nodded and left them. Kitty took Dr. Grant-Stewart to her husband's bedroom. He gave the body only a cursory examination and Kitty looked at him with tears in her eyes. ''When I think of all the fun they used to have. Parties every weekend; all the young men from the best London families. I'm afraid it will be very messy when you reveal all the details.''

He cleared his throat and said, ''I think it would save you a great deal of pain, my dear, if I just signed the death certificate. We'll put down 'accidental death.' Inquisitive people will assume it was a hunting accident, and I see no reason why you should disabuse them of this idea. I'll make the burial arrangements for tomorrow.''

At last she could think about sleep. She looked at the bed. The last time she had slept there, she had been clasped safe in Patrick's embrace. God! How long ago that seemed. She sank into the bed and pulled the covers over her head to blot out the daylight. She slept for the next twenty hours. She awoke to find Terry shaking her. *"Acushla,* are you all right?"

She looked up into worried brown eyes, smiled sleepily and said, "I thought you were Patrick. As soon as the funeral is over, we're going to Julia's in London. When Patrick returns from America, we'll be married."

"Are you certain he promised marriage, Kitty?" he asked dubiously.

"Of course he did!" she said, stiffening. "What are you getting at?"

"Well, it's easy to promise marriage to a woman who has a husband. I've done it myself. You just keep promising, 'when you're free,' knowing full well she may never be free!"

"It wasn't like that!" Kitty protested. "He swore he would get me free and I really believe that Patrick would have killed Simon if there were no other way," she said earnestly.

Terry chuckled rather unpleasantly. "Well, love, in that case it seems like you've saved him the trouble. You've done the dirty work, so to speak, and like all the bloody wealthy masters of this world, he's managed to keep his hands clean."

"I thought you admired Patrick," Kitty said in bewilderment.

"Oh, I do admire him, but that doesn't mean I'm blind."

"Underneath, he is exactly the same as us—black Irish," she insisted.

He laughed scornfully. "What a bloody recommendation! Think back carefully, Kitty, to your hours in bed together. Make sure he used no slipping-out phrases. Did he promise or didn't he? Do you have a contract with his conscience?"

She blushed at his words but said with a finality that settled his doubts and her own, "We exchanged vows."

Simon was buried in the same grave as his father. Kitty listened dry-eyed to the curate recite the funeral service, "I am the resurrection and the life. . . ." She leafed absently through her prayer book, and two sentences stood out and screamed their words at her: "Thou shalt not kill" and "The wrath of God is upon him that committeth adultery." She had done both!

She looked up and saw two strange men standing a short distance away. She was surprised to find they followed her. They were creditors! She was astonished. How had word gotten to the city so quickly? She fobbed them off with a tale of a will being read and assured them if they would return tomorrow they would be paid what was owed them. Half of the money Patrick had given her was already gone, so she was determined that not another penny would slip through her fingers to pay off Simon's obligations. Brandywine had been gambled away long ago and Brockington had taken the only other decent horse in the stables. "Terry, we'll have to take it in easy stages by the looks of these poor animals."

He reassured her, "They don't look much, but they won't let us down. Neither one of us is a heavyweight."

"It will be good to see Barbara again," mused Kitty.

"Barbara?" Terry went white.

"Yes, of course. She's staying with Julia while Patrick is in America."

Kitty knew that Barbara was crazy about Terrance, but realized wisely he was feeling very unclean at the moment and could not contemplate a romance with the innocent young girl who obviously adored him. Kitty changed the subject quickly and prayed his sensitivity would lessen as time passed.

* * *

With every mile she traveled closer to London, the hope
grew that she would be in time to catch Patrick before he left.
How marvelous it would be to tell him of the horror she had
gone through and let him take over and comfort her. A longing grew within her that she had never experienced before,
and it grew until it obsessed her. She wore a thin black muslin dress. It was a poor excuse for a mourning gown—the
neck was low enough to expose the rise of her breasts—but it
was the only thing that came close to observing the strict
rules laid down for a widow. As they rode through the London streets, Kitty felt as shabby and strange as the day she
and Terry had arrived on the wagon in Bolton. Things really
were not so different now. Everything she owned was in one
pathetic bundle, and still she had no home of her own to go
to. She straightened her back and knew at least she had hope
to cling to. She had a purse full of money, and maybe, just
maybe, Patrick still would be at Cadogen Square.

They left the horses at the stable and walked up the steps
to the front door. The butler, usually so stiff and proper,
broke into a smile when he saw her. "Miss Kitty, welcome
back. Miss Barbara and the mistress will be home any minute. Make yourselves comfortable in the library, and I'll
serve you some tea." He hesitated. "You won't be alone;
there's someone else waiting in the library. . . ." Kitty
needed no further words. She dropped her bag and ran
breathlessly down the hall to the library. With his broad back
and dark head, the library's occupant didn't hear her enter
until she cried out, "Patrick! Thank God you're still here!"
She ran toward him with arms outstretched. Sir Charles
Drago turned from the fireplace to see the most beautiful girl
he had ever seen. At the sight of his face, a look of unbeliev-
ing dismay came into her eyes. Her legs turned to water and
she knew she was going down into a vortex from which there

was no escape. She knew she was too late! The walls closed in on her, and the floor rose up to hit her in the face.

Charles sprang forward instantly and caught her in his arms. She was in a dead faint and as he gazed at the lovely mouth, drooping just inches below his own, saw the black lashes shadowed on the creamy pallor of her face and felt the soft body relax against his, he felt the stirrings of desire. He was completely surprised at his physical reaction, as he hadn't been able to achieve this state for over two years, and he had greatly feared that that part of his life was completely finished.

Charles looked helplessly at Terrance and said, "Why did she faint? Is she ill?"

Terry said quietly, "We buried her husband only yesterday. I'm afraid it's all been too much for her."

Charles was startled. The girl didn't seem old enough to be a wife, let alone a widow.

At that moment Julia and Barbara entered the library. Julia cried, "Sir Charles, how lovely to see you again. Good Lord, what's happened?"

Barbara cried, "Oh, it's Kitty!" and looked helplessly toward Terrance for an explanation.

Charles said, "The poor child has fainted and I don't even know who she is."

Julia, who had been expecting Kitty for days, said carefully, "She's Kathleen, our Irish cousin, and this is her brother, Terrance. Put her here on the sofa, Charles. Barbara, get some brandy. Whatever can be the matter with her?"

Once again Terrance said, "There was a shooting accident. We buried Simon yesterday."

"Good God, no wonder she's ill," said Julia.

"I think she's coming round," said Charles, rubbing Kitty's hands and looking at her anxiously. She opened her eyes and looked into his kind face. She could tell he was genuinely worried.

"Excuse me, I'm very sorry to be so much trouble. I thought you were Patrick, and then when you turned round I was so surprised to see it was someone else, I made a shocking display of myself," apologized Kitty.

"Not so, my dear. We offer our sincere sympathy for the loss of your husband. It's delayed shock. Are you feeling better now?"

"You are very kind," she whispered, and thought, What a gentle man, and how strong his hands are.

Barbara gave her the glassful of brandy and said, "Oh, Kitty, Patrick sailed yesterday. You've missed him, but you must rest and get well and he'll be back with us before your mourning period is even over."

"So Patrick's gone to America again, has he? Then I've missed him too," Charles said regretfully.

Julia, very conscious of Sir Charles Drago's position, said, "I had no idea you were in England. Is your governorship of St. Christopher's over?"

"No, I'm afraid I have another year to serve before I can come home to stay. Unfortunately I returned because my father was dying. We buried him two days ago in Ireland."

"I'm so sorry, Sir Charles," said Julia.

"Oh, your Grace, that makes you the new Duke of Manchester!" cried Barbara.

"If you ladies will excuse me, I know you are wishing me at the ends of the earth at this moment. I'll call again tomorrow to see how the lass is," and he gave Kitty a meaningful look.

As soon as he was gone, Kitty insisted on getting up. "I'm sorry I was a bother, but I feel perfectly fine now."

"Patrick insisted I put you in his room when you arrived, so up you go and stay out of my way until dinner. I'm in a

wretched mood. I have a million things on my mind, and
Charles Drago has to pick today to pay a call on us. I'll tell
you one thing, Kitty: I should have married that man who
was here today instead of that idiot I saddled myself with. I
could have been a duchess today—just think of it, a duchess!''

"Julia . . . about Simon,'' Kitty began, but Julia held up
her hand imperiously.

"Not one word. I don't know what you and Patrick have
cooked up between you, and I don't want to know. This is
Patrick's house, and I have no doubt you'll be mistress of it
when he returns. Until then, make yourself at home. You
know you are one of the family, so I shan't treat you like a
guest, but for God's sake don't involve me in this business
about Simon!''

"Where's Terry disappeared to?'' asked Kitty to change
the subject.

Barbara answered, "He's taken his things to the room over
the stables. I told him he would be more comfortable in the
house, but he would rather be around the horses than three
women, I think.''

When Kitty was alone in Patrick's room, she opened his
closet and touched all his clothes. She held a velvet coat
sleeve against her cheek and whispered, "Wherever you are
at this moment, my love, I hope you are thinking of me.''
She gazed into the mirror that had held his reflection so
often, and after a few moments' concentration she conjured
up his image so lifelike, she reached out her hand to touch
the crisp black tendrils of hair. She could see the blue
shadow that appeared on his jawline when he hadn't shaved.
Depending on his mood, his mouth could be cruel, arrogant,
sensual or curve into an unbelievably sweet smile in a tender
moment. When she felt tears well up, she quickly turned

from the mirror. The bed dominated the room, just as Patrick would have done if he had been there. She realized she felt a sensual pleasure in sleeping in his bed, which provoked thoughts of erotic fantasies fulfilled and those yet to come.

Chapter 17

Kitty was awakened with flowers from Sir Charles Drago, accompanied by a note that begged her to drive out with him at eleven. When she entered the breakfast room Julia accidentally broke her cup and saucer and shouted, "Blast everything!"

Kitty spoke up quickly, "Sit down. I'll get you another cup of coffee."

Julia shouted, "Goddamn that man to hell!"

Kitty, at a loss said, "Do you mean your husband?"

"Yes, God rot him! I think I'm breeding again. He did it on purpose!"

A housemaid came to see what damage had been done and to clean up the mess. "Get out! Can't you see I'm having a private conversation? Tell them in the kitchen to stop cooking that bacon immediately. The smell permeates the whole house and makes me feel sick!"

The maid had barely closed the door when Julia continued with her tirade. "I told Jeffrey I wasn't having any more for at least two years. I'm so damned careful! When he demands to sleep with me I absolutely insist he withdraw."

"Withdraw?" asked Kitty, startled. "You don't mean withdraw before . . . before . . ."

"A fat lot of good it would do after!" shouted Julia.

"Oh, but surely that would be distasteful to you both, and besides, you would miss all the . . ."

"Pleasure?" asked Julia sarcastically.

Kitty blushed. "For me it was an indescribable joy."

"Then how in the name of God have you escaped getting caught? It only takes once!"

"Once?" echoed Kitty.

"Don't be so bloody obtuse! Whatever method have you been using?" Julia asked curiously.

Kitty was stunned for a moment. "I have to confess I never thought once about becoming pregnant. I'm ashamed of my ignorance," said Kitty.

"That's how men like to keep us! Selfish to the core. They take their pleasure where they find it, then go off merrily about their own pursuits and we are left to bear the fruit!"

A cold hand gripped Kitty's heart. A wave of dizziness swept over her as she thought of the classic case of the unwed Irish servant girl in trouble by the master. Now that she thought of it, the smell of bacon cooking did definitely produce the symptoms of morning sickness! She fervently wished that she was not going to have a child, but deep down inside she felt such a strong premonition, she knew she was caught.

She excused herself and went upstairs, where she could be alone to think. It had been six weeks since she had last had her menses. How could she have overlooked something so important? She wondered with amazement. She pushed the thought away at once and sought out Barbara.

"I hate black, Barbara. Lend me a pretty dress, will you? His Grace has invited me out for a drive. Tell me what he's like."

"Oh, he's a darling man. He and Patrick are great friends. His wife has been dead for years, so I never met her. I saw a great deal of him when I was a little girl, but he's lived in the tropics the past few years. He's enormously rich, owns lots of houses here in London and estates all over England and Ireland. He'd be a wonderful catch if he weren't so old!" said Barbara ingenuously. Kitty thought privately that he was a very comfortable age; a man you could lean on. She knew she shouldn't consider going driving with a gentleman while she was in mourning, and under no circumstances should she go unchaperoned, but she didn't give a damn for the conventions and knew she never would.

Charles was surprised to see her appear so quickly. His eyes smiled down into hers as he said, "Kathleen, I know this is a sad time for you, but let's try to be happy today?"

"Please let's be comfortable with each other. If I have to keep saying 'your Grace this' and 'your Grace that' the conversation will be so stilted I couldn't bear it. I have a confession to make: I'm not a lady of quality, and I'm absolutely penniless. Now, I can put on airs and graces, but not with you, Charles! Can we be friends?"

He leaned over and kissed her soundly.

Her eyes widened. "Is that what you've been wanting to do ever since we met?"

He nodded "yes."

"My God, all men are alike!" she said and laughed.

"But not all women, thank the Lord. You are unique! There is one kind of woman frightens me to death. Deliver me from society's debutantes. I should know—I was married to one," he said dryly.

They came to a large estate, but the house seemed to have been closed for the season, and the knockers had been removed from the doors. The park stretched out before them with magnificent shade trees, flowering shrubs, arbors, fish ponds and miniature bridges. Beyond the park, the lawns swept down to the river. "Belongs to a friend of mine who's out of the country," he explained.

Kitty knew instinctively it was his.

"It's so green it reminds me of home," she said with a little sigh. She turned to him eagerly. "How is it in Ireland now?"

"Well, it's a bit better. I think they'll have crops this year, but things still are bad," he said sadly.

She took his arm and said, "I'm still homesick for it, though."

"Homesick? Lass, you don't know the meaning of the word. There've been times in the tropics when the heat dances and shimmers off everything and the hours of sunshine seem to go on and on until you think darkness never will fall. I've often looked about me at the jungle gaudiness and thought nature must have gone mad in that part of the world. Just the effort of thinking makes your clothes damp with sweat and your throat always feels parched for just one more rum punch. It's times like that Ireland beckons. For just one hour of its softness a man would trade away his very soul."

"Tell me, Charles: Is it very frightening out on the Atlantic?"

"I can't lie to you, lass. There are times when it can be frightening if you meet up with a gale, but if you avoid sailing during the bad-weather months, why, it's like having a holiday, it's so pleasant."

"How much does it cost?" she asked curiously.

"Well, that depends on where you are going," he said and smiled.

"Say I was sailing from Liverpool to America," she said, pretending to pick a place at random.

"Passage shouldn't cost more than fifty pounds. Of course, if you wanted a private cabin, it would cost more."

"Can a woman book a passage on her own? I mean, would a ship take her without a man?"

"Some would," he conceded.

She decided to change the subject before he became suspicious.

"Has anyone ever told you that you resemble King Charles II?"

He threw back his head and laughed. "Many times! Me and my father before me," he said and winked. "I think it likely there's Stuart blood in us—wrong side of the blanket, of course." Kitty laughed at his aside and he said, "That's the sort of remark I shouldn't be able to make if you were one of these Victorian females who shock easily."

She tossed her head and said, " 'Tis all hypocrisy, anyway. At every social function in London the women compete with each other to see how much of their breasts they can reveal, yet a glimpse of ankle and their reputations would be gone; they'd be fallen women!"

"To show your ankles is to invite seduction." He twinkled at her.

She sighed and said, "If you hadn't said that, I would have taken off my shoes and stockings and gone wading."

He felt a terrible pang of regret at her words, yet he didn't even know if she was being serious or just teasing. They came to a fallen log and Kitty sat down on it and patted the place beside her. He was sitting so close to her he could smell the subtle fragrance of her skin. Once again he felt a tightness in his loins that he knew was more than mere imagination. He looked down at her and said, "You haven't the faintest idea how exciting you are to a man."

"What do you mean?" Her eyes widened.

"I can't tell you without using blunt, explicit language," he smiled.

"Tell me," she urged.

"You are so young, almost still a child, yet you have had experience in the marriage bed. That's a very exciting combination."

Immediately she wished she hadn't pressed him to tell her.

"Well, I asked for that one, but now I shall return to conventional behavior. It's time I returned home, your Grace."

"I've offended you, Kathleen, and I'm sorry. I'll take you home immediately, but you will come driving with me again, won't you?"

She hesitated.

"I've only got a week, Kathleen. Say you will come?"

She relented. "I've enjoyed it as much as you; perhaps more," she said and laughed.

"I doubt that, lass," he said.

When Kitty returned to the house, Julia almost dragged Kitty up to the privacy of her bedroom and began asking questions as soon as the door was closed. "Kitty, you must help me! Who else can I turn to? How can I get rid of this child I'm carrying?"

Kitty was confused. If Patrick had known Julia was thinking of such a course, he would have slapped her silly. If her husband, Jeffrey, knew, he would be incensed. However, Kitty felt it was wrong for a man to impregnate a woman when she didn't want a child. "Julia, I don't know very much about it. I do know that in Bolton the mill women jump off the kitchen table or even deliberately fall down the stairs, but in spite of it, most babies stick, no matter how they try to shake them loose. I knew an old woman who used to perform some obscene operation with a crochet hook, but a lot of girls died from it," said Kitty sadly.

"I know there is something you can buy. It's very expensive, but I have lots of money, Kitty. I need to know the name of it and where it's available. Help me, Kitty!"

"I promise I'll try to find out for you."

* * *

She watched all evening for her brother. "Terry, I have some questions, and I'm wondering if you know the answers."

"I'll try my best, sweet," he answered affably.

"I want to know what that stuff is a woman can take to get rid of a baby, and I want to know if there is any way of protecting yourself from conceiving a child," she plunged in.

"Christ Almighty! That bastard Patrick has got you in the family way." He was livid and snarling with anger.

"He has not!" she denied hotly, knowing full well she was telling a lie. "Terrance Rooney, if I were having a child, I wouldn't be after destroying it! To me it would be a sweet burden."

He sagged to the bed in relief, but then his lips tightened and he said almost primly, "Such subjects aren't for young ladies. I won't speak of them with you."

"Terry, your narrow-mindedness shows up your working-class background!"

"Indeed?" he asked calmly. "Well, a gentleman might discuss things of that nature with you, but only if you were his whore!"

"Forget it. It was only curiosity, anyway. What I really came to say was I'm thinking of going to Patrick in America. I'm free now, so why should we wait to get married?"

His eyes narrowed. "I thought you said he hadn't gotten you in trouble."

She stamped her foot and blurted out, "For God's sake, it's Julia who's with child. Oh, I shouldn't have told you! Now you'll tell Jeffrey and there will be hell to pay."

"Jeffrey's been generous to me, Kitty. He's offered me a job. However, if you really want to go to America, that's what we will do," he offered.

"No, no, love. I want to go alone. Stay and work with

Jeffrey and by the time I return as Mrs. O'Reilly you'll be on your way to making your fortune.''

"I can rave and curse and forbid you, and after it all you'd have your own way no matter what. You're a willful little bitch, Kitty. I pity the man who marries you.'' He laughed and held out his arms to her.

"I must visit Grandada before I go, and by God, when Patrick comes back I'm going to get Swaddy out of that slum, if it's the last thing I do.''

The next day Sir Charles had arranged for a picnic in the countryside. After they had eaten, Charles said, "Do you mind if I smoke, my dear''

"Oh, please do! Do you grow tobacco on your island?''

"Yes, but its main crops are sugar, bananas, coffee and spices. These cigars come from Cuba.''

She watched him light up and said mischievously, "Would you be shocked if I asked you for one?''

He laughed indulgently. "I've seen many women in the islands smoke, so I wouldn't be shocked. I wouldn't advise you to smoke, though. Not because it's unladylike, but because your breath would no longer be sweet, and it would spoil your pretty teeth.''

"Oh! Then I shan't smoke,'' she promised. "Do you own any ships?'' she asked innocently.

"Well, now, not officially. However, at the risk of shocking you, I will admit I've financed a few pirate ships in my time.''

"How exciting! I thought piracy had been outlawed.''

"It has,'' he said dryly. "So has slavery, but sometimes I have to turn a blind eye to that also.''

"Oh, no! I cannot approve of slavery. How could you?'' she asked reproachfully.

He sighed and said, "Well, morally I'm opposed to it too,

lass, but the whole economy of the islands is based on it. You can't run a plantation without slaves. If I enforced the letter of the law, the economic structure would collapse and thousands would starve. So I'm left to choose between two evils, as is so often the case in life.''

"I see," she said sadly. "Patrick is in partnership with a shipowner in Liverpool. I just forget his name, but I think he makes quite a good profit off them."

"Aye, that would be Isaac Bolt. That Patrick has a business head on his shoulders. Profit is his middle name," he said and laughed.

She had gotten the answer to one of her questions easily enough, so she decided to ask him the other questions that were puzzling her. She put her head on one side and regarded him archly. "Sir Charles, you're a man of the world and I'm woefully ignorant of some things. Would you tell me honestly the answers to some rather intimate questions?"

"Well, we've made a habit of being truthful with each other. What do you want to know?"

"Is there a substance you can buy that will rid a woman of a child she is carrying?"

He looked at her for a penetrating moment and asked quietly, "Is it for you, Kathleen?"

She took both his hands into hers in a sort of pledge and looked straight into his eyes. "No, it isn't for me, Charles."

His features relaxed. "Yes, there is then. It's called Penny Royal. You have to buy it from an apothecary shop."

She took a deep breath and said, "And the other thing I want to know is, How can you prevent conceiving a child in the first place?"

"Well for the woman there is a little sponge with a ribbon attached that you put inside before you make love, and for the man there is a linen sheath that he can wear."

"I see! Thank you for being so frank with me, Charles."

His eyes twinkled. "And I suppose that isn't for you either?"

"Well, you have to admit it's useful information for a woman to know," she said and laughed.

"Kathleen, I've only a couple of days left. Would you consider . . ."

She put her hand over his mouth. "Oh, please don't spoil it by asking me to sleep with you," she pleaded.

"Lass, I wouldn't ask that of you. I want you to come with me!"

She shook her head sadly. "It would be a great adventure, but I won't be any man's mistress, Charles."

"I swear, I had nothing so dishonorable in mind. Kathleen, I want you to marry me."

She stared at him in disbelief. "Marry you? My God, that would make me a duchess! No, Charles, they'd never accept me."

"You would be my choice, my lass; they'd accept you," he swore.

"Charles, no one has ever done me a greater honor, but I cannot."

He looked at her sadly. "I understand. It's too soon after your loss. A lass can't replace a young virile husband she loved deeply with a middle-aged man she hardly knows."

She wanted to cry out a denial, but she let the words lie undisputed.

Chapter 18

The weather had suddenly changed, and changed drastically. Summer was over. The wind blew from the north so fiercely and the rain had come down in sheets all night. Autumn was here with a vengeance and the leaves were shedding from the trees by the thousands. Kitty wrapped her cloak about her and stepped out into Cadogen Square. She walked quickly up to Knightsbridge and on past Hyde Park Corner. There was a little man in a cocked hat he had made out of the *Times*. He carried a placard that read: "Less Meat . . . Less Lust." In spite of the biting wind, Kitty stopped to listen for a moment. He equated meat eating with carnal lust and was handing out leaflets advising people to eat more fruit and vegetables and thereby become pure. Kitty bit back a question about rabbits and their breeding abilities and covered a smile with her gloved hand as she hurried along Piccadilly. She turned up Half-Moon Street, with which she was somewhat familiar, and into Shepherd's Market, where she remembered there was a very fancy apothecary shop. As she opened the door a bell rang above her head and an elegant gentleman with a very pronounced Mayfair accent offered to assist her. For a moment she wanted to ask for something else and leave quickly, but her courage didn't quite desert her. She was amazed to hear herself asking for Penny Royal, but she couldn't keep her face from coloring deeply as he gave her a sly, knowing look of sneering condescension. He left her alone while he went into the back of the shop. She waited and waited and would have left without what she came for except her feet wouldn't seem to carry out her wishes. When he finally returned, he was still measuring powders into packets and as she waited patiently he kept casting her knowing glances.

Kitty's Irish was up as she observed his carefully concealed bald spot and expensive clothes. Finally when he handed her a tiny packet and asked for twelve guineas, she knew he had her over a barrel in asking such a ridiculous price. Her pride wouldn't allow her to haggle over the cost, but she couldn't help giving him a setdown. She looked at him blandly and said, "I've heard this stuff is good for baldness," then turned on her heel prettily and departed unruffled but pleased with herself.

"I want a few minutes alone with you, Julia. Will you come up to Patrick's room, where we won't be overheard?"

Julia, intrigued, followed her upstairs.

"Please don't interrupt me until I'm finished, Julia. I've made up my mind to do something which no amount of arguing will change. I'm going to America, to Patrick. I hope to sail next week. I'm a widow now and I see no reason why I should wait months for him to return."

Julia opened her mouth to speak, then closed it again.

"Please don't waste your breath trying to dissuade me."

"Then all I can say is *bonne chance.*" Julia smiled kindly.

"Now then, I have a present for you." Kitty reached into her reticule and handed Julia the packet. Her eyes widened as she realized what Kitty had done for her. Then tears of relief and gratitude mingled and fell down her cheeks. "I've also learned of a simple device to use to prevent conception. I'll write it down for you."

Barbara came running in, breathless with excitement. "Oh, Kitty, Terrance has just told me. I think you're the bravest person in the whole world!"

Kitty started to laugh, almost hysterically. She was quite

willing to bet she was the most terrified person in all London. Her insides were jelly when she thought of the terrifying sea voyage that was ahead of her. Then there was the child. She couldn't even allow her thoughts to wonder what she would do if Patrick would not marry her. An illegitimate child in Victorian England was so sinful its stigma lasted a lifetime. Beyond this was the dark fear of childbirth. Her own mother had died giving birth to Terry and the thought was enough to make her mouth go dry and her knees turn to water.

"I want you to help me pick out some traveling clothes, Barbara. Then maybe we can dine at that new fancy restaurant after the shops close this evening. I don't think Julia is feeling too well, and I think she'd like to be left alone for a few hours."

Kitty bought an amber velvet gown with a square neckline and puffed sleeves. At another shop she purchased a pale green wool with long sleeves and a dark green velvet cloak with a heavy quilted lining. Queen Victoria had set the fashions to disguise her many pregnancies. Kitty was glad of the full skirts, for though she hadn't started to expand yet, they would be useful in the months ahead to camouflage her condition.

Barbara and Kitty didn't return to Cadogen Square until after eight that evening. As soon as Kitty deposited her packages in her room she went along to Julia's bedroom.

"May I come in for a moment?"

Julia's voice rang out, "It worked splendidly, Kitty, but by God I've gone through hell this afternoon. The worst seems to be over but I'm still having awful cramps."

"I think you will have, but I suggest we have the doctor come and have a look at you just to be on the safe side."

"But, Kitty, he'll know!" she protested.

"Very likely he'll have his suspicions, but there isn't a damned thing he can do about it, is there? He can't put it back, can he?"

"But what if he goes to Jeffrey with the story?"

"The best thing is for me to send him a note telling him you've miscarried and we've sent for the doctor. He'll come dashing home from his club or wherever he's gotten to at this time of night, filled with guilt and showering you with sympathy."

"You know a lot about men, don't you, Kitty?" asked Julia with admiration.

"Do I?" wondered Kitty, surprised.

"Please see baby Jeffrey gets to bed without me tonight and send that note off to his father right away. Terrance probably can run him to earth."

While Barbara and Kitty bathed the baby, Kitty observed him closely. He was all O'Reilly, exactly as Patrick must have been. He had a head full of black, silky curls, a very red mouth that was either chortling with laughter or screaming his displeasure with those about him. He was a robust, sturdy baby with all-knowing Irish eyes, and not one speck of his father's blue blood showed up in his physical appearance. She prayed that her own baby would be half as lovely.

The next morning she took a hansom cab to The Swan with Two Necks in Lud Lane. They owned sixty coaches and over a thousand horses. To sit up on top cost three pence per mile, while a seat inside cost five pence. The weather was too miserable for Kitty even to consider an outside seat. The trip from London to Bolton would take twenty-eight hours, with a stop for the night at Leicester. The coachman would expect a tip of at least a shilling, and the guard would want half a crown. Doing mental arithmetic, Kitty allowed five pounds for the trip. The generous amount Patrick had given her had shrunk to such minuscule proportions that Kitty felt guilty. What had seemed like an adventure soon deteriorated into a wearying trial of endurance. The seats were so hard you could get relief only by shifting about, but the passengers were packed so tightly you had to sit still to avoid encroaching on your neighbors. The roads were so bad with the constant downpour that all the passengers had to disembark every time the coach came to a steep hill because the horses couldn't climb and pull in the mud. Although her cloak was sodden and her shoes and stockings wet through, Kitty pitied the horses and felt annoyed at the complaints of the other passengers, most of which came from the men, she noted with contempt. The next morning her clothes still were damp when she embarked at Leicester. The sky was leaden, but at least it had stopped raining. When the coach finally unloaded at the Packhorse Hotel in Bolton, Kitty stumbled and could hardly walk. Resolutely she picked up her bag and walked down the dirty, narrow streets that led to Spake Hazy. It was after dark, but the lamplighters had done their rounds and the gas lights shone their brave yellow along each cobbled street.

After Kitty had been sitting in front of the fire, laughing and chattering for an hour, it was almost as if she had never been away. Everything was the same, except Ada had produced another child and by the looks of her, she was off again. When the household retired, Kitty and Swaddy were able to be private at last.

"Well, my beauty, you're off to America, are you?"

"Patrick promised to marry me, and I don't see the need to wait months and months until he sails home. Do you?"

His eyes twinkled. "Well, lass, if he's been at you, it would be a good idea to get that ring on your finger."

"Grandada, don't reproach me. I've been wildly in love with him since I was a child."

"Couldn't you have satisfied yourself with that young husband you wed?"

"No, I'm afraid not. He married me only because he fell in love with Terry."

"Then he deserved to die. Remember, beauty: no guilt."

Kitty pressed ten pounds into his hand before she curled up for the night.

"Thanks, *acushla*. Make an effort to behave yourself in the future, lass. You have an uncanny knack for getting into scrapes."

She laughed and said, "Patrick will look after me."

He shook his head and thought, "A man would need to wear his jackboots to control you, lass."

It was teatime the next day when Kitty walked past the posh Adelphi Hotel in Liverpool. Inside, waiters in white gloves and frock coats served wafer-thin cucumber and watercress sandwiches to the elite who politely listened to a twenty-five-piece orchestra hidden behind a jungle of foliage. Kitty hurried past and bought a pie from a pieman hawking his wares. Liverpool was peopled with seamen from all over the world, lascars, black men and at least half the population seemed to be Oriental. A large directory on the wall of the Lyver Building told Kitty where Isaac Bolt had his offices. She knocked and walked in. A clerk asked her her business and she told him she wished to speak to Isaac Bolt.

"I'm afraid he's occupied at the moment, ma'am." He hesitated. "His daughters are with him."

"Well, I'm sure if you told him that the sister of his partner, Mr. O'Reilly, was in his waiting room, he would see me," she ventured.

"Oh, I'm pleased to meet you, madame. Mr. O'Reilly is a great favorite around here. I'll tell Mr. Bolt right away that you are here."

She was shown into an office with large, ugly furniture.

Isaac Bolt was in his sixties with graying mutton chop whiskers. The eldest daughter was quite pretty, but the younger one had slightly protuberant eyes with hooded lids. Kitty knew immediately that she was very shrewd. Kitty held out her hand to Isaac Bolt and smiled. "I'm Patrick's sister, Barbara. How do you do, Mr. Bolt?"

"A pleasure, my dear. These are my daughters. Alice is the pretty one, and this is Maude. Maude is the fey one, but what she lacks in beauty she makes up for with brains." He laughed heartily and Maude stood up on tiptoes and whispered something in his ear. "Exactly so, exactly so, Maude. What service may I render you, Miss O'Reilly?"

"I'm going to join Patrick in America. I would like passage to Charleston on the first available ship."

"I do admire an adventuress. Let's see now: Big Jim Harding is sailing tomorrow or the next day. I can issue your tickets right here."

"How much is the passage, Mr. Bolt?"

"Well, let's see now. It's forty pounds, or if you wish a cabin to yourself and first-class service, it's fifty pounds."

"Oh, that's fine," said Kitty, carefully extracting fifty pounds from her purse.

"Are you traveling alone?" he asked with raised eyebrows.

"Yes. You see, my maid took sick on the journey from London, so I left her at our house in Bolton," she improvised quickly.

"I see. Well, just a moment and I'll validate this ticket for you. Now, you must stay with us tonight. We're on our way home now. My girls will be delighted to have you, my dear."

"Ah—well, I was planning to put up at the Adelphi Hotel,'' she lied, ''but you know how they frown on women traveling alone.''

''Just so, my dear, just so.''

Kitty smiled to herself as she sat down to dinner. Boiled meat, boiled potatoes, boiled cabbage. It was all so unappetizing. Kitty realized it was fortunate she hadn't developed a delicate palate. She marveled at Isaac Bolt, who seemed to have the digestion of a horse. When dessert arrived, he exclaimed with relish, ''Ah, spotted dick!''

Kitty laughed aloud, not at the quaint name he had given it, but at the fact that the pudding also was boiled.

After dinner, her father insisted Alice sing for them. He requested all the mawkish, sentimental Irish ballads and Alice delivered them in her high, too-sweet voice, while her father beamed fatuously. The evening seemed endless, until Kitty wished she had spent the night under a hedge. Somehow the evening came to a close.

''I'll take you down to the ship in my carriage in the morning and see you safely aboard. Maude here will show you to a guest room. Breakfast is at seven sharp. Alice, come.''

When they were alone, Maude looked at Kitty and said, ''Excruciating, wasn't it?''

Kitty's lips twitched appreciatively and she came close to liking Maude. On impulse Kitty said, ''When I came into the office today, what did you whisper to your father?''

''I said, 'If that's Patrick's sister, I'm a Chinaman!' ''

Kitty blushed vividly. ''Then why did he let me continue with the deception?''

Maude shrugged. ''Don't worry about Father; his whole life's a deception.'' She jerked her head toward the stairs and said, ''He's having her, you know.''

"You don't mean . . . you can't mean . . . his own daughter? I don't believe it!"

Maude laughed. "Believe it! I'm the youngest of twenty-one children he's had out of four different wives. When the last one died, the family all got together and decided to put a stop to him having droves of wives and children. There's twenty-one of us to divvy up when he goes to that great shipyard in the sky, so Alice was the logical sacrifice."

"But that's unheard of!" said Kitty.

Maude chuckled. "Aye, unheard of, but a common enough practice all the same. Think now, surely you know one or two families where a widower has one of his daughters fill his wife's place?"

"Only socially," protested Kitty.

"Socially and privately," assured Maude.

"Does Patrick know what's going on?" asked Kitty, scandalized.

"I'm certain he doesn't; however, we all could stand on our heads and smoke Indian hemp and he wouldn't show a flicker of interest in us personally. He's all business. In fact, you are a very big surprise to me. I've often wondered about Patrick's woman. I pictured either a toffee-nosed daughter of a peer, or a plain-faced girl as rich as Croesus. I never thought he'd let his heart overrule his head in a million years."

"Well," Kitty said with a laugh, "that's a very pretty compliment. Thank you."

"Save the thanks, lass; you aren't wed yet!"

Chapter 19

Kitty took one look at the captain, Big Jim Harding, and felt terrified. He was a huge man with a barrel chest. He had a full beard of golden curls, but his head was shaved bald. When he raised his voice to shout orders to the men, it could be heard from one end of the ship to the other. His laugh was full-bellied and his mouth showed the glint of gold teeth. "Jemmy! Jemmy! Take this lady to the small cabin next to mine. Ma'am, I'll be sailing on the evening tide, I'd be obliged if you can keep to your cabin until after we sail." He nodded a curt dismissal and Kitty followed the cabinboy below decks. The cabin was small with a neat wooden bunk built into the wall. There was a tall sea chest, which doubled as a table with a stool beside it. There was no cupboard or wardrobe for her clothes, but only wooden pegs on the walls. The floor was bare boards without covering, and the room boasted only three things to add to her comfort: an oil lamp, a tin bowl for washing and a chamber pot. Kitty was quite pleased with the cabin. It smelled salty fresh. The floorboards had obviously been scrubbed with seawater, and she was thankful the bed was clean. When she lay down on the bunk to rest, the gentle rocking motion of the water lulled her to sleep. She awoke when Jemmy brought her supper. The food was good. When she finished there was a knock on the door. Captain Harding entered and filled the room with his presence. Kitty gave a little gasp of fear, at which he laughed. His presence was so overpowering in the small cabin, Kitty could hardly breathe. He was so male, it was tangible in the air.

"Are you Isaac Bolt's woman?" he asked bluntly.

"Of course not!" she said angrily. "I'm no one's woman!"

"Then how's your sex life?" he said and grinned.

She gasped. "Captain Harding, how dare you show me such disrespect?"

He threw back his head and laughed. "Go on with you, I'm just pulling your leg! Don't you think I know how Victorian girls are brought up in England? Damned unnatural. All them clothes you wear from your earholes to the floor. I tell you, seductions have become damned difficult, so take that worried look off your face," he said with a laugh.

"I assure you, Captain Harding, I never . . ."

"I'll bet you never," he said, grinning. "You don't know what you're missing. Why, do you know, in certain parts of the world the young women run about naked?"

She was sure he enjoyed shocking her, so she said repressively, "Please, Captain, I should like to be alone. Was there something you wished of me?"

"Call me Big Jim. Do you know why they call me Big Jim?"

She paled visibly.

"No, no, it's not what you're thinking! Mine's no bigger than the next man's." He laughed, then winked. "It's just harder!"

"Good night, Captain Harding," and she blushed over his name.

After he had gone, she found that she was trembling. "Such a coarse, uncouth man. So vulgar and . . . and . . . male!" she said to herself. She feared she would be raped in her bed before the night was over, and lay for hours not daring to close her eyes. She was awakened by a knock on the cabin door.

She was amazed to find it was morning. She let Jemmy in

with her breakfast and said, "I was afraid it was the captain."

"You are never afraid of the captain, are you, ma'am? He's a wonderful man!"

"Yes, I am afraid. He's so big and coarse and vulgar. He scares me out of my wits with that shaved head of his."

"Oh, his looks are deceivin', all right. I could see where he'd frighten you if you met him in a dark alley, but once you get to know him, he's a real gentleman."

"Gentleman? That's not how I'd describe him! What do you mean?"

"You should see him in port when he walks down the street. If he meets a little girl, he gives her a flower; a little lad, and he hands out money."

"Really?" she asked.

"That's the captain. Now, eat hearty before it's stone cold!"

Kitty pulled up the little stool to the table and cracked open her boiled egg. The tea began to slosh about in the cup and splashed over into the saucer. The plate slid about on the tray, and the tray slid about on the table. The table seemed to be heaving up and down, and all at once her stomach was keeping time with it. She moaned and covered her mouth. She feared she was going to be sick, but as her insides churned miserably for such an interminable length of time, she began to fear that she wasn't going to be sick and obtain blessed relief. She arose and as she moved toward her bunk, the floor went up under her right foot and down under her left. At last she vomited into the washbowl. All seemed well for a moment. She wiped her mouth on the towel and leaned against the wall. She began rolling with the ship, and the nausea arose again. Acid, stinging her throat; sour smell assaulting her nostrils, she vomited again. She shuddered at her own nastiness and sank down upon her bunk.

Jemmy took away her dirty bowl, ignoring her protests that she could clean up her own mess. She drank a little water and lay down again. The seasickness was with her all the next day. She refused all food but kept down some water.

Late in the afternoon, Captain Harding came into her cabin. "You need some fresh air. Come on, now, out of there and get up on deck."

"Please, just leave me," she begged feebly.

"No chance. You are going up if I have to carry you."

She got off the bed under her own steam. She went slowly up the steps to the deck, and as she did so Captain Harding below her was given a delicious display of ankles. He reached up to caress one of them, but Kitty felt too wretched even to protest. The brisk wind smashed her in the face! She struggled to the rail and began to retch. In an instant he was holding her. One arm secured her safely, while the other held her stomach rigid and miraculously her guts stopped trying to turn themselves inside out. He massaged her knotted stomach muscles until they began to relax. Even though she felt so sick, she didn't want any man seeing her vomit. As she looked up at him, she saw his mouth curved with compassion and was very thankful for his help. She heard him murmur, *"Pauvre petite."* She thought vaguely that he was too uncultured to speak French.

"Now," he said briskly, "once around the deck. Take my arm. I wouldn't want you to be swept overboard."

The entire crew leered at her as she made her way along the deck. They looked more like criminals than sailors. One man was standing so close that she knew she would have to walk around him if she was to avoid brushing up against him. Jim Harding's arm shot out and the man was sprawled on the deck. Kitty noticed the captain had fists like hams, and the impact had made a sickening thud. Not one word was exchanged.

He searched her face for some sign of color, but although the wind whipped her cloak and hair about, her pallor was almost ethereal. The protective urge soared in his breast as he bent his head to caution her, "Never walk alone, day or night. Never forget to secure your cabin door."

She nodded her understanding, afraid to open her lips. He feared she would faint, but at last they had circled the deck and he led her down to her cabin. He went into his own cabin and returned with wine. "Drink this, slowly now. It will stay down better than water, and it will restore you. Good girl! Now then, into bed with you and sleep the clock round. I'll have Jemmy bring you dry biscuit to nibble on; that won't make you queasy." He turned swiftly to the door and bade her, "Lock this after me."

She whispered "Thank you" so low she wondered if he had heard.

It was into the second week before her seasickness departed. She kept to her cabin unless Captain Harding was free to take her up on deck. Sometimes in the evenings he would invite her to dine with him, and after interminable days of her own company, she was glad to do so. Her eyes widened in surprise the first time she had dined in his cabin. Snowy, starched cloth and napkins, tall silver candlesticks, heavy lead crystal goblets and Sèvres china graced his table. The captain himself was attired in a very formal dark suit and stiff shirt, which made him look uncomfortable rather than elegant. However, he had done it for her and she was glad she had worn the pale green woolen dress and the dark green velvet cloak. Watching her, he said, "The eye also dines."

Kitty soon discovered that he wanted nothing more than someone who would listen to him. When he was crude and used thinly veiled innuendos to shock her, she serenely ignored his words and pretended she hadn't heard them. She looked at him often now and wondered how she could ever have thought him ugly. His golden beard was magnificent, and when he smiled, tanned, crinkled lines gathered about the startling blue eyes. Proximity had turned strangers into friends. He loved nothing better than to sit with her, spinning yarns of his voyages, especially the fights which pointed out his physical strength.

"Guess how much I measure about the chest?" he challenged.

She hid a smile and guessed a deliberately small forty-two inches.

"Ha! Fifty! More if I expand it. You don't believe me. Go! Go on, fetch your tape measure and I'll prove it to you."

There was nothing to do but get the tape measure. Then he insisted she measure his biceps. Enormous!

He said now, "Did I ever tell you about the time I was in the fanciest brothel in the world?"

She ignored his coarse talk.

At other times he quoted poetry or Shakespeare. Once he intrigued her by speaking at length of a book he had been reading.

"It's called *Ecstatic Voyage*. It was written in 1656 by a philosopher called Athanasius Kircher. He went on a celestial voyage to the planets. Venus was the best place he visited. Its air was perfumed with amber and musk, where beautiful young angels sang and danced while strewing flowers about. I've seen places like that, Kitty. He could be describing Ceylon."

"What about the sun? I love the sun," said Kitty, listening raptly.

"The sun is inhabited by angels of fire who swim in seas of light round a huge volcano. I've seen places like that in the South Seas. Saturn is full of evil spirits who spend their

time meting out divine justice to the souls of the wicked."
The lines crinkled around his eyes. "Genius or crackpot?
Who's to say? Not me, Kitty, not me."

She looked at him and pinpointed his attraction. He was a
paradox. So coarse on the outside; so fine within.

"Are you married, Jim?" she asked.

"I was once," he said reflectively. "She was unfaithful to
me. She liked to go dancing. She picked up with this fellow
who took her dancing."

"Dancing with him doesn't mean she was unfaithful," she
said gently.

"Oh, aye, she was. I followed them one night and copped
him with his pants down! I half killed him. The next day they
found him on the high road. They thought he'd been run over
by the mail coach. I don't miss her, she was a whore, but I
miss my children unbearably."

She looked at him with compassion and saw that he was
crying.

During the second month out they ran into a hurricane.
Jemmy came into Kitty's cabin and found her huddled in a
corner.

"The captain ordered me below till it blows over. I know
I'd be safe enough up there, but Captain Harding's afraid I'm
such a lightweight, I'd get swept overboard."

They sat in the cabin for over an hour and finally Kitty
could stand it no longer. "I've got to go up and see what's
going on. I can't stay below like a rat."

"It's not safe up there, ma'am, you have no idea what it's
like," he shouted over the roar of the storm.

Kitty opened the cabin door and crept up toward the deck.
Her eyes opened in amazement as a wall of water as high as a
mountain towered above them, while the ship seemed to be
down at the bottom of a deep valley. Suddenly, without

warning, everything switched positions and the ship was perched on the precipice of a mountainous wave, and a gorge opened up in the sea below them and threatened to engulf the ship once it plunged from its great height. Kitty was rooted to the spot, too terrified to move. A terrific crack like thunder rent the air, and the mast fell amid shouts and screams. The bloodcurdling screams continued until a gunshot rang out. Kitty scurried like a rat back to the cabin.

After the storm, when the sea was calm again, Jemmy went to see what the damage was. He came back to tell Kitty the mast had fallen on one of the crew, and the captain had shot him to put him out of his misery.

"My God, how could he shoot down a man in cold blood?" she demanded.

"He had to. His legs were gone, he was almost cut in half!"

The captain locked himself in his cabin for three days.

On the third morning Kitty took the captain's breakfast tray from the cabinboy and after a perfunctory tap on the door, she plunged through the doorway with a confidence she did not really feel. Big Jim sat on the edge of his bunk with a brandy hangover. He swiftly averted his eyes from the tray of food and said, "Get shut of that, for starters!"

Without a word she put it outside the door and reentered. "Are you all right, Jim?"

"My mouth tastes like I've been sucking on a shepherd's stocking." He grimaced. He hauled himself across to the washstand. He looked in the mirror and said, "Christ! My eyes look like two piss holes in the snow!"

Kitty's lips twitched. The Irish could be vulgar, but not one had quite the coarse touch that Big Jim Harding lent to a phrase. She knew she could leave him now and everything would return to normal.

Dismay clutched Kitty's heart when she discovered her

money was missing. She went up on deck and accosted the captain in front of his men. He could have cursed her and ordered her below, or delivered a stinging slap to silence her tongue, but instead he swept her up into the air, planted her firmly with a kiss and carried her below to his cabin.

"Filthy, thieving bastards!" she shouted. "I should have known something like this would happen!" she screamed.

He eyed her appreciatively as she spat and fumed, cursed and threatened.

"Are you finished? Then listen to me. When a woman comes aboard a ship, traveling alone, the first thing she should do is choose the biggest, strongest sailor of the lot and he will protect her."

"In return for certain favors!" she spat.

"Kitty, everything in life must be paid for," he said quietly. "Now, the biggest, strongest sailor aboard is myself. Be my woman, Kitty?" He took her hands in his and bent to kiss her full on the mouth. It was a nice kiss; a good kiss. His lips were firm and dry, his soft beard brushed her cheek gently. His eyes were kind, his aroma was pleasant, his hands gentle, yet she pulled away and said, "Please don't force me! I'm still a maiden," she lied. "If you force me, you'll lose your job," she threatened.

His eyes narrowed. "Who is your man?"

"Patrick O'Reilly," she whispered.

The captain threw back his head and laughed. "I'd do more than lose my job, I'd lose my life, girl! The O'Reilly has sailed with me, and I have his measure. Kitty, what I feel for you is love, not lust. If you've chosen the O'Reilly to be your man, I'll send you to him untouched." His eyes sparkled with mischief as he held her purse and money aloft. "Just for safekeeping and the hope of a reward, you understand." He held it too high for her to reach until she gave him the kiss he wanted.

* * *

That night, as she lay in her bunk, she admitted to herself
that she was tempted. She realized you could feel different
kinds of love for different people. With Patrick it was special,
wild, passionate. It was all highs or lows, no in-betweens.
Ecstasy or hell, pleasure or pain. With Jim Harding it was so
disconcerting to have a man who looked ferocious enough to
kill you, but who put you on a pedestal and worshiped you.

He set himself the task of amusing her, and she really did
love him for it. They had been at sea so long, cut off from the
rest of the world, they had formed an attachment for each
other. When the weather was bad, Jim did everything from
steadying her with his strong hands to making her laugh so
she would forget her fears. As the sun began to get warmer,
Kitty's skin darkened into a healthy tan. Her baby was beginning to show, and though she cherished it in private and
spoke to "him" quite often, when she went up on deck, she
concealed her stomach with her large cloak, and when she
took supper with Jim, she was always careful to drape a
shawl about her.

One night after dark, one of the seamen grabbed her. She
managed to tear herself away and run like someone de-
mented. She crashed into Captain Harding, who led her to
her cabin to wipe away her tears and still her frantic pulse.
He held her securely and murmured soothing words until her
tears stilled and she began to relax.

In a quiet voice Jim began to quote Shelley's "Love's
Philosophy":

> The fountains mingle with the river
> And the rivers with the ocean,
> The winds of heaven mix forever
> With a sweet emotion;
> Nothing in the world is single,

All things by a law divine
In one another's being mingle—
Why not I with thine?

See the mountains kiss high heaven
And the waves clasp one another;
No sister-flower would be forgiven
If it disdain'd its brother;
And the sunlight clasps the earth
And the moonbeams kiss the sea—
What are all these kissings worth,
If thou kiss not me?

When their lips sought and found each other it was the most natural thing in the world. His arms were both strong and gentle, his lips tender and firm. His hands were sure, his touch magically arousing. It felt so natural to go to a reclining position, where they could lie in each other's arms. Inevitably, Jim's large body covered Kitty as he rolled her onto her back. The child within her turned over and "quickened" at that moment and she was swept with such a sudden wave of nausea that, groaning uncontrollably, she tried to sit up. Jim immediately sprang up, thinking he had hurt her. Kitty wasn't quick enough. Before she could struggle upright, she had begun to vomit. It covered her dress and even the bed where they had been lying. Jim fumbled with the lantern in the darkness, finally managing to illumine Kitty's miserably huddled figure in a corner of the bunk.

"Please, Jim, go away and leave me. I don't want you to see me like this."

He waved away her pleas with an impatient hand and briskly poured water into her washbowl and brought over a fresh towel. He took hold of the soiled dress and took it off over her head. Kitty was too weak to protest and allowed herself to be undressed like a rag doll.

"Sweetheart, you're with child! Why didn't you tell me?"

She shook her head miserably and began to retch again.

"Hush, now; hush, lass," he murmured as he washed away the filth. He found a clean nightdress and slipped it over her head.

"You can't sleep in this bunk until it's been stripped and cleaned. Come on, sweetheart, I'll carry you to my bed. You can't stay here. It stinks!" He put a glass of wine to her lips and slipped her into his bed. He couldn't have treated her with more loving care had she been his child. In that moment she loved him with all her heart. He bade her rest and went off with his incredible energy to strip and scour her cabin. No sooner was her bunk made up clean and the air made sweet-smelling again than she fouled Jim's cabin as she had her own. With infinite compassion he washed her again, changed her nightgown and carried her back to her own cabin. Each time she awoke, Jim's comforting presence was beside her.

In the early hours of the morning he asked, "Are you feeling better, lass?"

"Yes, Jim. I'm sorry about what happened," she said, embarrassed. She awoke later to find Jemmy taking his place. He looked at her kindly and said, "Have your ideas about the captain changed, ma'am?"

"Jemmy, that man's a saint."

He grinned. "Don't let him hear you say that. He prefers to think he's the devil."

She smiled a secret smile. "We know differently."

After breakfast, Captain Harding returned and sat on the edge of her bunk. "Why didn't you tell me about the babe, lass? Your little belly looked so pretty, all rounded and swollen with the sweet burden you carry. I'm fond of you, lass, but it just wasn't meant to be. You've found your man and

I'm not one to come between a man and his woman. Still, it would have been an adventure—two Gypsies sailing the seven seas. I'll think of it on lonely nights.''

She reached up and touched his face where his beard curled softly. ''I'll think of it too, Jim.''

''Rest now. We'll sight land tomorrow.''

Chapter 20

Patrick had arrived in Charleston a full month before Kitty. He quickly arranged for the disposal of his profitable cargo and so was free to make plans to fill the ship with goods to take back to Liverpool. He would buy cotton from Bagatelle, travel to Wilmington to pick up tobacco grown in Virginia, then sail to Philadelphia and New York to the branch offices of the Hind Food Company, which was expanding faster than he had ever dared hope. He purchased a carriage and a fine team and arranged for a young seaman, Rob Wilson, to drive him to the Carolina plantation.

When they arrived at Bagatelle, Patrick was surprised to find that Jacquine had not remarried. He couldn't believe that a woman of her passions could lead a celibate life, so kept his eyes peeled for evidence of her bedfellow. Surprisingly, he found none. He took young Rob aside and spoke seriously to him. "There's an extra fifty pounds in it for you, Rob, if you stick to my side like glue."

Rob cocked a questioning eyebrow at him.

"It's very simple. I don't wish you to leave me alone with the widow," he said with a laugh.

"She looks like a grand piece. Willing, too!"

"Too damned willing, that's the trouble. You've heard the expression, 'She'll have your guts for garters'? Well, this one would have your balls for earrings!"

Kitty's face was ever before him. His thoughts dwelled on the times she had been warm in his arms. The scent of her lingered in his dreams, and many had been the night on the long voyage when he had tossed sleepless upon his narrow bunk while her vision teased him with a burning, consuming desire. She was in his blood now, never to be denied. She was his love; his only love. The thought of other women was like ashes to him. His one thought was to get away from the plantation as soon as possible.

Jacquine was burning with impatience to get him alone, but when Patrick kept up a steady conversation with the common seaman who accompanied him, her pique smoldered beneath the surface.

The table was being set only for two. Patrick quirked an eyebrow at Jacquine. "Surely there will be three of us for lunch, or aren't you joining us, madame?"

She gasped audibly. "I presumed your servant would dine in the servants' hall, Patrick."

He fell back on southern prejudice, which he knew would be strong. "A white man—to dine with the Negroes? I think not, my dear. Rob is not merely my servant, he is also my friend, and therefore my guest."

She masked her annoyance immediately. Patrick O'Reilly was arrogant, dominant, used to getting his own way and best of all, he had a deliciously cruel streak. If she angered him now, she realized she was in danger of losing him, so she became all smiling, gracious hospitality.

Patrick laid the groundwork for an early departure. "Unfortunately, I am already behind in my schedule. We must press on immediately at dawn tomorrow."

She licked her lips and pouted, "I think you are ungallant to put your work before me, *chéri.*"

When he didn't respond to her sally, she decided on a more direct approach. "I beg a few words with you in private, *monsieur?* I must retire while the sun is so hot. Please excuse me?"

He sidestepped the brazen invitation. "Good! That will give me a chance to show off your lovely plantation to Rob."

In the stables Patrick explained to Rob, "We'll ride; it's far too large to cover on foot. You have no idea how vast this plantation is."

The farther they rode, the more astounded Rob Wilson became. "I knew there was wealth in the world, Mr. O'Reilly, but I've never seen it on a vast scale like this before."

"It took my breath away too, the first time I saw it," acknowledged Patrick.

"All this could be yours, couldn't it?" quizzed Rob.

Patrick smiled ruefully, "I suppose it could, but at what a price, lad, at what a price," and he silently shook his head.

Inside the mansion Jacquine summoned Topaz to her bed-chamber. "Go to the compound and tell Colossus that under no circumstances must he come up to the big house tonight." Topaz knew without further explanation what was required of her. There were no secrets on a plantation. "I think also once dusk has descended you can go up to our young visitor's room. You may tell him he has my permission to pleasure you." Topaz veiled the hatred in her eyes and stepped quickly from the room.

Since the heavy meal had been served at dinnertime, supper was a light, cold meal. Afterward the two men lit cigars and relaxed with a drink as the sky outside gathered into a thick darkness.

Topaz slipped out of the house and hurried down toward the compound. Colossus was striding past the row of cabins, as he did every night on his way to the big house. No one paid much attention, even though everyone knew where he was going and why. Topaz came up with him under a beautiful live oak draped with moss.

"The mistress says you're not to come up to the big house tonight."

"Why not?"

"Her fancy Englishman has come visitin' so she can't have no nigger in her bedroom."

He went to brush past her and took another two steps toward the house, but Topaz was after him in a flash. "Colossus, no! She'd strip the hide off me," she cried.

He reached down and gripped her arms. "You can take her place, Topaz."

"You're too big for me," she said fearfully.

"When is this Englishman leavin'?"

"Tomorrow. I heard him say he's leavin' tomorrow for sure."

"All right, gal, go on."

Jacquine grew very impatient as she watched the men laughing and smoking. Finally she arose and stretched sensuously, "Time for our little tête-à-tête, Patrick," she said suggestively.

Able to evade her no longer, Patrick smiled lazily. "Lead on, my dear." He followed her up the stairs to her boudoir and closed the door behind them. He went over to an array of bottles and glasses and poured two Bourbons. "Try it my way with a little bitters; it adds a subtle flavor," he offered.

"*Chéri*, you know I'll try it any way," she said and laughed.

"I'm sorry I have to leave so soon, Jacquine, but when I return we'll have lots of time to . . . talk."

"How long will you be gone, *mon amour?*" she asked.

"Three weeks, a month at the most, I think." He refilled her glass. "Why didn't you marry?" he quirked a dark brow at her.

"None but you could satisfy me, of course," she said, laughing.

He sat beside her and slipped one arm about her. He took the drink from her hand and put it to her lips.

"How many have you tried?" He grinned.

"How many at one time, you mean?" Her eyes were growing heavy as he watched her closely. Already her pupils were dilated enormously. He picked her up and carried her to the bed. Patrick began to undress her. He was provocatively slow about it, kissing and biting each part of her flesh as he exposed it. The low moans died in her throat as she slipped into unconsciousness. Patrick blew out the lamps and left quickly, patting the vial concealed in his pocket.

Before Kitty sighted land, she could smell it. It was a curious mixture of spice and greenery. The birds came out to meet the ship, and the inevitable signs of man, bottles and garbage were spotted floating in the water. The pale blue harbor came into view, with waves washing up the seawall. The docks were crowded and Kitty could see that most of the faces were black. She made out a government building with cannons, and the waterfront warehouses and markets. The houses were different shades of pastel, with iron railings surrounding them. The sunlight dazzled her eyes, while the humid heat made her gasp. Captain Harding took her ashore, where Kitty knew the first thing she had to do was buy a lighter gown. She felt better the moment her feet touched land, but her heavy dress and cloak were suffocating. Big Jim directed her along East Bay Street until they came to a dress shop. Her pregnancy was quite obvious now, so she chose a loose gown of pale green lawn with a matching parasol that was quite inexpensive.

"Tell me, is it always this hot?" she asked the saleswoman.

"Hot? Why, it's barely spring, child," the woman said and laughed. "Wait until summer!"

The breeze rattled the palm leaves, and the streets and gardens were filled with pink and red blossoming trees. Big Jim took her to the Battery Carriage House and left her to her own devices. When he returned they had to meet in the front parlor, as visitors were not allowed up to guests' bedrooms. "Are you feeling better, lass?"

"Oh, yes. I fell asleep hours ago. Were you able to find me transportation, Jim?"

"I looked about the livery stables, but I think I have a better idea. There is a government mail coach goes north from Charleston tomorrow. It stops at the outlying plantations and goes right past Bagatelle. They sometimes take passengers, so I took the liberty of saying you'd travel with them."

"That sounds wonderful. What would I do without you?"

"You'll find out tomorrow, won't you?" He laughed. "Now, here's your ticket and I'll write down the address for you. You just walk down the South Battery to the building next to the Court House."

"I know I'm keeping you from your duties, so we'd better say good-bye." Her eyes glittered with tears.

"Well, I hate sentimental good-byes, they're not in my style, so I'll just kiss you for good luck. Remember, if you ever need a ride back across the pond, just ask around the waterfront for me." He drew her to his massive chest quickly and bussed her on the forehead. "Don't go walking about the city alone, Kitty. Good-bye, love."

Jacquine awaited her overseer on the front veranda.

"Simmons, I want you to get word to the slave buyer right away that I have a prime hand I wish to sell."

"Yes, Miz LeCoq. Which one do you have in mind?"

"Colossus, but I don't want any trouble, so he mustn't find out about it until the slave dealer is actually here."

"But ma'am, he's our best field hand, he's worth mor'n half a dozen others put together," he protested.

"Are you questioning my orders, Simmons?" she asked coldly.

"No, no, ma'am," he stammered, "you know best what you want to do with your own slaves. We should get a good dollar for him," he suggested placatingly.

"You can pick out a couple of young striplings to go with him; this place is nigger rich!" She dismissed him with a cold nod. She hoped there was no delay in finding the slave dealer; she had to get Colossus off the place before Patrick returned.

Two men rode on the mail coach: the driver and his guard, who carried a rifle across his knees. Kitty was the only passenger. They would follow the Cooper River all the way out past Bagatelle and up to Georgetown, then return by way of the Ashley River, making a circle. They assured her she was going to view the most beautiful country she had ever seen. The mail coach stopped at the main gates of each plantation but didn't turn into them from the main road. The plantations were so large and the driveways so long it would have added many hours to their weekly trip. Kitty was enthralled by the beautiful gardens. Live oaks draped with moss gave everything a fairy-tale appearance, and the tall cypress trees had their roots in the water. Everything seemed to be in bloom.

The coach was very hard and bumpy and to Kitty the heat was unbearable, but every time she thought she couldn't sit one moment longer, the sight of a delicate white dogwood would take her breath away. Finally the mail coach stopped outside a tall pair of white gates.

"Hi there, Josh. We got mail and a visitor for up at the big house."

"Hold on while I unlock the gate."

Kitty opened the coach door and stepped down. "Thank you for a beautiful ride, gentlemen. Have a safe trip." She smiled.

The young boy Josh took the mail pouch in one hand and Kitty's bag in the other. "I had no idea the plantation would be this big," said Kitty, taking in the acres of formal, manicured lawns that swept down on both sides of the driveway. The boy was too shy to answer her, so he just grinned. They had walked a considerable distance before the mansion came into view, and Kitty stopped in her tracks to gaze at it. "Oh, it's simply breathtaking," she cried. Josh grinned.

When they arrived at the front door, Kitty felt suddenly that she should not have come. How was she even going to walk into the splendor of Bagatelle and explain who she was? Then her natural optimism took over and she knew everything would be all right the moment Patrick saw her.

Josh knocked on the door and Ebony, the butler, opened the portal wide. He bowed stiffly, "Won't you come in, *madame*. I will inform Miz LeCoq." Kitty followed him into the spacious entrance hall.

Her knees felt weak and she began to tremble from the long walk in the heat. At that moment a tall, striking figure appeared at the top of the stairs and paused dramatically to gaze down upon her. Jacquine descended the stairs slowly, never taking her eyes from the beautiful girl who waited below. A presentiment clutched at her so strongly that by the time her feet touched the bottom step she knew beyond a shadow of a doubt who she was. She extended her hand smoothly, a smile upon her lips. "How do you do. I'm Jacquine LeCoq. Can I help you?"

"How do you do. I'm Kitty Rooney. I'm looking for Mr.

Patrick O'Reilly, and I'm afraid this is the only address I
have for him in America.''

"Ah, yes. The moment I saw you I knew you were looking
for Patrick. I'm afraid he's left for the North on business, but
do not worry your head, my dear, he will return to Bagatelle.''

"Oh, dear. I'm sorry to be a nuisance, *madame.* I've traveled all the way from England, and to be truthful I'm at a
loss to know what I should do next,'' said Kitty, her heart
tumbling with her disappointment.

"Allow me to extend the hospitality of Bagatelle. You are
most welcome here. It gets lonely, as you can imagine. Come
into the salon. You must be exhausted.'' Kitty smiled her
thanks and followed Jacquine into the deliciously cool room.
"Topaz, bring a palmetto fan,'' she ordered the black girl
standing in the corner.

"Thank you. I'm not used to this heat,'' said Kitty.

"Tell Ebony to prepare two juleps with lots of ice,'' Jacquine ordered.

"Thank you,'' murmured Kitty, sinking back into a pea-
cock chair. Her mind sought desperately to put things in
order. This woman who was so friendly and hospitable on the
surface had the hardest mouth Kitty had ever seen. The corners turned down and deep lines of what? . . . discontent?
ran downward to the jaw.

"Patrick would be very angry with me if I didn't take the
best care of you, I'm sure. I propose that you rest today.
Bathe, lie down for a good sleep. I'll have a tray sent up so
you needn't come downstairs at all this evening. Tomorrow
we will talk. You can decide whether you will wait here for
Patrick's return, or go North and try to locate him at his
place of business, *n'est-ce pas?*''

"You are very kind, *madame.* The drink was delicious;
I've never had ice before.''

"Wherever have you been—the convent? How old are you, fifteen?"

"I'm twenty-one," lied Kitty, her eyes sparking with anger. "Ah, perhaps . . . but certainly hotheaded!" Jacquine said and laughed. "Topaz, take this lady upstairs and get her settled."

When they were out of earshot, Jacquine summoned Ebony. "Have one of the gardeners dig a grave. Under the magnolias where my husband is buried will do nicely, thank you."

Ebony knew better than to question her. She was a woman of bizarre caprices. All he had to do was make sure it wasn't for him. All else was superfluous. Kitty took off her pretty green dress and hung it in the wardrobe. She lay on the bed without even washing.

"You must know Patrick. When did he leave?"

Topaz looked frightened. "The mistress gets mad if I gossip about white folks."

Kitty closed her eyes, trying to come to a decision. Her money was gone. The logical thing was to stay and await Patrick's return, but she was filled with a vague anxiety.

Jacquine ordered a horse saddled. When she returned, she had vented a good deal of her frustrated anger by the liberal use of her riding crop.

It was not Topaz, but the butler who brought up a tray to Kitty's room. The food was delicious and for the first time in weeks it didn't produce the nausea that had been plaguing her. After she had eaten she felt a good deal better. She bathed from head to toe and brushed the tangles from her hair. The mirror showed it to be a mass of frizzy curls from the humid air, and her skin had a deep, healthy tan. She wished Patrick could see her, for she knew she looked extremely pretty.

Tomorrow, after a good night's rest, she would have to

face that formidable opponent. She did not doubt for a moment that Jacquine was her opponent in an important game, with Patrick the prize. She knew a great plantation like this would be a temptation to a man with Patrick's ambition, but she believed that deep down he would abhor slavery and all it stood for.

Ebony lit the candles so his mistress was no longer sitting in the dark, then said, "*Madame,* Mr. Simmons and another gentleman would like a word with you." She put down her glass and said, "I'll see them in my office."

"Miz LeCoq, ma'am, here's Mr. Logan; I got hold of him as soon as I could."

"I remember Logan when he did business with my husband. You may leave us. I am capable of handling the affairs of this plantation without male advice."

"As you wish, ma'am," he nodded and left.

"Well, Logan, have you seen him?"

"Yes, they've got him secured at the compound. I'll admit he's a fine specimen." He said with narrowed eyes, "What's wrong with him?"

"Wrong with him? Are you mad?"

"My guess is he's a runner," he suggested.

"Wrong! We have no runners here, Logan," she contradicted. "They were dead men the minute we got them back."

"He's powerful big, probably hard to handle," he suggested.

She smiled slowly. "I never had any trouble. He's worth three thousand."

"Could be, but I'm not paying three thousand for him. He's flawed somehow, or you wouldn't be selling him."

"Logan, I can see you drive a hard bargain, so I'll be honest with you. I'm to be married shortly. For purely per-

sonal reasons I want Colossus off the place before my future
husband returns.''

''I see! Top dollar—two thousand, no dickering.''

''Done. The two boys you can have for five hundred
apiece. You should be able to turn a profit.''

''There is always a good market for young females. Anything you can let me have in that line?'' he asked.

''My house girls are trained to my every command; I
couldn't possibly spare any. It would be much too fatiguing
to retrain new girls.''

She was glad to get the business concluded so she could
concentrate on what to do about her other problem. It would
be so simple to show Patrick Kitty's grave. So easy to con-
coct a tale of fever. What could he do once it was a *fait
accompli?* How to go about it; that was the problem. There
was no one on the plantation who would commit the murder
for her. If only the wench wasn't so young and pretty. She
stopped. Logan was looking for light-skinned wenches! She
sat down at the desk and thought out each step of her plan.
The girl certainly was dark enough, exotic as some of the
''fancies'' black and white blood often produced. Who
would deny her, except the girl herself? She could make out
papers that none would question. She reached for a slave bill
of sale and filled in the name. She carefully sanded the paper
and placed it in her bosom for safekeeping.

''Topaz, follow me,'' she said. They went to the back of
the house to a storeroom. Here were kept linens and a supply
of brightly colored cotton garments the slaves wore. Jacquine
selected a brilliant orange cotton shift with a matching
tignon. ''Listen carefully to what I want you to do. First you
must make absolutely certain that the girl upstairs is asleep.
Then I want you to remove every article she brought here
with her and leave this orange shift in their place. If you
overlook one article of clothing I will lash you smartly.''

Jacquine arose early. When Logan came she greeted him almost warmly. "Ah—Logan, I've been thinking over what we were discussing last night, and I have decided to let you have one of my female slaves."

"Well, that depends on what you're asking for her. I'm a little low now that I've paid you the three thousand."

"That's the best part. If you can guarantee me that she won't be sold to anyone in Charleston or thereabouts, I'll throw her in for nothing."

"What's wrong with her? What's the catch?" he asked bluntly.

"Such a suspicious man! I want her away from here. Ship her to the islands and keep whatever you can get for her. She's even got a sucker in her, Logan, a white man's sucker, so I don't think you'll refuse my generous offer, will you?" At this moment Kitty came running down the stairs. Her eyes were blazing in anger. She was wearing the shapeless orange smock and brandishing the scarf in her hand.

"What the hell is going on here? Where are my clothes and by whose authority were they removed from my room?" she demanded breathlessly.

Jacquine ignored her and turned to Logan. "Well, what do you think of her?"

"I think you're one smart woman to sell her before your man returns," he said and laughed.

"Sell? What are you talking about? What's going on here?" cried Kitty.

Still ignoring her, Jacquine took out the crackling document: "Here is her paper, transferring ownership to you. Her name is Kitty and she is an octoroon."

"Octoroon? That's a damned lie! My skin is dark because I'm a Gypsy. You must be mad!" Kitty flew at Jacquine's face, but she eluded the attack and sent Kitty a stinging blow to the side of her head.

"Control her, Logan; she's your property now."

Logan took the bullwhip from his belt and shook it threateningly under Kitty's nose. He took her arm and shoved her violently toward the door. "Outside, girl." Logan pushed Kitty across the veranda toward his wagon. He took out a set of leg irons and clasped them about her bare ankles.

Kitty turned burning-mad eyes on Jacquine and screamed, "Hecate! Nebo! I call up the powers of darkness. I damn you everlastingly. I curse your immortal soul!"

Two young black boys were being loaded into the wagon when Kitty saw him. The gigantic black man came forward in chains. He made no protest, but the look of pure contempt he bent upon the assemblage was enough to put fear into all of them. Kitty's eyes were starting out of her head. Never before had she beheld anyone so ugly. He was the size of a monster. When they brought him forward and shackled him to Kitty, she went down into the vortex of oblivion.

Chapter 21

The first thing she became aware of was the relentless sun beating down upon her face. She tried to open her eyes but was instantly blinded by a brilliant flash of yellow, which turned to orange and then fire red behind her closed eyelids. She was on the tailgate of a moving wagon, being pulled by one heavy-set mule. The enormous black man walked behind the wagon, his long, even strides keeping pace. His wrists were shackled with irons to the wagon, so he had no choice. Colossus opened his mouth to say something to Kitty, but she shrank away from him in horror.

"Tie that tignon round your head, or you're gonna get sunstroke for sure." Logan stopped the wagon. "So, you're awake at last, eh, Sleeping Beauty? You can walk the rest of the way. I'll take these leg irons off and fasten you by your wrist to Colossus here."

Terror made her heart beat so loudly inside her eardrums, she was momentarily deafened. "No, please!" she begged, but Logan only laughed suggestively as he tied such a small female to such a large male. They were on a dusty back road. Colossus was observing her dainty white feet as she struggled to keep up. As the miles passed slowly, a terrific thirst grew within her that was like torture. About noon, when the sun was at its fiercest, Logan stopped the wagon outside a house that was sort of a general store. He paid for food to be brought out to his slaves. The young boys laughed and jumped about, enjoying themselves immensely. Colossus also looked pleased at the sight of food, but when Kitty was handed a dish of boiled greens floating in a greasy mass of fat-back pork, nausea arose in her throat. She tried to hand it back to the serving woman, but Logan said threateningly, "Eat it. You have a long way to walk before dark."

"I'm very thirsty," she said.

"You can have a cup of water after you've eaten, not before." The smell of grease rose up in a miasma, but she tried to ignore it and took a morsel of the fatty pork in her fingers and put it into her mouth. The moment she swallowed it, her stomach revolted and she vomited into the dirt. Her retching continued until she had the dry heaves. Colossus took her tin plate away and handed her his cup of water. She took only one mouthful when Logan knocked it from her hand.

"I told you to eat! You need strength for walking. I won't have you riding on the wagon tiring my mule, you black bitch!"

They had only been traveling for half an hour when Kitty was overcome with exhaustion and knew she could walk no farther. Colossus picked her up without a word, and matching his pace to the wagon's, supported her against his massive chest. Some of her fear of him began gradually to seep away as the fierce sun burned down upon them. As soon as she felt able she made him put her down again so she could walk by herself.

The giggling and playful wrestling going on up front confirmed for Kitty what she had suspected of Logan from the first. She knew she had nothing to fear from him sexually, but Colossus was another matter. Virility oozed from every pore. It was so potent and tangible you could almost see, hear, touch, smell and taste it. The wagon drew up beside a pecan grove. Logan unlocked Kitty's wrist shackles. He put an iron on her ankle and chained the other end to Colossus' ankle.

"We're gonna have a little siesta," Logan said and grinned. "You can take her behind the trees. I know you must be in need by now, boy.'' He was well aware that Colossus wouldn't be able to escape with the exhausted female shackled to him.

Kitty was rooted to the spot with fear, but Colossus took her by the hand and pulled her into the pecan grove. She trembled from head to foot, her thirst and exhaustion almost forgotten. Colossus stretched out on the ground. Kitty stood terrified before him. ''Lie down. I won't touch you,'' he said simply.

''I don't believe you!'' cried Kitty.

''You too small for me; I'd kill you.'' He smiled to himself. '' 'Sides, I don't fancy you.''

Her eyes opened wide in disbelief. ''What do you mean?''

''You've got funny eyes and your nose is all thin and pointy. You're a white woman.'' She was dizzy with relief. She fell down beside him and relaxed. She slept almost immediately. She awoke with a gentle hand on her shoulder. ''We have to go now.''

It was dark before they finally reached Charleston. They went down the back streets to the warehouses by the docks. Colossus and Kitty were locked in a cell-like room, and Logan gave the woman with the keys a few coins for their supper. He departed with the two black boys, saying he would return for the male and the female in the morning. As the last of her physical resources drained away, Kitty fell into a stupor from dehydration. After an hour had elapsed with no sign of the meal they had been promised, Colossus hammered on the door and shouted, ''This wench will die if she don't get food and water.''

Kitty was floating in a detached state of mind. The candle flickered across Colossus' face and she wondered how she had ever thought him ugly. He had the noble face of a warrior. His skin was a beautiful shade of ebony and the full lips were attractively molded over strong white teeth. His rippled body was beautiful. "Magnificent," she murmured and slipped into unconsciousness. Frantically he felt for her heartbeat and listened for her breathing. It was so shallow, for a moment he thought she had slipped away. He gathered her against him and willed the strength of his body into hers. The gigantic slave could not have explained his own reasons for his concern for the small girl at his side. Perhaps he saw in her an innocence he had never had, perhaps he pitied her vulnerability, but he was determined she would not die.

When the door was unlocked for Logan, he found an avenging angel standing between himself and the female. "This wench almost died. We got no food or water; that woman cheated you."

"That's a lie!" the woman snarled, but quickly retreated as Colossus took a step toward her.

"How're you gonna sell this fancy wench if she's half dead?"

Logan bethought himself of the demand for fancies lately, and if he livened her up a bit, he would be able to get a better price.

"Calm down, boy, we'll look after the wench. Woman, you get this boy a good breakfast—double portions of everything, mind you. I'm taking him up to Chalmers Street for the auctions today. This gal now is another thing altogether. Her stomach is delicate-like. Bring her some juice and some fresh fruit. Then I want you to fill a tub for her to bathe in and wash her hair. You cheat me again, woman, it be the last time you ever cheat anybody."

It was late afternoon when Logan took Kitty down Chalmers Street to the slave auction. She entered the compound with the other black women who were to be sold. A young girl was up on the auction block and Kitty watched with fascinated horror as the girl was stripped and handled by prospective buyers. She could never go through such degra-

dation; she felt sure she would die first. Shortly, Logan returned with a man who took a critical interest in her. She
heard him say, "You sure she's black?"

"Got her papers here to prove it," Logan assured him, but
they winked at each other.

"I'm always on the lookout for girls for Molly Maguire.
Don't find many, her being so particular, but this one is
exquisite. Let's talk price."

When the other man led Kitty away, all she felt was a vast
relief that she hadn't been made to mount the auction block.
They walked over to Market Street, then down to the foot of
Water Street Pier. Kitty looked in vain for Big Jim Harding.
She was led onto a ship called *Island Queen*. He put her in a
tiny cabin with one other girl who was very slim and tall with
jet-black skin. When Kitty spoke to her, she answered in a
foreign tongue, so Kitty gave it up.

It became warmer each day, but the sea was never rough
enough to make Kitty sick again, and with regular meals and
plenty of sleep, she was beginning to feel quite recovered.
The other girl did not speak to her, but held herself aloof
from any contact with her fellow passenger. Kitty was quietly
gathering strength for the ordeal ahead. By now she suspected she was being shipped to a brothel, and she would
need her strength and agility to make a break for it. She filled
her mind with happy musings about the child she was carrying to block out thoughts of her future.

But when land was sighted, she knew her time was running out. In a desperate move, she cried out to the ship's
captain one day when she passed him on deck. "Please, sir,
please, you must believe me. I'm white, I shouldn't be here.
Help me, please help me!" she begged.

"Do you take me for a fool, woman? You've been sold to
Molly McGuire's whorehouse. The fanciest knocking shops

in the islands are here on St. Kitts. Now, out of my way; we're about to come into harbor.''

''St. Kitts,'' said Kitty wonderingly, and her eyes lifted across the ship's rail to where tiny boats dotted the harbor. Great rollers were breaking on the beach between long jetties where porters and ship's clerks milled about, waiting to meet the ships. Her eyes swept the town of Basseterre and beyond to the north, where Mount Misery reached into the clouds. Hope budded and blossomed inside her chest. Surely St. Kitts meant Charles Drago!

Kitty and her companion were taken into a small warehouse office and locked in a cell with bars. After about an hour, Kitty felt the heaviness of her pregnancy and clutched the bars to keep herself upright. The sound of a woman's laughter reached her ears, and a small party came into the office.

''I'll take their papers from you, boyo, when I've had a look at the bloody merchandise! God almighty, don't tell me they're both flaming well colored,'' she said with a tinge of disgust.

''Now, Molly, I didn't know you had anything against colored gals,'' the captain said with disbelief.

''Oh, flaming hell, of course not, it's just that men always have contempt for what there's too many of, and on St. Kitts there's just a shade too many colored gals.'' At the sound of the Irish brogue, Kitty broke down in tears.

''Don't cry, *acushla*. Welcome to the Paris of the West Indies.''

''Mavourneen'' was all Kitty could whisper.

''That's Gaelic! You're Irish! What the flaming hell are you doing here?''

Kitty's Gypsy blood pounded in her veins as she lied, ''Charles Drago, the governor of this island, is my fiancé. I sailed from England to join him and I was kidnaped. Please, if you will get word to Charles that I am here, he will reward you generously, I'm certain.''

Molly knew Charles Drago from the years when he was first sent out as governor. He'd been a frequent visitor at her establishment, but she hadn't seen him in well over a year, she was sure. Molly made a quick decision. If Charles Drago acknowledged this young woman in the orange cotton shift, who was literally barefoot and pregnant, she must indeed mean a great deal to him. It would pay her to be as discreet as possible. She couldn't embarrass the governor by visiting him openly, so she decided to stay with the girl and send a note to the back door of Government House with her man, Jean-Paul.

It amused Molly to think an Irish waif could capture the heart of the governor and perhaps become a duchess. As they waited, Molly wondered how they would discreetly convey Kitty to the governor's mansion without so much as a cloak to cover a multitude of sins.

Charles Drago swiftly made his way from his carriage into the warehouse office. "Kathleen! This fellow was telling me the truth after all. I can't believe it!''

"Oh, Charles, thank God you came so quickly. Oh, my God, I can't believe it's over,'' she cried.

He put a protective arm about her and spoke to Molly in a warm, natural manner. "I can't thank you enough, Mrs. Maguire. I'll send my man of business around tomorrow. You'll never regret this kindness. My word on it.''

Without a thought for embarrassment, Charles picked up Kitty and strode outside. He helped her into the carriage and jumped in beside her.

"Charles, let me explain how I come to be in such a predicament.''

"You don't have to explain anything to me, and we're

certainly not going to have explanations until you are completely recovered.'' He smiled happily. "My governorship lasts another six months, so you're going to be stuck with me that long anyway.''

"Oh, Charles, words fail me. I just don't know what to say.''

"Don't say anything. Enjoy the beautiful view. See, there's the cathedral. It's the building with two turrets. The houses here are called châteaux; notice they all have red tiled roofs and no glass in the windows. That's to catch the cool breezes off the sea. Why am I running on like this when I can see all you need is a bed? You're close to exhaustion.''

"When I'm stronger, you can show me everything. I know I'll love it here.''

The governor's residence was a startling white with a terra-cotta-tiled roof. At the front, royal palms waved in the cool breeze from the sea. There was no glass in the windows; instead, jalousies were used as shutters if the evening became too cool. In the center of the house was a tiled courtyard with a splashing fountain. Brilliant flowers banked the courtyard; tubs overflowed orange lily, and hanging baskets trailed purple and pink bougainvillea everywhere. Her steps were reluctant as she hesitated to meet the staff unkempt as she was, but Charles took her hand and propelled her through to a delightfully cool sitting room.

The servants were friendly and showed a desire to please, which put Kitty at ease immediately. They spoke some English and Kitty decided she would try to learn some French. The bathroom had a square sunken bath with beautifully ornate faucets. The warm, perfumed water filled the room with an exotic, heady fragrance and they left her to relax and went in search of a garment in which she could sleep. As her tensions melted, the tears slipped down her cheeks and she became engulfed with great shuddering sobs. Charles heard and stayed the servants from going to her assistance. He realized that all the pent-up fears connected with her ordeal would be better out than in. Eventually she became still. The girls helped her into a white silk shift and led her to a bed-chamber.

"Please don't burn my orange smock. I want to keep it lest I forget one moment of my slavery."

"I wash and iron and wrap up in parcel," the girl called Mimi said.

"No!" said Kitty. "I want it just the way it is, stained and filthy!"

She sank against the pillows and looked about her at the light furniture. The bedroom suite was made from bamboo. Kitty could sense the exquisite taste of these furnishings when she compared them to the heavy, dark pieces of Victorian furniture she had always seen in England.

Charles came through the doorway with a tray in his hands. Before she could protest he appealed to her generosity.

"Please don't banish me to dine alone another evening; I swear I'll run mad if you do. I promise not to force any food upon you. However, if there's anything on the tray you fancy, I'll look the other way while you help yourself." Without any embarrassment, he perched on the side of her bed as if they had lived together for years. He got her to try the matoutou of crab, the chicken with coconut, and mangoes simmered in wine and cinnamon. "Well, what do you think?" he prompted.

She laughed and said, "It's all far too rich, you know."

"Kathleen, you are so refreshing. My guests fill my ears with flattering compliments for my cuisine here at Government House, but now that you've brought it to my attention, they are rather indigestible messes!"

Kitty laughed, then covered a yawn daintily.

"You're tired; I'll leave you now. Good night, my dear. I am so delighted to have you here."

When she was alone, she couldn't dispel thoughts of Patrick. Since the first moment she had seen him, she had been determined to marry him, and because of that she had made a mess of her life. First, her disastrous marriage, then her flight across the ocean when she learned she was carrying his child. He hadn't wanted her on her terms, but she had to admit he'd been honest and warned her that he would marry someone who would at least bring him a bleachworks. Well, he'd be getting a plantation now, but at the thought of the woman who went with it, her blood ran cold. God help him! Well, she gambled and she had lost, but at least she had the best part of him. Her hand slid over the mound the child inside her made. Her love for this baby was fierce and protective. She was bitter against Patrick and she hated the Frenchwoman, but she had to be honest with herself. She could not hate Patrick, because she loved him.

The next few days blurred together for Kitty, with lots of bed rest and exotic food. Charles had found a new purpose in life. The months that were left of his governorship had stretched endlessly before him, but now he couldn't leave his office fast enough each day. As soon as he got rid of each visitor, his thoughts returned to Kitty. He imagined he knew the panic she must have felt when she discovered she was with child by a husband who was in his grave. A hypocritical society would point a shameful finger at a young widow growing large with child, and she had fled rather than face the gossip. He had a hammock slung between two shade trees in the garden and often watched her swing lazily with a deep contentment.

His footsteps quickened as he left his office and hurried down the corridor toward the sitting room. He discerned tears in her eyes. "My dear, please don't cry." He took her hand and gently led her to a settee. "I know you must grieve unbearably for your young husband, especially when you think about his child, whom he never will be able to see, but it does no good to dwell on these things."

Kitty was speechless for a moment. Then she realized Charles thought her child was a result of her marriage. It was a perfectly natural assumption.

How shocked he would be if he knew the truth, she thought. "I didn't mean to greet you with tears, Charles." She arose but kept hold of his hand. "Come and see what's for dinner. I've been giving instructions all the afternoon."

They were served roast fowl. "You've no idea how strangely they looked at me in the kitchen when I insisted it should be cooked without all that oil and garlic."

"I know exactly what you mean. We have such beautiful fresh fish available, but instead of poaching it or broiling it, they disguise it with such rich sauces, my palate was ruined in no time."

"We are going to have fruit salad made with bananas and what's that other fruit called that's yellow and tangy?"

"Pineapple, I think you mean."

"Yes, pineapple! Isn't that a delightful name?" she asked.

He looked at her for a long moment. "Kathleen, you are beautiful. I'd quite begun to hate this place, but it seems to suit you very well; you're positively blooming. What do you like about St. Kitts?"

"Oh, it's so different, Charles. For instance, look at this beautiful white batiste dress. The material is so delicate. I adore wearing white; it's such a contrast from the dark clothes we wear at home. The colors here are so brilliant. I remember when I saw Lancashire for the first time, everything was black." She laughed as she went on. "The food is unusual, the native people are delightful and I've been trying to learn French." He poured her some rum and she held up her hand and said, "Just a *soupçon*," and they both laughed. "I'm looking forward to exploring the island and seeing the volcano"—she lowered her eyes—"of course, I mean after the baby is born."

"I want to talk to you about that, Kathleen. Come into the garden with me." He placed a shawl about her and led her into the fragrant evening. "I think we'd better let my doctor have a look at you. I don't mean to alarm you, but I think the time is drawing near."

"I'm not alarmed, Charles. I'm frightened of the pain, of course, but I want this baby so much, I can hardly bear to wait."

"Kathleen, I want to give this child my name."

"Oh, Charles, I realize how difficult it must be for you. Everyone you know must be whispering about me being here, but it's too big a sacrifice just for propriety's sake."

"Sacrifice? What are you talking about? It's my dearest wish to make you my wife. You're the most desirable woman I've ever known; you tempt me every time I look at you."

"Marriage is out of the question. I wouldn't be a suitable wife for a man in your position. Here where life is so relaxed, the romantic atmosphere has lulled you into thinking it would be like this, but just stop and consider what it would be like in England. I wouldn't be accepted; I'd be beyond the pale. You are a duke!"

He threw back his head and laughed. "How innocent you are. English society is completely hypocritical—once you possess the title of duchess they'll fall over each other beating a path to your door."

"Charles, I couldn't bear it if you thought I'd been trying to maneuver you into a proposal."

"I know full well that isn't so; in fact, my age probably makes me distasteful to you. I know you can't love me, especially when you've had a handsome young husband, but I'd cherish you all my days, and I'm looking forward to having the child almost as much as you are. I've wanted a son for many years and thought it impossible until now. Think about it; don't say no. I won't plague you anymore tonight. After the doctor has a look at you, we'll talk again.''

Chapter 22

When the doctor examined Kitty, he told her that she should be delivered in about two weeks. Charles doubled his efforts at persuading her to marry him before the child was born. As the time drew closer, the housemaids filled her ears with lurid stories of death from childbirth, and Kitty began to panic at what would happen to her child if she did die. She thought seriously about accepting Charles' proposal, but it seemed such an unequal bargain to her. She would be gaining wealth, a title, security for her child and couldn't even offer love in return. She firmly rejected the idea, only to have the most appalling nightmares of living in the slums where everyone screamed "bastard!" at her child.

Charles had to work late one evening, and when he returned he went straight to Kitty and said, "I've been thinking how selfish it is of me to keep pressing this marriage upon you, my dear. It's so one-sided, with all the advantages going to me. I'd be getting a beautiful young wife and a child I could pass my title to and all I'd be giving in return is financial security. There are hundreds of men who could do that, all of them closer to your own age." He stopped when he noticed how white she was about the mouth.

"Charles, don't get cold feet, just when I was about to accept you."

"I'll send for the priest immediately, but in years to come, don't recriminate me for taking advantage of your fear and vulnerability—even though it's true." He smiled.

Though she was trying to conceal it, he could tell that she was experiencing pain, so as soon as his heavy gold ring was on Kitty's finger, he lifted her into his arms and hurried upstairs.

"Into bed with you, my duchess; the doctor's on his way."

Kitty smiled through her tears.

She was not smiling fourteen hours later, when she still was in hard labor but had not delivered. There he was again anxiously hovering over the bed. Poor Charles! His face was haggard; his eyes clearly showed the misery he was feeling. A great surge of anger arose at Patrick. He should be the one pacing the floor in a fever of anxiety over their unborn child. "I bet he's enjoying himself this very moment." She stuffed the sheet into her mouth and bit down hard. "By God, I'll make him pay for this!" she vowed.

When she became conscious the first sound she heard was her son screaming for food. She opened her eyes and looked at the most beautiful creature who had ever existed. Granted, there was an angry red mark on his forehead, left by the forceps, but his eyes were dark blue and he had an appealing crop of black curls. The relief showed clearly on Charles' face, the grim lines softening as his eyes rested upon mother and child.

"How do you feel?" he asked softly.

"Tired . . . happy . . . quite brilliant, really, like I've accomplished something worthwhile."

"And so you have, my dear. Now, Katie here is going to be the baby's nurse; also, the doctor recommended a wet nurse who delivered a couple of days ago."

Her eyes were closing sleepily and she stifled a yawn. "Whatever is a wet nurse, Charles?"

"Well . . . er," he colored slightly, "wealthy ladies usually don't feed their babies at their own breasts, since it spoils the figure, so a wet nurse is substituted."

Kitty laughed delightedly. "Oh, Charles, you make up the most absurd stories to amuse me."

Charles smiled to himself. She didn't even believe him, so he might as well keep quiet and let nature take its course the way it was meant to. He kissed her brow. "Rest, my darling. I'll come back later."

She was up and about in a week. She had a new reason for being alive, which was obvious to everyone who saw her. To Charles she was a delight. She wore ruffled white dresses with vivid red hibiscus blossoms in her hair, and she sang constantly to the baby.

"Are you happy, Kathleen?" he ventured one evening after she had put the baby to sleep in his cradle.

"Charles, I can't remember feeling so secure and content in my life."

He smiled. "We should get him christened."

"Yes, we will call him Charles . . . Charles Patrick."

"You know, that would please me above all things. Are you sure?"

"Yes, very sure," she said firmly.

"When the baby is a month old, we'll have our wedding reception. The island society is dying to meet you. I receive questions about you every day from the planters and their wives."

"Won't it seem awkward having a wedding reception so many weeks after the wedding? I don't want to be an embarrassment to you, Charles."

"You're not an embarrassment; you're my salvation. If you like, it can be a large dinner party, but *we* will know it's our wedding reception. You shall have a whole new wardrobe." He hesitated. "Kathleen, you aren't sorry you agreed to be my wife?"

"As a matter of fact, I'm looking forward to being introduced as your wife, and after the reception I'm going to move into the master bedroom, where I belong."

"Sweetheart, there's something I should have told you,

but it's such a source of shame to me that I've kept putting it off. I'd die if this information ever got about—in fact, one of the reasons I wanted a wife was to show her off to the world. Now I have a son, and of course everyone thinks it's my child, and that's exactly what I want them to think.''

''I don't think I understand,'' said Kitty.

''The thing is, I don't honestly believe I'm capable of having a child, but I wish the world to think that I am. Is that very despicable of me?''

''I'm delighted to have you as the father of my child. I've never met a kinder man, or one I liked more.'' She smiled.

He took her hand. ''Kathleen, you've been married before. May I speak freely about what happens between man and wife?''

''Do you mean in bed?'' she whispered.

He nodded. ''Yes. I've had difficulty in the past. I'm hoping with all my heart that it won't be so with you, my darling. If we do have trouble along those lines, perhaps not now, but in future years, I beg you never let my dark secret out.''

''Charles, everything will be just right, you'll see. We made vows to each other, and no matter what happens, I'll never break mine.''

''May I hold you?'' he asked humbly.

She ran to him eagerly and he curled up with her in his lap. She smoothed the worry lines from his brow, relaxing against the warmth of him. He took her hands in his and kissed her fingertips, then her wrists. His lips traced a pattern up her throat and then quite naturally his lips sought hers. Their kisses grew bolder. Kitty was pleasantly surprised at how nice his mouth was. It was firm and dry and he made it very plain that he adored her. Charles was deliriously happy as he felt the blood surge through his veins, giving the lie to the secret fears he harbored. When he left her to her slumber,

he had no doubts that everything would be fine on the night
of their wedding reception.

Charles decided to hold the reception at four, so that it
would be over at a reasonable hour. Some of the planters'
parties lasted all night. Of course, they were huge drinking
binges where the women retired and left the men to it. He
was determined this affair would not degenerate into such a
brawl and thought a good way of keeping decorum was to
make everything as formal as possible. The men would kick,
but the women would adore every moment. He wanted to
dispense with any dancing. For one thing, it was too hot for
such exertions, but primarily he didn't want his bride danced
off her feet by every loutish planter on the island. He considered setting up card tables, but rejected the idea immediately.
They'd never leave once they started gambling. No, he'd
have to come up with some sort of entertainment. They'd
open up the gardens after dinner so people could stroll about
in the evening breezes. Something to keep the men entertained; perhaps native dancers in their brief costumes. For the
ladies, perhaps those fellows who walked on fire. Then something that bored them all to tears so they would take their
departure.

"Collins, I hear your wife has a wonderful program of
Italian opera she entertains with at parties?" he remarked to
his secretary.

The chef's helpers at Government House had all come
from the island of Martinique, and the kitchens rang with a
mixture of French and Creole. Kitty took great pains with the
menu, begging Charles' superior advice whenever she was
unsure.

"My darling, the best advice I ever received, I'll willingly
pass along to you. When in doubt, do nothing! It's done
wonders for my career," he said with a laugh.

"I'm so ignorant, Charles!" she wailed.

"Why do you suppose I pay the chef such exorbitant wages? Because he's an expert, so just let him get on with it. What about your gown?"

"You are just trying to change the subject, and besides, it's a secret. I'm going to impress you immensely with my taste. My choice has to be impeccable, something in which the governor's wife will be the epitome of respectability."

"Respectability is bourgeois," he teased.

"Trust me about the gown. Now, do you think clear turtle soup would be acceptable?"

He sighed. "Oh, love, don't you think it's a bit warm for soup?"

"Oh, please, Charles, it sounds so elegant!"

"Ah, so that's to be the criterion, is it? Then we should have *ratatouille!* Does that sound elegant enough for you?"

"Oh, yes, please. What is *ratatouille?*"

"Sweetheart, I'm a beast to tease you so. That means poor stew, bad stuff, a mess."

She laughed with him and he slipped his arms about her and drew her down onto his knee. "That reminds me of the time I was invited to dinner in Lancashire—there're some incredibly bad cooks in Lancashire, by the way—and believe it or not, everything they put on the table was . . ."

"Boiled!" she finished his sentence for him.

"Exactly! When they brought the dessert it was a huge congealed mass of boiled treacle pudding. They eat so much treacle pudding in Lancashire, their feet stick to the floor when they walk," he said and laughed.

"Oh, but, Charles, when you're ravenous, nothing gets rid of hunger pains faster."

He looked at her tenderly. "Let's go up and have a look at our son."

* * *

Kitty's gown was eggshell georgette, delicately fluted and pleated. Tiny buttons ran up the back and from wrist to elbow. Charles brought her orchids.

"You're so lovely you take my breath away," he whispered.

"Charles, I'm so nervous about meeting everyone, I'm terrified of making stupid blunders, and I do so want you to be proud of me," she said anxiously.

"Come. Our first guests are starting to arrive. I assure you that you pass muster."

"You go on; I'll be along in a moment, dear."

Katie was in the adjoining dressing room with the baby. His cradle had been moved in earlier. Kitty had moved her things into the master bedroom, and now that she was alone, she looked the room over apprehensively. The bed loomed large in the center of the room and she wondered how she was going to bring herself to share it with her new husband. The ordeal of the crowd below seemed small by comparison, so she took a deep breath and went down to meet her guests. Charles awaited her at the foot of the stairs, smiling encouragement. He took her arm and together they stood in the reception hall. Kitty was amazed when the gentlemen bowed deeply to her and the ladies curtsied and murmured a reverent "Your Grace." At first the women were dismayed when they saw how beautiful she was, but when they watched her turn aside their husbands' compliments without attempts at flirtation, and when she addressed herself almost exclusively to the wives, they relaxed and included her in their conversations about servants, children, the weather, the crops and the latest fashions.

The menu she had chosen brought many compliments as the servants brought in silver platters heaped with delicacies. The wine flowed into tall goblets and she noted with surprise that Charles drank only mineral water. She thought she would do the same, since she was unused to wine and its effects. After dinner the guests wandered into the gardens to get the sea breezes. Kitty sought out Charles. "I have to go up and feed the baby. Do you think they will miss me for a little while?"

"Of course not, sweetheart. So long as the liquor flows, your guests will be happy. We won't start the entertainment until you come down."

When she was alone she picked up her child and nestled him against her. He nursed hungrily and she gazed at the robust child with wonder. He looked exactly as Julia's baby had, with the stamp of O'Reilly all over him. He closed his eyes and his long black lashes made shadows on his cheeks. She went quietly back into the larger bedroom and poured some scented water from the ewer to bathe her hands and face. She looked toward the baby's room and told herself over and over that she had done the right thing in marrying Charles. She picked up the lacy nightgown that had been put ready on the bed and replaced it in the bureau. Instead she took out a more modest one of heavy satin and put it on her pillow.

She went back downstairs to the evening's entertainment. It was all a colorful blur to Kitty. The music, the dancers, the costumes were all a noisy jumble; however, everyone seemed to be enjoying themselves immensely. Everyone came indoors when Mrs. Collins was ready to sing, and as Charles had hoped, the crowd quickly became bored, and after three selections some of the guests began to take their leave.

By ten o'clock the last guest had departed, and Charles took Kitty by the hand and led her upstairs. Katie came out of the dressing room when she heard them. "The baby is asleep, ma'am."

"Thank you, Katie. I'm sorry you missed all the merriment. It was very kind of you to stay with him."

As soon as the door was closed Charles picked up Kitty and swung her into the air. "You were magnificent, my darling. Everyone loved you! I'd swear you were born to the purple."

She blushed vividly and murmured, "Please, I must check on the baby." She hurried into the dressing room and Charles followed her. She stood gazing down at the child and said wistfully, "He's asleep."

"And you'd rather he was awake? Well, go on, wake him up and say hello."

"Oh, no, I wouldn't disturb him for the world," she said quietly.

He took her hand and led her back into their bedroom. He sat down in a large, comfortable armchair but kept hold of her hand. She stood before him with downcast eyes, for all the world like a virgin to the slaughter.

"The name Drago is Latin for dragon. Do you think me a dragon, Kathleen?"

"No, I'm not afraid of you, Charles," she said very meekly.

"Then you're just apprehensive about this business of sleeping with me?"

She nodded her head, miserably. He pulled her into his lap.

"My darling, don't be afraid. I promised to cherish you, and I shall. I'll always be gentle with you. I promise never to hurt you in any way. Look at me, Kathleen. Ah, that's better. I love you with all my heart." His lips brushed her hair and he held her to his heart. She was beginning to feel better. His arms were so protective and comforting.

"I'm just nervous. I'm sorry I'm being so silly."

"It's perfectly understandable. You're not in the least silly, but I suspect you're worn out from the rabble we've been entertaining." He sought her lips, and when she didn't pull away, he was encouraged to kiss and caress her as he had longed to do for weeks.

"Now, the first thing we have to do is get you out of this uncomfortable gown. Turn around, love." She turned her back to him and he undid all the little buttons down the back. "You need something to make you relax. I'll just go down and get you a glass of wine. Put your nightgown on and slip into bed, sweetheart. I'll be right back."

She had worried so much about undressing in front of another man, but it had been accomplished without any embarrassment. Her breasts were very large and firm at the moment, and she had no idea how beautifully they were revealed in the satin gown. Charles was back before she was in bed, so she quickly slipped under the covers, but not before he had taken in every detail.

"Here, darling, this will make you sleep." He turned the lamps low and undressed quickly. Kitty averted her eyes and drank her wine. "It's delicious. Thank you."

He took the empty glass from her fingers and set it aside. Then he gathered her into his arms and buried his face in her breasts.

"You're incredibly lovely. I've longed to hold you like this since the first time I saw you."

He kissed her slowly and made love to her so gently it wasn't an ordeal for her after all. Later, when he was asleep, she half smiled at the complete power she had over him. She would have to be very careful never to hurt him. Her heart ached for betraying Patrick. She closed her eyes to shut out the guilt she felt.

Charles slipped from the bed early in the morning and came back with a breakfast tray. "Sit up and see what I've brought you."

"Mmmm, I can smell chocolate."

He took a long envelope from the tray and held it carefully.

"I want to give you your 'morning gift.'"

"What is a 'morning gift'?" she asked.

"It's an ancient tradition. When a husband is pleased with his bride, he gives her a 'morning gift.' You please me very much."

She smiled at him gently.

"At first I thought of giving you jewelry, but that's such an ordinary gift. I decided to give you something that would be more meaningful to you." He held out the envelope.

"What is it, Charles?"

"It's the deed to one of my Irish estates. It's yours free and clear, to do with as you wish. You mustn't save it for Charles Patrick, because he will get all of my lands. This is yours to keep or to sell, or even to give away, if it so pleases you."

"Why, I . . . I don't know what to say. Are you sure you want to do this?"

"Absolutely sure." He laughed to lighten the mood. "Now you can leave me if you want to. You're not dependent on anyone anymore, not even me."

She was crying and in a moment he was in bed with her, holding her and laughing. He tipped back her head and kissed her.

"Charles, the servants will see us," she protested.

"Mmmm, I hope so," he murmured against her neck.

Much later, when she was alone, she vowed that she would be a good wife to Charles. She knew it would take an extraordinary effort on her part to fulfill the role of a duchess. She would start by putting away her tarot cards. She would help her husband make decisions about their son and their life and stop consulting the cards every time she had a decision to make. It would never do for her to go about telling fortunes now that she was married to a duke. She wanted him to be proud of her and swore she'd make every effort to be a lady.

Chapter 23

Patrick was nearing Bagatelle Plantation at last. He regretted his decision to ride. The heat was unbearable; he'd never been so affected by it. A wave of dizziness swept over him. He steadied himself with his knees and wiped the sweat from his eyes. As he came into view of the plantation, he sagged with relief. He'd been in the saddle for two days and every muscle in his body ached. He dismounted awkwardly and entered the house.

He knew at once that something was wrong. He could not identify what it was he saw in the faces of the house servants —fear? Jacquine greeted him with a brilliant smile, but her eyes were filled with compassion for him. He walked toward her with a sense of impending doom. "Patrick, sit down. I have some shocking news for you."

He sat down and waited.

"A young woman came looking for you. I know it was someone very special to you called Kitty. When she arrived she was very sick—boat fever, I believe—anyway, I did everything I could to save her, but it was hopeless from the beginning."

He laughed. "Kitty? Here? That's impossible! Where is she?" he demanded.

"I told you, Patrick, it was hopeless. She died from the fever."

"It wasn't Kitty. There's been some mistake, some mixup!" he denied quickly. "It's not true, you're lying!" he shouted.

Without a word she turned quietly and went upstairs.

When she returned, she held out the traveling bag containing Kitty's belongings. He snatched it from her and rummaged inside. His mind denied these things belonged to Kitty, but when his fingers closed on the pale lavender silk, he knew. He breathed in her fragrance deeply, and the delicate details of their lovemaking rushed back to him as his fingers caressed the silk.

"My God, what have you done with her? When did she arrive? Why wasn't a doctor called to help her?" he raved.

"Patrick, you look ill. All these questions are only upsetting you. She is dead, you must accept it. Take this brandy."

He ignored her outstretched hand. "Show me where," he said more quietly.

He followed her to the private cemetery plot and saw a small new mound of earth with a plain wooden cross.

"Leave me," he said.

When he hadn't returned to the house after two hours had elapsed, she went in search of him with two male house servants. She would use force on him if necessary. They found him unconscious on the ground, beside the grave. He was soaked with his own perspiration. She knew he had a raging fever and instructed the men to carry him up to bed immediately. She sent down to the cabins for Lucy. "If he dies—you die," Jacquine stated flatly. "When you know for certain one way or the other, you will come and tell me."

Lucy worked over her patient day and night for a week. It was not an easy task. He was well over six feet of raving, cursing, struggling male animal. Her emotions ran the gamut of fear, hatred and finally compassion for the man in her charge. Finally he looked at her with comprehension. She was startled as he hissed, "Why didn't you let me die?"

She ran for her mistress, who came with such caring haste he would never know she hadn't attended him once since he fell ill.

Her smile was tender, her hands gentle as she fed him broth to bring back his strength. He remained coldly indifferent. His eyes were narrow slits whenever they rested upon her for a moment, and she knew she would need to become the consummate actress ever to break through his iron carapace. She plied him with liquor, hoping he would indulge in a gigantic drunk to drown his heartache and emerge with his sorrows behind him. Patrick disappointed her. He set glass after glass aside with hardly a glance. She knew he didn't wish to ease the pain of Kitty, but to hold it close. When he was well enough to leave his bed, he kept to himself. He was silent and remote and she had to double her efforts to reach him. The grave held a fascination for him; he visited it both night and day. He took solitary rides; she rode out after him many times, but could never capture more than a fleeting glimpse as he thundered through the forest. She fell into the habit of riding off her own frustrations after dark. Sleep became elusive. She watched covertly as he returned to the house on foot.

"He has been at the damned graveside again," she said to herself jealously. She walked over to the burial ground and stood gazing down. "I have a garden filled with perfect roses and camellias, but he prefers to gather wild flowers for her." Her mouth twisted downward in a derisive laugh as she thought of the empty grave and the hoax she had perpetrated. Men were such sentimental fools! When would he get on with the business of living? He showed signs of becoming restless and she feared it would only be a matter of days now before he would announce his return to England. Her mind twisted and turned for some small shred, some weakness in his makeup that she could fasten upon and turn to her own advantage. It did not take her long to find an idea.

"Mon chéri, we must speak. Things cannot go on as they are."

His eyes narrowed. He lit a cheroot and allowed the smoke to mask his expression.

"Don't you think the time has come when you must return to England?"

The moment he hesitated, she knew she had won. "I know how much you must have loved her. She was so very young, you cannot bear to leave her here alone while you return to England. There is still a bond between you which even death cannot sever."

He crushed out the cigar and let her see the naked pain in his eyes.

"Stay here, marry me and you will own all this land. Then you may be near her all your days. We would make good partners. You would be the first to acknowledge this if you were thinking clearly."

During the next few days her words came to him again and again. The truth was that he had wanted to leave for over a month now, but he could not abandon Kitty. He began to look upon the plantation with speculative eyes. He even had an occasional smile for the house servants these days. When Jacquine returned from her ride each evening, her eyes went up to the balcony outside his window.

"Ah, well," she thought, "not tonight, but soon he will send out an invitation, soon."

Jacquine went for her usual evening ride, leaving Patrick still at table with a large brandy. Topaz came in to clear the dishes and she smiled shyly. "Can I get you something else?"

"I'll just help myself, Topaz. I don't want you waiting on me, child."

"It's always a pleasure to do for you. sir," she said and smiled.

"I'm glad you feel that way, Topaz. I've been thinking about staying here. I think we're going to have a wedding."

Her face crumpled. "You can't!" she blurted, then quickly covered her mouth.

"Topaz, what's wrong?" he reached out and touched her cheek. The gentle gesture undid her. Tears flooded her eyes.

"Oh, sir, your Kitty's not dead." He jumped up so quickly the chair went over backward. His eyes blazed. "Where is she?" he demanded.

"The mistress sold her to the slave buyer."

His face went ashen and he slumped to his knees before her. "Sweet Jesus, I've prayed that she was alive and now I wish to God she was dead!"

"Oh, lord, sir, she'll kill me for sure!"

"Stop crying, Topaz, I won't let her harm you. Where did he take Kitty? The slave auction in Charleston? What's the slave master's name?"

"I can't remember, sir. Oh, lord, she'll kill me."

"Go to bed, Topaz," he ordered quietly.

Jacquine rode full gallop up to the house and drew rein under Patrick's balcony. He looked down upon her and struck a match to light his cheroot. The flame flared up and outlined his naked body against the darkness. She smiled up at him and dismounted quickly. She picked up the hem of her habit and ran up the stairs eagerly. He was there before her, splendid in his manhood. She reached out her hands and ran them up his arms and along his muscled chest. He took her in his arms, lifted her high above his head, then brought her crashing down across his uplifted knee. A crack rent the air as her backbone snapped and her body crumpled to the floor, quite dead. Calmly he washed his hands and slipped into his clothes. He lifted her body and took it down to her horse. She rode like a madwoman; it would be natural to assume she had

killed herself in a fall. In the stables he caused no stir as he
saddled a horse for himself. He knew how impossible was
the task that lay ahead of him. He feared he would never find
her, but he had to try.

Little Charles caught Kitty's eye. He pulled himself up by
a chair leg and tottered over to her, threatening to lose his
balance with every step. She chuckled at his progress
through the packing cases. Their departure had been delayed
a couple of months before the new governor had arrived. She
was supervising the packing of Charles' art collection to take
back to England with them. She would feel a pang of regret
at leaving here, because she had been happy. Charles was so
good to her. He treated her as a precious possession, constantly giving her tokens of tenderness to show his love.
Often she felt she was cheating him because he made few
demands of her in bed. She knew he wasn't indifferent, but
she knew he feared failure and embarrassment. Perhaps
things would change when they were aboard and he had left
behind the heavy responsibilities of his governorship. Kitty
longed to see her brother again. As soon as they were back
she planned to have her grandfather go back to Ireland to live
on the estate Charles had deeded her. Terry could manage it
and even breed horses, which always were his first love.

"I did the right thing," she assured herself as she thought
of the happiness she would bring to her family when they
learned they could go back to where their hearts had always
been.

Kitty dressed carefully and picked a large hat that shaded
her face well. She walked swiftly and surely from Government House, through the business section of Basseterre and
up through the posh residential area where each mansion was
more imposing than its neighbor. The last house was larger

and more impressive than the rest. Without hesitation she went through the gateway and up to the massive front doors. She pulled the bell and waited patiently. After a few moments Molly Maguire answered the door herself. Her eyebrows rose in surprise when she saw Kitty.

"Well, I'll be damned, it's the governor's lady. Come in, honey. It's not every day I get a visit from flaming nobility." She led Kitty into a small salon furnished in exquisite taste, and rang for a serving girl. When she came, Molly ordered tea and gave orders that they were not to be disturbed.

Kitty spoke for the first time. "We are sailing for home in a few days. The new governor is already here."

"Oh, I've had the pleasure. This is one of the first stops gentlemen make when they arrive on the island," Molly said.

"Well, that really shouldn't surprise me, should it?" said Kitty, laughing and feeling more relaxed.

"I don't often get the chance to entertain a lady. Aren't you afraid someone will see you visiting such an unsavory place?"

"Not at all. I couldn't leave the island without thanking you for all you did for me when I arrived. You saved my life, Molly. I came to say good-bye." She hesitated.

Molly looked at her keenly. "You seem as if you would like to ask me something but don't quite know how to go about it."

Kitty laughed nervously. "You're very observant."

"I don't wish to pry, but if I can help you with something, all you have to do is ask. Don't be embarrassed."

"Well, there was something I was going to ask your advice about, but it doesn't seem important now. I'd better go," said Kitty.

"Sit right where you are! It's something intimate, isn't it? Something isn't right between you and your husband. Tell me," she urged.

"Well, it's just that, he doesn't . . . he can't . . ." Kitty stopped.

"Listen, Irish, I've seen every sex problem in the world. Sometimes a man can't get an erection." She knew from Kitty's face that she had guessed right. "Usually the easiest way to cure that is to take it into your mouth for a minute and run your tongue along . . ."

Kitty jumped up, outraged. "I couldn't do anything like that!" she cried angrily.

Molly threw back her head and laughed. "I've shocked you! Well, listen to me, Miss High-and-Mighty, if you were passionately in love with a man, doing something like that wouldn't disgust you so much."

Kitty thought of Patrick and silently admitted that what Molly said might be right.

"I'm sorry. I didn't mean to look down my nose at you. I came for advice and then acted like a prude when you were good enough to speak plainly."

"It's not your fault. I'm so used to dealing with whores, I forgot myself. Now, for a man who has trouble getting hard in the first place, you sort of have to set the mood. Undress in front of him, be very seductive. Kiss him, touch him, manipulate him with your fingers. Allow him to explore your body and play with your breasts. A beautiful girl like you shouldn't have any difficulties, unless of course his tastes are perverted in lovemaking. That's an entirely different thing."

"No, I can assure you that isn't the case," replied Kitty.

"That's good! With the nobility you never can be sure. Give me a man from the working class every time—he always prefers his sex straight."

Kitty stood up and extended her hand. "We'll probably never meet again, but I shall always remember you. Good-bye, Molly."

"Good-bye and good luck, Irish."

* * *

Patrick walked down the wharf in Charleston. He was thinner, and the lines in his face were deeper. He'd searched every pleasure palace from New Orleans to Natchez. He'd done it knowing it was hopeless, but he wouldn't give up. Finally, he'd come full circle back to Charleston, without a trace. He collided with a burly sea captain.

"Well, I'll be damned! Patrick John Francis O'Reilly, himself! Let me buy you a drink, boss; you look like you could use one."

"Big Jim, I haven't seen you in years. Did you just make port?" asked Patrick.

"Aye, aye, sir. By God, you're looking rough. It has to be a woman!"

"We can get a drink in here, Jim. I've some questions to put to you."

They sat down at a table and ordered rum.

"Have you been to the islands lately, Jim?" asked Patrick, getting straight to the point.

"I've just come up from down there."

"I've been going mad looking for a young woman. . . ."

"Our glorious Kitty!" cut in Jim.

Patrick sprang up. "How the hell do you know Kitty?" he demanded.

"She sailed with me from Liverpool last year, that's how I know her."

Patrick groaned and sank down, his head in his hands. "She's been sold as a slave, probably shipped to one of the islands."

Big Jim let out a bellow of laughter that was deafening.

"What in Christ's name are you laughing at, you bloody fool?"

"A slave! That's bloody rich, that is! Well, the laugh's on both of us, boyo. She wasn't good enough for me, and by the looks of it she wasn't good enough for you, either. She sold out to the highest bidder, Patrick, my lad. She's a bloody duchess!''

"Duchess? Make sense, man!" Patrick demanded angrily.

"Two months back I made port at St. Kitts, and who was sailing for England but the Duke of Manchester and his duchess. Traveling like a bloody queen, she was, with enough sodding baggage to sink a freighter.''

Patrick sat stunned.

"What you need is a woman. Come on, I was just on my way to Dirty Annie's.''

"Dirty Annie's be damned!" replied Patrick. "I'll take you to the fanciest goddamned whorehouse in Charleston— La Maison de Joie.''

Chapter 24

After a week's rest in London, Kitty was launched into a whirlwind of social activities that dispelled forever her fear about being accepted. They were immediately deluged with invitations by those who were vying for a return invitation to the Duke and Duchess of Manchester's. Charles couldn't resist showing off his son for all their visitors. Kitty allowed him to show off his new son because it gave him obvious pleasure and pride.

The first thing Kitty had done on her return was to make sure Terry took their grandfather to her estate in Ireland. After that every moment was taken up with fittings for new clothes, making the rounds of the shops for new pieces for the house and entertaining Charles' friends. They went to the ballet, the opera and the theaters. Kitty began to enjoy herself. At first she had been nervous of society, but Charles encouraged her to be herself and she bloomed under this encouragement. She didn't affect any airs, but spoke to any and all with her natural exuberance. Charles chuckled to himself when he heard two of his friends discussing her at a party. "Remember this: The bluer the blood, the bluer the language, I say. The girl's descended from royalty—wrong side of the blanket, of course." Sometimes Charles accompanied her shopping and she became very familiar with Hatton Garden off Bond Street. It was a dark shop with a room behind where they kept their stock of diamonds, and the tellers in Coutts' Bank knew her on sight. Men were very attracted to Kitty, but soon she acquired a witty repartee that kept them in their place. However, there were one or two ready to step over the line the moment she gave them the slightest encouragement. At buffet suppers, they rushed to help her select the tastiest dishes.

"Do try some of the cucumber salad, my dear," said Lord Macklesfield, standing much closer than he needed to.

She fixed him with a direct look and answered, "A cucumber should be well sliced, dressed with pepper and vinegar and thrown away."

"*Touché,* my dear," he said with an appreciative twinkle. "You can't blame a chap for trying!"

Granville, a rather small man, overheard them and cautioned Lord Macklesfield, "Patience is bitter, but it bears sweet fruit."

Kitty winked at Lord Macklesfield and said, "Never listen to a man with short legs—brains too near his bottom."

"I won't tangle with you, your Grace; your tongue has a decidedly sharp edge to it," he said and laughed.

The Duke of Portland, whose job it was to engage all the royal footmen, saw Kitty coming toward him. He turned to Lady Chatham and said, "Here comes an angel, and by God I'd like to clip her wings. I do believe she fancies me, you know. She always singles me out for a compliment or two."

Kitty gave him a dazzling smile, "How do you do it?" she asked sweetly.

"Do what, my dear?" he bridled.

"Delude yourself practically every day of your life."

Lady Chatham hooted with laughter. "You're incorrigible! Come, let's find that husband of yours. I think he went into the card room with the dowager Duchess Gresham."

"Good God, not that horsey woman! Did she have Mr. Weatherley's stud book under her arm?" asked Kitty with horror.

"She doesn't go anywhere without it, does she?" laughed Isobel Chatham.

"We must rescue him at all costs. The last time she cornered me I had to get away from her before I was wormed or served!"

Kitty slipped behind Charles' chair and put her hands on his shoulders.

"Darling, I was hoping you'd take me home. It's a terrible crush tonight."

"Excuse me, Maude, duty calls," he said politely.

After the theater, they often invited a few friends back for a light supper. Kitty enjoyed these intimate evenings because the conversation always was lively and interesting. She became famous for her devastating imitations of people in the inner circle.

"Where were you last evening? I missed you at the opera," said Lady Derby.

"Viscountess Palmerston's soiree in Charlton Gardens," answered Charles.

"Oh, it was lovely," said Kitty, "except I got cornered by the Duchess of Sutherland. She uses all those double words. What do you call it, Charles?"

"Reduplicative," he said with a smile, knowing what was coming.

Kitty mimicked, "Pish tush, I say! The whippersnapper talks claptrap. He's a wishy-washy, namby-pamby nitwit. What a mishmash it is tonight, nothing but riffraff and ragtag. Tut-tut, girl, drink up, chin-chin, no more chitchat, don't shilly-shally. Oh, fiddle-faddle, here's the major so I'll say ta-ta."

Her appreciative audience clapped their delight at her take-off.

"Isn't she marvelous? Kitty, do the Foreign Secretary."

Charles cut in smoothly, "I don't think that would be wise. Kathleen is to be presented to Her Majesty next week."

"Oh, marvelous; she'll take an instant dislike to you of

course—far too pretty. Remember, no bright colors; it's an unwritten rule that all the ladies wear sober attire. What shall you wear?''

''Oh, bottle green, or something equally hideous, I suppose,'' Kitty said and laughed.

Patrick's sister Julia lost no time rekindling her friendship. Kitty suspected it had a great deal to do with her new status, but she did find Julia's social advice invaluable. The London Season was upon them, and social activities reached a frenzied peak. Charles paid careful attention to dressing the evening his wife was to be presented to the Queen. He was vying for a new appointment, and although he didn't think he'd get to be Chancellor of the Exchequer, he thought he stood a good chance for customs collector for the Port of London.

Inside the anteroom the gentlemen handed their capes and top hats to footmen on the right, while ladies went to the left to remove their cloaks. They came together again to be announced as they entered the state ballroom. As he turned, Charles was shocked to see Kitty standing resplendent in flame-colored silk with crimson poppies in her hair.

He thought wryly, There goes my appointment.

''Their Graces, the Duke and Duchess of Manchester,'' rang out across the room, followed by a shocked silence that seemed to stretch out for minutes. Inwardly she wished with all her heart that she hadn't done this stupid, impulsive thing. Then a gentleman separated himself from a group of courtiers and walked down the ballroom toward Kitty. He bowed low in front of her.

''May I have the next dance, madame?''

''Thank you, Prince Albert, You are the most courageous man in the room.'' He raised her quickly and everyone

ENTICED

around them gave a collective sigh that she had been accepted.

Later, when she danced with Charles, she told him she regretted her whim. "Now I shall have to learn how to dismount gracefully from my high horse. Darling, I'm sorry if this queers your chances with the Queen."

"Nonsense; she'll probably take pity on an old man like me, saddled with such an incorrigible snip of a girl for his wife," and he squeezed her hard before letting her go. She dreaded the moment coming and when at last she was face to face with Victoria, Kitty sank into a curtsy and waited to be spoken to first.

"Irish, are you not?" inquired the Queen.

Kitty nodded and began. "Your Majesty, I'm sorry . . ."

"No need to apologize; you'd stand out anywhere, rather like a tiger lily at a funeral."

Kitty had many offers to take her in to supper. She chose Lord Liverpool, who joked that Liverpool and Manchester should always go arm in arm. "Here comes the Prime Minister," hissed Lord Liverpool.

Lord Palmerston, with a fatuous look toward Queen Victoria, said, "Ah, ladies, your cause has come a long way because of our gracious Queen Victoria. Because one of your own fair-sex rules, womanhood has come out of the dark ages."

"I don't agree, Mr. Prime Minister," said Kitty. "The Regency and the Georgians were frankly bawdy. Victoria's suppressions have turned us all into hypocrites."

"However do you mean, madame?"

"Well, for example, take an innocent thing like afternoon tea."

"My dear lady, you aren't suggesting . . ."

"Of course I'm suggesting! Big overstuffed sofas are more comfortable than featherbeds! Now, here's where the

hypocrisy comes in. The Victorian woman is one mass of
pads, cushions and corsets from head to foot. Frilled trailing
skirts prevent a man from going up and boned necklines
prevent him from going down, so what is the very latest
fashion? Why, the tea gown, of course! That miracle garment
which falls loosely about the figure and can be discarded in a
trice. Our society is based on the hypocrisy of not being
found out. Why, the last weekend we had in the country I
needed a bloody program to keep the players straight as they
went from one bedroom to another!''

''Brava, brava, my girl,'' cheered Lady Derby. ''Taking
tea with other men's wives is a shameful custom.''

Lord Palmerston bowed to Kitty with a twinkle in his eye.
''Your husband is a lucky man, and I shall tell him so when I
confirm his new appointment.''

The London House in Strand Lane had lawns that sloped
down to the river. Kitty and Charles Patrick were running
back up to the house. His shoes were muddy from the riverbank and he played tag so fiercely with his mother that his
hair stood on end. The dampness had given them both a wild
look. She took tea in the nursery with him and by the time he
was finished, jam had smeared up his cheek and into his
curls. His mouth opened in a cavernous yawn.

''I think you're tired,'' she said.

''Not!'' he protested stubbornly, but at the same time he
yawned again.

''Look, you be a good boy and have a nap now, and later,
when nurse gives you your bath, I'll come up and watch.''

''Can I splash you?''

''No, not in this velvet dress you can't.''

''I'll splash nurse,'' he countered.

''You little bugger, I bet you will,'' she said and laughed.

''Daddy?'' he asked hopefully.

"I suppose he'll let you," she agreed and lifted him into bed, fully dressed, minus the muddy shoes.

"I love you," she whispered.

"Love you," he answered sweetly.

She slipped into her bedroom to smooth her hair before Charles arrived. It was almost five and she could count on his arrival like clockwork. She was on the upstairs hall landing when she heard him.

"Kathleen, come and see the surprise I have for you!" he shouted happily.

She lifted her skirt and began a rapid descent when his next words caused her to hesitate.

"Can you imagine the damned fellow being in England months and not visiting us?"

Her eyes sought out the dark figure beyond Charles, and she stopped dead from the sudden shock.

"You're not seeing a ghost—it's your cousin Patrick."

He looked as reluctant as she was for this meeting as he took a stiff, tentative step forward.

"Bumped into him this afternoon and practically had to drag him here," continued Charles in a hearty tone.

She swayed visibly and caught hold of the banister to steady herself. Time stood still as she confronted the man who stood before her. His mouth was set in a grim line, his body tense. His eyes were sharp as a hawk's; they would miss nothing. His aristocratic face tilted arrogantly and he said in a deliberately bored voice, "How are you, cousin?"

Anger began to swell inside her and she moved down the staircase with eyes blazing. "Weren't you able to pull off marriage with the American, then?" she asked cuttingly.

"I leave marriage to others," he said dangerously.

"Ah, you don't know what you are missing, my boy," said Charles, who had no idea how inflammatory the remark was.

Virginia Henley

Patrick stiffened visibly as he watched Kitty through narrowed eyes. She could feel his hatred but could not comprehend it. It was she who had the right to hate him after what he he had done to her.

Charles was putting glasses of sherry in their hands and ushering them into the drawing room. "Here's the best part. Wait till you see my son. You'll be jealous as the very devil," he said and laughed, already heading toward the stairs.

"Charles, no!" cried Kitty. "He's having a nap and you know how I hate you to disturb him," she pleaded.

"Nonsense; whatever's gotten into you? You know I can't resist showing him off to all and sundry." He winked at Patrick affectionately. Patrick murmured, politely, "I heard you'd had a child."

They stood alone like two protagonists unable to control events that swirled about them. Neither spoke. The muscles in Patrick's jaw clenched like a lump of iron. Kitty's bottom lip trembled until she caught it between her teeth. Each could feel the heat of the other's anger.

"Here we are. Come and see your Uncle Patrick. He's come all the way from America," urged Charles.

Patrick looked up and saw the little boy walking down the stairs dragging a dirty stuffed donkey with its tail missing. His eyes narrowed, puzzled at the child's age. Kitty, thinking her son would be terrified at the dark, forbidding figure, picked him up protectively and Patrick said, "Good God, I thought he was a baby."

"Not a baby!" cried Charles Patrick, soundly thumping Patrick with a jam-smeared fist.

Patrick's eyes widened in comprehension as he looked over the black curls into Kitty's eyes. God help me, he knows! thought Kitty.

Patrick's face softened as he gazed at the child with wonder. He finally realized Charles Patrick was using his finger to make a sticky jam pattern on his velvet lapel. "I don't suppose they beat you, but they ought to," he said softly. The boy gave him such a sweet smile that he had to resist the impulse to take his child in his arms.

Kitty said hurriedly, "Charles, please take him to bed; it's wicked of us to spoil him like this."

"Come on then, old son, Mother's all straitlaced disapproval tonight." Charles flashed an apologetic look at Patrick. "Usually she's off and running at the first madcap suggestion."

"I remember," said Patrick acidly.

When they were alone again, Patrick said, "I shall be at Half-Moon Street tomorrow evening. I demand a reckoning."

"I shan't come!" she retorted with outrage.

"I don't believe I heard you correctly," he said in a tone so quiet and menacing she felt her blood run cold.

Charles returned. "Well, what do you think of him?"

"He's a fine young cockerel, to be sure," answered Patrick truthfully.

"Stay for dinner. Believe it or not we're entertaining Julia and Jeffrey tonight," invited Charles.

"Can't be done, Charles. Like nothing better, but there it is, old man," he lied desperately.

"All right, I know you've probably got so many irons in the fire you haven't time for your old friends, but I'm warning you, we'll catch up with you one of these days and spend the whole evening together."

Patrick shot Kitty a meaningful look. "Yes, very soon, the whole evening."

That night at dinner Kitty changed the subject every time Patrick's name was mentioned. Although she pretended to listen to Julia, her ears strained to catch what Jeffrey and Charles were saying.

"He's sold all three mills. He's finally out of the cotton business for good," said Jeffrey.

"I wonder what he'll invest the money in? I only ask because if we followed Patrick's lead, we wouldn't go wrong," said Charles.

Julia said, "He has vast shipping interests these days with that Bolt fellow in Liverpool. I hope he puts the money into slaves. The profits are unheard of."

Kitty went cold. She put her fork down and pressed her napkin to her lips. When she was able to speak she said, "Charles, you don't believe he would do such a thing, do you?"

"Darling, I can understand your repugnance for such dealings, but in the past I haven't been above a bit of slave trade myself; as Julia says, it's very profitable."

She wanted to walk out on them all, but instead she politely changed the subject. Later Jeffrey put his hand on her arm and said quietly, "She's only speculating, you know. You don't think for one moment Patrick consults Julia about his dealings, do you?"

"Of course not." She gave him a quick, reassuring smile, but she was far from reassured. She'd have to see him now. She had sworn she wouldn't attend the command performance Patrick had ordered her to, but now she knew she had no choice.

She knew before she opened her wardrobe door what she would wear. It was a burnt-orange walking suit edged in deep brown sable. It had cost the earth. She brushed her hair until the black curls cascaded down her back, and perched the matching fur hat on a saucy angle. She took a parcel from the bottom bureau drawer and marched forth to do battle.

Patrick opened the door himself; she noted there were no servants in evidence. An expression of satisfaction, quickly veiled, came into his face when he saw her. "I knew you'd come."

"You infuriating bastard, I didn't come because you ordered me to," she spat. He looked at her with distaste. "If you live to be a thousand, you'll never become a lady," he said quietly. "At least wait until you're over the threshold before you start screaming like a banshee."

She trembled with rage, but at the same time realized he had the advantage so long as he kept rigid control of his temper.

More calmly she stepped inside. "It appears you delude yourself with the idea that you are the aggrieved party and deserve some sort of explanation. Let me quickly disabuse you of any such notion, Mr. O'Reilly."

His temper flared. "You shallow little bitch, you think a simple explanation on your part is enough to set everything right when you've done your damndest to destroy me and almost succeeded."

She looked around for a seat. "I might as well make myself comfortable while you bore me with an interminable catalog of grievances."

He towered over her, his wrath frightening her more than a little. She had had to sit down because her trembling legs had threatened to collapse.

"It was the simplest request in the world. All you had to do was wait for me. I gave you money and I gave you my word that I would return and we would be married. But oh, no, you acted the thoughtless, selfish, willful child and came racing headlong to America. A more stupid act I can't conceive of. They say the Irish are thick, and by God they're right! I should have known better than to pick you out of the bog! You're as wild and uncivilized as a bloody aborigine from a rain forest and always will be!" He caught his breath and her beauty stabbed him to the heart. "The great pity is

you have no conception of the pain and heartache you've
caused me,'' he went on in a quieter tone. ''They told me at
the plantation you had died from the fever and showed me
your grave. I kept vigil and mourned at that graveside like a
faithful dog! I didn't want to stay in America, but I couldn't
bear to leave you in the cold ground alone. It almost turned
my brain. I came to the conclusion that my only way out was
to join you in death. Then I discovered you hadn't died but
had been sold as a slave. There are no words to describe what
I went through then. I had rather you were dead a thousand
times over than sold to some brothel.'' The quiet voice was
deceiving; it masked a fierce temper. He sneered now. ''I
should have known not to worry about you. You can take
care of yourself better than anyone who ever drew breath,
can't you, Kitty? Well, I hope you're pleased with yourself.
Because of your blind ambition for a title, you've deprived
me of my own son!''

''Permission to speak, milord?'' she asked with heavy sar-
casm.

''Granted.'' He nodded and settled back with a cheroot,
exhaling the smoke to mask his expression.

She did not use an accusing tone but decided to set forth
the facts as simply and quietly as she could.

''The same night you left me, I was frightened out of my
sleep. I discovered my husband and his friend raping Terry. I
shot my husband through the head. It was an accident, of
course, but even so took a great deal of explaining on my
part. I went to London after the funeral, hoping you'd been
delayed. I met Charles there. He was kind and compassionate
and asked me to marry him. The idea of marrying any but
you was unthinkable, even when I discovered that you had
gone away and left me with child. My one thought and desire
was to reach you as soon as possible. Some notion of honor
kept me from wanting to be the mother of a bastard. Your

whore shackled me to a black man and sold me to the slave trader. I was resold to a brothel in the islands, but before I could be delivered, Charles rescued me. I stood before Charles in this shift, my belly distended with your child, and he took me to his heart and cherished me." She handed him the parcel and tore it open for him. He pulled out the orange rag caked with dirt and encrusted blood. Instead of recoiling from it, he held it to his cheek and said, "Forgive me."

"You are probably right. Most of the blame is mine. Damn if I cry, I'm undone," she said, dashing away her tears. He pulled out his handkerchief and wiped her eyes.

"Please, I insist, let me be the villain," he said and smiled.

"A bloody role that suits you down to the ground!" she cried, snatching the hanky from him and blowing her nose.

"Darling Kitty, we've hurled accusations at each other, spat out our hatred and venom, and after all the blood and tears, it still boils down to one thing: You're mine, and I want you!"

"Patrick, it's too late for that," she said wearily.

"Listen to me, kitten. I've murdered for you. Killing brutalizes a man and reduces his quality. I'll stop at nothing to have you. Besides, it's clear you want me too."

"Patrick, you must listen to me. The only reason I came here tonight was because Julia said you might invest the money from the mills in slaves. I came to beg you to have nothing to do with slavery. I don't want you to destroy your soul."

"Julia's a bitch! She lies to amuse herself. Besides, America is on the threshold of a civil war. Mr. Lincoln will put an end to slavery." He began to undo the buttons on her pelisse.

"Don't do that, Patrick. I'm not staying."

She put her hands out to stop him and felt the knotted muscles in his arms quiver. His voice roughened with desire as his lips found her neck. "You don't think I'm going to let you go, do you?"

As the old remembered tingling sensations started, she panicked and tried to pull away. She managed the top half, but his strong hands slid quickly to her buttocks and pressed her into his thighs. She could feel him hard and ready. As he bent his head to take her lips, he was shocked to see the look of fear in her eyes.

"I'm frightening you," he said, and reluctantly withdrew his arms.

"Patrick, you're so strong, I know you can force me, but I didn't come here so you could make love to me tonight."

"I don't want you just for tonight; I want you every night and I want my son. I want you to come away and live with me. It's love, not lust I feel for you, Kitty. Why are you afraid of me?"

"You have such dangerous weapons you can use against me. I can't leave Charles and come to you. He's such a fine person and he's been so good to me. He dotes on Charles Patrick; it would kill him to deprive him of the boy. I couldn't be that cruel."

"Believe me, kitten, you are quite capable of cruelty," he said pointedly.

"Patrick, I love you with all my heart and soul, and I'm so guilty about it, but I never could leave Charles."

A look of triumph came into his eyes. He tipped up her chin with his fingers. "I'm content for now. You'd better leave; you're completely aware of how much you arouse me, and I'll curse myself for a fool the moment you're through that doorway." The next morning she received a basket of tiger lilies. The card read: Somewhere, Somehow, Someway, Someday!

Chapter 25

Kitty had trouble sleeping. She tossed and turned, banishing dark night thoughts. Her nerves seemed to be on edge to a point where she wanted to scream. There were nights when she was so jumpy her skin felt too tight for her body. At social functions, she spent more time in the card room than on the dance floor. Gambling was becoming an obsession with her. Charles was wise enough to realize that things usually ran their course before they stopped, but he did keep an eye on her. They were having what appeared to be a cozy afternoon tea together when Charles Patrick fell from the last two stairs.

"Take those damned things off immediately!" shouted Kitty.

"Whatever's wrong, sweetheart?" asked Charles, who'd never heard her raise her voice to the child before.

"He's always got those damned riding boots of yours on. It's the third time he's fallen down the stairs this week. If you fall down one more time, those damned boots go on the back of the fire! All he ever talks about is the horse you've promised. He'll break his neck!"

"Charlie, go upstairs and take the boots off. I'll try to coax Mummy out of her bad mood. Now what is it, Kathleen? Come and talk to me—we've always talked things out before. You know you can tell me anything."

"I've been gambling and losing. I lost those lovely earrings you bought me, and worse still, I came within a hairsbreadth of losing that country cottage in Kent you gave me last month, and I haven't even seen it yet. I don't like myself very much these days, Charles. I don't know what's the matter with me.''

"I do," he said simply. He patted the couch beside him. Slowly she went to him and sat down. He put his arm about her and hugged her reassuringly. "You're young and beautiful and bursting with life. You're not being fulfilled and it's making you restless."

"I don't understand, Charles. What do you mean?"

"You're young and I'm not. I can't satisfy you in bed. The fires of my blood have died out, but yours are just beginning to burn. No, don't look so shocked, darling, it's perfectly true. I'm a realist and I knew it would happen one day. You need a lover. I'm not so selfish as to deny you such diversion. I only ask that you be discreet."

She looked at him with wide eyes. "Do you mean you wouldn't mind?"

"I shall mind like the very devil, so be sure to keep me in ignorance."

"Oh, Charles, you can always make me laugh."

"And a good thing, too. You were sulky as a bear with a sore arse. That child probably is crying his eyes out upstairs," he teased.

"You lie through your teeth. You know I can't dampen his high spirits."

Her words were punctuated by a loud clatter. She ran to pick her son up, and he protested, "It isn't the riding boots, Mummy, it's that damned beeswax the bloody servants keep polishing the stairs with."

"He has a salty vocabulary for someone who hasn't reached his third birthday. Speaking of birthdays, you're about to celebrate one shortly. Why don't we give a costume ball?"

* * *

Kitty was wise enough to take the suggestion her chef offered for the buffet-style supper. Charles had refused all blandishments to get him to wear a costume. He wore his dark evening clothes and told Kitty, "If anyone objects, you can tell them I'm supposed to be Beau Brummell."

Most of the ladies went all out with rather grand costumes. There were many Marie Antoinettes, and many medieval ladies, each one in a steeple headdress. Julia, resplendent in red wig, made a magnificent Elizabeth and contrasted well with Kitty's authentic Gypsy dress. Everyone wore masks, so it took a few minutes to recognize some people. Kitty was surprised to find the man in the common seaman's striped jersey was none other than the Prime Minister. She winked at him. "Always predicted you would amount to nothing—glad to see you've fallen far below my expectations."

Charles found her sparring with Julia. "You are audacious to dress as a Gypsy girl, Kitty. I think it's demeaning to the duke."

Kitty laughed as she tipped back her third glass of champagne. "Careful what you eat, Julia; we cooked one or two hedgehogs this morning."

"It's midnight and there's no sign of anyone leaving. I think it's been an unqualified success, darling," said Charles.

"The masks definitely allow people to have more fun. Everyone still will be here at breakfast time," she said happily.

"I think I'll go up now. I'll slip away quietly so people won't get the idea we want them to leave," he said.

"There's no fear of that. This lot will see the dawn arrive. Why don't you open up a card room?" she suggested.

"Wouldn't be able to fill it. Too much competition from that moonlit garden. I won't spoil your party with cards, I'm off to bed. Enjoy yourself, darling."

"I'll come up with you for a moment. They wouldn't miss me if I disappeared altogether," she said and laughed. "Are you sure you wouldn't like me to stay with you?'' she asked him.

"Kathleen, I'm very sure. I'm going to have a brandy and a cigar. You get back to the rabble and I'll see you tomorrow."

She closed the door on the peaceful scene, and before she reached the staircase, the great noise of the party came up to meet her. Steadying herself with the banister, she warned herself not to have any more champagne and descended the stairs. The French doors to the garden stood open invitingly. A tall, masked figure slipped his arm about her and drew her into the night. She turned her face up to him with a polite refusal on her lips, but before she could utter a word his mouth was upon hers demanding a response.

"Patrick, whatever are you doing?'' she gasped breathlessly.

"Abducting you, darling,'' he whispered deliciously against her ear.

She pulled back reluctantly, so he quickly lifted her into his arms and strode off into the darkness.

"What are you going to do?'' she cried.

"You know,'' he promised softly.

"Put me down immediately or I'll scream my head off,'' she threatened.

He chuckled and said, "You can scream bloody murder, and who will attend?''

"Why are you doing this?'' she cried.

He murmured softly, "Because you tempt me and I cannot resist.''

His carriage was in darkness, but it had a driver waiting. In spite of her struggles, he lifted her inside with amazingly gentle hands.

"I can't just leave my own party. I'll be missed! They'll call the police.''

"Your guests will think you are upstairs and Charles will think you are downstairs. I'll return you in the morning, and none will be the wiser."

"Why are you doing this to me?" she demanded angrily.

He easily lifted her against him. "Come to me, darling, while I explain."

Her skirt and petticoats twisted behind her and she was trapped against him in a reclining position.

"Tonight was a fantasy for you, pretending to be that little Gypsy we both knew, wild and free. I'm completing the daydream where your secret lover comes to steal you away and carry you off."

She could feel his manhood throbbing through the thin material that covered her thighs. Her senses were being aroused against her will. His voice was coaxing and persuasive. "I'll make a bargain with you. Give me one last time, sweetheart, and I give you my oath I'll never bother you again."

She was being swayed against her better judgment, but his word was his bond and she knew he would keep it once he had pledged himself.

"Patrick, let me breathe. I can't think coherently when you are touching me."

"You have the same effect on me, kitten; like heady wine!"

He allowed her to sit up. She immediately missed his warmth and shivered. Wisely he kept his distance. She moved toward him of her own free will. "I'm cold," she said shyly.

He took his cloak from the opposite seat and wrapped her tightly. The carriage stopped and he jumped out and lifted her down.

"You are a devil to bring me here," she protested when she saw they were at his house in Half-Moon Street.

He caught her earlobe between his teeth and said, "Then

that's another fantasy you can fulfill—bargaining with the devil for your soul,'' he said and laughed.

"It's the height of arrogance to bring me here for a tryst," she said with more anger than she really felt.

He set her down on a velvet couch while he lit the gaslight. The light flickered up across his face, so incredibly handsome she had almost forgotten its powerful attraction. "Stay with me tonight, love. Don't leave," he begged seriously.

In a far-off corner of her mind she realized it was hopeless to oppose him. He always had his way. "He has hypnotized me," she thought wildly, then ruefully admitted the strong attraction she felt for him was love inevitable. To be here alone together was paradise. He touched her hair and it curled possessively about his fingers.

"Let me make love to you tonight, so we'll always remember. Let me play with you. I'll start with your fingertips and stop at your toes," he said, pressing quick kisses into the palm of her hand. He kissed the silky flesh on the inside of her arm. "Be generous with me, sweet; you know I'm madly in love with you." He found her lips and kissed her deeply. His hand caressed her breast. "Chamade," he whispered hoarsely, "the heart wildly beating in surrender." Very gently he undressed her, kissing each part as it was uncovered to him.

"Now you," she murmured, reaching for his shirt buttons. She performed the same ritual for him and by the time they were both naked, they were dizzy with rapture. He lifted her from the couch, high above him and let her slip down his body. The head of his shaft penetrated her and he cupped her buttocks so she could sit on him and savor the exquisite feeling it gave to both of them. The tip of his tongue slipped inside her mouth and she felt she would die from the twin sensations of penetration and withdrawal their bodies made. She wrapped her legs around his back and he slowly walked to the bed with her in that position. He bent down until she was on the bed, then she playfully rolled away and buried her face in the pillows. In a flash he straddled her and showered kisses on her back. As he rolled her over to face him, their playful laughter ceased and they became very serious. The awe of the moment dawned upon them as they fully realized the deep love they felt for each other. Their lovemaking had a delicious newness about it, while at the same time they were repeating the ritual mating they had shared years before. With hardly a pause he repeated his lovemaking to make up for all the nights they had lived without it. Afterward they lay entwined and talked.

"I think it will be easier for us if I go away," he said.

"But you said war was about to break out in America," she said, frightened.

"There's money to be made in war, darling."

"Not gunrunning, Patrick," she said fearfully.

"No, not gunrunning. I can leave that up to my partner. You forget Hind's is a food company. We can get army contracts. That's why I sold the mills. There will be an embargo on cotton and all our food factories are in the North. My sympathies lie with the South, but I have more sense than to align myself with the losing side."

"How can you possibly know who will lose?"

"I know. I'm far enough removed to see things objectively. The North is vital, alive, industrious; the South is indolent," he said.

"Let's not speak of war," she begged.

He kissed her hungrily and she responded immediately.

"Am I right to think you love-starved, darling? Does Charles . . . no, I'd rather not know! I can't bear to think of you together. All that really matters is that he's good to you."

"He is good to me. To Charles Patrick also." She bit her lip because she knew she gave him pain. He crushed her to him. "Never stop loving me," he demanded.

Patrick knew a deep need to put his brand upon her to blot out the thought of all other lovers, ever. He knew he must make love to her as if it was their first time, and their last. How could he show her what she meant to him in one short night?

He pulled her on top of him to lie along his hard length. "I have so much I want to give you, but we only have till dawn. Take it from me hungrily. Make demands on me. I'll give you everything and take everything in return."

Suddenly Kitty was seized by a dark, violent passion. Only Patrick could arouse her to such madness. It was their secret that when they shared a bed they became shockingly wild and untamed.

They gave each other pain and pleasure, torture and bliss. They shared love and lust and raw carnality. Licking, sucking, biting. Fierce. Savage. Ferocious. Cruel. It took more than once to slake their need. Then their lovemaking became gentle, sweet, tender, heartbreakingly poignant. All giving, sharing, cherishing surrender.

They lay spent, totally exhausted from an excess of love. He stroked her gently and they drifted into slumber.

She awoke with a start. "Patrick, wake up, darling, I have to leave." She shook him gently.

He masked the regret her words brought to him. "Let me dress you."

Inside the carriage he held her in his lap so they could savor their last precious moments together. The carriage stopped. The moment had come. Her lips were beestung from too many kisses, so he kissed her forehead, "Don't look back." She stood in the cold light of dawn and wrapped his cloak tightly about her. A few carriages still were there.

One couple actually was getting into a punt at the water's edge, each carrying a champagne bottle. Kitty shuddered. She made her way toward the house, hoping to reach her bed without having to face anyone.

Chapter 26

Three weeks later Kitty sat at the breakfast table with Charles. She toyed with her food as she sorted out her thoughts. She was worried about Charles. He looked old. She couldn't hurt him by telling him so, but she couldn't remain silent any longer.

"Charles, you don't look well to me. Please, dear, see your doctor. I think you've been working too hard."

"I'm all right. Just a little tired. As a matter of fact, I've been worrying about you. Look at your plate—not enough on it to feed a bird and you keep pushing that about from one side to the other. I think you've lost weight. Perhaps the boy's getting too much for you. I think it's time we channeled some of that energy. He'd better have a tutor before he becomes unmanageable."

"He's just a normal boy, but I do agree that it's time for a tutor. A little discipline wouldn't be amiss," she said and smiled.

"That's better! I love to see you smile, and you've looked so sad lately." He cocked an eyebrow at her. "I don't believe you took my advice, did you?"

"What advice was that, Charles?"

"About finding yourself a nice young man."

"Ah, that's my secret," she teased. "You know the husband is always the last to know. But you're diverting attention from yourself. We were discussing how tired you look."

"Why don't we have a holiday. It would do us both good. What we need is a dose of Ireland! We'll visit my seat, Drago Castle in County Armagh."

"It sounds marvelous. I've never been to that part," she said excitedly.

"It will give Charlie a chance to run wild before we saddle him with a tutor. I'll charter a boat to take us up to Dundalk Bay. Your cousin Patrick keeps a yacht in Liverpool at the ready to take him wherever he wishes."

She pulled a slight face. "How decadent of him."

"Kathleen, you have a blind spot when it comes to Patrick," he said.

"What do you mean?" she asked faintly.

"Well, you never have a good word for him, and a more worthy fellow I can't imagine," he told her.

"Worthy?" she questioned.

"Well, I'm not supposed to bandy it about, but at this very moment he's taking secret messages from our government to Mr. Lincoln's government in America. An occupation that could very easily get him shot."

An ice-cold hand gripped her heart. Patrick's words drifted back to her: "One last time . . . I'll never bother you again." Surely he didn't think he was going to his death. He hadn't seemed worried, but then again that was the impression he gave—never caring if he won or lost!

Drago Castle was foreboding, but it fascinated Kitty. Only one wing was habitable. The rest was damp, dark and quite forbidding. The suite of rooms Charles and Kitty used were kept cozily warm by blazing fires night and day. Katie and Mimi, the servants Kitty brought, were deathly afraid of the place and swore there was a ghost around every corner.

Charles said, "When I was a child the place terrified me, so I can understand how the girls feel."

"Well, I don't want them frightening Charlie with their ideas. I'll soon put a stop to it," she promised.

Mimi came to her not ten minutes later. "Ma'am, I hear

footsteps following me whenever I go to bring anything from the kitchen. I dare not go again." She trembled. "Ah, I see I shall have to tell you the story of the castle ghost. It seems that Charles' grandfather had a darling little dog when he was a young boy. It had such an enormous appetite for a tiny dog that whenever the servants brought food from the kitchens, it followed them every day. It was such a familiar sight that around the castle, mealtimes weren't the same unless the little dog trotted about after the servants. The legend is that if someone comes into the castle who is extremely kind to animals, they can hear the little dog pattering about behind them."

"Oh, the dear little thing! That's not very frightening, is it?" said Mimi, and she went from the room without trepidation.

Charles was bemused. "And what happened to the dear little dog?"

Kitty made claws and growled at him. "The dragon ate it!"

Charles chuckled. "I think she believed you."

Kitty shrugged and said, "People usually believe anything you tell them."

He studied her for a minute. "You'd never fob me off with a pleasant story, Kathleen. You'd always tell me the truth, wouldn't you?"

She regarded him quietly with her head on one side, then said softly, "Not if it would break your heart, Charles."

The autumn air was crisp and tangy. Kitty rode every day. She finally allowed her son to ride a small pony, which put him in his glory. Charles took the dogs and went hunting. Kitty noted the fresh air must be doing him good, as he certainly lost the tired look and seemed quite relaxed.

Kitty visited one middle-aged woman who looked after

orphaned children. After she left, she felt ashamed at the way she had frittered away her time in London in a whirl of social functions. Plans were already being formed to get money for this orphanage and others by having charity functions. She knew so many people who were far too heavy in the pocket. It would be like doing them a favor to lighten them a bit. She hired one or two girls who came up to the castle looking for work. A few more came and she wondered how the household could absorb any more young girls. Kitty felt a definite obligation to these young women who desperately needed employment. By the time she had agreed to take back five girls with her, the stream had turned into a steady flow of colleens eager to take their place in domestic service.

Charles chided her, "I think you're running an employment agency, my dear." She began to write letters to her friends in London to try to secure places for them. Finally she called half a dozen aspirants together for a word of warning she knew had to be said.

"You will be alone for the first time in your lives. You all seem far too young and innocent to be going to a worldly place like London. There are dangers to be avoided at every turn." Kitty hesitated, she was on the brink of warning them of money matters and traffic, when she let out a heavy sigh and said, "A young pretty maid is almost the property of her employers. The sons of the family will take liberties every chance they get. And it's not just the sons," she warned, "the master of the house will do his best to seduce you every time the mistress turns her back. They'll attempt to lift your skirts in every dark corner they can catch you."

The girls blushed and giggled, but she went on, "Be determined never to let anyone make a victim of you and you'll manage fine in London, or anywhere else, for that matter."

Kitty purposely kept herself so busy all day that she had no idle time to sit and daydream. Whenever the brisk autumn

weather permitted she went out riding. Then the dreams
started. The first one found her in vaguely familiar surroundings. She wore only an orange cotton shift. She was mana-
cled to a man whose body was so close, their thighs brushed
together. She opened her mouth to scream in terror, but it
was Patrick she was shackled to and as she clung to him with
relief, his manhood hardened against her thighs and he took
her on the hard ground. She awoke, still feeling his rigid
fullness inside her, and let out her breath on a sob, not knowing if she was happy or sad to find it was only a dream.

A few nights later her dream began in a beautiful bedroom. She felt truly at home there. The curtains were drawn
over the tall windows, and a blazing fire warmed the spacious
room and cast its flickering shadows across the huge four-
poster. She brushed her hair before a dressing table, while a
smile played about her lips and anticipation made her spine
tingle. Suddenly she heard a noise, and the doorknob turned.
She was afraid until she reassured herself the door was securely locked. Suddenly there came a curse and a splintering
of wood. Patrick stood in the doorway in a towering rage.
"To lock the door against me, madame, is to invite rape!"

Charles had thoroughly enjoyed his sojourn in his native
land, but the day arrived when he could put off his return to
London no longer. "You must be eager to see your own
estate. Why don't we stop on our way through to the coast—
it's not far out of the way—and you can have a nice visit
with Terry."

"Oh, Charles, that would be delightful. I've longed to see
Windrush ever since you put the deed in my hands."

He kissed her. "That was one of the happiest mornings of
my life." He ran his hand lightly across her breast and she
blushed at the unaccustomed intimacy.

"I've been well pleased in you," he whispered.

* * *

When the entourage arrived at Windrush, Kitty was enthralled with it. It was very similar to the estate the O'Reillys had owned by the River Liffey, giving her the feeling of coming home. The sight of her grandfather deeply shocked her; he had become so frail and thin. She confided her fears to Charles.

"If you feel like staying here awhile, my love, it's perfectly all right with me. Charles Patrick can stay with you; Katie and Mimi will help you. I'll come and meet you when you're ready to come home."

"But it doesn't seem fair to you, Charles. I'm supposed to take these young girls to England, and that means you'll get stuck with making all the arrangements."

He leered and said, "If I can just get rid of you, it'll be like having a harem. I'll push on in the morning while the weather is holding. The Irish Sea is a bugger once the winter gales start."

Her grandfather soon was too weak to be up and she had the servants lift him to bed. She slept downstairs, next to him. When Terry came in that night, Kitty spoke to him about getting a physician up from Dublin.

"I think that's what we'd better do. We have to overrule his objections and do what we think best." He looked at her kindly. "Having you here has cut my worry in half."

The physician told them bluntly there was nothing that could be done. He diagnosed a tumor and told them it would be only a matter of days. Kitty begged for something for his pain, and the doctor gave her the only thing he could.

The laudanum worked like a miracle. One dose at bedtime assured that he slept the night through. The doctor was wrong about the time, though. It went on and on and his pain grew more severe. Each time he dirtied the sheets, she would gently wash and change him and hold his hand. She wrote to tell Charles that she would be in Ireland for the whole winter. She knew he would understand that she was staying until the end. In spite of the emotional drain, Windrush was a haven to her. She loved everything about the old house. It seemed to draw around her and comfort her. It was a place that had always known life and death, joy and sorrow, love and pain. Death finally came on the second day of February while winter still gripped the land. She could mourn his passing; but it was such a blessed release.

As soon as she got the letter from Charles, she packed up her family and left immediately. He had a touch of bronchitis, but as soon as the doctor gave him permission to travel, he would come for her. The carriage couldn't go fast enough to suit Kitty. The moment it stopped before the mansion in Strand Lane, she dashed out and flew up the steps. She was dismayed to see him standing in his overcoat with his traveling case in his hand.

"You should be in bed. Wherever are you going?" she demanded.

"My dearest, I'm on my way to get you from Ireland, but as usual you have anticipated me."

"Oh, Charles, I've been worried to death. Are you recovered?"

"All except for a slight cough. No, no, don't kiss me, darling, I'm probably still infectious."

That evening as they sat before the fire, he told her, "You'll never know how much I missed you. I've never known such a dreary winter in my life. You are my dearest delight."

She kept a surreptitious eye on Charles' cough, even though she began immediate plans for a charity ball to raise money for the orphanages in Ireland. Julia was delighted when asked to assist, and the two spent a whole day together discussing their strategy.

"There's so much organizing goes into one of these affairs, I don't know where to begin," said Kitty.

"I'll get a committee together; there're only two things I need you for, Kitty. One is your ducal coat of arms to head up the invitations, and the other is to show up on the night of the ball. Patrick's back in London," said Julia happily.

"Thank God he's safe. He wasn't wounded or anything, was he?" asked Kitty. Julia threw back her head and laughed heartily. "Oh, you do come up with some absurd notions, Kitty. He's escorting some Americans about London. One of his business associates sent his wife and daughter over to escape the dangers of war." Julia rolled her eyes heavenward. "What a complacent fool to think his womenfolk would be safe with Patrick."

Later that evening Kitty recalled with irony Julia's words about not needing her help. Charles' bronchitis had taken a turn for the worse. She insisted he go to bed, then sent over to Harley Street for his personal physician. Julia would have to look after the running of the charity ball after all.

"I'm afraid his Grace has a slight touch of pneumonia. Keep him in bed, keep him warm and we'll see if he's any better tomorrow."

He wasn't. Kitty slept on a couch she had moved into his room. She did everything for him herself and allowed everything else to slide. Gradually Charles began to improve, but she didn't lessen her vigil during his convalescence. Then Charles Patrick got a hacking cough. She whisked him to bed immediately and started nursing her second patient.

Charles remonstrated, "You're tired to death; if you don't get some rest you'll be ill yourself. My darling, you've had so much sickness to cope with all winter and now this. You mustn't worry about me. Spend your time with the boy, but don't sit up all night, every night with him."

She smiled gently at his concern. "That's what mothers are for."

The doctor finally declared that the child was out of danger and that Charles also was better. The doctor said reassuringly, "Medicine is the practice of keeping the patient entertained while we let nature heal. I think the boy is at the stage where he needs to be amused."

Kitty tirelessly read to him, played card games and cut out paper dolls. She made his and her false moustaches, and another one when he insisted the dog must be included. She unstuck the black cardboard from her top lip with dismay as she realized the date.

"Katie!" she screeched at the top of her lungs. "My God, why didn't someone remind me of the ball?" demanded Kitty.

"I thought you'd given up any idea of attending; you must be worn out."

"But I'm the patroness of this affair; I must attend! Good heavens, I never ordered a dress or anything."

She flung the wardrobe doors wide. "I haven't even looked at these dresses since last summer. Oh, they've been so sadly neglected. That pale green one is a favorite, and this lavender, but look how they are soiled. Where are all the clothes I took to Ireland last autumn? Don't tell me they're still in my trunks! Good God, things should be run better than this; the place must have over a score of servants and yet there's none to keep my clothes in order."

"How about this lovely apricot satin?" asked Katie.

Kitty slipped it over her head and it fell off her shoulders and gaped back and front. "It always was loose on me, but I've lost weight, I suppose, and now it hangs like a sack. The gold lace on this one actually is tarnished; the same with this silver tissue."

"What about this wine brocade? I don't remember you ever wearing it."

"Oh, I suppose it will do, Katie. I think perhaps I was too preoccupied with clothes and my appearance. Somehow this winter has put things in a new light. I was a social butterfly, so vain I had to outdo everyone."

"Excuse me, ma'am, but what about your hair?"

"Good God, it hasn't been dressed in ages. I've grown so used just to twisting it into a bun. It's so wild if I let it free. I'll just roll it into a chignon and wear one of those nets over it. See if you can find me one that matches the dress."

She looked at herself in the mirror with a critical eye. Her throat was scratchy and there was a spot in her chest that burned like fire. She thought ruefully, The Gypsy's showing; I'm as sallow as a guinea.

In the carriage she wished she'd made a different selection of dresses. What she first thought was a rich wine, she now realized was a hideous maroon. When she glanced across at Charles, thoughts of herself took flight. "Do you think you should have come tonight, Charles?"

"It's my turn to look after you, my pet. You look completely done in to me," he said tenderly.

She did not dare tell how she really felt, for she knew he would have the carriage turned around immediately.

They arrived at the Banqueting House at Whitehall Palace amid a crush of people. As she traversed the ballroom, graciously acknowledging greetings, the room became stifling. Her chest was on fire and for a moment she thought she might faint. Julia sailed up to her with Jeffrey quietly following in her wake.

"Oh, Julia, you look magnificent," said Kitty sincerely. Julia was gowned in purple velvet with bishop sleeves. She looked down at Kitty. "Too bad I can't return the compliment; you look a positive dowd."

Kitty's lips twitched in amusement. "Well, it's not easy for a scullery maid to look like a duchess."

"We can't stand together; we clash horribly," said Julia.

"We always did," bantered Kitty.

"Don't look now, but we've just been invaded by the Americans," said Julia.

Kitty glanced across the room. Patrick had a beautiful blonde on each arm. The younger woman, no more than eighteen, wore an exquisitely designed rose pink crinoline. Every curl was in place, and her fair skin glowed as she looked admiringly up at her escort. The older woman was slimmer but just as beautiful. She wore a most sophisticated black silk. Kitty murmured, "I wonder which one he's after?"

"Probably servicing them both at the same time if I know Patrick," sneered Julia.

Jeffrey spoke up immediately, "That's a disgusting thing to say, Julia."

She laughed lightly. "Oh, you know my little jokes. I love my brother very much, in spite of his taste in women." She looked pointedly at Kitty.

Kitty was dismayed to see Patrick bringing the younger lady over to introduce her. He bowed stiffly before Kitty and said, "May I present Her Grace, the Duchess of Manchester, Miss Amanda Astor."

The girl's laughter trilled out. "Oh, Patrick stop!" She turned to Kitty and said, "Patrick thinks I'm so gullible, I'll believe anything he tells me."

There was a stunned silence for a moment as the people around them couldn't quite believe what they'd heard. Kitty's lip trembled for a moment, but she caught it between her teeth and said softly, "I thank you sincerely for coming tonight, and I welcome you to England. I hope you are graciously received wherever you go."

She turned to Charles and said, "Please excuse me," and fled to the ladies' room.

Patrick gave his companion a cold stare. He turned to Charles and asked, "Is her Grace unwell?"

"Patrick, lad, I'm worried to death about her. She's had the devil's own time of it lately. Buried her grandfather in Ireland, then dashed home to nurse me with pneumonia. To top it all off, Charles Patrick had a bad bout with bronchitis and she's been up every night for a month."

"Is he out of danger?" asked Patrick worriedly.

"Now, you know she wouldn't be here if he wasn't better," assured Charles.

"Please convey my deepest sympathy to your wife, Charles," said Patrick, crushing the impulse to run after her and comfort her. "Perhaps she's caught the boy's cold."

"You may be right. I'm going to take her home to bed."

The muscles in Patrick's jaw clenched as he bit back the jealous retort that almost rose to his lips. He burned to go to her, but he wouldn't break his bond. He had to be content with the knowledge that if she needed him, she would seek him out.

In the powder room Kitty smiled through her tears, "When he presents that dumpy little fat woman as Queen Victoria I hope she takes him at his word!" She despaired when she looked in the mirror. "He couldn't have caught me looking worse!"

Chapter 27

After a week in bed her strength came back. Charles found a tutor for Charles Patrick, and the boy took an immediate liking to him.

"Charles," Kitty said, "Mr. Bromley is a lovely young man; he's so easy to talk to."

"Yes, he fits in well. Patrick recommended him," he said offhandedly.

"Damnit all, does he have to meddle in our lives?" she stormed.

"Why, darling, we never see him." He smiled indulgently. "However, I'm well aware you jar on each other's nerves. The air fairly bristles whenever you come face to face."

The following week she and Charles were just coming out of Humphrey's Print Shop when she spotted Patrick with an entirely different woman on his arm. She quickly took Charles Patrick's hand and crossed to the other side of the street.

"Kathleen, that was Patrick. You just cut him dead!" said Charles.

"What do you expect when he's out with one of his whores?" she demanded hotly.

"Sssh," Charles cautioned as he looked askance at the boy.

The following week, when young Charles was out with his tutor, Patrick was delighted to run into the boy. He eagerly scanned the dark head and handsome features of his son. Young Charles' friendly curiosity got the better of him as he

eyed the young woman with Patrick. "You must be one of
Patrick's whores!"

Mr Bromley was aghast. "Forgive him, sir; he has no idea
what the word means."

"But that's what my mother called her," protested Charlie.

Patrick was at pains to calm the woman. She was incensed,
for that's exactly what she was.

As collector of customs for the Port of London, Charles
was kept busy. Kitty was so proud of his achievements, but
the extra work load kept him away from home long hours,
and he traveled constantly among ports.

Kitty knew a great restlessness within her. When she saw
Julia, she invited her to come out of London for the hot
months. "I'm planning to go to my country place in Kent.
We could ride every day, and why don't you bring young
Jeffrey along; the boys would be great company for each
other," enthused Kitty.

"Are you mad? What would I do in the country? I spent
too many years in the backwaters of Bolton. London is my
whole life. You go and become a rustic if you wish, but for
God's sake leave me out of your plans."

Kitty laughed. "You make it sound so boring, but it's the
loveliest place in the world, except for Ireland, of course."

"Ireland!" Julia said with a shudder.

"How about Barbara, then? Do you think she will come?"

"Barbara's off visiting a friend in Cornwall or somewhere.
I can't keep track of her these days."

When Kitty returned at the end of August, Julia lost no
time coming around for afternoon tea.

"You look disgustingly domesticated," she told Kitty.

"Bring me up to date with what's happening in town," said Kitty.

"Well, let me see," Julia said thoughtfully. "Oh, yes, the Duchess of Marlborough is entertaining next week. Have you ever been to Marlborough House in Pall Mall? I'm having the most expensive gown made. Oh, yes, and bye the bye, Patrick has a new interest."

"Just one of his flirts," said Kitty lightly.

"Ah, there I beg to differ. This isn't one of his whores. On the contrary, quite a respectable young woman, from what I've seen. I do hope something comes of it; he should have been married years ago."

"Who is she?" asked Kitty, feeling a sickness begin in the pit of her stomach.

"Oh, lady somebody or other. He was after some land in Ireland her father owned or something. He doesn't discuss his business with me, you know. Now, what will you be wearing to Marlborough House?" asked Julia avidly.

Later that day Kitty visited her friend Lady Derby and casually brought the conversation around to Patrick.

"Who's this woman I've heard so much about?"

"Oh, you mean Lady Patricia Cavendish?"

Kitty laughed lightly. "Determined to get her hooks into him, is she?"

"Oh, she isn't like that, Kitty. She's a lovely young woman, very well bred. You should see her clothes. I'd love to know who does them for her."

"Showy female, is she?" asked Kitty, growing angry in spite of herself.

"I certainly wouldn't describe her as showy. Everything she wears is in exquisite taste, you know what I mean. Simple, quiet good taste."

Damnit, what's that supposed to mean, Kitty wondered, that I'm too flamboyant? Well, you've seen nothing yet!

* * *

Kitty pored over sketches at the dressmakers' in Bond Street the following day. "No, no, that's so old-fashioned, my grandmother wouldn't be caught in it," Kitty told the Frenchwoman.

"Perhaps this one, your Grace. The crinoline has a full seventeen yards in it."

"That's the whole point; I heard the crinoline was on its way out," said Kitty.

"Well, not exactly, but I do have the latest design from Paris. It is called the bustle. Very *outré;* the material fits the contour of the body and is gathered behind into the bustle."

Kitty's eyes opened wide as she looked at the sketch. "Oh, yes," she breathed. The shop boasted taffetas, moirés and brocades in shades from apricot through amber, lemon to primrose and coral to chartreuse. The moment Kitty spied it, she knew that was the shade that would do the most for her dark coloring. It was a turquoise as brilliant as the South Seas that caressed the white, sandy beaches. She stood absolutely still while the material was draped about her. "I want the skirt tighter," she said.

The seamstress smoothed it across her hips, "But your grace, if I make it tighter, you cannot walk."

"Put a slit up the back," said Kitty recklessly. "Now the neckline needs to be lowered three more inches and we'll have a creation worthy of you, *madame.*"

The woman shook her head but pinned the neckline lower as Kitty asked.

"I hate being conventional in my clothes. I like to set my own style. See this black velvet? I've always wanted a pair of riding britches made out of such material. I could wear boy's britches, but they are unfeminine. Now, if you fit the velvet across the rounded contours of my derriere, I think it would be most fetching! Make me up a pair; I have a fancy for them.''

The woman knew immediately she was setting the trap for some man, so when Kitty glanced at the nightgowns, she knew instinctively what to suggest. It was a sheer wisp of gossamer embroidered with forget-me-nots.

On the day of the ball, Kitty luxuriated in the bath for hours, then oiled, perfumed, powdered and painted. Her curls were swept up to match the bustle with one or two artfully arranged in playful disarray. The only jewelry she wore were earrings—aquamarines encrusted with diamonds. Her tiny whaleboned corset was laced so tightly that when she put on the gown her breasts swelled over the top like delicious melons. She put on her high heels and practiced walking and turning a full half hour before she felt confident to handle the new tight gown.

Charles came in. "You look magnificent! Now I'm sorry I won't be there to see their faces when you walk in.''

"There's still time to change your mind,'' she urged.

"No, no, I'm off to Southampton tomorrow and I've dozens of customs documents to look over. Off you go; have a happy time. Enjoy, enjoy!'' he admonished.

At Marlborough House, Kitty was on pins and needles in case Patrick didn't show up. She caused quite a stir among the guests but seemed hardly aware of the cold glances from the women or the hot ones from the men. She spotted him arriving and immediately relaxed and started to enjoy herself. One glance at the woman next to him told her that this was the paragon of breeding, Lady Patricia Cavendish. Kitty smiled up at Lord Palmerston, who immediately responded by asking her to dance.

"Is Charles not here this evening? Then I shall take advantage of you,'' he promised suggestively.

Patrick's eyes were drawn to her like a magnet. He held

his breath. Each time she turned in the waltz he thought her breasts would come out of her gown! Without hesitation he strode across the dance floor and cut in on the older man.

"That took a great deal of courage, to steal me from the Prime Minister," she said prettily.

"He's a known womanizer and a lecher," he said bluntly.

"Will I be safer with you?" she teased.

Anger and lust raged a battle within him, but lust was winning as he feasted his eyes upon her as a man starving. As the music finished he released her reluctantly. Kitty eyed the serene young woman who came to stand by him. Kitty's eyes took in the expensive eggshell satin with the modest neckline and the gentle face devoid of any makeup.

"Patrick thinks he has to protect me, but I could give lessons in how to handle men," Kitty said provocatively. "I always know exactly what effect I'm having on them," and she cast a deliberate, sideways glance at the bulge between his legs. Patrick's eyes narrowed dangerously, but she ignored the warning. "I hear you are looking for land in Ireland, Patrick. I have an estate there I might be persuaded to sell. Why don't we go over next week and I'll show it to you?"

"Well, I'll be damned," thought Patrick, "she's seducing me, right here in public." He responded eagerly as his warm glance held her possessively.

"I'd love to see anything you'd care to show me."

"Good! Shall we say next Wednesday? I'll drop you a note giving directions to Windrush."

"Will we travel across together? My ship is anchored at Liverpool."

"I don't think so. I'll be waiting for you when you arrive," she told him.

Patricia Cavendish accepted an offer to dance. The moment she moved away, Patrick put his finger under Kitty's chin and grinned down at her wickedly.

"She wasn't any competition for you, kitten; we were just friends."

"Ha!" said Kitty as she swept past him regally, her mission accomplished.

Kitty swept aside Mimi's offer to accompany her to Ireland. "No, no, I'd rather you stayed with Charles Patrick. It's just a whim to see Windrush again in the autumn."

Charles could overhear them from the next room. "Irish people get very, very homesick," he told Mimi.

Kitty refused to entertain the guilty feelings that threatened to trap her. She pushed them out of her mind and admitted to herself she was as excited as a child at the thought of Christmas.

She arrived on Tuesday. It had rained in the morning, but the afternoon sun mellowed the bricks of Windrush to a misty rose. She knew she'd never get enough of the place as she opened her own front door and carried her valise inside. She heard a girl's footsteps running to see who had arrived and looked up expecting to see a maid. "Barbara! Oh, my God, you haven't?" Kitty asked, dismayed.

"I'm afraid I have," she said, glancing over her shoulder as Terry came up behind her.

"Have you been here all those months you were supposed to be in Cornwall?"

"She has," answered Terry, slipping his arms about Barbara and nuzzling her neck.

"You know who'll get the blame for this bloody lot, don't you? Me, that's who!" she shouted.

"Blame?" said Terry, puzzled.

"Patrick's coming tomorrow. How the hell do I keep him from finding out?" she demanded.

Barbara giggled. "Take him to bed as soon as he arrives and keep him there."

"Barbara!" cried Kitty, thoroughly shocked.

"To hell with it," said Terry, "I'm tired of sneaking about. We might as well have it out."

"Well, thank you both very much!" she said with arms akimbo. "I plan a secret little tryst and in its stead I get a big stinking family fight!"

Barbara ran to her. "I'm sorry, Kitty."

"Oh, so am I. I love you both very much and I understand that you fell in love almost the first time you saw each other, but coming here and sleeping with him—my God, Patrick will run mad!"

She took off her hat and coat and sat before the kitchen fire, planning strategy. "You can come and go as you please today, Barbara, but tomorrow I want you out of sight completely. I expect him in the afternoon, and you will dine with us, Terrance, and entertain him tomorrow evening."

"But he'll want to be alone with you," protested Barbara.

"Precisely! Here's lesson Number One, my girl: You don't give a man everything he wants. Where are you sleeping?"

"In the west wing, right above this kitchen, I think," said Terry.

"Oh, that's good. The two large bedrooms at the front are far enough away; we'll use those."

"I don't think Patrick will stand for separate bedrooms," said Terry, winking.

"You just let me handle Patrick if you know what's good for you. Now, is everything clear? Tomorrow Barbara becomes invisible and you help me entertain our guest. He's coming here to buy Windrush."

"What a bloody charade; you wouldn't sell the place if you were down to your last penny!"

"You keep a civil tongue in your head and go along with

whatever I tell him. You're both going to need someone on your side when your little bubble bursts, speaking of charades," she said sarcastically. "Where are the servants? I hope everything is being run properly around here."

"Stop worrying, Kitty. The household runs as smooth as glass. They aren't in evidence because we like to be alone."

"I want to speak to the manservant. Call what's his name, Mr. Burke! How could I have forgotten after that day last year when I fired the housekeeper and put Mr. Burke in charge?"

Picking up her overnight case, she went in search of the man. He was warm and friendly. "Welcome home, ma'am."

"Thank you, Mr. Burke. I'm expecting a gentleman tomorrow. Will you help me get everything ready? You were such a help to me when I was nursing my grandfather."

"It will be my pleasure, ma'am."

She headed toward the stairs. "We'll use the two large bedrooms at the front of the house."

He opened the door to the first room and they both went inside.

"It's a beautiful room; a welcoming room. Will you see that someone builds me a fire? You needn't light the one next door until tomorrow." She went to the door that connected the two bedrooms, opened it wide and stepped through to look about with satisfaction.

"Let me see; I want you to bring a decanter of brandy and glasses. He smokes, so you'd better find some ashtrays. When he arrives, make sure there's plenty of hot water for a bath. And I think he shaves twice a day, so he'll need hot water again at night."

She walked back into her own room. "Make sure the beds are aired. Oh, yes, the most important thing of all, Mr. Burke. I'd like a key for this connecting door so that I can lock it."

"I'll send a maid for some towels, ma'am."

"Mr. Burke, I want you to keep the maids busy downstairs. I see none in evidence at the moment, but once Mr. O'Reilly comes through that front doorway, I have an idea they'll be thick as moths around a candle. I'm up on all their little tricks, Mr. Burke. I used to be a maid myself."

"An attractive gentleman, I take it?" he asked with a straight face.

"Mr. Burke, he'd charm the ducks off the pond," she said and smiled.

"I'll get you that key," he said with a twinkle in his eye.

When he returned with the brandy, he lit her fire. She was looking from the tall bedroom windows over the green paddocks where horses grazed lazily. "I love Windrush. It's so peaceful. Does everything run as smoothly as it seems on the surface?"

"Just like clockwork. Terrance runs everything outside and I run everything inside. Smooth as glass."

"Really? You can expect some ripples then, Mr. Burke. The gentleman I'm expecting is Miss Barbara's brother."

"Oh, dear. I take it he is in ignorance of the situation?" he asked.

She nodded. "And I intend to keep him in ignorance as long as it's humanly possible."

"I see. I believe we have some Irish whiskey in the cellar, ma'am."

"I think the brandy will do nicely, Mr. Burke. I don't want to render him unconscious."

"I see, madame," he said solemnly.

"I'm sure you do, Mr. Burke," she said saucily, and turned the key that locked the connecting door and slipped it into her pocket.

* * *

The next morning she was up with the larks, singing and humming happily. She decided to pick some flowers. She chose a mass of Michaelmas daisies for Patrick's room and some late-blooming roses for her own. They filled the air with a heady fragrance. After lunch she put on the black velvet riding pants and went down to the stables.

"I'd like to ride. Which one would be best?" she asked Terry. He cast her an amused glance. Poor Patrick didn't stand a chance against this little witch.

"Most of the mares are in foal. You can take Lady Jane here; I don't think she caught the last time I put her to stud. I'll saddle her up for you, but don't go too far. I don't want to get stuck with Patrick."

"I'll watch for him, but remember I expect your company at dinner. I want you to stick like glue even if he tries to get rid of you!" she admonished. She returned from her ride feeling more alive than she had in years. The breeze had brought the roses into her cheeks, and her hair billowed about her shoulders in wild disarray. She trotted along the fence of the paddock. The horse inside snorted wildly and reared into the air. This sleek, black stallion was Terry's pride and joy and there obviously was something wrong. She dismounted quickly and looped the reins over her arm. The stallion's eyes rolled wildly and his scream rent the air. She ran toward the gate and lifted the wood.

"Kitty, no!" a voice thundered. Patrick's hand shot past her and slammed the wood home in the gate. A stableman ran up to them and took away the horse that Kitty had been riding. She looked up at Patrick in confusion. "The stallion wanted to mount the mare. He would have trampled anything that stood in his way."

Terry came running. "Is she all right? By God, Patrick, I'd no idea she was so ignorant."

The moment of danger was forgotten as Patrick drank in the sight of her.

Terry hid a smile as he wondered how many seconds would elapse before Patrick would have his hands on her.

"Welcome to Windrush," breathed Kitty.

The cooling breeze rustled her silk shirt, and her nipples stood out in clear relief. Patrick's hand stole to her waist and his fingers immediately discerned that she was indeed naked beneath the silk. Terry turned half away, pretending to be unaware of the byplay that was going on.

Kitty easily slipped out of Patrick's grasp and took Terry's arm. "Let's take Patrick up to the house and get him settled."

Patrick said quickly. "We're taking him away from his work, Kitty."

"Nonsense! He's never too busy to welcome a guest," she assured him.

Patrick gave Terry a warning glance, but Terry shrugged helplessly.

"Windrush will steal your heart; you'll never want to leave. Don't you love it?" she asked.

"Yes, it's beautiful," he said, never taking his eyes from her.

"Shall I ring for some tea?" she asked brightly as they entered the house.

The look of dismay that came over the men's faces at the thought of sitting through afternoon tea filled her with amusement.

"How silly of me," she relented. "You'd probably much rather have a drink up in your room."

His eyes burned into hers until she lowered her lashes.

"Mr. Burke," Kitty called out to the hovering servant, "please take Mr. O'Reilly's bags up to his room."

Terry watched her lead Patrick on and hoped she realized

Patrick wasn't one to follow, but would seize command at the first opportunity. Mr. Burke led the procession, and Kitty followed. Patrick, coming up behind her on the staircase, could control his actions no longer. He reached out and caressed her bottom.

She remonstrated, "You trespass, sir!"

"Then lead us not into temptation," he said irreverently.

Mr. Burke set the bags down and tended the fire. Kitty splashed brandy into a glass and handed it to Patrick. He sipped it impatiently, waiting for the servant to leave, while the heat of his eyes roamed over her figure and came to rest hungrily on her mouth. The servant turned from the fire to leave.

Quickly Kitty said, "Wait, Mr. Burke, I'll come with you. I must see about dinner."

"Dinner?" Patrick said blankly.

"Of course, dinner," said Kitty innocently. "You didn't think you'd retired for the night, did you?"

Mr. Burke went through the door, but it was swiftly closed before Kitty could follow him. Patrick's body came full up against hers as he flattened her against the door. His voice came raggedly, "Oh, God, don't play games with me." His mouth came down on hers in a heated, crushing demand. The ache of passion so long denied rose up in her until she was ready to yield to him.

Then suddenly Mr. Burke was back at the door. "I brought hot water for your bath, sir."

"Damn," swore Patrick angrily.

She slipped from his embrace. "The hot water will ease away your stiffness," she said outrageously.

He leaned against the closed door in agony. The craving hunger gnawed at the pit of his belly. He clenched his fists and ground his teeth. Would he never be able to master the physical effect she always provoked in him?

* * *

The dinner was a simple affair suited to a man's taste. The
broiled beefsteak and vegetables were followed by a fruit pie
and cream. If Patrick had been questioned about it, he could
not have recalled what he had eaten. All he tasted was Kitty

They dined at a small table in a cozy room off the main
dining room. She poured both men a brandy after the meal
and when Patrick took out a long, slim cheroot, she bent
toward him intimately to light it. His fingers covered hers to
steady the light, and his eyes met hers with an intensity that
took her breath away. Terry nudged her under the table. She
was enjoying this small cruelty she was inflicting on them
both. She yawned delicately.

"I'm sure Patrick must have a thousand questions he
wants to ask you about Windrush, Terry, so I'll leave you to
your brandy and cigars." Terry looked angry enough to kill,
and Patrick's brow lowered dangerously.

"I'll say good night." She arose. "Oh, Patrick, I'm in the
room next to yours if there's anything you desire."

He choked on the brandy. She moved swiftly, knowing it
would be only minutes before each sought an excuse to retire. She closed the long drapes over the windows and poked
the fire until it blazed high. By the time she hung her clothes
in the wardrobe, she could hear Patrick moving about in his
room. She took out the sheer nightgown and slipped it over
her head. Her pulse raced madly as she heard Patrick's footsteps come to the connecting door. She brushed out her hair
and in a few minutes she heard him come again to the door
This time he turned the knob. Silence. She shivered at the
thought of his touch.

"Kitten," he called softly through the door. She held her
breath. Her eyes widened as she realized this was the room
she'd dreamed of long ago. Now she knew why she was

goading him into breaking down the door. She wanted him to fulfill all her dreams and fantasies.

The door gave way under a resounding crash. He was prepared to do battle, but his anger melted away like snow in summer as the impact of her lithe body assaulted his senses. As he advanced into the room the fire in his blood throbbed along his veins, and his eyes blazed as they noted that the nightgown had flower petals embroidered on the breasts, and the centers of the flowers were her pink nipples, provocatively exposed.

He crushed her in his embrace, held her away to gaze down at her in wonder, then took her inside his robe. The shock of his lean, hard, naked body against hers made her cry out. Her legs trembled beneath her. As she leaned against him for support, he gathered her up and took her to the bed. Love words tumbled from his lips and he was astounded to discover she must have hungered for him every bit as much as he had hungered for her. Her response was eager and hot. She obeyed his demands implicitly, but he was delighted when she made demands of her own. Her cries shattered the stillness of the house as he entered her, swollen to the full with passion. Beginning slowly, his movements built in a silken rhythm that carried them both higher and higher in pleasure until Kitty thought she could bear it no longer. She bit his shoulder and he groaned aloud, but he hadn't even felt her bites. He shuddered as a crescendo exploded, and then he felt her implosion draw the nectar of love from his shaft.

"I didn't know it could be like that," he whispered in awe.

Her face was wet with tears. Her release had been so great, a sob shuddered through her whole body.

"My God, we can't go on like this, Kitty. It's killing us both. You've got to leave him. I won't live without you any longer."

"Oh, please, darling, our time is so short, so precious, we mustn't waste it with angry words."

"I'll leave it for now, but it's something you are going to have to face up to," he said with finality.

Just before dawn, Patrick stirred. He marveled at finding his love in his arms. He looked his fill at the lovely face. Black crescent lashes lay still on her cheeks, her hair fanned out across the pillow. This was what he missed most—the luxury of awakening in each other's arms, the intimate, peaceful moments of the early morning before the world intruded. It was not just the lovemaking he wanted. He wanted it all; to share the same bed until morning, to spend days in close companionship, to watch their son grow, to have more children. She stirred and moved closer. He whispered softly and cuddled her close. She snuggled into the crook of his arm, laying her cheek against the dark mat of his chest, and he touched her temple with soft whisper kisses. She drifted back into slumber, sensing the safe watch he would keep over her. He tried to sleep, but as his senses stirred, the familiar ache started in his loins. He controlled himself for over an hour; then, just as he could stand it no longer, he looked down at her still face. It was sweet torture, but he couldn't bear to disturb her. Very gently he arose from the bed and crossed to his own room. He gazed out the windows across the beautiful meadows below him. His heart sang; he could never recall feeling such elation. He heard the household begin to come to life. He slipped on his pants just as he heard a low knock on the outer door. He quickly rumpled the unused bed as a voice said, "Your hot water, sir."

Patrick called, "Come in, Mr. Burke. Thank you. I hope you haven't been kept waiting; I overslept this morning." Patrick scrutinized his demeanor and was satisfied that the man didn't suspect a thing. "Terrance probably is wondering where I've gotten to. Tell him I'll be down directly."

"No need to rush, sir; Master Terrance hasn't gone down-
tairs yet."

"Really?" asked Patrick, surprised.

The servant closed the door, and Patrick turned to the
mirror to shave. He was momentarily dismayed to see the
iny crescent bruises that ran across his chest to his shoulder.
The teeth marks had been clearly visible to Mr. Burke. Pat-
ick grinned shamelessly. How did the fellow keep a straight
ace? he wondered.

He went back to Kitty's room and sat on the edge of the
bed. She stretched luxuriously and lifted her arms around his
neck. "Mmmm, you're already bathed and shaved."

"I should hope so; it's after ten," he said and smiled.
They gazed deeply into each other's eyes, trying to find
words to convey their pleasure.

"When you came through that door last night, you looked
like a stallion who would trample anything in his way."

Patrick was entranced with her. "Your cries of delight
while having your pleasure last night must have awakened
the household. I hope Terry's room isn't too close to this
one," he said and laughed.

She giggled. "No, he's in the west wing."

"Good. I'll just go over there and drag him out of bed. Do
you realize he isn't up yet?"

It took a minute before his intention was clear to her, but
by then Patrick was already through the doorway. She
jumped from the bed and threw on his robe.

"No, wait, Patrick don't!" she cried.

She followed his quick strides down the hallway and
across the landing.

Patrick threw open the chamber door and stopped dead on
the threshold. The startled young couple sat up in bed, their
nakedness forgotten. A stool crashed savagely into the far
wall as Patrick exploded, "What in Christ's name is going

on here?'' His face was murderous. ''You dare to use my
sister for your whore?'' he thundered.

Terrance shot naked from the bed. ''You dared use mine!''

The words incensed Patrick to an even greater rage, while
Kitty stood helplessly behind him. ''You young bastard, I'll
kill you,'' spat Patrick.

Terrance was just as angry. ''Don't you think I've begged
her over and over to marry me? But because of you, you
bloody tyrant, she refuses. She's afraid of you; everyone's
afraid of you!'' shouted Terry.

''By Christ, you don't seem to be!'' Patrick blazed.

''I won't see our whole lives ruined by our being kept
apart!'' shouted Terry.

''Your whole lives?'' sneered Patrick. ''My heart bleeds
for you! How old are the pair of you? Nineteen? Twenty? I'm
past thirty. My life should be settled, but I'm denied a wife,
I'm denied the pleasure of watching my own son grow up.
The pair of you make me sick!'' He turned from the naked
couple, struggling with his anger. His eyes swept over Kitty.
''Cover yourself,'' he demanded savagely, as he stalked from
the room.

Barbara pleaded, ''Kitty, go after him.''

''Are you insane? He's trying to control a black rage. I
wouldn't dare to go near him.''

Barbara reached with trembling fingers for her nightgown.
''I must have been blind not to know Charles Patrick was my
brother's child. I'm sorry, Kitty.''

''We've all made a mess of things,'' said Terry ruefully,
his anger dissolving.

Patrick was gone most of the day. At teatime Kitty bade
Barbara eat something. ''Come, you've had nothing all day.
Join me now, for I certainly don't intend for the four of us to
dine together this evening.''

"Patrick's back. He and Terry have had their heads together, but Patrick didn't even have a look for me," said
Barbara.

"Naturally! Women must be punished. We must be kept in
our place for fear we might invade the men's territory. So
he'll ignore you, but by God he won't ignore me! Now eat up
and then make yourself scarce. Men are very prickly where
their sisters are concerned. The state of their own morals has
absolutely nothing to do with it."

Patrick dined alone. The thought of a conspiracy which
perhaps Kitty had authored still rankled, but the thought of
her hiding in her room annoyed him. He wasted no time on
brandy and cigars, but went upstairs immediately after dinner. He gave a low knock on her door and entered. She
wasn't there. Perplexed for a moment, he went through to his
own chamber. She was in his bed! His lips twitched, but he
was silent. He undressed leisurely, taking all the time in the
world, but there was no movement from the bed. Finally he
got into bed and lay with his hands clasped behind his head.
After all this time he knew she never would make the first
move. "You are the most provoking wench! You crawl into
my bed so I can't ignore you, then do your damndest to
ignore me. Feigning sleep will do you no good whatsoever,
kitten." In a flash he lifted her on top of him. Her eyes shot
open and she tried to roll away but he held her firmly pressed
against the length of him. His hands slipped up the backs of
her legs under her nightgown. When they reached her hips,
he clamped her firmly to him, ensuring any wriggling on her
part would only bring added pleasure.

"What about Barbara and Terry?" she asked faintly.

"To hell with them," he said. "What about Patrick and
Kitty?"

She giggled.

"There's no hope for Barbara, anyway. Once you've bedded with a Gypsy, no other mate is wild enough for you,'' he teased.

''Oh, really? And what about the O'Reilly blood? I'd say it's too hot to be considered normal,'' she said and laughed.

''Would you?'' he sounded most pleased. ''Are you going to use your nails and teeth on me again, you little witch?''

''That just proves I'm more passionate than you,'' she provoked.

''Is that what biting proves?'' he asked and promptly took her nipple into his mouth. She screamed in mock terror.

After their desires had been sated she stretched against him like a cat.

He whispered erotically, ''When I give you cream, you purr.''

She sat up and threw the covers back.

''What are you doing?'' he asked.

''Going back to my own bed. We can't have the servants find me in here.''

''Get back into bed. Now lie down,'' he commanded. ''An hour is no good to me; I'm going to keep you abed for a week.''

When they arose the next morning Kitty discovered the young pair had left. She puzzled over their whereabouts, hoping Patrick's temper hadn't driven them away.

Kitty had horses saddled for Patrick and herself and they rode about the estate; she dreamy-eyed and languid, he bound by the spell of her beauty.

''This must be one of the most beautiful places on earth. You know I never could buy it from you,'' he said.

''I don't want it to be yours, nor mine; it's ours. Ours to share forever,'' she said wistfully.

When the evening closed in and darkness descended, Kitty peered out the window for signs of the missing pair. Patrick had disappeared into the kitchen an hour past. All of a sudden the door burst open and a radiant Barbara announced, "We were married!"

"How? Where?" asked Kitty, completely taken by surprise.

"Patrick arranged a special license for us," said Terry.

"The four of us are going to have a wedding celebration!" shouted Patrick, coming through the doorway with a bottle of champagne in each hand.

"Where in the world did you conjure that from?" asked Kitty, amazed.

"Didn't I tell you last night I could perform tricks that would leave you breathless?" He winked.

She blushed at his meaning.

Terry laughed and said, "What's a wedding without a coarse jest or two?"

Patrick shouted, "Did you hear the one about the duchess who . . ."

"Enough of that, you rogue!" screeched Kitty, throwing a cushion at him.

The wedding supper was a delightfully happy time, with toast after toast being drunk to the newlyweds.

Much later, in love's afterglow as Patrick caressed the silken curve of her back, he said, "God, how I envy them! I'm going to go to Charles when we get back and ask him to release you."

"No, Patrick you mustn't!" she cried. "Promise me you won't! If you love me, you won't!"

"You seek to tie me hand and foot. Don't you understand I want all or nothing?" he demanded.

"Promise me!" she insisted.

He groaned, "I promise not to confront him, but I'll do everything in my power to separate you from him and bind you closer to me." He crushed her in a demanding embrace.

Patrick swept the covers from her and knelt above her in a

towering passion. His face was hard and dark, his eyes stained with desire. "Lord God, how I'm going to make you quiver," he vowed.

His tongue annointed her from throat to thigh, every silken inch, every secret cleft, until Kitty lay in a love-drunk sprawl. "I'd love to do these wicked things to you if it weren't so wrong," she breathed huskily.

He murmured openmouthed against the soft inside of her thigh, "When we share a bed there is no such thing as wrong, no such thing as sin, no such thing as forbidden." He drew her hand to his shaft to show her the enormous effect she had on him. Her fingertips brushed across the velvet head, drawing forth drops of liquid love juice.

Kitty knew an overwhelming desire to taste him. She raised her fingertips to her lips and sucked the taste of him from them. It was a mix of salt, spice and smoke, all heavily scented with pure male animal. Without coherent thought she slid down his body and drew him whole into her hot, wet mouth.

Patrick's cry echoed round the bedchamber and she knew an insatiable need to hear the dark, hoarse, intimate sounds again. Patrick was determined not to waste his seed in such a frivolous way. He pushed her back down on the bed and entered her with a thrust that sent him deeper than he'd ever been before. As he felt his seed start he groaned, "You know I cannot give you up now. Not even if you beg me."

As his white-hot life poured into her, she was too far gone in rapture to even hear him.

Their time together was over. Kitty lay cradled in his arms inside the coach. They were traveling to the coast together, but she insisted on taking the public ferry back to Liverpool.

"Give me time?" she begged with tears in her eyes.

He kissed her temple and murmured:

"Tonight I am coming
To visit you in your dream
And none will see and question me—
Be sure to leave your door unlocked!"

She surrendered her mouth to his, half faint with the thought of separation.

"I feel I am dying of love," she wept.

"I have the cure," he promised. He opened the window and called to the driver, "Stop at the next inn. My lady is ill and in need of attention."

The couple who kept the inn were consumed by curiosity when the well-dressed gentleman swept in with a woman in his arms and demanded their best bedroom. They spent the next three hours conjecturing what was happening above-stairs.

Chapter 28

Kitty was worried. She counted again to make sure there was no error in her calculations.

"It's not possible," she told herself, but an inner voice contradicted her mockingly. "Not only possible, but probable after such wanton behavior. But Patrick would have been careful. He would never have been negligent in such matters, not again," she told herself.

Then his voice came to her loud and clear: "I'll do everything in my power to . . . bind you closer to me."

"Oh, no; please, Lord, no! Don't let him have deliberately gotten me with child," she prayed silently.

"Let's see: It happened at the end of September, beginning of October . . . that would make it . . . seven, eight, nine . . . end of June, beginning of July. I'm only frightening myself! Next month everything will be back to normal," she promised herself fervently.

In November her menses again proved elusive. With many sighs, Kitty resigned herself to the inevitable. At least she wouldn't be big enough to show before Christmas, when social activities couldn't be avoided. She really didn't know what she hoped to accomplish with her secrecy, and the mocking voice from within kept repeating, "Ignore it as much as you like, it won't go away!" So far she had managed to avoid Patrick by becoming almost reclusive, and whenever his words came back to her about demanding that she leave Charles, she pushed them resolutely away. The scandal she would bring down upon their heads frightened her. Not for herself; she had never given a tinker's damn what anyone said about her, but Charles would be devastated. She could never hurt him so cruelly. Then there was Charles Patrick. How could she take him from Charles? It was unthinkable. She would sacrifice her own happiness a thousand times over before she would do that. "Oh, Patrick, why can't you understand?" she asked silently.

The morning sickness began; in fact, it lasted most of the day. Just before Christmas, Charles came upon her gazing unhappily through their bedroom window. He came up behind her to see what held her solemn attention on the ground below. She was watching the birds eat some crumbs. "Remember the blue and yellow parrots that flashed through the trees on the island? Do you miss them sometimes?" he asked.

"Oh, no, I love the starlings. They make me laugh when they run on their little red legs."

"Then why are there tears on your cheeks?" he said softly.

"Well, they also make me feel sad, especially when they lift one foot up and tuck it underneath them because the ground is so cold."

"It all sounds most fanciful to me. Come and tell me what's ailing you, darling," he coaxed gently.

"I'm with child," she blurted.

He stared at her in amazement.

"You're shocked," she said.

"No, only surprised, and I shouldn't be surprised after pushing you to seek diversion, should I?" he asked gently.

"Charles, I wish with all my heart that I didn't have to hurt you like this," she said wretchedly.

He patted the sofa. "It isn't the end of the world, Kathleen; come while we consider it carefully. If there's one thing I've learned in life it's that everything in the world has its advantages and its disadvantages. Charles Patrick needs a brother or a sister; it will do him a world of good. My stock in society will go up as they whisper, 'There's life in the old dog yet,' and you will just adore another baby.''

''And the disadvantages?'' she asked faintly.

There were crinkles around his eyes. ''I can't think of any.''

Kitty wrung her hands. ''Damn you, why are you so saintly? Why don't you beat me, or throw me out?'' she cried.

He came to her and held her close. ''I cherish you. If anything ever happened to you I wouldn't care to live.''

Now, at least, she didn't have to lace so tightly or disguise the fact that she was feeling wretched. She knew she could put off seeing Patrick no longer. She sent a note around to Half-Moon Street, but it was returned with a note from his man that he was out of town for the New Year's holiday and would be returning about the middle of January. As it happened, Charles got to see him before Kitty did. They met at the club when Charles was with a couple of government colleagues. The conversation was all war and how to make profits from it. Patrick was always good for a few tips that would swell the old coffers. Patrick turned to Charles. ''Will you be coming to Julia's party Friday?'' he asked almost too casually.

''I think we'll have to send our regrets. I'm worried about Kathleen. She's such a little thing. The doctor says she's not strong; far too thin.''

''Doctor'' Patrick was alarmed. ''Is she ill?'' he demanded.

''Well, not really ill. Confidentially, she's in a delicate condition. I don't think she wants anyone to know about it just yet, so don't let on.''

Patrick was stunned. She'd kept it from him for four months! He cursed himself for his careless inconsideration.

She was having a bad time, too. No wonder she hadn't been near him since they returned from Ireland.

The next day, while he was writing her a carefully worded note, he was relieved when his man told him that the duchess was there to see him.

He looked down at her with longing. It took an iron will not to crush her in his arms. She was definitely thinner; there was no way he could have guessed she was carrying a child.

She began in a rush of apology for not seeing him, and the excuses fell from her lips in bright little phrases. It began to dawn on him, incredibly, that she wasn't going to tell him! "You do understand that the stolen moments we shared must never be repeated?" she said in a rehearsed little speech.

"What about my baby?" he asked slowly.

She flew at him with clenched fists, her composure shattered. "You did do it on purpose! Oh, I just could knock you down. If only I were a man!"

He held her arms to her sides to ward off the blows. "You weren't going to tell me, were you? You know damned well I'd insist on claiming my children and you!"

She completely broke down at his words. "God help me, Patrick, I can't walk out on him. I have too much pity and compassion for that. You are so strong, Patrick. No one ever could pity you," she said, sobbing.

"Thank God for that," he said quietly. Her plight touched his heart; he was so vulnerable where she was concerned. "My own love, I brought you pain when I told you to decide between us. The pity of it is, it was just male pride. I know you love me. I respect you for standing on your principles." He kissed her brow.

She clung to him desperately. "Principles are a trap door; when you do stand on them, you go straight through." She looked suddenly stricken. "I'm afraid I'm going to be sick."

He helped her to the bathroom. Afterward he washed her face gently.

She gave him a tremulous smile. "I bet you're thankful you've been saved from a terrible fate."

He didn't laugh. "If you don't take care of yourself, you're going to lose this baby, Kitty. I couldn't bear that and neither could you. I want you to go home and rest, and for God's sake, eat! You're so fragile, you look like you're going to shatter. Try to be calm; think beautiful thoughts, and don't worry your head about me. My God, am I such a bastard I've got you worrying your guts to fiddle strings? He brushed her lips with his. "Go now. I'm here if you need me."

The May afternoon was warm and sunny. Kitty had spent endless hours with Old Tom, the gardener, planning a butterfly garden. The old man had been so skeptical when she told him that in the islands they planted certain flowers to attract different varieties of butterflies.

"We'll use showy sedum, sea holly and Jacob's ladder with scabiosa behind. Then the little rock plants in front like creeping phlox, moss pink and rock cress. There're some good annuals we'll need to attract the prettiest ones, like naughty Marietta, verbena, cosmos, wallflowers and what's that red stuff . . . fireweed!"

"It won't work in England; we've no butterflies—only them white things that eat cabbages!" he said stubbornly.

"Oh, Tom, you're a gardener. How can you say that? We have red admirals, painted ladies, Milbert's tortoiseshell, spring azures, and mourning cloaks, to name only a few."

She walked heavily now, under her burden, but she looked happier and more contented. Charles Patrick came running. She took his hand and they went off to feed the swans.

"When you have the baby, I won't be the baby anymore, will I?" he asked happily.

"Good heavens, you haven't been a baby for ages," she wisely assured him. Later that night, as she gazed down at her sleeping son, she whispered, "Little Patrick, how exactly like your father you are, and now, God help me, I'm about to bring another little O'Reilly into the world."

Charles moved quietly out of the shadows and went into his bedroom. A report sounded through the house. Kitty looked up startled, then she ran along the hall toward Charles' bedroom, a gathering fear clutching at her heart. She was calling for Katie at the top of her lungs, long before she reached the bedroom door. Her hand turned the knob reluctantly, knowing what she would find. Katie was behind her as she opened the door and quickly slammed it shut again in horror.

"Get a doctor! Hurry! Hurry!"

As Katie ran down the stairs, she said, "What's his doctor's name? It's gone clear out of my head."

"No, no, his doctor lives in Harley Street. Quickly, go across the square. The big house at the corner has just been bought by a doctor," she said breathlessly.

Mimi came running upstairs. "Was that a gunshot I heard?"

"Yes, yes. There's been a terrible accident. Go to Charles Patrick; make sure he doesn't leave his room!"

Kitty had gone a ghastly shade of putty. Her mind screamed, "No, Charles, no!" all the while she was giving directions. Two menservants came, but she waved them back. "I'll go in to him. Stay here, please."

She went into the room and began to talk to Charles. "It's all right, darling, I've sent for help. It's all right, you're not going to die. I won't let you." There was no blood. The gun lay on the floor beside Charles. It was such a tiny hole, it couldn't possibly have done much damage. He lay very still. Her pregnancy prevented her from getting down on the floor.

She pulled the comforter from the bed and draped it around him to keep him warm. "The doctor's coming, Charles. Hang on, for God's sake, hang on," she begged. She lifted his hand and held it tightly. All the while she knew that he wasn't just unconscious, but she clung in desperation. If he hovered anywhere between life and death, she would bring him back. She looked up dazed as Katie ushered the doctor through the bedroom doorway. She was hallucinating! This had all happened before! Otis Grant-Stewart stopped on the threshold. Recognition dawned on him as he looked at the young woman before him.

Kitty raised her hands in supplication. "Please help him!" she begged.

He gave the body a cursory examination.

"We meet again under identical circumstances, madame," he said coldly.

"He can't be dead," she said firmly.

"He is quite dead, madame," he said.

"Do something, anything!" she ordered.

"Indeed I shall, madame. I shall inform the police and the coroner's office. I shall order an autopsy and an inquest into this shooting. When one's husband is found with a bullet in his head, the circumstances are regarded with suspicion. When one's subsequent husband is found with a bullet in his head, the circumstances are damning!"

"What will you do with him?" she asked, all her thoughts still with Charles.

"I shall inform the coroner's office. Attendants will come and remove the body. I bid you good evening," he said curtly.

"I bid you good riddance!" said Kitty, coming out of her trance. She called in the menservants. "Lift him up onto the bed, please. Be very gentle," she admonished. When they left she brushed back her husband's hair, all gone gray now.

"Why must we always hurt the ones we love?" she asked him. "Good-bye, Charles," she whispered tenderly. "May you be half an hour in paradise before the devil knows you're dead."

She stayed beside him until they came to collect the body. Afterward, she sat so still Katie didn't know what to do.

"Ma'am, do you realize the serious trouble we are in?" she asked fearfully.

The child kicked hard. "Life and death," mused Kitty, putting her hand to the baby. "It's a matter of life and death, isn't it?"

"That doctor should have done something for you. He could see what condition you were in. Let me help you to bed."

Kitty ignored her words. "I want the carriage brought round. Bring me a cloak, Katie."

"You can't go out alone, you're in shock!" She stopped when she saw Kitty's face. "I see you are determined," she said with resignation. "I'll come with you."

The carriage stopped in Half-Moon Street. Katie left Kitty in the carriage while she went for Patrick. She was back in a minute and told the driver to go on to Cadogen Square.

"He has business at Julia's," she explained quickly.

This time Kitty could not wait in the carriage, but went up to the door herself. When the butler opened to them she swept past him toward the sound of voices. The three people were in a heated conversation about shares and proxy votes. They broke off abruptly as Kitty entered.

Patrick came to his feet immediately. "What has happened?"

Kitty said with disbelief, "Charles has killed himself!" Patrick was beside her in two strides. She felt his comforting hand at the small of her back, and she said, "It's my fault!"

Julia cried, "You've been trouble since the day Father

brought you into our home. I wouldn't be surprised if you hadn't killed him too!''

A slap rang out. Jeffrey stood before his wife and said pointedly, ''At least she didn't murder her own baby, madame. Leave this room at once or I won't be accountable for my actions!''

When Julia had gone Patrick said angrily, ''It's about time you were master in your own household.''

''I apologize for my wife. I will do anything I can to help you both. I'll leave you so you can have some privacy,'' he said, taking Katie from the room with him.

Patrick led Kitty to a chair, then fetched her some brandy. He knelt beside her and guided the glass to her lips. She choked as the fiery liquid touched her throat and Patrick took the glass from her trembling fingers.

''I was saying good night to Charles Patrick . . . my thoughts were all of you . . . I was thinking aloud . . . Charles must have heard . . . he shot himself.'' She looked at him helplessly. ''There was nothing I could do . . . there was nothing anyone could do.''

He clasped her hands between his and found her hands like ice. He knew there was more, but he waited for her to tell him without his prompting.

''It was like a nightmare . . . I sent Katie for a doctor . . . it was the same doctor who came when Simon was shot.''

She closed her eyes against the ugly memories. Patrick brought her a footstool. He gently eased her back in the chair and lifted her feet.

''He's ordered an autopsy, an inquest . . . he thinks I killed him!'' she cried.

''No, no, that's simply routine in the City of London. Under the circumstances he had no choice whatsoever,'' he reassured her. ''I use the best barristers and solicitors in

London. We'll get you counsel. You won't have a thing to
worry about. An inquest is just a hearing, remember, not a
trial.''

"I'm in ignorance of these things," she said wearily.

"That won't matter in the least. You must place yourself in
the hands of your counsel and say whatever he tells you to.
I'll arrange everything myself. The important thing, the only
thing that matters is you. You must be very strong, because
even though I am with you, I cannot physically stand beside
you. They mustn't find out about us or you will be cruci-
fied.''

The truth of his words hit her. "I shouldn't have come
here tonight.''

He shook his head impatiently. "You came to Jeffrey and
Julia. Jeffrey and Katie will take you home later and he will
be our go-between. All our messages to each other can be
carried through Jeffrey. Trust no one else," he cautioned.
His eyes lingered on her belly. "How is everything with our
baby?''

She reached for his hand and placed it beneath her heart.
The child kicked beneath his fingers and he was filled with
awe at the mystery of it all. He pulled up another easy chair
beside her. He sat back, keeping hold of her hand. "Have a
little rest. Let me be with you for a while. Heaven knows
when we'll be able to be together again.''

Chapter 29

The autopsy concluded death was caused by one gunshot to the brain. Whether self-inflicted or otherwise could not be determined. Kitty was served with a paper notifying her the inquest would be three days hence. London was agog with the news. Reporters from the newspapers waited outside her front door to glean lurid details for their dailies. Her counsel assured her they would delve into Charles' business affairs and also the state of his health to find a valid reason for his suicide. A reason must be found, she was assured, so that no suspicions could fall upon her. He gave her advice on what to say, what to wear, her comportment and so forth.

"It's all so contrived, like staging a play," she protested wearily.

"That's exactly how you must think of it. You must catch their sympathy and hold it. You must awaken a desire to protect you, not only in the magistrate, but also in every human being who is there to observe you. They are your audience, your Grace, and they will judge you."

She ached for Patrick. His notes were cold comfort when she needed his physical strength to lean upon.

Her counsel came again the following day. "We have nothing to go on. The duke's business affairs were above question. His private life has no sordid affairs that would suggest any form of blackmail," he said with disappointment.

"I should hope not!" she snapped.

"His doctor gives him a clean bill of health; no fatal illnesses lurking about. It's really too bad."

"Jeffrey, the man offends me. He wants to walk all over Charles' memory with muddy footprints. I must speak with Patrick," she demanded.

"He's absolutely adamant on that point, Kitty. He will not jeopardize your reputation by coming to you," said Jeffrey. "He's right, Kitty; it's not just your reputation that's at stake here, it could be your life! Patrick will have my hide for frightening you this way, but if they don't find just cause for suicide, they could start looking for a motive for murder!"

The day before the inquest Charles' doctor came to the house. Counsel met him. "I've been asked to testify regarding Charles' health. Could I speak with her Grace?"

Counsel said, "I am in charge of the case, so it would be best to communicate any information you have with me."

"Well, there is one thing I could say that probably would help you, but it's rather indelicate and I'd like her Grace's permission before I divulge such personal matters."

"Speak up, man. What have you got? It may save her from a murder charge!"

"Well, I treated him for impotence."

"That's it! Good man, good man. Nothing like the spice of bedroom details. We'll have them eating out of our hands."

In the back of her mind, Kitty thought that when the day of the inquest arrived, the birth of her child would mercifully prevent her from being there. The day dawned and with it came the realization that the ordeal must be faced. Jeffrey and a much-subdued Julia arrived early to accompany her to court. Her counsel was already there, giving her last-minute advice.

"It's not seemly for a lady in your condition to be seen in

public. Thankfully, the crinoline will help to disguise your condition. Keep your cloak on at all times. Now, remember to keep your eyes down; you must be meek—a supplicant. The 'tragic widow' is a most sympathetic figure.''

''I shall be the pathetic creature you have ordered me to be, even though it goes against the grain,'' she flashed.

As she entered the courtroom, a wave of whispers swept around the room. She was surprised to see the room filled mostly with men. There were some newspaper reporters but largely they were Charles' peers. Her eyes searched the crowd for Patrick. She was surprised when he ignored her and gave his attention to the smartly dressed woman on his right.

The inquest opened with a few words which the coroner addressed to the jury. ''We are here to determine the cause and circumstances of the death of Sir Charles Drago, ninth Duke of Manchester. Whether it was suicide or whether it was a greater crime.''

The first witness, Charles' business secretary, was called and sworn in. He testified that all monies collected for the Port of London were accounted for and that all business matters were in complete order, down to the last detail. Otis Grant-Stewart testified how he discovered the body, and the results of the autopsy were officially put into the record of the inquest.

Then came a succession of servants, ending with Katie, who testified that they heard the gunshot. Katie perjured herself by claiming she saw her mistress run to the bedroom door after the shot was fired.

Charles' doctor was brought to the stand to testify about the state of his patient's health. When he concluded that it was excellent, a murmur went around the court.

Kitty kept her eyes lowered. She tried to pay attention to every word spoken but she caught her mind drifting over and

over again. She wondered when her labor would begin and
hoped she had done right engaging a midwife rather than a
doctor. Her mind snapped back as her counsel asked Charles'
doctor about treating him for impotence. The room was
hushed. The doctor was asked to step down. Before she could
utter a protest, she heard her name called out and she moved
forward as one in a trance.

"I call on Kathleen Drago, Dowager Duchess of Manchester, who will corroborate the testimony just given."

"Repeat after me: I swear by Almighty God that the evidence I give shall be the truth, the whole truth and nothing
but the truth."

She placed her hand upon the Bible and so swore.

Kitty looked about the room at the avid faces. It was the
one thing Charles had dreaded. He had made her promise,
right after their marriage, never to divulge his secret. She
never had, not even to Patrick. She knew she would always
carry the burden of guilt for Charles taking his life. She had
betrayed him in life, but before Christ she would not betray
him in death!

When the question of his impotence was put to her, she
stood and threw off the cloak. Her pregnancy was revealed to
every eye. Gone was the meek figure. It had been replaced by
a fiery woman who spoke with passion. "That's absolutely
ridiculous," she said triumphantly. "We made love almost
every night!" A roar went up in the courtroom and the judge
had to bang his gavel repeatedly to bring order. Kitty sat
back down. She ignored her counsel and instead turned to the
judge and said, "My husband was cleaning his gun when it
went off. It was an accident, pure and simple."

They broke off for lunch at this dramatic point. Patrick did
not meet her eyes. She saw him slip from the back of the
room with the woman on his arm.

Julia flashed her a pleased look that filled Kitty with dread, but Jeffrey patted her hand. "Not to worry, that's the judge's wife."

The verdict of accidental death came as a surprise to none after the morning's dramatic testimony. An emotionally drained Kitty went home to await the birth of her child, while Londoners read of the "dragon lady" and the "notorious duchess."

Chapter 30

Her pains began around ten o'clock at night. Katie said to Mimi, "I'll stay with her; you fetch the midwife."

By midnight, hard labor had begun in earnest, but no matter how they struggled, the child would not make its appearance. The midwife refused to panic. These things took time and ran their own course, and the lady was not built for childbearing.

Katie put on her cloak and slipped out the doorway. It was just striking one when she returned, a tall, dark figure close upon her heels.

Arguing voices came to Kitty through a haze of pain. The deep timbre of Patrick's voice started to curse and she called out to the midwife, "He's no respecter of persons; let him come to me."

He knelt beside her, taking her hands. It lifted her heart to see how deeply concerned he was. He stayed beside her for four hours. When the child finally was born, Patrick was dizzy with relief.

"We have a daughter," he whispered tenderly. Kitty was too exhausted to speak. He turned to the midwife. "How long will she be abed"

"A lying-in is always a fortnight," she told him.

He turned back to Kitty. "One month, one month from today I'll return. I'll come boldly for all the world to see; no more climbing the back stairs for me, Kitty."

She closed her eyes and nodded her understanding.

* * *

Flowers came every morning especially chosen by Patrick. There was no need for any card; she knew who sent them.

A full month hadn't quite gone by when he came striding into her private sitting room. She had just finished feeding her daughter and was rocking her gently to sleep. The energy he brought into the room with him almost made the air crackle. "Kitty, it's all settled," he said, laughing, as he waved a telegram in the air. "You're looking at the new president and chairman of the board of Hind of New York. If you don't like New York, we can live in Philadelphia. The gossip won't follow us to America. We'll be married before we sail. When can you be ready?"

She watched him talking and laughing. How handsome he was! Patrick was at his best when he was in control, directing everyone about him like some young god.

Kitty said very quietly, "I'm not going."

He stopped laughing and turned to look at her. "Not going?" he questioned her.

She sighed deeply, reaching for words that would make her explanation less painful for him. "A trip across the Atlantic would kill me right now," she said sadly.

He looked closely at the small, black-clad figure before him. Her cheekbones stood out so prominently, they looked like they might pierce the skin. Her wrists were so fine-boned they were skeletal. He knew her words told the truth. He was at a loss for the first time in his life.

"I'm going home," she said simply.

He knew he could rave and shout until he was blue in the face. It would alter nothing! Her mind was made up. He crumpled the telegram into his pocket, bent down to place a kiss on his daughter's brow and left quietly.

It took a week to pack the belongings she wanted shipped to Ireland. She put the huge house in the hands of her bankers and asked them to sell it for her. Katie and Mimi both agreed to accompany her to Windrush.

A small cavalcade stepped off the boat train on an evening in July. A chilly breeze blew off the Irish Sea, making Kitty thankful she had worn her furs. She carried her baby daughter, while her son, grown out of babyhood, walked beside her. Two young women followed, each struggling with a heavy case. Kitty tried to hail a porter to transport their luggage onto the overnight ferry, but before she had given him her instructions, two men strode purposefully along the platform toward them. She looked up startled as the tall figures loomed out of the darkness.

"Patrick!" she gasped.

He tipped his hat and swept her a mocking bow. He handed the cases to the man standing beside him. He took the baby from Kitty and placed her in Katie's arms; then he swung Charles Patrick to his shoulder and commanded, "Follow me!" Kitty had to walk very quickly to keep up with him, but her heart was beating wildly and singing at the intoxicating nearness of the man.

"Madame, there are some women who are willing to sacrifice everything and follow a man to the ends of the earth. Ah, but how many men do you know capable of such a grand gesture? None, you say? Ah, there you are wrong, madame! Permit me the luxury of the supreme gesture." He took his letter of appointment and contracts from his pocket and tossed them into the wind.

"But, Patrick," she protested, "what do you intend to do?"

"Marry you, madame, before you elude me again," he said with a wolfish grin.

They went up the gangplank of his ship, and he swung his son to the deck. "It's time our children were in bed. We'll see to them together tonight," he said with relish.

The maids soon were settled in their cabins and the children fed and put to bed. The anchor was lifted. They were going home!

Patrick picked up Kitty's furs and wrapped them about her closely. Then he took her hand and led her out on deck. "This has to be done by moonlight," he explained. He took her into his arms and bent to claim her lips, shuddering with his great longing. "Kitty, will you marry me?" he asked humbly.

Soft and tender-eyed and sighing, she answered, "Yes, my darling. When?"

"Now! The captain awaits us in the cabin below."

When they were finally alone, getting ready for bed, she was still breathless. He had again swept her off her feet, giving her little time to decide her fate. He could not get enough of looking at her. When she was ready for bed, he stooped and caught her in his arms, lifting her against his heart. Ecstasy thrilled within her. At long last she had her heart's desire. Under the covers he came close against her back and gathered her in his embrace.

"Patrick, what will you do now that you have thrown your career away?"

He nibbled the silky flesh of her shoulder. "I don't know. Go into politics, perhaps, start another business, I don't know. And I don't care. Right now all I care about is you." The faint, sweet perfume of her hair stole to him. "What have you decided to name our daughter?" he asked, trying to control his mounting desire.

"I'm going to call her Pagan! Pagan O'Reilly!"

"Good God, kitten, a name like that is just asking for trouble."

She slipped around in his arms to face him. "I do always ask for trouble, don't I?" She kissed him seductively. "And you always manage to give it to me."